DIANE CHAMBERLAIN

is a multiple *SUNDAY TIMES* and *NEW YORK TIMES* bestselling author, beloved by readers around the world for stories that are rich with emotion, laced with secrets and that inspire thoughtful conversations. Born and raised in New Jersey, Diane obtained a master's degree in social work in San Diego. She then worked in hospitals before opening her own private psychotherapy practice, focusing primarily on at-risk teenagers. This background as a psychotherapist has given Diane great insight into the secrets that families hold beneath the surface and how destructive they can be when they come to light. She has observed firsthand the ability of those under tremendous pressure to tap into their inner strength – a resilience that inspires her most-loved characters.

Diane Chamberlain has written twenty-eight bestselling novels, and her books have been published in more than twenty languages. She makes her home in North Carolina with her partner, photographer John Pagliuca, and her Shetland Sheepdog, Cole.

Also by Diane Chamberlain

The Good Father

The Midwife's Confession

The Lies We Told

Secrets She Left Behind

Before the Storm

The Lost Daughter

The Bay at Midnight

Her Mother's Shadow

The Journey Home (anthology)

Kiss River

The Courage Tree

Keeper of the Light

The Shadow Wife (formerly *Cypress Point*)

Summer's Child

Breaking the Silence

The Escape Artist

Reflection

Brass Ring

Lovers and Strangers

Fire and Rain

Secret Lives

Necessary Lies

The First Lie (eBook short story)

The Silent Sister

The Broken String (eBook short story)

Pretending to Dance

The Dance Begins (eBook short story)

The Stolen Marriage

Secrets at the Beach House (formerly *Private Relations*)

The Dream Daughter

Big Lies in a Small Town

The Dark End of the Street

DIANE CHAMBERLAIN

brass ring

REVIEW

First published in Great Britain in 1995 by Little, Brown

First published in paperback in 1997 by Sphere

Reissued in 2012 by Sphere

This edition published in 2020 by Headline Review
An imprint of HEADLINE PUBLISHING GROUP

Cataloguing in Publication Data is available from the British Library

ISBN 978 1 4722 8278 1

Offset in 11.73/14.27 pt Bembo by Jouve (UK), Milton Keynes

Printed and bound in Great Britain by Clays Ltd, Elcograf S.p.A.

HEADLINE PUBLISHING GROUP
An Hachette UK Company
Carmelite House
50 Victoria Embankment
London EC4Y 0DZ

www.headline.co.uk
www.hachette.co.uk

To the coyote and his pups

Harpers Ferry, West Virginia
January 1993

Claire Harte-Mathias believed you could be forced to endure only one major catastrophe in your lifetime. Once the trauma had passed, you were safe. Jon had suffered his own catastrophe long ago, and so Claire stayed close to him always, as if she could make his tragedy her own, thereby warding off one for herself. She had held tight to this notion ever since meeting Jon twenty-three years earlier, when she had been barely seventeen.

So, it never would have occurred to her that the snow falling outside their hotel in Harpers Ferry might present a danger to her and Jon on their drive home. Most of the other conference attendees were staying an extra night at the gently aging High Water Hotel to avoid driving in the storm, but Claire simply could not imagine anything other than safe passage for their sixty-mile trip home to Vienna, Virginia.

The young woman behind the time-worn wooden

counter wore a frown as Claire settled their bill. "It's treacherous out there," she said.

"We'll be fine." Claire looked toward the stone fireplace, where an enormous blaze burned, warming the lobby and its cozy assortment of antique and reproduction furniture. Jon sat in front of the hearth in his wheelchair. Behind him, the snow fell steadily through the darkening sky. Jon was bending forward, elbows on knees, engaged in an animated discussion with Mary Drake, the vice-president of the Washington Area Rehabilitation Association. He was already wearing his brown leather jacket, and he held his gloves in his hand. The flames from the fire laid a sheen of gold on his cheeks and glittered in the silver that laced his brown hair. Watching him, Claire felt a rush of desire. For a moment, she entertained the idea of spending one more night in the turret room, where their bed was nestled in a circle of windows, where she could be nestled in the warm circle of Jon's arms. It would be a relaxing night. The conference was over. They could forget about work.

"Are you sure you don't want to stay the night?" the young woman asked.

Claire let go of the fantasy, replacing it with thoughts of Susan. She smiled at the receptionist. "No," she said. "Our daughter's going back to William and Mary in the morning. We want to be there to say good-bye."

She signed the credit card slip with the new, jade green fountain pen Jon had given her for her fortieth birthday and began walking toward the fireplace.

Ken Stevens suddenly appeared at her side, catching her arm. "You and Jon were an inspiration, as always," he said. "Doesn't matter how many times I hear the two of you speak, I always get something new out of it."

"I'm glad, Ken. Thanks." She embraced him warmly, his shadow of a beard scratching her cheek. "We'll see you next year."

Jon was laughing with Mary Drake, but he looked up as Claire approached. "Ready?" he asked.

She nodded, zipping up her red down jacket. Through the wavy glass of the hotel's front windows, she could see their blue Jeep in the circular driveway. She had moved it there an hour earlier and stowed their suitcases inside.

"You guys are crazy to drive in this stuff." Mary stood up and followed Claire's gaze to the window.

Claire pulled her black knit hat low on her head, tucking her long, dark hair inside it. "It's going to be a gorgeous drive." She gave Mary a hug. "And we'll have the road to ourselves."

Jon zipped up his own jacket. He took Mary's hand and squeezed it. "Say hi to Phil for us," he said, and Mary bent low to buss his cheek.

"Drive carefully," she said, and as Jon and Claire made their way to the door, those words were echoed by a half dozen of their friends in the lobby.

Outside, the cold air felt good, and the snow fell quietly from the dark sky. A thick white blanket layered the earth, illuminated by the lights from the hotel windows and puckering here and there over shrubs and other unseeable objects. "It's so beautiful out here." Claire stretched out her arms and tipped her head back, letting the snow chill her face for a moment.

"Mmm, it is," Jon agreed as he wheeled through the snow. He stopped to look at the snowman Claire had coerced a few people into building with her that afternoon. He laughed. "It's great," he said.

The snowman, sitting in his snow wheelchair, had lost his features under a mask of white. Claire dusted the snow from the round face so Jon could see the gravel eyes and holly-berry lips. Then she turned toward the edge of the cliff, longing for one final view of that steep drop to the rivers below but settling for the memory. She could picture the rivers crashing and tumbling together in a rush of black water and white foam before finally surrendering to each other and slipping quietly into the mountains.

Jon opened the door on the driver's side of the two-door Jeep. Claire held his chair while he picked up his legs and set his feet on the floor of the car. He grabbed the steering wheel, gathered his strength, and pulled himself up to the seat. Claire hit the quick disconnect button on the side of the wheel and had the chair disassembled and tossed into the back of the Jeep before Jon had even closed his door. She brushed the fresh snow from the windshield, then climbed into the passenger seat beside him.

Jon turned the key in the ignition, giving the Jeep a little gas with a twist of his hand control, and the engine coughed, breaking the spell of the still, white night. He looked over at Claire and smiled.

"Come here," he said, and she leaned toward him. He kissed her, tugging a strand of her thick, dark hair free of her hat. "You did a great job, Harte," he said.

"And you were fabulous, Mathias."

The Jeep appeared to be the only moving vehicle in all of quiet, tucked-in Harpers Ferry. The roads were covered with white, but they were not very slippery. Nevertheless, Jon used the Jeep's four-wheel drive on the steeply descending main street through town. The darkened shops that lined the road were barely visible behind the veil of falling snow. Jon would have difficulty seeing the white line on the highway, Claire thought. That would be their biggest problem.

They had done a great deal of talking the past few days, with each other as well as with the participants at the annual conference, and now they were quiet. It was a good silence. Comfortable. Their part in the conference had gone exceedingly well. It was always that way when there were many new, sharp, fresh rehabilitation specialists in the audience, hungry to see them. Being in a workshop led by Jon and Claire Harte-Mathias was viewed almost as a rite of passage.

Jon drove slowly along the street that paralleled the Shenandoah, and Claire knew he was testing the road, getting a feel for how bad conditions were.

The Jeep skidded almost imperceptibly as they turned onto the bridge that rose high above the river, and Jon shifted into four-wheel drive again. The long ribbon of white in front of them was untouched by tire tracks. Overhead lights illuminated the falling snow and the hazy white line of the guardrail, and Claire had the sensation of floating through a cloud. She felt a little sorry for Jon that he had to concentrate on driving and could not simply relish the beauty of this drive across the bridge.

They were nearly halfway across the river when she spotted something in the distance. Something ahead of them, on the left, resting at the side of the bridge. At first, she thought it was a piece of road equipment covered with snow. She squinted, as though that might help her clear her vision, and the piece of equipment moved.

"Jon, look." She pointed toward the object. "That's not a person, is it?"

"Out here?" Jon glanced toward the side of the bridge. "No way." But then he looked again. They were nearly even with the object now, and Claire clearly saw a snow-covered arm lift into the air, glowing in the overhead light before dropping back again to its resting place.

"God, it *is* a person." Jon stopped the Jeep in the middle of the road.

It was a woman. Claire could see the long hair, clotted white with snow, and she thought: homeless? mentally ill? out of gas?

"She's outside the guardrail," Jon said.

"You don't think she's planning to do something stupid, do you?" Claire leaned forward for a better look. "Maybe she just likes to come up here when it's snowing. I bet she has an incredible view from there."

Jon looked at her with amused disbelief. He might as well have called her Pollyanna, as Susan frequently did.

"I'm getting out." Claire opened her door and stepped out of the Jeep, her feet sinking into the thick layer of snow.

"Be careful," Jon called as she closed the door behind her.

The snow was wild this high above the river, caught in the wind that blew wet and blinding against Claire's face as she plowed her way across the bridge.

The woman wore a light cloth coat covered with a thick crust of snow. How long had she been out here? She wore no gloves, no hat. Her hair—blond?—was hidden beneath a veil of white. She had to be freezing.

Claire reached the guardrail and could see that the woman stood at the very edge of the bridge, high above the black abyss, untethered to anything.

"Miss?" Claire called.

The woman did not turn around.

Claire leaned over the railing. "*Miss*," she called again, but the snow swallowed the word.

"*Hello*," she tried. "Can you hear me? Please turn around."

The woman stood still as an ice sculpture.

There was a narrow break in the railing a few yards from where Claire stood. She glanced behind her at the Jeep, her view obstructed by snow and darkness. She could not see Jon clearly, could not signal him to call the police on the car phone, but surely he was doing so. Surely he would think of that.

Tugging the collar of her down jacket closer to her chin, Claire walked toward the break in the railing. She stepped onto the platform, which was nothing more than a few feet of slippery metal separating her from the ice and rocks and water far below. She had the immediate sensation of suspension, of hanging in the air high above the river on a slender thread of concrete. She had no fear of heights, though. She did not feel the magnetic pull of the open space the way others might.

She clung to the guardrail as she made her way toward the woman. Afraid of startling her, she walked very slowly. When the woman finally turned her head in Claire's direction, though, she did not seem surprised to find her there, and for a moment, her eyes locked fast with Claire's. She was young—late twenties or early thirties. In the overhead light of the bridge, her eyes were translucent, like gray ice on the surface of a midwinter lake. Her lashes were white with snow. Flakes battered her cheeks and her eyelids, yet the woman did not blink or make any attempt to brush them away.

Claire held tight to the rail with one mittened hand and reached toward the woman with the other. "Let me help you come behind the railing," she said.

With an air of indifference, the woman turned slowly away from her. She looked out into the darkness expectantly, as though she could see something that Claire could not, and Claire lowered her hand to her side. She glanced down at the woman's legs. The dark pants were far too short. Her feet were clad only in white socks bunched around her ankles and in tennis shoes. The toes of those sodden-looking shoes extended an inch if not more over the edge of the slippery platform, and for the first time in her life, Claire felt the sickening pull of vertigo. She tightened her hands on the railing, but it was hard to get a good grip with her mittens. The snow had turned to tiny icy pellets that stung her cheeks and blurred her vision, and deep inside the layers of her down jacket, beneath her sweater and her turtleneck, her heart beat like that of a captured bird.

She swallowed hard and tried again. "Please," she said, "tell me why you're out here."

"Leave me alone." The woman's voice was soft, muffled by the snow, and Claire dared to take a slippery step closer to hear her better. She could touch her now if she wanted to, but she kept the fingers of both hands curled around the metal railing. There was no feeling left in her fingertips.

"Please come back," she said. "You'll fall."

The woman let out a soft, bitter laugh. "Yes," she said into the air. "I suppose I will."

"But you'll die," Claire said, feeling stupid.

The woman raised her head to the sky, shutting her eyes. "I died here a long time ago."

"What do you mean?"

She did not answer.

"This is crazy," Claire said. "Nothing can be so bad. There's always something to live for." Slowly, Claire let go of the railing with her right hand and reached toward the woman. She circled her hand around the woman's wrist, struck by how reed-thin her arm was inside her coat. The woman did not react to Claire's touch. She did not even seem to notice.

Suddenly, she cocked her head to one side. "Do you hear it?" she asked. "Chopin?"

"Chopin?"

"Nocturne in C-sharp Minor."

Claire strained her ears but heard nothing other than the muted sound of falling snow. "No," she said. "I'm sorry. I don't hear anything."

"That was his problem, too. He could never hear the music."

"Whose problem? Chopin's? What do you mean?"

The woman did not answer, and now Claire thought she *could* hear something other than the snow. She listened hard. Yes. A siren, far in the distance. A city sound, out of place here as it sifted toward them through the black-and-white night.

The woman heard it too. Her head jerked toward Harpers Ferry, and Claire felt a spasm run through that slender, birdlike body. The woman gave Claire the look of someone betrayed.

"You called the police," she said.

Claire nodded. "My husband did."

"Let go of me," the woman said evenly.

"Tell me what you meant about the music," Claire prompted. Her own legs were trembling, and the stinging snow pelted her eyes. "Tell me what you can hear." Tell me *anything*. Just don't jump. Please.

The siren cut through the air, through the snow. Glancing over her shoulder, Claire saw a red light flashing at the entrance to the bridge. *Hurry*.

The woman locked her gaze with Claire's again, but now her eyes were wide and full of fear. Claire tightened her grip on the bony forearm. "It's going to be all right," she said. "You're going to be safe."

The woman twisted her arm beneath Claire's hand in its black mitten. "Let go of me," she said. The first siren was joined by a second. One of the police cars screeched to a stop behind the Jeep. "Let *go*!" the woman shouted now.

Claire only locked her hand more securely around the woman's wrist. "Let me help you," she said.

The woman raised her head high again, her eyes still riveted on Claire's, and when she spoke, her voice was even and unflinching. "Let go," she said, "or I'll take you with me."

She meant it, Claire knew. Behind them, there was a squeal of brakes, a rush of voices. A horn honked. The woman did not shift her eyes from Claire's for even a second. "Let go now," she said.

Claire opened the fingers of her hand, and the woman offered a small smile of victory, or perhaps gratitude. She did not leap so much as fly from the bridge, or fall so much as be lifted and carried by the snow. The streetlight glittered in the thousands of ice crystals clinging to her hair and her coat, and Claire thought she was watching an angel.

She did not think to scream. She barely breathed, suspended between the earthbound sounds of the men and machines behind her and the drifting, fading glimmer of the angel below. She barely noticed the heavy, gloved hands that wrapped around her own arms, her own shoulders. Hands that struggled to tug her back from the edge of the bridge. She tried to block out the voices, too loud in her ears, as she stared into the snowy abyss, because—at least for a second—she thought she heard the music after all.

2

Harpers Ferry

Jon could hear Claire's teeth chattering nonstop during the two hours they spent in the police station. The police had questioned her at length, not in an interrogatory style but gently, and Jon felt grateful to them for their sensitivity. Claire was in no shape to be raked over the coals.

Someone—he could no longer recall who—had draped a gray wool blanket over Claire's shoulders, and she sat on one of the metal chairs lining the wall of this small office. He had moved another chair out of the way so he could wheel close enough to put his arm around her. Her shoulders felt stiff beneath his arm, though, as if she could not relax enough to take comfort from him.

The police had driven her to the station, while he'd followed in the Jeep. They'd wanted to take her to the hospital. She was in shock, they'd told him. But Claire had adamantly refused to go, insisting she was fine. They were overreacting, she'd said. Jon knew, though, that Claire was not fine. He had seen her in the emergency room after Susan's grisly bicycle accident. He'd seen her seconds after she'd discovered her mother's lifeless body in their living room. Yet he had never seen her like this. So shaken. So shivery. She hadn't cried, but that was not unusual. She never did, at least not in front of him. She was a soft touch at movies or when reading sad books, but in real life she held those tears inside her as though they might turn to acid once on her cheeks.

They were waiting now for the police to find them a place to stay for the night. They could have returned to the High Water, but the thought of having to explain what had happened to them tonight to so many friends and colleagues was overwhelming.

He kissed the side of Claire's head, his lips brushing the dark hair where it was beginning to give way to silver. "We should call Susan," he said, and she nodded. The sound of her teeth chattering made him want to wrap both his arms around her. He pulled the edges of the blanket more snugly across her chest, then tried to meet her eyes, but her gaze only darted past him on its way to nowhere. He looked at Detective Patrick, the burly, kind-faced officer behind the desk.

"May I use that?" He pointed to the phone at the edge of the desk.

"Help yourself."

Jon wheeled forward a foot or two and lifted the phone into his lap. It was nearly eight o'clock. He thought Susan might be out with her friends, but she answered on the fourth ring.

"Hi, Susie."

"Hi. You still in Harpers Ferry?"

"Yes. We're going to have to stay here the night, hon."

"Oh, sure. No problem. It's pretty awful out."

He thought he detected relief in her voice, and he felt a jab of pain. Susan had reached the age—nineteen— where she needed them far less than they needed her. Sometime during this past year, he'd finally admitted to himself that she had labored to graduate early from high school not because she was brilliant or an over-achiever but because she was anxious to leave home, anxious to escape from him and Claire. He had never shared that thought with Claire. He would let her believe they had an ambitious daughter, hungry for college.

"We were on our way home, but . . . " He let his voice trail off as he collected his thoughts. He was going to have to find a way to tell this story. This would not be the last time he would have to recount the events of this evening. "There was a woman standing on the bridge outside of Harpers Ferry and we stopped to try to help her, but she . . . she jumped off while Mom was talking to her."

Susan was quiet for a moment. He could picture her leaning against the kitchen counter in her tight jeans and oversized gray sweater, her long brown hair falling in a shiny swath over her shoulder. A cloud would have fallen over her large dark eyes and she would be frowning, two delicate lines etched into the perfect fair skin of her forehead. "You mean, this lady committed suicide right before your eyes?"

"I'm afraid so. Right before Mom's eyes, anyhow. Mom was out on the edge of the bridge with her, trying to talk her out of jumping."

There was one more beat of loaded silence from Susan's end of the line. "What do you mean, out on the edge of the bridge?" she asked.

"Outside the guardrail."

He heard a sound through the phone—a book being

slammed onto a table, perhaps—before Susan spoke again. "God, why does she do things like that?" she asked, her voice rising. "Is she there? Can I talk to her?"

He glanced at Claire. "She's a little upset right now, and—"

Claire shook her head and reached for the phone, the blanket falling from her shoulders to the chair. Reluctantly, Jon relinquished the receiver.

"Hi, honey," Claire said cheerfully. Detective Patrick looked up from his desk at the transformation in her voice. "We're *fine* . . . Hmm?" She frowned at Jon as she listened to her daughter. "No, Susan, I don't think I can save the world," she said, "I just thought I might be able to help one person." She nodded. "Yes, I know. And I'm so sorry we won't get to see you tonight. I'm going to put Dad on again, okay?"

He took the phone back and immediately heard a volley of chatter from Claire's teeth, as though they were making up for the minute and a half they'd had to be still while talking with Susan.

"Susie?" he said into the phone.

"She could have gotten herself killed." There was a small break in Susan's voice, and Jon heard the love behind her words. He ached to see his daughter, to hug her, before she took off for school again.

"Mom's okay," he said. With a little surge of joy, he thought of the snow. Susan would not be able to drive back to school until the roads were clear. "I guess we'll still get to see you tomorrow," he added. "You can't drive to school in this weather."

"Yes, I can. Or at least, I've got a ride. I'll have to come back in a few weeks for my car, though."

"Who are you riding with?"

"There's this guy here who has some kind of four-wheel-drive wagon. He's taking a bunch of us down."

Jon winced at the thought. "Well, tell him to drive carefully, all right?"

She let out one of her exasperated sighs. "Right."

"I love you."

"Okay. You drive carefully, too."

He hung up the phone, setting it back on the desk, and Claire let out a sigh of her own. "I'm going to the rest room," she said. She stood up, pulling the blanket once more around her shoulders.

After she had left the room, Detective Patrick raised his eyes to Jon's. "Do you mind a personal question?" he asked.

Jon shook his head.

The older man looked down at his desk, rubbing a hand over his jowly chin. "Well, I'm asking this because my nephew just got a back injury." He lifted his eyes to Jon's. "A spinal cord injury, they call it."

Jon nodded again.

"And, you know, you see people in wheelchairs and you don't think about it much until it happens close to you, and now it looks like he's going to be paralyzed and ... well, do you mind if I ask what happened to you?"

"It was an accident in my case, too," Jon said. "My family and I were in a plane crash." He wouldn't tell him that it was his family's private plane. He did not want this man to focus on wealth. "I was sixteen. My parents and sister were killed, and I was in a coma for a few months. When I woke up, they told me I'd never walk again."

The detective's eyes were wide. "Shit," he said.

"And your nephew?"

"Motorcycle. They say he's a T-four. Do you know what that means?"

"Yeah." Jon touched his own chest at the level of the boy's spinal cord injury. This kid was not going to have an easy time of it. "I'm an incomplete L-three," he said, although he doubted that would have much meaning to the detective.

He questioned the man about the rehab program his nephew was in and offered to make a call to the program director—a woman he'd known well for many years—to check on the boy.

Detective Patrick wrote his nephew's name on a business card and handed it to Jon. "I feel better talking to you," he said. "I mean, it seemed like it was the end of the world for the kid, you know? But now I look at you"— he gestured toward Jon—"and you get around okay and you've got a pretty wife and all. And you must have met her after you were . . . " The officer pointed to Jon's wheelchair.

"Yes. We met in high school."

"Aha." The man smiled. "High school sweethearts, huh?"

Jon smiled himself, remembering. "Not of the usual variety." He had moved in with an aunt in Falls Church after his six-month stay in a rehab program, transferring into Claire's public high school after a decade of being pampered by private schools. He could still, if he let the memories in, taste the bitterness of that year after the accident. He had lost everything. But then Claire drew him under her protective wing. They began dating. Neither of them ever dated anyone else again.

"And you have a kid?" The detective nodded toward the

phone, his voice tentative, and Jon laughed. He knew exactly what the man was thinking.

"Yes, she's mine," he said. For years, he and Claire had counseled couples where one of the partners was disabled, and they had learned that sharing personal experience was sometimes more helpful than anything else they might say. He could talk about Susan's parentage without an ounce of discomfort, but Detective Patrick colored.

Jon worried he had given the man false hope. "I was very lucky," he added. "It's rare for a man with a spinal cord injury to be able to father a child, and we weren't able to have other children."

The older man shifted in his seat. "Well, that's great you got the one." He poked at a stack of papers on his desk. "Do you think my nephew stands a chance in that department?"

Jon drew in a breath. "I wouldn't want to guess. Everybody's different." He saw the pain in the man's eyes. "He'll do okay," he said. "He's in a fine program. They'll take good care of him."

Claire had walked back into the room as he was speaking, and he was struck by her pallor. She was still beautiful, though. She was one of those women who was far more striking at forty than she had been at eighteen. Her sharp features had softened. Even the vivid green of her eyes seemed to have mellowed over time.

Struggling to smile at him, she sat down again and took the hand he offered. Her fingers were cold and damp.

A female officer appeared in the doorway to let them know they had a room at a nearby bed and breakfast, one that was ramped for a wheelchair. Claire stood up, folding the blanket, and faced the detective.

"When you find out who she is," she said, "will you call and let me know?"

"Sure will," he said.

Outside, the snow had nearly stopped, but the air was still blustery and cold. Claire was quiet on their cautious drive to the bed and breakfast, and she was merely polite to the owners of the small inn, when her usual style was to make instant friends of anyone she met. Jon was scared by her silence. It wasn't until they were lying under the thick comforter in the canopy bed that she began to talk.

"I should have held on to her," she said.

Jon pulled her close to him. "You did as much as anyone could have done."

"Maybe if I'd held on, she wouldn't have jumped. And then if she did jump, I could have simply let go of her at the last minute." She was quiet a moment. "It's like I gave her *permission* to do it, Jon. I let go, and said, fine, go ahead, end your life. I was the last person to have a chance with her and I failed. Maybe if we hadn't called the police. That's when she freaked out."

"Are you aware that you're talking nonsense?"

She shivered. "I can't get warm." She'd worn nothing to bed, and her skin felt chilled against his chest.

"Do you want one of my T-shirts?"

"No. Just keep holding me, please."

He rubbed her arm. "Shall we try the carousel?"

"Mmm." She snuggled closer to him. "Yes."

Jon closed his eyes, pressing his cheek against her hair. "Once upon a time, on a big and beautiful farm in Jeremy, Pennsylvania, there was an enormous red barn."

Claire cocked her head against his shoulder. "Do you

think it really was enormous, or do you think I just remember it that way because I was so small?"

"Does it matter?"

She nearly giggled. "No."

"It looked like an ordinary barn, although certainly a very well-cared-for barn, because the farmer who owned it was the type to take very good care of the things and the people he loved."

"Yes."

"This farmer had two little granddaughters who loved going into the ordinary-looking barn, because inside there was an *extra*ordinary carousel. There were many beautiful horses on the carousel, and some empty spaces where more horses would go when the farmer had finished carving them out of the big blocks of musky-smelling wood he kept in his workroom."

"At the side of the barn."

"Yes. The workroom at the side of the barn. One of the little granddaughters had a favorite horse—a white horse with a wild golden mane—named Titan. And she liked to—"

"And he was a jumper," Claire added.

"Yes. He was one of the jumpers on the carousel. That's why his mane was so wild. And Claire liked to climb on his back and pretend she was a cowgirl."

"And try to grab the ring."

"Right. She'd try to grab the brass ring so her grandfather would let her go around again."

"It's working," Claire mumbled against his chest. "You're so good at this."

He knew it was working. Her body was growing warm next to him. The tension was gone.

"The organ played 'By the Light of the Silvery Moon,'

and the little granddaughter would gallop around the barn on her beautiful horse, and she'd feel the most extraordinary sense of joy and peace, there on her grandfather's carousel."

"Mmm. I love you so much, Jon."

"Love you, too."

Within minutes she was asleep. Her body was warm and heavy next to him, her breathing almost too soft to hear. The air in the room was dark and still; if there was any light outside the windows, the heavy shades did not let it in. He lay awake, staring at the black ceiling, wishing he could fall asleep and escape the sense of powerlessness that had been haunting him all evening.

He had long ago come to grips with his limitations, but the helplessness he'd felt tonight as he watched Claire struggle with the woman on the edge of the bridge had been different. It had felt like an enemy, a taunting foe he could never defeat. He had watched that scene unfold in terror, thinking that both women would slip on the icy platform, both women would plunge to their deaths. For a long, dark moment, he'd thought he would lose his wife, and although he had been no more than a few yards from her, he had been powerless to save her. He could not recall another time in his adult life when he had felt so utterly helpless.

The image of the woman and Claire seemed etched on the ceiling of this room. He closed his eyes, but the scene sprang to life on the backs of his eyelids. No matter how hard he tried to wipe the memory from his mind, it slipped back in, again and again, and he wished he had a carousel of his own to carry him through the night.

3

The phone rang on Claire's office desk. She was about to ignore it, but then remembered that Jill, her secretary, was not in today to pick it up. Most of the foundation's employees were still digging out from the storm.

Claire lifted the receiver to her ear.

"Harte-Mathias Foundation."

"I'd like to speak with Mrs ... uh, Harte-Mathias, please?" The raspy male voice sounded vaguely familiar.

"This is she."

"Uh, hello. This is Detective Patrick in Harpers Ferry. You wanted to know when we identified that suicide."

"Yes." Claire sat up straight. "Did you find out who she is?"

"Her name was Margot St. Pierre, and she—"

"Margot, with a 't'?"

"Yes."

Claire jotted the name on a notepad.

"They finally found her late last night. The body'd

gotten caught in the rocks about a quarter mile from the bridge. She fit the description of a woman who'd been reported missing from Avery Hospital in Martinsburg. That's a mental—uh, a psychiatric hospital."

"How far is Martinsburg from Harpers Ferry?"

"Twenty-five, thirty miles. She'd just walked out of the hospital Sunday morning, according to the staff there. No one realized she was missing until that evening. They didn't have her in a locked ward, because she'd never given any indication of being a danger to herself or anyone else in the three years she'd been there."

"Three years?" Claire looked out her office window at the leafless, ice-coated trees.

"Yeah. Don't know why she was in that long. So, anyway, a fella picked her up outside Martinsburg. She had her thumb out and said she wanted to go to the bridge in Harpers Ferry. The guy called us late last night. Said he'd read about a woman jumping off the bridge and thought he'd better report what he knew. He said he refused to drop her off at the bridge, what with the snow and all, so she told him to take her to a certain house nearby, which he did. He didn't see her go in, though. We checked at the house. No one there knew of her, and she never went inside. Trying to throw the guy off her trail, I suspect."

Claire tapped her pen on the top of her desk. "Is there any family?" she asked. "Someone who cares about her, who should know what happened to her?"

"I don't have that data right in front of me, ma'am. Sorry."

They talked for another moment or two, but it was obvious that Detective Patrick had little other information to offer.

Claire hung up the phone, her eyes on the name she'd written on her notepad. Margot St. Pierre. A beautiful name. If she had heard it spoken by a stranger on the street, the name would have stayed in her mind for days. The fact that it belonged to the woman on the bridge meant she would never be able to forget it. No matter how much she wanted to.

It was nearly noon. Claire's morning had been long and full, despite the quiet, abandoned climate of the foundation offices. She had called the rehabilitation therapists she usually supervised on Tuesdays to cancel their meeting because of the weather, but Kelley Fielding, one of the graduate students doing her internship at the foundation, had broken into tears at that news. Needless to say, Claire had invited her to come in.

She'd listened to Kelley berate herself over her inability to work effectively with the angry, belligerent young men who made up the bulk of the foundation's rehab patients. They scared her, she said. She was useless with them.

Claire tried to get the young intern to see that her patients' hostility was only a mask for their fear. "Imagine waking up one day and having your life completely changed," she said. "Changed for good. Forever. The plans you had for yourself are gone. The goals you'd set for yourself are out of your reach. You can't work at your former job. You can't even go to the bathroom the way you used to. And you certainly can't make love the way you used to. These guys were macho and independent at one time. Now they wonder if they'll ever be able to do anything for themselves again. They're terrified men trying to cope the only way they know how."

"I just wish they could be a little less *combative*," Kelley had said.

"They have fight in them." Claire pounded a fist on her desk. "That's terrific. It gives you so much to work with."

Kelley had looked relieved and relaxed by the end of their meeting. She told Claire that she'd applied to do her internship at the foundation primarily to be able to work under her supervision. "I've never known anyone who could turn a negative into a positive the way you do," she said. "And you always manage to get me to see things through my patients' eyes."

It was easy for Claire to understand what Kelley's patients were going through. She was married to someone who'd been there.

Now, with the long morning behind her, Claire dialed the number for Jon's office on the other side of the building.

"Are you ready for a break?" she asked.

"Sure am."

She ran a fingertip over Margot's name on her notepad. "I just heard from the Harpers Ferry police."

"What did they say?"

"I'll tell you when I get there."

She got off the phone and stood up, and the room whirled around her for a second before coming to a standstill. That dizziness—that sudden vertigo—had seized her several times over the last two days. Twice last night, she'd awakened with a start, thinking she was still suspended on the slippery edge of the bridge.

She walked toward the door, knees trembling. There was a stiffness in her shoulders and back. She'd spent the afternoon before shoveling snow from the walks around their house while Jon rode the snowblower in the long driveway that stretched through the woods to the main road.

Leaving her boots in her office, she padded through the maze of gray-carpeted hallways in her socks. The glassy, three-story foundation building was set high above a small pond in a wooded section of Vienna. Jon's office was in what they referred to as the "financial side" of the foundation while her office was in the "service side." Jon was head of the financial side, determining what rehab-oriented programs would receive foundation funds, while she supervised the therapists working with the foundation's outpatient program. There was a great deal of overlap in their work. They were a team. They planned the foundation's annual Spinal Cord Injury Retreat together. They never spoke at a conference or led a workshop or counseled a couple without one another. People expected to see them together, and they had learned to play off each other's cues very well.

She glanced into Pat Wykowski's empty corner office as she passed it, wishing the foundation's part-time psychologist were in today. Pat might have been able to offer some insight into Margot St. Pierre's behavior—or maybe into her own. But Pat, whom Jon affectionately referred to as a party animal, was still up in Harpers Ferry with a few other die-hard conference attendees, dragging out the recreational element of the conference, making the most of the snowstorm.

Claire stopped at the kitchenette, picked up their bagged lunches and a couple of Cokes, then walked into Jon's office. He was sitting in his wheelchair behind his desk, talking on the phone. Claire pulled their sandwiches from the bags, along with his apple and her orange, and set them on paper plates. Then she sat down across the desk from him. When he hung up, he sighed.

"Are we overbooked for next month or can you handle one more workshop?" he asked.

"Where?"

"At Georgetown."

She laughed. "Do you need to ask?" They never turned down an opportunity to talk to students. Never.

"And guess what?"

"What?"

"We've got an invitation to the Accessibility Conference in Baltimore next month."

"Fantastic." She tried to get some zest in her voice, without success. It was truly terrific news, but she could not seem to shake herself free from Detective Patrick's phone call. "Would you like to know what I learned from the police?" she asked.

"Of course." If he was put off by her lackluster response to his news about the conference, he didn't show it. He took a bite from his sandwich and looked at her expectantly.

She repeated the information Detective Patrick had relayed to her, and he listened with interest. He even asked a few questions, but when she had told him all she knew, he glanced at his watch.

"We'll have to figure out the best way to handle the Accessibility Conference," he said. "We have to make the most of this invitation. Do you think we should host a reception in the hotel?"

His voice sounded far away. She rubbed her temples with the tips of her fingers. "I'm sorry, Jon. I'm having trouble thinking about anything other than Margot right now."

He looked at her over the rim of his Coke can. "You sound as though she was a personal friend. She was a stranger, Claire. And you did all you could for her."

She sighed, looking down at the untouched sandwich on its paper plate. "I know."

Jon leaned forward to reach across the desk, and she met his hand halfway with her own. "I think about the other night sometimes, too," he said. "It feels like a dream to me. The snow. The darkness. I feel as though it didn't really happen."

She wished she shared that sense of unreality. Every detail of those few minutes on the bridge was sharp and clear in her mind, and her body jerked involuntarily just thinking about it. She tightened her grip on his hand.

Jon was looking at her oddly. "Are you all right?" he asked.

"I'm fine." She let her hand slip from the desk to her lap. "I just wish I knew what her diagnosis was. Why was she in the hospital for so long?"

"Well, we can guess." Jon shifted in his chair. He seemed tired and restless, as he always did when he'd missed a few days at the gym. "Three years is a long, long time. She was delusional. Hallucinating. Obviously psychotic. And obviously a danger to herself."

Claire leaned forward. "But was she always that way? And who was she really? Did she have any family? Did she leave any children behind?"

Jon gave her a wry smile. "You really can't let go of this, can you?"

She ran her fingertip around the rim of her own Coke

can. "I think I need to understand, for my own peace of mind, why she would do what she did."

Jon balled up his lunch bag and tossed it, with perfect aim, into the wastepaper basket in the corner. "Two points," he said with a satisfied nod of his head. He looked at Claire again. "Maybe you need to prepare yourself for the fact that there might not be any answers."

She barely heard him. She looked out the window at the snow-covered trees. "Margot St. Pierre," she said. "Someone once cared enough about her to give her a beautiful name."

4

Seattle, Washington

A cold Seattle rain was falling outside Lassiter Hospital for Children as Vanessa Gray stepped through the automatic doors into the lobby. She closed her umbrella and pulled the scarf from her straight blond hair before walking toward the elevator. The traffic had been abysmal, and she was going to be more than a little late for rounds. But then, she was the attending physician in the adolescent unit; they would not start without her.

The four men and two women, all in their early to mid-twenties, were sitting in a half circle on the plastic and chrome chairs in the small conference room. The junior resident, one fellow, two interns, and two medical students all wore their white jackets, crisp and bright against the dark blue chairs. They were laughing when she opened the door, but quickly sobered. They had started their new rotation in adolescent medicine a couple of weeks earlier. None of them was certain yet how much levity she would allow. She knew they had heard about her. She was certain they'd been subjected to numerous tales of her mercurial temper, her attention to detail, her high expectations of her staff, and her unrelenting advocacy for her patients.

She sat down in the empty chair nearest the door. At thirty-eight, she felt far older than any of these green young doctors and students, and the feeling was not in the least unpleasant. She nodded across the room to red-haired Pete Aldrich, the resident. With pale, lightly freckled hands, Pete opened one of the charts resting on his lap.

"Couple of new admits," he said. "A new anorexic in one-oh-three. Fifteen-year-old female. Electrolyte imbalance. Bradycardia. Dehydrated. Eighty-three pounds at five-three. She's—"

"Does she have a name?" Vanessa interrupted him. She had one mounting concern about Pete Aldrich. He was bright—perhaps brilliant—but he tended to see his patients as little more than symptoms and diagnoses and treatment plans.

"Shelley Collier. She's a pacer. Paced the halls all night. Actually tried to run through the unit, but the nurses stopped her."

Vanessa sat back in her chair and looked around the group. "So, what should we do about Ms. Collier?"

"Prohibit exercise?" The female medical student spoke timidly.

"The nurse should be with her while she eats," the fellow added.

"She threw up her breakfast," Pete said.

"She can't use the bathroom for an hour after her meals," Vanessa said. "If she won't eat, give her osmolite. If she doesn't drink the osmolite within fifteen minutes, tube-feed her. Has a psychotherapist been assigned to her yet?"

"She was in to see her this morning."

"Good. Keep me posted on her. Who's the other admit?"

Pete opened a second chart. "Fourteen-year-old male CF, in for a tune-up. Been having increasingly hard time breathing at home. Hasn't been able to go to school and"—Pete caught himself and quickly glanced at the name on the chart—"Jordan Wiley," he said.

"Ah, Jordy." Vanessa let a sad smile pass over her face. Jordan Wiley had not been admitted to the hospital in two, maybe three, months, but he had been a regular visitor during the three years she'd been at Children's. The thought of him being once again under her care gave her both pain and pleasure. He was a terrific kid whom she could not help but admire. She had never seen such strength and courage in a patient. But no amount of bravado would save Jordy from the inevitable. He had cystic fibrosis. His breathing was always a struggle. It was anyone's guess which admission to the hospital would be his last. Leaning forward, she questioned Pete closely about his condition.

Pete looked down at his notes. "He's very small for his age—looks about ten or eleven—with a deformed chest. He's having trouble breathing, but he's not cyanotic. Nail beds are pink."

She could picture those nails, overlarge and thick from lack of oxygen. She remembered the rounded shoulders and protruding sternum—the result of Jordy's struggle to draw in air.

"Really junky lungs," Aldrich continued. "Coughing up huge amounts of mucus. Good appetite, though. He ate an enormous breakfast—I mean, this kid can pack it away— and then threw it up after he was percussed."

"He shouldn't be percussed too soon after his meals," Vanessa said.

"That's exactly what he said." Pete looked amazed at hearing the same words from her mouth. "He's really an irritating kid. He tells you what you should be doing for him, and he asks questions about everything. What kind of antibiotic is he getting, shouldn't the dosage be different, and on and on. Thinks he knows more than we do, you know?" He looked at one of the interns for support, and the young woman nodded in agreement.

Vanessa crossed the circle to take the chart from Pete's hand. "I would guess he *does* know more than you about his condition," she said, sitting down again. "He probably knows more than the six of you put together. Possibly more than the seven of us. He's been studying cystic fibrosis longer than you have, Dr. Aldrich." She opened the chart but did not look inside. "He's an expert," she said. "I suggest you listen to him."

She wanted to see Jordy herself. After rounds, she walked to the room he was sharing with another young-looking fifteen-year-old, a kidney patient. She stood in the doorway. Jordy was sitting in his bed, hunched over a pillow. He was turning the pages of the comic book lying on the mattress in front of him. He looked worse than she had ever seen him. He was a tiny, gaunt figure in the large bed. His skin was a pasty, papery white. His frizzy dark hair was pulled into a small ponytail at the back of his neck. She masked her distress at seeing him look so sick.

"Hey, kid," she said from the doorway.

He looked up from the comic book and grinned. "You gotta get me out of here, Dr. Gray. My scout troop is going to this midwinter encampment in two weeks, and I've gotta be there."

She smiled as she walked toward his bed. He had timed this. A typical "tune-up" for a typical CF kid was fourteen days. He wanted to be in the best shape he could for his encampment. She pulled the curtain between his bed and that of his sleeping roommate.

"Dr. Aldrich said you had to stop going to school."

"Is he the one with the red hair? He wouldn't listen to me. I told him I'd puke if I had percussion after breakfast."

"I heard. It won't happen again."

"You can sit." Jordy scooted toward the side of his bed to make room for her as she sat down. She would never have sat there without his invitation. She had chewed out more than one medical student for sitting on a bed without the permission of its occupant, invading the only space these kids had to call their own.

"So what's this about school?" she asked again.

Jordy let out a ragged-sounding sigh. "It's worse than ever," he said, and she knew he was referring to his condition. "I can't lie down anymore. I can't breathe that way. Have to sleep sitting up. And I can't get up the stairs."

"Should you have come in sooner?" She thought— although could not have sworn to it—that there was a faint bluish tint to his lips.

"Probably," he admitted.

She noticed the small gold hoop in his left ear. "Where'd this come from?" She touched it lightly.

"You like it? Kinda cool, huh?"

"Kinda." She felt the threat of tears in the back of her throat and behind her eyes. He would never fit in, this boy. At one time, when he was very small, he had. But his classmates had grown and played hard and flourished while he had stayed small, his body weakening, almost month by month. The earring was his attempt at normalcy. "You are definitely one of the coolest kids I know, Jordy."

"Jordan." He corrected her with a grimace.

"Oh. Jordan." She had a vague memory of him telling her during his last hospitalization that he no longer wanted to be called by his nickname. He thought it made him sound too young.

"So, um, who else has been in?" There was trepidation in his voice, as there always was when a CF kid asked about other patients he might remember from previous hospitalizations. She rattled off a few names of kids he knew, updating him on how they were doing, before telling him, gently, that Holly Marx had died during her last stay.

"Damn." He shook his head and looked down at his comic book. A patch of red formed on his throat, and his nostrils flared. "That sucks, man," he said. "That really sucks."

Vanessa nodded. "I know."

He looked up at her, the look in his eyes a mixture of anger and fear. "Dr. Gray?"

"Yes?"

"I really want to go on that encampment."

She smiled, squeezing his knee as she got to her feet. "We'll do our best to get you there, Jordan," she said.

It was dark when she left the hospital that night, but she took the time to stop at a stationery store to pick up a card for Brian. He would be home when she got there, after five days on the road. She wanted to celebrate, as she always did, his safe return. She hated those trips, knowing he was almost constantly in the air. Despite the safety record of commercial flights and the fact that he was one of the best pilots ever born, she could not relax until he was securely grounded in the town house they'd shared for the past two years.

She read more than a dozen cards before finding one that had the right tone. It was clearly, strongly, loving, but without demands or expectations. Brian regularly invited her to ask more of him, but she was not yet ready to make herself that vulnerable.

It was after seven when she pulled into the garage of their town house, the garage her car shared with the metal pipes from Brian's soccer goal, along with his varied collection of balls and bats and tennis rackets. He'd finally given up rugby this year—the week after he turned forty—but as far as Vanessa could tell, Brian Everett had simply channeled his passion for rugby into the other sports he loved.

Stepping out of the car, she could smell the aroma of something Oriental—soy sauce and sesame oil—and she smiled to herself. He was cooking. He was in a good mood, as happy to be home as she was to have him there.

He greeted her at the door, spatula in hand, and pulled her into an embrace. Soft piano music from the stereo in the den filled the air around them as she kissed him, slipping the card into the wide pocket of his smock-style apron for him to find later. Brian liked surprises.

"I've missed you something fierce," he said.

She stepped into the kitchen and took off her coat, draping it over a chair. Then she wrapped her arms around him again, and for a moment she was aware only of the warmth of his body against hers, the sensation of his lips pressing hard and hungrily on her own.

He drew away from her. A lock of brown hair fell over his forehead, and there was a smile on his boyish face. "Let's skip dinner," he said.

"But it smells so good."

"Later." He turned off the heat under the wok, then put his arms around her again. "How about right here in the kitchen, huh?" He nuzzled her neck. "Have you ever made love on the kitchen floor?"

"Uh-uh." She had, but not in a very long time. She barely remembered the man, and "making love" was probably not an accurate description of what had occurred between them.

She tapped her foot on the tile floor. "It'll be awfully hard, though," she said.

"It's extremely hard." He took her hand from around his neck and drew it toward the front of his pants. "Want to see?"

She laughed, and their hands butted up against the card in his pocket.

"What's this?" He pulled out the card and opened it, reading it to himself. His face grew serious for a moment, and he pulled her back into a crushing embrace. "I love you, too, Van." His voice was husky, and for the second time that day she felt the threat of tears.

It was another minute before Brian let go of her. "So," he said, "the floor? I have to warn you, though. I've been replacing your birth control pills with placebos."

Vanessa shook her head with a smile, taking his hand. "Come on." She led him toward the hallway, and without protesting further, he followed her into the bedroom.

She made a quick stop in the bathroom, and by the time she emerged, Brian had lit a candle and set it on the dresser.

She undressed and joined him on the queen-sized water bed. They kissed for a long time, so long that her body began seeking more from him. Her legs twined around his; her arms circled his back to pull him closer. But just as Brian's hand came to rest on her breast, his fingers grazing her nipple, the phone rang on the night table.

She lifted her head to see which line was ringing. The red light blinked above line two—her hospital line. It had to be important. She groaned.

"Ignore it," Brian said.

"You know I can't." She reached for the telephone and spoke into the receiver. "Vanessa Gray."

"Van, it's Darcy."

Vanessa rolled onto her back, frowning. This could not be urgent. Darcy Frederick was the executive officer at Lassiter responsible for a variety of tasks, including fund-raising and legislation related to children. She was also Vanessa's after-work running partner. It was unusual, though, for Darcy to call her at home.

"What's up?" she asked. Brian was playing with her hair, lifting it up, letting it fall from his hand. In the candlelight, she could see the strands of gold slipping through his fingers.

"Bad news, Van," Darcy said. "Sorry to bother you at home, but I wanted you to hear it from me first."

Vanessa braced herself. She knew that Darcy was not talking about a patient; she was talking about the hospital's purse strings. The administrators had been meeting for days to determine where to make cuts.

It felt suddenly chilly in the room, and she tugged the sheet up over her shoulders. "Spit it out," she said.

"The AMC Program."

Adolescents Molested as Children. Vanessa shut her eyes.

"What about it?" she asked, although she was certain she knew.

"I'm so sorry, Van. They cut it."

"You mean, completely?" Vanessa opened her eyes to find Brian looking at her, a frown on his face.

"Yes."

"Uh-uh." Vanessa sat up. "That is absolutely unacceptable."

"You talk like you have some say in the matter," Darcy said.

"They cannot cut the AMC." She heard Brian groan as he realized what she and Darcy were talking about.

"I fought for it, Van," Darcy said, "but I was alone out there. I know it's your pet project, but they just don't get it. 'Lassiter has bigger fish to fry.' That's a direct quote."

"But it's a *preventive* program," Vanessa argued. That had been the approach she'd taken when she'd initially started the fight for funding not much more than a year ago. The thought of going through that all over again was exhausting. Yet the arguments poured out of her mouth easily. "The kids who try to kill themselves, or starve themselves, or—"

"I know, I know." Darcy interrupted her. She sounded tired, and Vanessa pictured her taking off her thick glasses, rubbing her blue eyes. "You don't have to sell *me* on it, Van. And you might as well save your breath with the other decision makers as well. The fact is, those kids are not the ones who generate a ton of sympathy, you know what I mean?"

Yes, she knew all too well. If the hospital had a dollar to spend and the choice was between some cute little five-year-old who was currently being abused by a stepfather and some oppositional, self-destructive, nasty-mouthed teenager who'd been abused at some time in the past—well, there was no contest. They could not get it through their heads that both kids were worth saving, that maybe they could prevent that teenager from becoming an oppositional, self-destructive, nasty-mouthed adult.

"Those idiots need to get their priorities straight." She felt Brian's warm hand stroking her back. She had almost forgotten he was there.

Darcy sighed on her end of the line. "I'm only the messenger," she said.

"We've barely gotten off the ground." Vanessa could not seem to stop herself from arguing. "We've had no chance to collect statistics, no chance to measure how effective the program is. Just two more years. Tell them that."

"They're firm about this, Vanessa. It was one of the cuts they were in complete agreement on. They think it's expendable."

"Right, and what if it was one of their own kids on the line? How expendable would it be then, huh? Assholes."

"*Van*," Darcy was losing her patience. "Chill out."

Vanessa lay down again with a sense of defeat. She was useless when her emotions got in the way. She could handle a battle from a controlled, logical, persuasive stance only so long before she was reduced to cursing, fist-pounding, and on a few humiliating occasions, tears.

She pulled in a long breath before speaking again. "I'm getting funding for the AMC somehow, some way, Darcy," she said. "That program is not folding."

Darcy was quiet for a moment. "I'll help you," she said finally. "You won't get it from Lassiter, but we'll put our heads together and come up with something else, okay?"

"Okay."

Vanessa hung up the phone and looked at Brian.

"Sorry, Van," he said. "It wasn't unexpected, though, was it?"

The honey-colored candlelight flickered on the high cathedral ceiling above the bed. "I guess I was hoping a miracle would happen," she said. From the moment she'd been hired at Lassiter, she'd fought for that program. Any kid who passed through the adolescent unit whose current problems might be linked to past abuse was screened to be put in the AMC. Vanessa could practically sniff those kids out. The rest of the staff marveled at her sixth sense.

"I think I blew it when I went for funding originally," she added. "I wasn't tough enough. Maybe what I really needed to do was to give them a dose of personal experience."

Brian touched her cheek. "Could you have done that?" he asked softly, and she shook her head.

"No." She stretched her arms toward the ceiling with a sigh. "No, I'm gutless."

Brian chuckled and rolled to face her, propping himself up on his elbows. "That's hardly the adjective I'd use to describe you."

"Yeah, well, the adjectives that describe me are going to be my ruin. I'm a stubborn, obnoxious woman, remember?" That was the phrase one of the administrators had used in reference to her the year before.

Brian kissed her lightly on the lips. "I would never use those words to describe you."

"Difficult, then."

"Determined."

She smiled at him. "I love you."

He gave her a rueful smile in return. "That phone call was a real passion-killer, huh?"

She reached for him, wrapping her arms around his shoulders. "No," she said. "I don't think so."

They ate dinner after making love, the stir-fried chicken and vegetables by this time sodden but delicious. Then they sat in the den by a glowing fire, comparing their schedules for the week. It was close to midnight when Brian finally persuaded her to go to bed for the night. She was afraid of bed, afraid that sleep would be elusive.

Once in bed, she tried to block thoughts of the AMC program from her mind, but they were replaced by images of Jordan Wiley, small and gaunt, bright and ever hopeful. Still, she fell asleep more rapidly than she would have thought possible. Around two, though, she was awakened by a nightmare so vivid in color and sound and motion that she lurched forward in bed, clutching her throat, gasping for breath.

It took her a moment to realize that Brian was sitting next to her, that he was holding her. "You're safe, baby," he said. "Safe in Seattle, Washington, a million miles from anything that can hurt you."

The music played in her head, and she pressed her hands over her ears as if she could somehow block it out.

"The carousel?" Brian asked.

She managed to nod her head, squeezing her eyes shut. The painted ponies with their wild angry eyes and open mouths still galloped and leaped in front of her. The brass poles shifted up and down, and the small oval mirrors on the inside rim of the carousel sent shards of reflected light to her eyes. The world spun past her, far too fast, and she felt sick to her stomach. And all the while, the hideous organ music filled her ears.

Brian let go of her to turn on the lamp, and she clutched his arm. "I'm right here," he said. "Not going anywhere."

She opened her eyes to the light and looked around the room. The mint green walls stretched up to the high cathedral ceiling, the mirror above the teak dresser reflected the painting of soothing green grass and red poppies that hung behind the bed, the water-bed mattress was warm beneath her legs. And slowly, the horses became pale and transparent, featureless. Finally they disappeared, along with the music.

"Shit!" Vanessa pounded her fist onto the bed. "Where the hell did *that* come from?" She looked into Brian's eyes and wrinkled her nose. "I'm sorry," she said. "Good old Vanessa, right? She's fucked up again."

"Stop it." He scolded her, then lay back on the mattress, pulling her down next to him.

She stared at the ceiling. "I thought I was through with that garbage." There had been other dreams, other nightmares. The one where they took Anna from her, where she searched the streets and knocked on doors and looked in dumpsters trying to find her again—that was the worst. But the carousel was a close second. She hadn't had that dream in more than a year, not since those miserable days when she was first fighting for the AMC program.

And now she was starting that fight all over again.

"It's not fair for you to have to go through this with me again," she said.

"I'm a big boy. I can take care of myself, Vanessa."

"I would understand if you wanted out. There's no reason for you to suffer just because I have to." She was always doing that, giving him permission to leave. Then, if he ever did go, she could tell herself it was her doing, not his.

"I have a better idea," he said. "Marry me and let's have a baby. Then maybe you'll get it through your thick skull how committed I am to you."

She managed to smile at him. "Someday, maybe," she said. She wanted both those things more than she could express to him, and she had thought she was nearly ready. Weeks, sometimes months went by when she did not once think of the possibility of Brian leaving her.

"Do you want the night-light on?" Brian asked.

She rolled her eyes. "I guess."

She reached low on the wall behind her night table to turn the little switch on the night-light while Brian turned off his lamp. Then she settled next to him, her arm across his chest. With her eyes closed, the night-light bathed her vision in a familiar, comforting deep violet, and she knew the light would keep her safe from the horses and the mirrors, safe from the spinning, reeling world of the merry-go-round.

5

Vienna

Claire and Jon spent the morning in Claire's office at the foundation, counseling a young couple, Lynn and Paul Stanwick. For the most part, the Stanwicks had adjusted well to the injury that had left Paul in a wheelchair, but when it came to the issue of sexuality, their basically solid marriage was creaking under the strain of too much left unsaid.

"He's never even mentioned sex since the accident," Lynn said, "so I figured he's just lost interest in it." She looked squarely at her husband from beneath her long, dark bangs. "I don't think you feel anything for me anymore. Any desire, I mean."

Paul groaned and looked up at the ceiling.

Jon laughed. "Can I speak for you, Paul?"

Claire knew what Jon was going to say. She could have said it herself, but the words would never have the same impact coming from her.

Paul nodded his permission, and Jon continued. "I'd be

willing to bet that sexual desire is so constant and so intense for you that you can feel it in your toes."

"*Yes*." Paul looked surprised.

"You long to express it, but can't," Jon said. "You used to know how, but not anymore. Everything's changed, and nothing's changed. Your body is completely different, but your needs are entirely the same."

Claire saw tears welling up in Paul's dark eyes, and she was pleased when Lynn reached over to take his hand. They would be all right, these two.

Of all her tasks at the foundation, this was Claire's favorite—working with Jon to help a couple meet the challenges that had been dumped in their laps. She loved watching Jon counsel someone. He was so good at capturing the feelings of whoever sat in that wheelchair and making those feelings safe to talk about. Claire always emerged from these sessions enormously glad that he was her husband.

She and Jon gradually led the Stanwicks into a discussion of experimentation, of discovering each other's needs and desires, of separating the possible from the impossible.

"I can have a reflex erection," Paul said. "It's not spectacular but—"

"I think it's spectacular," Lynn interjected.

Jon laughed. "Well, then you can experiment with intercourse, too."

"But he can't ejaculate," Lynn said. "It doesn't seem like it would be fair to him."

"I'd like to try, though." Paul looked at his wife. "You'd enjoy it, wouldn't you? I'd like watching you enjoy it."

Claire was touched. This guy was a sweetheart.

"I'm not saying it won't be frustrating, Paul," Jon said.

"The truth is, a lot of your pleasure will come from Lynn's."

Jon had once told Claire that when she was happy, he was happy, when she hurt, he hurt . . . and when she came, he came. She'd felt a flash of selfishness then, but he'd said those words with no sorrow or self-pity, and she'd tucked her guilt away.

Jon *could* come, in a sense. Sometimes. It was unpredictable, both the occurrence and the sensations it produced. Unlike Paul Stanwick, Jon had suffered an incomplete injury to his spinal cord. At times, his numbness gave way to a prickling, burning feeling or to what he described as "minifireworks" that shot off when and where he least expected them. He'd once said that having some feeling was worse than none at all. But he'd never said it again, and she did not believe he'd meant it.

Claire had something she wanted to say to Lynn Stanwick. She debated quickly whether to bring it up here or to wait until she had a session with the woman alone. This couple could handle it, she decided.

"Lynn." She leaned toward the younger woman. "Paul's not going to have the ability to move the way he used to. You'll probably have to take responsibility for your own orgasm if you want to have one during intercourse."

Lynn's eyes widened. "You mean . . . masturbate?"

Claire nodded, and Paul groaned.

"Sorry, kid." Paul gave his wife a wry smile.

"No problem," Lynn said, but from the expression on her face, Claire knew it would take Lynn a while to get used to the idea.

After the Stanwicks had left her office, Claire walked over to Jon and bent low for a hug.

"Good session, Mathias," she said.

He wrapped his hand around her thigh. "Made me kinda hungry for you, Harte."

"Tonight," she promised.

He let go of her leg as Jill ducked into the office to hand Claire a stack of pink message slips. Claire noticed the name on the top slip: Detective Patrick.

Jon wheeled past her to the door. "Are you ready to come to my office to work on the retreat?" he asked.

Claire stared at the pink slip in her hand. She could toss it out. Forget it. It had been nearly a week since that night in Harpers Ferry, and she had just proved to herself that she could get through an entire counseling session without a single thought of Margot. That was rare, though. More often that not, she found herself fighting the memory of that night on the bridge, along with the vertigo that accompanied it.

"I'll be there as soon as I return these calls," she said.

She closed her office door after Jon left, then walked to her desk and dialed the number for the Harpers Ferry police.

"I thought you'd want to know this right away," Detective Patrick said. His raspy voice was tinged with a boyish excitement. "It turns out that the other night was not Margot St. Pierre's first experience on that bridge."

Claire sat down behind the desk. "What do you mean?"

"Well, it seems as though she grew up in Harpers Ferry, and twenty years ago—to the very *day* that she jumped— she and her brother were playing on that same bridge when the brother fell off and was killed."

"*What?*"

"Right." There was some pleasure in his voice, as though

he enjoyed passing on a good piece of gossip. "I don't know a whole lot more about it," he said. "We got this piece of information from the social worker at the Avery Mental Hospital, and she didn't know much more herself. Though she did say that Miss St. Pierre fell, too. Not into the water, but more towards the embankment. Hit her head on the rocks. They think that might have been part of what was wrong with her."

Claire looked out the window, where the sunlit snow still blanketed the ground and clung to the banks of the pond. What was it Margot had said to her: *I died on this bridge long ago*? Something like that. "It's been haunting her all these years, poor thing," she said.

"Looks that way. The social worker said they were some kind of musical geniuses or something."

"Who were? Margot and her brother?"

"Right. You know, that kind of kid who can play the piano as good as an adult?"

"Oh!" Claire recalled more of Margot's words. "Chopin."

"What's that?"

"Nothing." She felt herself getting sucked in deeper. The more information she was given about Margot, the more she seemed to need. "Do you think I could talk to the social worker at the psychiatric hospital—if I should decide I'd like to?" She turned the pink message slip over and picked up a pen.

"Don't see why not." Detective Patrick gave her the woman's name, along with the number for the hospital. "This case is closed for us," he said. "A suicide, cut-and-dried. But I thought you'd want to know this piece of it before I put the file away."

Claire stared at the message slip for a long time after getting off the phone. She was thinking. Plotting. She got up from her desk and walked quickly through the maze of corridors to Jon's office.

He was leafing though a stack of papers on his desk when she walked into the room. "Ah, good," he said. "We need to talk about who can run the driving workshop at the retreat this year. Lillian's going to be on maternity leave, and—"

"Jon?" She sat down on his green sofa.

He stopped shuffling the papers on his desk, raising his eyebrows. "Yes?"

"One of those calls I returned was from Detective Patrick. He told me that twenty years ago, Margot and her brother fell from that same bridge. The brother was killed, and Margot was injured."

Jon's eyes were wide. "No kidding? Was she trying to join him or what?"

"I don't know, but I would really like to find out. Would you mind if I took the rest of the day off?" He did not respond, and she rushed ahead. "I know we have retreat stuff to get done, but I can work on that tonight." They would be swamped with "retreat stuff" from now until the weekend of the annual retreat itself, to be held, as always, in September in the Shenandoah Valley. "I want to go to the library in Harpers Ferry to see what I can find out about that incident."

She could not read his face. The miniblinds at his window cast lines of shadow across his cheek. He looked down at the papers on his desk, shoving one of them with the tip of his finger. "I didn't realize you had so much Nancy Drew in you," he said.

"Neither did I." She tried to smile.

He was quiet again, tapping his fingers on the papers. When he looked up, he spoke quietly. "I don't think I've ever seen you like this," he said.

"What do you mean?"

"I mean, you don't usually carry stuff around with you. Shit happens, and you say, *que sera, sera*, and get on with your life."

She sat back on the sofa with a sigh. He was right. "I don't know what it is, Jon." She lifted her hands and dropped them into her lap. "I feel as though she's not going to let go of me unless I follow this through."

"Could you wait until tomorrow?" Jon asked. "I could go with you then. But I can't get away today."

"That's all right. I don't mind going alone."

"Maybe Amelia could go?"

She considered the idea for a few seconds before discarding it. She usually relished spending time with Amelia, her neighbor and longtime friend. But not today. When she'd told Amelia about Margot's suicide, Amelia had said that perhaps Margot's death had been for the best. "She sounded so disturbed," she'd said. "So miserable." Claire heard the words she herself had spoken so often to other people—*Maybe it's for the best*—and suddenly the phrase made her bristle. No, she didn't want Amelia with her. Or Jon. She wanted to do this on her own. She was the only person who really cared what she unearthed in that library.

"I'm going by myself." She stood up and walked over to Jon's desk, bent down, and kissed him. "Am I acting crazy?"

He reached up, his hand circling her shoulder, and

tugged her down for a second kiss. "Crazed, but not crazy," he said. "I'll see you tonight."

It was a warm day for January, a beautiful sunlit day, the snow melting along the side of the road as Claire neared Harpers Ferry. She felt relaxed and calm, and so she was unprepared for the dizzy, sick-to-her-stomach sensation that accompanied her as she drove across the too-familiar bridge above the Shenandoah. In the daylight, the bridge held no visible threat. The road was clear of snow, the sky was an unbroken expanse of azure blue, and the bright afternoon sun glittered on the guardrail. A few other cars crossed the bridge with her, but she was certain she was the only driver for whom that stretch of concrete seemed unending, the only driver to feel the ominous pull of the river below.

Her heart was pounding in her throat by the time she reached the other side, and she had to pull to the side of the road to catch her breath. She extracted a tissue from her purse and wiped the beads of perspiration from her fore-head. How was she going to cross that bridge again to go home? Crazy. This was crazy.

She found the library easily. The librarian set her up in a small room with several cases of microfilm. For ten min-utes, she scrolled through newspapers from the second week of January 1973, and she was beginning to think that Detective Patrick had gotten his information wrong. But then, suddenly, there it was, on the front page of the January 14 edition.

The article was one column, about seven inches long. CHILD DIES IN FALL FROM BRIDGE, the headline read. Claire turned the knob on the microfilm machine to bring the fine print into focus.

There had been a severe snowstorm the night of January 10, the article stated, and the bridge had been empty of traffic. Details of the fall itself, though, were sketchy. The dead boy had been Margot's twin brother, ten-year-old Charles. Another brother, Randall, age fifteen, had also been present. After Charles fell, Randall and Margot tried to scale the embankment to reach the boy. During that climb, Margot herself fell and was knocked unconscious. Randall carried her home, a mile from the bridge. The end of the article stated that Margot remained in a coma at a nearby hospital. It was not known how extensive her injuries were or if she was expected to recover from them.

A good two-thirds of the article was devoted to the twins' impressive, albeit short, biographies. Their father was a classical pianist, and the twins were considered child prodigies. They had appeared in a Young People's Concert the previous year at Carnegie Hall and had been accepted at Juilliard for the following year.

It didn't fit, Claire thought. She could not imagine these little musical geniuses living in a tiny West Virginia hamlet like Harpers Ferry.

It was after dark when she pulled into her driveway. From inside her car, she opened the center door of the three-car garage. Driving in, she got a deceptive rush of delight at seeing Susan's red Toyota parked in its space, and she had to remind herself that her daughter was not home. Susan had called the night before to tell them it would be a couple of weeks before she could get back to Vienna to pick up her car.

Jon had bought a roasted chicken at the supermarket and a container of potato salad, and she joined him at the kitchen table. She told him what she'd learned at the library, and he asked appropriate questions, but he was uncharacteristically subdued. He was not interested in Margot St. Pierre; she had to accept that. After dinner, she shifted their conversation to the retreat and saw his usual animation return.

In bed that night, he pulled her close under the down comforter. "I was worried about you driving out there by yourself," he said.

"I was perfectly fine."

He ran his hand slowly over the bare skin of her back. "I know how upset you were the last time we were in Harpers Ferry. I thought being there again might bring some of that back. I didn't like to think of you alone."

"It was no big deal. It was a beautiful day for a drive." She touched the corner of his mouth. She wanted to see him smile. Jon circled her arm lightly with his fingers. "Do you think you can lay Margot to rest now?" he asked.

Claire hesitated. She wished he hadn't asked. "I want to, but there's one more thing I need to do," she said. "I'd like to talk with the social worker at Avery Hospital about her. Then I think I'll be done with it for good."

Jon slipped into silence. Outside the closed bedroom windows, a branch snapped on a tree somewhere in the woods.

"What's the point to this, Claire?" Jon asked finally.

"I'm not sure." She ran her fingertips across the light tracing of hair on his chest. "I try to block thoughts of her and that night from my mind, but they keep creeping in."

He stroked his fingers across her cheek. "That must be very frustrating," he said.

"It is. And I think the only way to put an end to them is to understand as much as I can about why it happened.

I was the last person to see her alive. I was the last one who had a chance with her."

Jon dropped his hand from her arm and said nothing. The silence swept around them for several minutes before she propped herself up on her elbow to look into his eyes.

"Are you upset with me over this?" She wasn't used to his disapproval.

He shook his head, touching her cheek lightly again with his fingers. "I wish it hadn't happened," he said. "But it did. And I guess you have to find your own way of putting it to sleep."

"I don't have to drag you into it, though." She could not bear his sullenness, his worry. She lowered her head to kiss him. "So," she said, "are you still hungry for me?"

"What? Oh." He smiled. "A little."

She kissed him again, then shifted on the bed to touch his eyelids with her lips, the tip of her tongue. She remembered him telling Paul Stanwick during their session that morning that Paul would discover erogenous zones he had never known he'd had. For Jon, it was his eyelids.

"Mmm," he murmured. "I can feel my appetite coming back."

With a rush of energy, he rolled her onto her back and kissed her, tenderly, nibbling at her lips. Her breathing quickened, keeping pace with his as he lowered his mouth to her throat, her breasts. She felt the warmth of his tongue on her nipple and slipped her fingers into his hair.

"So," he said, his breath warm against her chest, "what feels good, hmm?"

"That does," she said, then arched her back as the tug of his lips grew stronger. "Oh, *yes*."

They had been lovers for twenty-three years. They

didn't need to ask each other what felt good. Yet they still, on occasion, bantered this way. Talking was an aphrodisiac, they'd discovered. An erogenous zone all its own. Talk alone used to be enough to make Jon hard and ready, but that phenomenon was rare these days. "It's a normal function of age," she'd reassured him, although she knew it was the injury at work. She was certain Jon was aware of that fact even more than she was.

Jon touched her with his hands and his mouth, moving down her body, teasing her as he took his time. He kissed the inside of her thighs so delicately and for so long that by the time he turned his head to give his lips and tongue free rein over her, she was already trembling with the early vibrations of an orgasm. She came quickly, but he did not stop touching her until she reached down to pull him up for a kiss. He supported himself on his arms above her while she slid her hand down his body to his penis. She stroked him, her touch practiced yet tender—despite his inability to feel it—and when her hand had filled with his firm warmth, she slipped her hips beneath his and guided him inside her.

She clutched his shoulders. The muscles in his arms were like iron, and she felt them tighten and catch beneath her hands as he rocked slowly above her, inside her. His strength excited her, as it always did. It seemed he could hold himself suspended above her that way forever as he watched her. Watched and waited. She had learned to set aside her inhibitions about being on display. He *had* to watch. For Jon, it was a large part of the pleasure.

She slipped her hand between their bodies, letting her fingers come to rest where his body was joined to hers. The image of Lynn Stanwick's wide and surprised eyes flitted briefly across her mind as Jon rhythmically pressed his hips against hers. She was aware of the softening of his erection, but it didn't matter. He was still inside her, still filling her, and she was lifting up, losing the sense of the bed beneath her head, her back. Jon was moving so slowly. Languidly. He knew how to move—oh, the wondrous hours of research that had entailed!—to let her body rise and fall, rise and fall, as it was doing now. He did not even pick up his pace as she began gasping for breath, or when she cried out, digging her fingers into his shoulder. And he kept his steady course as she flew into that brilliant shower of light—the light he could experience only through her.

There was peace in the room after a while, a peace that seemed hard-won and badly needed, and Claire lay next to Jon, her cheek against his shoulder. She was almost asleep when he broke the silence.

"Claire," he said, "I want you to tell me the things you learn about Margot. It might not mean as much to me as to you, but I'll listen."

She wrapped her arm around his waist, smiling. "I love you, Mathias," she said, and she snuggled closer to him, secure in the expectation of a contented night's sleep.

The weather had turned cold again by the following Monday, and the threat of snow hung low in the morning sky as Claire made the hour-and-a-half drive to Avery Hospital. The old brick building seemed to sag in the gloomy daylight as she pulled into the parking lot, and she felt compassion for Margot, for anyone who had to call this depressing building home.

She'd had to manipulate this meeting with Ginger Stern, the social worker who had worked with Margot. Ginger had been reluctant to talk about her former patient until Claire began connecting to her on a professional level. She was a fellow social worker, Claire said, although that was not quite the truth. She and Jon had both majored in social work at Catholic University in Washington, D.C., not far from where they lived now, but while Jon had graduated with honors, Claire had barely made it out of the program with her degree. She had gained a reputation among her instructors as a young woman with her head too much in the clouds to deal well with reality. In an evaluation of her skills, one of her professors had written, "Miss Harte is not able to accept that, in their day-to-day interactions, people do not always keep one another's best interests in mind. This attitude may prevent her from offering appropriate help to her clients." Or, as one of her fellow students put it, more succinctly and to her face, "You're a terrific person, Claire, but a lousy social worker." Claire had shrugged off the comments the way she shrugged off anything she did not want to hear.

In graduate school, she majored in rehabilitation therapy, where her positive attitude toward life was better appreciated, while Jon worked on a double master's in social work and health administration. It was the mention of Jon's name that finally got her the appointment with Ginger Stern.

"Jon Harte-Mathias?" Ginger had exclaimed. Apparently the Harte-Mathias name had not registered when she'd heard it attached to Claire. "From the foundation?"

As it turned out, Ginger's brother had gone through a rehab program funded by the foundation. She knew the story of the foundation's birth: A young man working in a rehab center inherited millions of dollars on his twenty-

fifth birthday—money that had been left in trust for him
when his parents were killed in a plane crash. He spent
little of the money on himself and his wife and baby,
instead pouring the millions into the development of the
Harte-Mathias Foundation. There were no inaccuracies in
Ginger's recitation of the story, but in the telling, she made
Jon sound like some sort of folk hero. It didn't matter. Here
she was, in the parking lot of Avery Hospital, about to
meet with the person who probably knew Margot St.
Pierre as well as anyone could.

Ginger was waiting for her inside the hospital. She was
an energetic blonde and much younger than Claire had
expected—probably younger than Margot had been by
several years. Despite her youth, though, she had an air of
self-confidence. Claire followed her into a small, win-
dowless office. Ginger sat down behind a stubby desk, and
Claire took the only other chair in the room—a small
wooden rocker that looked as though it had been discovered in a garage sale.

Claire rested her hands on her knees. "Now that I'm
here, I'm really not certain what I'm looking for," she said,
an apology in her voice. "I just can't seem to stop thinking
about her."

"That's understandable," Ginger said with a smile. "I'd
heard you went out on the bridge with her. I couldn't
believe anyone would do that."

"It was one of those things you do without thinking."

Ginger looked at her with curiosity. "You know that
what happened is not your fault, don't you?"

Claire sighed. "On some level, I know that's true. I just
wish I could have gotten her to wait a few more seconds.
The police were so close."

"You tried. That's more than ninety-nine percent of the population would have done. And Margot"—she shook her head—"Margot had a mind of her own." Ginger let out a sigh and moved to the edge of her seat, as if she were about to stand up. "Would you like to see her room?" she asked.

Claire nodded. She left her coat on the rocker and followed Ginger out of the office. They walked down a long, dim hallway, the walls painted a pale, dingy green. She remembered something she'd learned in college, something about psychiatric institutions using color to alter the moods of the patients. She wondered what this green was supposed to do. Certainly not lift anyone out of depression. Claire felt herself sinking lower with each step.

"Margot had been ill for a very long time," Ginger said as they walked. "Ever since losing her brother on the bridge. Her mother cared for her after that, but when her mother died, her father had her committed. He simply couldn't handle her. He visited her once in a while, but he died a year ago." She opened one of the doors that lined the hallway and stepped back to let Claire pass through. "This was her room."

The room was a small rectangle furnished with two twin beds, two night tables, and two small, squat dressers. The faded green walls on the near side of the room were covered with posters of Elvis Presley, and the three embroidered pillows on the bed all bore his likeness.

"She was an Elvis fan?" Claire said, incredulous.

"No." Ginger laughed. "That's Nonnie's half of the room. Nonnie was Margot's roommate."

Claire shifted her focus to Margot's side. The walls were bare, the bed neatly made with a thin green spread. "Margot's things have already been cleared out, then."

"Well, actually, no." Ginger walked across the room to Margot's bed, where she smoothed her hand across the bedspread. "Margot wasn't much of a decorator. She never put a thing on the walls, at least not during the couple of years I've worked here. She had exactly one picture." She opened the drawer of the night table to pull out a framed photograph, which she handed to Claire across Nonnie's bed.

It was a family portrait, a faded, five-by-seven black-and-white, obviously taken by an amateur photographer. A man and woman stood on the steps of a white house, the size and shape of which could not be determined from the close-up angle of the camera. Three children stood in front of the couple: a blond girl and boy of about equal height and a taller, dark-haired boy.

"Her brother brought this to her when she first came to the hospital," Ginger said.

"The tall boy?"

"Yes. Randy. He owns a restaurant in Virginia. In Arlington. That's near where you live, right?"

"Yes. Not far."

"The Fishmonger. Have you heard of it?"

Claire nodded. She had heard of it but had never eaten there.

"Apparently he visited Margot pretty regularly that first year or so, trying to get through to her somehow," Ginger said. "That was before I came here, so I don't know for sure. But she paid as little attention to him as she did to everyone else, and by the time I started working with her, he was only visiting once every couple of months or so. He gave up, I guess. Can't really blame the guy."

"What was their relationship like?"

"Margot didn't have much of a relationship with anyone, I'm afraid. I called to tell Randy about her committing suicide. He was very quiet. Just thanked me, told me to donate her things to Goodwill, and that was it." She took the framed photograph back from Claire's hands. "I've been meaning to send this to him, though." She looked down at the picture. "He felt helpless, I think. I did, too, sometimes. It's hard to work with someone you just can't reach."

Helpless. The word described well how Claire had felt in her few brief minutes with Margot. She could imagine the depth of helplessness her brother had felt.

Ginger nodded toward the door. "I'll show you where she spent most of her time."

Claire followed the younger woman down another long, green hallway until they reached a large, open room. Windows lined three walls, and Claire imagined that on a sunny day, the room would be awash with light. She felt as though she'd walked into the fresh air after being trapped in a closet.

Nearly a dozen patients were in the room, some watching the TV in the corner, a few playing cards at a small table. Only a couple of them looked up when she and Ginger walked in, and they quickly returned their attention to the cards and TV.

Ginger pointed to the upright piano against the far wall. "That was Margot's hangout. Everyone misses the music. Always classical, although one time—" Ginger smiled. "This was so weird. One time, when Nonnie walked into the room, Margot started playing 'Love Me Tender.'"

Claire laughed.

"It was positively the only show of humor I'd ever seen

from her, though." Ginger looked thoughtful. "She never spoke to anyone. Not the staff, not her fellow patients."

"But she spoke to me on the bridge," Claire said. "It didn't make much sense, but she was talking."

Ginger nodded. "Oh, she'd utter a few scattered words here and there, but nothing of substance. I know she was *able* to talk. I always got the feeling she didn't feel like it was worth the bother. She was bright, though."

"How do you know she was bright if she didn't speak?"

"She read constantly. We have a little library here, mostly paperbacks, and I bet she read every one of them. Fiction, nonfiction, it didn't matter. And she wrote, too."

"Really?" Claire was intrigued. "Stories?"

"No, or if she did write stories I didn't know about them. She wrote letters to other patients. They were often quite long and well written, although her handwriting wasn't very good. Lack of practice, maybe, or it might have been the medication she was on. She'd usually give advice in the letters. She was the Dear Abby of ward C. During group therapy, she'd hear someone talk about a problem they were having, and of course she'd offer nothing during the group, but later she'd write out her thoughts to the person."

"Wow. Was her advice on target?"

Ginger grinned. "Surprisingly insightful. Except for the fact that she'd say that God had told her what to write, or sometimes it would be her dead brother, Charles."

"Oh." Claire smiled. For a moment she had forgotten why Margot had been a resident in this sad place. "If you like, I could take the picture to Margot's older brother," she offered impulsively. She pointed to the photograph, still in Ginger's hand. "Save you mailing it. I'd like to talk with him."

Ginger hesitated. She looked at the picture again. "I suppose that would be all right," she said, handing it to Claire. "I'll call him to let him know you have it."

Once she'd stepped outside the hospital again, Claire gulped in the cold, clean air with relief.

She should have called Jon to let him know she was on her way home, she thought as she got into her car. He was worried about her these days. She could hardly blame him. She would stop somewhere on the road to call him.

She set the photograph of Margot and her family on the passenger seat of her car and looked again at the taller boy. Randall. Randy. With his dark hair and his adolescent gawkiness, he did not quite fit in. He squinted in the sunlight, and from between his dark lashes, his eyes seemed to be looking directly at the camera. At her.

She glanced over at the picture from time to time during her drive back to Vienna, her gaze drawn to the narrow-eyed boy. He had tried to get through to Margot, Ginger had said. He had tried to save her, too. Who better than Randy St. Pierre could understand how it felt to fail in that effort?

6

The lunch crowd at Carney's Café was boisterous as usual, but Jon had requested a table in the rear of the restaurant, and he and Pat were at least able to carry on a conversation. Carney's was their favorite lunchtime restaurant, despite its perpetually fevered level of activity. Like Jon, Pat Wykowski used a wheelchair, and Carney's had an easily negotiated ramp to the front door and plenty of open space between the tables. The fact that the food was palatable was merely a bonus.

Claire was on her way home from West Virginia. She'd called him from the road a few minutes before he left the office and told him about her meeting with the social worker at the psychiatric hospital. He'd listened to her as patiently as he could. He did not understand her preoccupation with Margot St. Pierre. Something was changing in Claire, and it worried him. She was not keeping up with her work at the foundation, and at home he'd catch her staring off into space. If this sort of obsession had occurred in anyone else, he might have been able to make some sense of it. But Claire was a woman who could rise above the worst experiences with a shrug of her shoulders and some cliché about no one ever promising her a rose garden. To someone who did not know her well, Claire could seem almost simple. But simple was not a word he could ever imagine applying to his wife.

The waiter stopped by their table to take their orders.

"My regular." Pat flashed her dimples at the young man with his long dark ponytail. The waiter nodded and turned to Jon, who ordered the grilled swordfish. Pat's regular, Jon knew, was the large, weedy-looking house salad. He felt a little sorry for Pat, his sympathy unrelated to the fact that her injury—sustained in a boating accident at the age of fifteen—was far more debilitating than his. He felt sorry for her because she could put on weight just by thinking about food. She was beautiful, although he supposed his assessment of her was colored by the fact that she was the person he felt closest to in all the world next to Claire and Susan. She had thick blond hair that fell in waves over her shoulders, and huge, sexy, green eyes in the sort of face men dream about. She was feisty, earthy, a little crass. And she was at least thirty pounds overweight. She dressed in drab colors and shapeless blouses that made her look as though she was carrying a sack of potatoes around in her wheelchair.

Driving to the restaurant in Pat's van, he'd considered talking to her about Claire, sharing his niggling concern about her preoccupation with Margot. Pat was the foundation's psychologist and a great listener. He'd changed his mind by the time they'd pulled into the parking lot. He was probably making too much of it. It had only been a week since that traumatic night in Harpers Ferry. He'd been safe inside the Jeep while Claire had dangled from the edge of the bridge. Who was he to judge how long it should take her to get over an experience that horrific?

Pat glanced out the restaurant window at the gray sky. "It's gonna snow again," she said merrily. "I can feel it. If I don't go skiing soon, I'll be crawling the foundation walls."

The waiter approached their table once more, setting Jon's swordfish in front of him and a bowl of rabbit food in front of Pat. Jon watched Pat dab the thick white dressing onto her salad with a fork.

"Do you have some ski trips planned?" he asked.

"Uh-huh. With the club. How about you and Claire joining us this year?"

He rolled his eyes. "When are you going to give up?" he asked.

"Never." She leaned toward him. "Come on, Jonny. You're always telling me what a hot skier you were as a kid."

He *had* been good, before the accident. When the mono-ski was invented a few years ago, Claire tried to lure him into going, but he resisted. It simply wouldn't be the same. And the thought of going with a club of paras and quads—a club funded by his foundation—was particularly unappealing to him. The club was Pat's outlet. What else did she have? No spouse, no lover, no family close by. He could not imagine the emptiness that waited for her at home each night. Pat was usually cheerful, but sometimes he caught a glimpse of that core of loneliness inside her, and he hurt for her.

"Well, I'm going to have a word with Claire about this,"

Pat said. "She and I will talk you into skiing. You two are always working, you know that? You never have any fun."

"Sure we do."

"When? Name it. When was the last time you took a trip together?"

He started to answer, but she interrupted him.

"*Not* related to work," she said. "When's the last time you just goofed off together or laughed until you peed in your pants? When, huh?"

"Peeing in my pants is not my idea of a good time," he said.

They talked about travel and vacations for a few more minutes before Jon managed to shift the conversation to plans for the retreat. But he couldn't get Pat's words out of his mind. Could she be right? He didn't need a break, but maybe Claire did. Maybe that was all it would take to wipe that night on the bridge from her memory.

It was dark as he drove home from the gym that night. The cold air still held the promise of snow, and as he turned onto the winding forested road leading to his house, a few flakes began to dust his windshield. By the time he pulled into his driveway, he had to turn on the windshield wipers. The snow was dry and powdery, though, and flew off the glass almost before the wipers touched it.

He pulled the Jeep into the garage, noticing that Claire had parked her car very close to his space, leaving him too little room to get his chair out. She must have been preoccupied. A bad omen.

He pressed on the horn a couple of times, the sound loud and sharp inside the garage. He waited in the Jeep, hoping against hope that the Claire who came out to move her car would be the same woman he had known and loved for the past twenty-three years and not her gloomy shadow. Maybe her afternoon at the hospital had provided her with a sort of catharsis that would allow her to close the door on Margot St. Pierre.

Claire did not appear. He backed the Jeep out of the garage and pulled his chair from behind the front seat. Snowflakes fluttered in the air around him as he got out of the car. With his briefcase in his lap, he wheeled through the garage toward the house. The ramp to the back door made his arms ache a little—he'd pushed himself harder than usual at the gym. He could feel his muscles stiffening up.

She was not in the kitchen. As he rested his briefcase on one of the chairs, he noticed the music. Claire favored old, old rock and roll. Not too heavy. Motown, mostly. Some rhythm and blues. But the music pouring from the stereo was classical. Piano.

Chopin, no doubt.

Damn it.

Claire walked into the kitchen. She was wearing tight, dark blue jeans, a baggy green sweater, and green tennis shoes. Her hair was loose, hanging long and dark over her shoulders. He caught its clean scent as she bent low to kiss him.

"This is the Nocturne in C-sharp Minor," she said. "Remember? The one Margot mentioned on the bridge? Isn't it beautiful?"

He looked up at her eyes. Her smile was enough to soften his irritation, and he wrapped his hand around her denim-covered thigh, squeezing lightly. "Yes," he said. "It's almost as beautiful as you are."

7

Seattle

Vanessa changed into her running clothes—the blue warm-up suit Brian had given her for Christmas and her Nikes—and took the five flights of stairs down to the ground floor of the hospital. She walked through the long hallway to the rear of the building and knocked on the open door to Darcy Frederick's office.

"Ready?" she asked.

Darcy looked up from her littered desk, her glasses slipping halfway down her nose. "Oh, Van." She used both hands to adjust the heavy, purple frames on her delicate nose. "I can't go today. I'm swamped."

Vanessa pushed into the office and dug Darcy's running shoes out of the canvas bag in the corner. She dropped them on the floor in front of her friend. "Off your butt, Darce."

They'd been running together for over two years, and both of them knew this routine. Darcy would probably never get out of the building if she didn't have Vanessa pushing her. Vanessa, though, would run with or without a partner. She had to. By the end of the day, she felt as though thousands of restless, prickly creatures coursed beneath the surface of her skin. The only way to settle them down was to do something physical. Aerobics would work, or biking. Anything. But running was easiest.

Darcy made a halfhearted attempt at straightening the papers on her desk before finally standing up. She took off her glasses and ran her fingers through her short, almost-black hair before picking up her gym bag and disappearing into the bathroom across the hall. In a moment she was back in a gray sweatshirt and black warm-up pants.

"Ready," she said, and Vanessa followed her out the door.

They walked the first block, then started an easy jog. Anyone watching them would have expected Darcy to be the faster, fleeter runner. She stood a good six inches taller than Vanessa, with broad shoulders and long legs, while Vanessa was slight and golden. But Vanessa was quicker by far.

"So, how're the kids doing?" Darcy asked as they turned off the main road onto a side street.

"Wasn't a great day. One of my CF kids is pretty sick." Jordan Wiley was no better, despite the antibiotics. It had been nearly a week, and she'd expected to see some improvement by now. "And we found laxatives stashed in one of the anorexic's teddy bear."

"You're kidding!" Darcy grinned, and Vanessa had to laugh herself.

"Yeah. I couldn't figure out why she wasn't gaining any weight. Kid's too clever for her own good."

They ran in silence for another block.

"Well." Darcy was beginning to lose her wind already. "I think I've figured a way for you to get federal funding for the AMC program."

"Really?" Vanessa glanced at Darcy, afraid to get her hopes up.

"Uh-huh. Have you heard of Walter Patterson? Senator from Pennsylvania?" The words came out between Darcy's puffs of breath.

Walter Patterson. The name was vaguely familiar. "Not sure."

"You need to contact him. You and your network. He's a zealot on programs that aid victims, and he's forever sponsoring legislation to help women and children. He can be an advocate for you, or at least he could point you in the right direction. But I think you should get the whole network involved. You know, make it a major deal."

Vanessa did not respond right away. She was thinking about the network—that informal group of physicians and health-care professionals she'd pulled together from around the country when she'd started working at Lassiter. They had in common their commitment to issues affecting adolescents, and Vanessa was their indisputable hub. She knew that hers was not the only AMC program being affected by cuts. Terri Roos's program in Sacramento was in jeopardy, and a particularly innovative project in Chicago had already shut down. Darcy was right—she should involve the entire network. She could check on this Patterson guy, then mobilize her forces to descend on him from all corners of the country.

"Federal money's so tight, though," Vanessa said finally.

"It was tight last year when my sister got money for the

Rape Counseling Program in Philadelphia. And it was Walter Patterson that got it for her."

"Really?"

"Really. My sister called him up with statistics on how many women she was reaching, et cetera, and filled out a few reams of paperwork and eventually got what she needed."

Darcy stopped running and leaned over to catch her breath while Vanessa jogged in place. It was rare for Darcy to give such high praise to a male. She was even critical—far too critical—of her own husband. Patterson must be a saint.

Vanessa started running again with a burst of energy fueled by a new glimmer of hope, and Darcy fell in next to her as they crossed the street. The long stone wall of a cemetery materialized next to them in the darkness, and a string of leafless maple trees bowed low over their heads.

"So all I have to do is call this guy and charm the money out of him?" Vanessa asked.

Darcy laughed. "You couldn't charm milk out of a cow, Van," she said. "Charm ain't your long suit."

"I suppose not," Vanessa admitted.

They ran along the wall in silence for a few minutes, and by the time Darcy spoke again, she was panting in earnest. "Well," she said, "you're not going to believe this."

"Believe what?"

"I'm pregnant."

Vanessa stopped running, but Darcy didn't. She teased Vanessa with the distance between them, leaving her with a disconcerting reaction of elation and envy, joy and loss.

Vanessa wanted Darcy the way she had her now—a child-free woman like herself, devoted to her work, able to run most evenings.

She started running again and caught up quickly. Catching Darcy by the arm, she pulled her friend into a hug.

"Congratulations, Darce." She felt like crying and bit her lip to hold the tears at bay.

Darcy drew away with a grin and leaned back against the stone wall, gulping air. "I thought it would never happen. All those tests. I mean, I'd look at you and Brian and see how good you two are without kids and think, 'Well, Dave and I can be like that, no big deal.' But the difference is that we really, really wanted them and you guys don't and it—"

"What makes you think we don't want kids?"

Darcy looked surprised. "I just figured. You're thirty-eight and Brian's forty—right?—and you haven't done it yet, and I figured the two of you made a decision that kids weren't important to you, and you were perfectly happy the way you are."

Vanessa leaned against the cold stone wall herself and breathed deeply for a minute before responding. "I would love to have a baby," she said. "More than anything."

Darcy studied her so intently that Vanessa realized she had never spoken to her friend this way, this confidentially. She knew all there was to know about Darcy. She knew about the first marriage that had ended in her husband's suicide. She knew about the abortion that had left her with problems conceiving and about Dave's long-ago drinking problem. Vanessa had shared little of her own past in return. She discussed those things with no one other than Brian.

And Marianne, the therapist she'd had until a year ago. Even then, even with those two people whom she trusted above all others, the telling had been long and hard in coming.

"Van." Darcy lightly touched her arm. "I didn't know that. Why haven't you ever said anything about this to me? I can't believe you've kept that to yourself after listening to all my trials and tribulations. Have you seen a specialist? I can tell you who's—"

"That's not it." Vanessa shook her head. "I can have a baby, as far as I know, even though I'm getting ridiculously old for it. And I assume Brian's capable of doing his part." She looked down the quiet, tree-lined sidewalk, away from Darcy's gaze. "I'm so afraid we'd split up, and the baby would only have one parent and—"

"God, Vanessa!" Darcy threw her arms up in exasperation. "You and Brian have been living together for over two years, but you always talk as though you moved in with him last week. Like you're still in the trial-run stage, or something."

She was right. It was irrational. Vanessa had known that for a long time, yet that knowledge did nothing to change her fear. She put her arm around Darcy and started walking in the direction of the hospital.

"Well, I'm as happy for you as I can be," she said, and she supposed there was something in her voice that told Darcy not to pursue the subject any further. They talked about sonograms and names and godparents, and Vanessa tried to concentrate on the conversation instead of the thoughts roiling in her head. She was as certain of Brian as she could ever be of any man, but trust was something that would never come easily to her. Trust in the future. Trust in other people. She expected to wake up one morning and find Brian gone. He had left his first wife, hadn't he? He hadn't walked out on her, exactly, but still, ending the marriage had been his idea. No matter how fervently he reassured Vanessa of his deep feelings for her, she knew something about herself that no words of love could change: She was the kind of person other people left behind.

8

Vienna

On Tuesday, nearly a week and a half after her harrowing encounter on the bridge, Claire called the Fishmonger Restaurant in Arlington and asked for Randy St. Pierre. The woman who answered the phone did not respond immediately.

"You must mean Randy Donovan," she said.

"Is he the owner?"

"Yes."

"Then, yes. I'd like to speak with him, please."

The woman left for a moment, and Claire paged idly through her appointment book where it lay open on her bed.

She heard a shuffling noise on the other end of the phone before a man said, "This is Randy Donovan."

The first thing that struck her about Margot's brother was his voice. Deep and rich and resonant.

"Excuse me for disturbing you," she began. "My name is Claire Harte-Mathias. I wanted to get in touch with you because I saw your sister just before she"—Claire wished there were some euphemistic way to say it—"before she took her life. I talked to her on the bridge."

Silence filled the line. Perhaps she had not explained herself clearly enough. She was about to try again when he spoke up.

"Yes," he said. "They told me about you."

Claire walked to the bedroom window and looked into the darkening woods. "Well, I'm finding that I'm having a hard time forgetting about her. I was wondering if we could meet and talk. I'd like to understand her better."

Randy Donovan cleared his throat. "I'm afraid you're asking the wrong person. I didn't understand my sister at all."

"Please? Also, I have something of hers for you." Claire looked across the room at the bed, where the framed photograph lay next to her appointment book.

He hesitated for a moment. "I suppose I could meet with you for a few minutes."

"Great." She walked back to the bed and sat down again, turning to that week's calendar in her appointment book. "You can say when and where," she said.

"How about tomorrow night?" he suggested. "It would have to be late. I'm rehearsing a play at the Chain Bridge Theater in McLean. Could you meet me there afterwards? Say about nine?" That voice. She tried to picture the man who would accompany it but failed to come up with a clear image.

She agreed to the time and place, and he gave her directions to the theater.

"And Mr. Donovan?" she asked.

"Yes?"

"I'm very sorry about Margot."

The diminutive Chain Bridge Theater had once been a small chapel. It was built of fieldstone and stood alone on a street corner, its slim white steeple piercing the night sky. Claire parked near a few other cars in the small gravel parking lot and walked around the building to the broad front doors. Pulling one open, she stepped inside.

She was in a foyer, cool and dark. From beyond the closed oak door leading into the heart of the theater itself, voices echoed. A sandwich-board poster, barely legible in the dim light, stood in one corner of the foyer:

The Chain Bridge Theater of McLean proudly presents The Magician of Dassant—*January 22–30*.

Claire shivered against the chill in the foyer and pushed open the heavy oak door. Inside, she stood still, letting her eyes adjust to the darkness. The stage was brightly lit, a rectangle of white in the dark cave of the chapel. A man and two women stood near the center of the stage, arguing loudly.

Claire unbuttoned her coat as she moved slowly down the center aisle. The pews of the little chapel now served as seats for the theater, and all were empty except for the front row, where a man and a woman sat facing the stage. Claire chose a seat in the center of the theater, laying her coat on the cushioned pew as she focused her attention on the drama taking place in front of her.

The actor onstage was short and squat. She had not pictured Randy Donovan fat; the boy in the photograph was slender. If he owned a restaurant, though, perhaps food was a ruling force in his life. He was in the midst of berating the two actresses, and his high, nasal voice was nothing like that of the man with whom she'd spoken on the phone.

A second man walked onto the stage. He was tall, solidly built, with medium brown hair and a beard and mustache so immaculately trimmed that from this distance it looked as though they had been painted on his face. The way he carried himself—his entire commanding demeanor— matched the voice on the phone. There was a self-assured dignity to him, and when he spoke, his voice swept across the theater and lingered in the dark corners. Claire sat up straighter. If there was indeed a magician in this play, Randy Donovan was it.

The squat man and two women listened raptly to his words, and Claire sensed that the scene was drawing to a close. After a moment, the other characters slipped back into the wings, and Randy Donovan stood alone, offering a soliloquy to his small audience, something about magic and community and loyalty. Claire was oblivious to the words themselves as she lost herself in his presence.

When Randy had finished speaking, the man and woman in the front row applauded. Randy walked down the steps at the side of the stage and spoke briefly to them before glancing in Claire's direction. Picking up a coat and a canvas bag from the edge of the stage, he started walking toward her. He slipped into her pew, reaching out with his hand.

"You must be Claire?"

She stood to shake his hand. There was something familiar about him. Something in the clear blue eyes. The scent of pipe tobacco was agreeably strong in the air around him. She felt as though she'd met him before.

"Yes, I'm Claire," she said. "You were excellent up there."

"Thanks." He motioned for her to take her seat again, then sat down himself. He rested his coat on the back of the pew in front of them, and she watched him brush an invisible piece of lint from the dark wool before he opened the canvas bag on his lap.

"I need some coffee," he said, pulling a green thermos and two Styrofoam cups from the bag. "I have an extra cup. It's decaf. Care to join me?"

"Yes," she said.

He poured them each a cup of very creamy coffee. "Sorry," he said, handing her one of the cups. "It's about half milk. I prefer it that way and wasn't thinking about anyone else's taste when I made it."

She took the cup and held its warmth between her palms. She sipped the pale coffee with a strong sense of comfort, unexpected and very welcome.

She should begin with small talk, she thought, not the probing questions she was longing to ask him.

"How long has this been a theater?" she asked.

"A decade." He looked up at the pitched ceiling, white crossed with dark beams. "My home away from home. The building dates from the early nineteenth century." He lowered his eyes from the ceiling and leaned back to study her. "Well," he said, "you look perfectly normal."

She laughed. "What do you mean?"

"I mean that Margot was my own sister, and I don't think I would have had the guts to hang off the edge of that bridge in a snowstorm to try to save her. I figured you would look either like some muscle-bound superwoman or someone with a few screws loose."

"Well, I only wish I could have succeeded in stopping her."

"You were doomed to failure," he said with a sigh. "One thing I had to admit to myself a long time ago was that Margot could not be saved. Unfortunately, she was smart enough to know what an empty existence she had. Life must have been unbearable for her. I don't really blame her for wanting to put an end to it."

There was a coolness to his words. A certain detachment that had probably rescued him from years of guilt over not being able to help his sister.

Three women walked up the aisle toward the exit. Randy waved good-night as they passed and told them he would lock up. Claire heard the heavy doors close behind the women, leaving her alone with Randy in the dim theater.

He looked at his watch, holding it into the stage light, and Claire quickly began speaking again.

"I think about her all the time," she confessed. "I've tried to tune her out, but my memory of that night seems to have a life of its own. That's why I wanted to see you. If I understood why she did it, maybe I could finally let go of her."

"I don't think it's possible to understand Margot," Randy said. "A dozen doctors sacrificed an inordinate number of their brain cells trying to figure out what made her tick, with very limited success."

Claire opened her purse and pulled out the framed photograph. "I brought this for you from her room," she said, handing it to him.

"Is that the picture I gave her?" He turned to hold it up to the light and laughed. "Does this look like a screwed-up family or what?"

"I thought it looked like a nice family," she said,

although she had not formed an assessment one way or the other.

"Which object does not belong in this picture?" he asked, as if he held a puzzle in his hands.

She leaned closer to look at the picture and stayed in that position a moment longer than necessary, breathing in the scent of his tobacco. "What do you mean?" she asked.

"I mean, me. Two beautiful little blond kids, this lovely blond mother, this handsome blond man. And this spindly-legged, dark-haired, big-toothed kid."

She studied the picture, knowing of course that he was right. She could see clearly that he did not fit in. He even stood a little apart from the rest of the family. A slice of the front door was visible between him and the others, and she felt sorry for the dark-haired boy. His smile in the photograph looked strained.

"You were in the awkward age," she suggested.

He set the picture upside down on the pew next to him and let out another sigh. "How can I help you, Claire Harte-Mathias?"

"Tell me about her. Tell me why this entire situation happened so I can make some sense of it and lay it to rest."

He looked away from her, back to the dark wool coat, and she was not surprised to see him pick at another obscure fleck of dust.

"Would you rather go someplace else?" Talking about Margot, about this family he felt no part of, was clearly not easy for him. "We could go to a restaurant or some-where—"

"Actually," he interrupted, "if I'm going to talk about Margot, I'd prefer the darkness."

Did he mean he might cry? Already she could see that

the smile had faded from his face. His lips had taken a downward curve.

"All right," she said.

"But I don't want to know the details of what happened between the two of you on the bridge." He raised his hands in front of him as if to thwart an assault. "Don't tell me her last words or any of that stuff. Please."

She licked her lips. "I'm sorry to put you through this," she said. What gave her the right to ask him to divulge his personal life to her? She thought about withdrawing her request entirely when he began to speak.

"The woman in the picture was my mother," he said, "but the man was not my father. My father had been a miserable shit—at least according to my mother. I don't remember him at all. They were divorced when I was three. She told me he was a chronic gambler, a womanizer, a liar, and a drinker, and that I was the spitting image of him."

"Oh," Claire said. "And that's where the name 'Donovan' came from?"

"Right. I was a constant reminder of someone who had messed up her life. So, then she met Guy St. Pierre, who was God in her eyes. He was a classical pianist who had toured with different orchestras before he developed arthritis and had to retire. They got married and had twins, Margot and Charles, who were, to be fair, incredibly gorgeous kids." He tapped the picture at his side. "Everyone fawned over them. They were *weird* though. My parents never treated them like children. Right from the start, they were tutored in reading and music. They were little robots. Articles were written about them. *Life* magazine did a story on them. And there is no doubt that they were gifted when it came to music."

"Excuse me." Claire interrupted him. "I don't understand why children who were this talented and about to go to Juilliard would live in Harpers Ferry."

Randy nodded his understanding. "Guy had come back to Harpers Ferry because his parents and sister were there. He met my mother, and kind of got stuck there, I guess. We were planning to move to New York, though. At the time of the accident, the house was on the market."

"I see."

"So, as I said, the twins were not normal." Randy pursed his lips. "Now I, on the other hand, was a normal kid." He let out a small chuckle. "My only gift was for screwing up and getting in trouble. The articles always mentioned me in a little aside: 'And the twins have an older brother, Randy.'"

There was a long pause before he spoke again. "I loved them, though," he said. "They were my baby brother and sister. They got bullied a lot because they were soft, and I protected them." He shook his head. "I once broke a kid's nose for tripping Charles on the sidewalk."

Stillness filled the theater again, and the air was growing colder by the minute. Someone must have turned down the thermostat on his or her way out. Claire thought of lifting her coat to her shoulders, but she did not want him to think she was ready to leave.

She looked at the empty stage, wondering how to word the question she could not leave without asking. "Would you mind telling me what happened on the bridge twenty years ago?" she said finally.

Randy swept his hand over the wool coat one more time. "I'll tell you," he said, "but that's it, all right? I'll talk about it this one time, and then I don't want to think about it again."

"Yes. Fine."

"I was fifteen at the time," he said. "The twins were ten. My mother had asked me to walk over to their piano teacher's house—they'd spent the night there because a big snowstorm hit during their lesson. It was about a mile from our house, across the bridge. So, I met them at their teacher's house, and we started walking home." He looked up at the beamed ceiling. "The bridge was covered with snow," he said. "It was beautiful."

"Yes," she said.

"We started throwing snowballs at each other. They were playing like normal kids for once. Charles got carried away, though. He was chasing Margot with snowballs and horsing around like an honest-to-goodness kid. But then he climbed over the guardrail. I have no idea why. I think he wanted to slide along the platform out there while he was holding on to the railing."

Claire caught her breath, remembering again the vertigo she'd felt on the bridge.

"We were yelling at him to come back, but he ignored us. Then suddenly, he was gone. He just fell out of sight. It happened so suddenly that, for a minute, I thought he was still joking around. We ran over to the side of the bridge and could hear him screaming, although we couldn't see him. We were too far from the edge of the bridge." He hesitated a moment. "I've always been glad of that. That I couldn't see him."

Claire nodded, although Randy wasn't looking at her.

"Margot flipped out," he continued. "She thought she could get to him somehow. She ran over to the spot where the bridge is built into the embankment and tried to climb down, but she fell and hit her head. Knocked herself unconscious and tumbled a few yards down to a rock."

"How terrible."

"I felt as if, in the space of a few seconds, I'd lost both my little sister and brother. And I was supposed to be walking them home to keep them safe. Terrific job I did, huh?" He glanced at her but did not wait for a response. "Anyhow, I climbed down the embankment and got to Margot. She was still breathing, but her head was covered with blood and she was unconscious. I half carried, half dragged her all the way home."

Randy suddenly let out a growl and rested his head back against the pew, squinting at the ceiling. "That damn bridge," he said. "I still can't drive over it. I hate that thing."

For the first time, Claire could see the pain inside him. He was circling it, edging closer. She had no desire to push him headfirst into it, but she needed to know the rest of the story.

"Margot was in a coma for a while?" she asked.

He sat up straight again and seemed to regain his composure. "She was unconscious for a couple of days," he said, "and when she came out of it, she was different. She couldn't handle losing Charles. He was her alter ego. She was extremely depressed, and afraid to leave my mother's side. Literally. My mother couldn't use the bathroom without Margot sitting right outside the door, waiting for her to come out."

"Could she go to school?"

"No, but she'd never gone to school in the first place. My parents taught her at home. Margot eventually wrecked my mother's marriage to Guy. If they tried to kick her out of their bedroom, she would sneak in and curl up in a ball and spend the night on their floor.

"My mother died of cancer three years ago, but Margot had lived with her until then. Once Mother was dead, it was obvious that Margot couldn't take care of herself. She would get into bed and stay there, not eating, sometimes not even getting up to use the toilet." Randy sighed again. "So Guy, who was living in D.C. at the time, and I got together to try to figure out what to do. He had remarried and had a new family and essentially wanted no part of her. I felt guilty about institutionalizing her, but I couldn't see us taking her in—she needed round-the-clock care. So we committed her. I'm still not sure that was the right thing to do, especially now, knowing she was able to get out and kill herself." He spread his broad hands flat on his knees. "Maybe I could have done more for her," he said. "I don't know. She was my sister, but sometimes I pretended she didn't exist. It was easier that way."

He fell silent, but Claire was too lost in her own thoughts to notice. Something he had said struck a chord in her.

"I have a sister, too." Her voice was as soft as a whisper in the cool, dark air of the old chapel.

Randy waited.

"She's two years younger than me, and I haven't seen her since I was a child."

"Why not?"

Claire shrugged. "Our parents divorced, and she went to live with my father in Washington State." With the entire country between them, it had required little effort to pretend she had no sister. Randy was right. It was easier that way.

Suddenly, an image passed before her eyes: a smooth, white surface—porcelain, perhaps?—smeared with blood. Claire's breath caught in her throat. The image disappeared as quickly as it had come, but she stood up abruptly, panicked.

Randy looked at her in surprise.

"I didn't realize it was so late," Claire said, although she had no idea of the time. "I have to go."

The theater was spinning, and she clutched Randy's arm as he stood up. Her stomach churned with the threat of nausea as he reached out to steady her, one hand on her shoulder.

"Are you all right?" he asked. "You've gone white."

She nodded, letting go of him. She felt his eyes on her. "Yes, I'm fine," she said, lifting her coat to her shoulders. Her legs trembled as she walked out of the pew, but once she reached the aisle, the vertigo had subsided, and she felt well enough to be embarrassed.

"I'm sorry," she said as they walked toward the foyer. "I guess I stood up too quickly."

"No problem." He held the heavy door open for her, and she stepped into the foyer. The poster announcing the opening of the play faced them from the corner.

She hugged herself through her coat. "You're playing the magician?" She nodded toward the sign.

"Uh-huh." He put on his long black coat and quickly regained that distinguished, sanguine demeanor he'd had onstage.

"And just what does the magician do?"

"Essentially nothing." Randy pushed open the outside doors, and a cold and welcome gust of air swept across Claire's face as they stepped onto the sidewalk. "He's not a magician at all, you see, but everyone *thinks* he is, and that's all that matters. He only has to stand back and watch the magic happen."

"Oh." She raised the collar of her coat up to her chin as Randy turned to lock the door. "I see, I guess." She looked toward her car, the only one still in the parking lot. "Do you need a ride?" she asked.

Randy pulled a pouch from his coat pocket. He removed a pipe from the pouch and slipped it into his mouth. Claire was mesmerized by the way he cupped his hands around the bowl as he lit it, and fragrant puffs of smoke rose into the air above his head.

"I prefer walking." Randy took the pipe from his mouth. "I don't live far." He motioned north of where they stood. The streetlight caught the blue of his eyes, and Claire had that sense of familiarity again, as if she had known him for a long, long time.

"Listen, Claire," Randy said. "I really am grateful to you for what you tried to do. It renews my faith in humankind that there are people out there like you. But forget about Margot. It's obvious that you're beating yourself up over something that was in no way your responsibility. Or your fault. You couldn't possibly have saved her."

"Thank you." She wanted to put her arms around him and bury her head in the brushed wool of his coat while he said those words to her over and over again.

Randy smiled and took her hand, holding it between both of his. When he let go, he turned and started walking away from her along the sidewalk. The street lamp cut an angle of light across the back of his coat, and she held her eyes fast to that silver light, watching as he crossed the street. He walked briskly, and soon all she could see was the white patch of his cheek moving through the darkness. Then, nothing. She stood numbly under the street lamp, her eyes still riveted on the distant point where he'd disappeared, and felt an inexplicable sense of loss and longing, as if he'd given her a chance to learn something she desperately needed to know, something she could never hope to learn without him.

9

Vienna

Jon was still at the gym, even though it was after ten on a Wednesday night. He'd worked late at the foundation, eating take-out kung pao chicken at his desk as he made phone calls to some of his West Coast colleagues. Usually on Wednesday nights, he and Claire made dinner together and rented a movie. Claire had begged out of tonight's date, though, to meet with Margot St. Pierre's brother. She'd asked Jon if he wanted to go with her, but he'd declined. This was Claire's business. Besides, he was tired of Margot St. Pierre. Ol' Chopin was beginning to grate on him, as well.

He was working out on a long row of exercise machines, all of which were open to accommodate a wheelchair. He had donated all eight of the machines to the gym several years earlier. The equipment faced a wall of mirrors, and he observed the comforting bulge and release of his muscles as he raised and lowered the weights. Great mirrors. Close enough to let him see the sweat glistening on his arms and shoulders, yet not quite close enough that he could make out the lines around his eyes.

The out-of-character vanity that had suddenly broadsided him this last year disgusted him. So, he was going to be forty in a couple of months. Big deal. Claire had turned forty a few months earlier, and she'd celebrated for days. She'd been positively boisterous. "Oh, it's *wonderful* to be forty," she'd told the world. "What a glorious age!" He would not be able to accept passage into his fifth decade with such ease.

He left the gym at ten-thirty. When he pulled into his long driveway, it was nearly eleven, and the sight of the darkened house disappointed him. She must still be out.

The garage door opened, and he saw her car in its usual spot when he pulled inside. Good. She was home. Probably went to bed early. He felt suddenly foolish for having stayed out so late himself.

He wheeled through the back door into the kitchen, where the small light above the stove cast a pool of white on the tiled floor, and he shut his eyes at the strains of Chopin coming from the stereo.

"Claire?"

"In here."

He wheeled into the family room. She was sitting on the sofa, in the darkness, and he felt an unfamiliar surge of fear.

"Why are you sitting in the dark?" he asked.

"I don't know. Just didn't get around to turning on the light, I guess."

He hit the wall switch and saw her wince at the intrusion. She had drawn her feet onto the sofa and sat hugging her knees.

"How about some different music?" he asked.

She shrugged. "Sure."

He wheeled over to the stereo and hit the disc-skip button. Otis Redding started singing about the dock on the bay, and Jon thought he had never heard a more refreshing, soul-reviving, sound.

Claire had lowered her head to rest her cheek on her knees, and she ran her fingers slowly over the pale tweed fabric of the sofa. What was wrong with her?

"Are you all right?" he asked.

She nodded without lifting her cheek from her knee.

He wheeled closer. "How'd your meeting go?"

"Okay." She sounded unsure of the answer, but she raised her head to look at him. "We met in this quaint little theater in McLean, and he told me about the night Margot and her brother fell off the bridge when they were kids."

She recounted the story to him, and he studied her face as she spoke. There was something unrecognizable there. Maybe it was the odd angle of the lighting. It illuminated her right temple and the small jut of her chin, leaving the rest of her features in darkness. Her face was not her own, and her voice was flat. That same intonation might have sounded perfectly normal in someone else, but in Claire, whose voice usually bubbled with life, the words sounded dry and stale.

He listened carefully and without comment until she had finished. Maybe she simply needed to talk, he thought. Maybe if she got every speck of it out, it would end. Every day he hoped it would end. Instead, she seemed to be getting drawn even more deeply into the pit of gloom Margot had dug for her.

Claire sighed when she had finished speaking. She stretched her arms toward the ceiling. "Anyhow," she said, "listening to Randy talk about Margot made me think about Vanessa."

"Vanessa?" Jon frowned. He did not see the connection, and he had not heard Claire mention her sister's name in years.

"Yes. Randy feels guilty for not doing more to keep the bond alive between himself and Margot. He thinks he took the easy way out. I'm doing the same thing."

"Oh, Claire, how can you say that?" He heard the impatience creeping into his voice and tried to tame it. "Margot's brother knew where she was, and he *chose* not to spend more time with her. You don't know where to find Vanessa. If you did, I'm sure you'd do everything you could to be a sister to her."

"But I have an address for her," Claire argued. "At least for where she was a few years ago."

"And you wrote to her, and she never answered. And you tried to find a phone number, and it was unlisted. What more could you do?"

She ran her hand across the sofa cushion again, her eyes lowered. "I could go to Seattle," she said. "I could show up at her door, or if she doesn't live at that address any longer, I could question her neighbors and track her down. There's got to be a way to find her, and I haven't done a thing about it."

"I think Vanessa doesn't want to be found." He had never met Claire's sister. After Claire's parents separated, her father simply took Vanessa and ran. He did not get in touch with Claire or with Mellie—his wife, and the girls' mother—again until his death twelve years ago. Just before he died, he sent a letter to Mellie, giving her Vanessa's address. Mellie flew immediately to Seattle, only to be rather brutally turned away at the door to her daughter's home. Heartbroken, she begged Claire to try contacting Vanessa. Claire wrote to her sister and heard nothing back, but she did not go to Seattle herself. Jon had been confused by Claire's easy surrender to her sister's wishes. Why hadn't Claire pushed a little harder? It was not like her to give up so easily. She was too busy, she'd said, and obviously Vanessa did not want to see her. At the time, he'd wondered if she was giving up out of sensitivity to him. His only sister— only sibling—had died in the plane crash.

"You know, I've always had this little fantasy." Claire sounded as if she were about to reveal a secret, and he leaned closer to her. "Vanessa and I shared such a wonderful childhood together. It would be such fun to compare memories." She ran her fingers through her long hair. "My fantasy is that she comes to visit, and we drive up to Winchester Village together to see Grandpa's carousel."

He smiled at the idea. A hundred times over the years they'd talked of going up to that amusement park three hours north of them in Pennsylvania. Somehow, though, they'd never gotten around to it. He would like to see that carousel himself after hearing about it for more than half his life.

"I'm forty," Claire said. "And Vanessa is my only sister. How long am I going to put off trying to see her?"

He wheeled a little closer and touched her knee. "You have a full life," he said gently, "and she probably has one of her own. Can you just forget it?"

"That's what Randy tried to do, and it's haunting him," she said. "He didn't say that exactly, but I could tell."

She sounded as if she and Randy were old friends, as if what this stranger thought and felt mattered to her. The disconcerting swell of fear washed over him again. He wanted to end this conversation.

"Well, I think I'm going up to bed," he said. "It's been a long day. Are you coming?" He held his hand out to her, but she didn't take it.

"In a few minutes," she said.

"All right." He lowered his hand reluctantly. He didn't like leaving her alone with the thoughts that were haunting her, the thoughts that were turning her into someone he didn't know.

Claire sat on the sofa for a while after Jon went to bed. She was finished with Margot now, she thought. It was over. Chapter closed.

The Otis Redding disc came to an end, and the stereo shut off, but still she felt glued to the sofa. The evening had drained her. Ever since leaving the theater, she'd felt as if she were moving through molasses.

Vanessa. She pictured the little girl everyone had called "Angel." Blond curls, like Mellie's. Laughing as she rode the carousel with Claire. Petite and delicate, Vanessa had never quite managed to reach the brass ring chute without some calculated help from Grandpa.

Claire rested her head back against the sofa and looked at the ceiling, an idea taking shape in her mind. She would write to Vanessa again. If she didn't hear back this time, she would go to Seattle, try to find her. Well, maybe she would write a couple of times first. Give her every chance to respond. She did not understand the hesitancy she'd always felt about getting in touch with her sister. It was way past time. She had taken the easy way out for too long.

She felt a rush of energy now that she had a plan of

action. Upstairs, she took a quick shower and put on her short blue chemise.

Jon was reading in bed when she walked into the bedroom. He looked beautiful, his eyes big and dark, the muscles of his bare chest and arms well defined. There was very little fat on his body, except for the spot low on his belly, which, given his injury, was impossible for him to tone. He ate carefully. He had an appreciation for his health most people never developed. Jon took nothing for granted.

Claire hopped onto the bed and straddled him above the comforter. He looked at her, surprised, grinning. She realized it had been a while since she'd seen that grin.

"What's this?" he asked.

"I'm gonna cheer you up," she announced. "It's Wednesday night, and we *always* do it on Wednesday night."

"Yes, well, we always make dinner together and rent a movie on Wednesday nights, too."

She was surprised by the hurt in his voice, and her throat quickly tightened. "I'm sorry, Jon." She bent down to hug him. "I'm so sorry."

"No." He sighed. "*I'm* sorry." There was remorse in his voice. "I know you had to see Margot's brother." Gently, he pushed her up by the shoulders until she was sitting above him once again. He closed his book, rested it on the night table, and turned off the light. She could still see his face clearly enough to know he was no longer smiling.

He reached up slowly to touch her cheek with the tips of his fingers, then let his hand run down her throat and over her shoulder before coming to rest lightly against her breast through the satin chemise. She felt the life in her nipples, the life in her groin. Raising herself to her knees, she started to pull the comforter from between their bodies, but he stopped her with his hands on her arms.

"Claire," he said. "I want you back."

She looked at him in confusion. "What do you mean?"

He held her arms tightly. "I'm not blaming you. I know this has been hard. But I feel as though you've been missing since the night of the suicide." His voice was thick, and in the faint light from the bathroom, she could see tears in his eyes. Had she put them there? She needed to rid him of them quickly.

"That's silly." She leaned forward again, this time to kiss him, but his lips were cool. "I'm here," she said. "I know I've been distracted lately, but I feel better now that I've talked to Randy. I can let it go now. It's okay. I'm okay."

She kissed him again, and after a moment he responded. But as they made love, her mind was filled with images of the snow-covered bridge and a child's innocent snowball fight. And of Margot flying, lit up like sparkling crystal, above the river. She tried to block the pictures from her mind. She tried to block the scent of pipe tobacco and the taste of milky coffee and the sound of the voice that had held her suspended in the chill air of the old stone chapel. But the images were vivid, the sensations powerful, and the more she tried to fight them, the more they drew her in.

10

Seattle

Vanessa had the phone to her ear and was about to make a well-rehearsed call to Senator Walter Patterson when Pete Aldrich walked into her office carrying a chart. Pete sat on the corner of her desk, wearing his usual frown beneath the mop of red hair, and Vanessa put the receiver back in its cradle to give him her attention.

"There's a kid in the clinic I'd like you to take a look at, if you've got a second," Pete said. "Her school counselor referred her to the AMC program, but I can't get anything out of her except that she doesn't want to be here." Opening the chart, he peered at the notes inside. "Physical exam is unremarkable, except for a bunch of self-induced cigarette burns on her arms. Sexually active, but doesn't want to talk about it. No alcohol or drugs, so she says."

Vanessa took the folder from him. "And does 'the kid' have a name?"

"Uh, yeah." He rose from the desk, pointing toward the chart, and she looked down at the label.

"Jennifer Lieber," she read.

"Right."

"Fine. Thank you." She waited for him to leave her office and then followed him down the hall to the clinic.

The girl was waiting for her inside the first examining room. She was strikingly beautiful, willowy, with long, golden hair. She sat on the table, wearing the flimsy hospital gown, her arms turned face-down on her lap, hiding the burns from view.

"Hi, Jennifer." Vanessa sat down on the stool. "I'm Dr. Gray."

The girl mumbled something unintelligible.

"Dr. Aldrich said that you're in good shape physically, except for the burns on your arms."

Jennifer made a face. "He's weird."

"Is he?" Vanessa kept her tone conversational. She didn't dare allow this patient to know how thoroughly she agreed with her assessment.

"Yeah. He's like Mister Science Project, or something. I thought maybe he was a robot."

Vanessa smiled. "I guess he can seem that way sometimes."

"He reminds me of Mrs. Kirby, asking questions that are none of his business."

"Mrs. Kirby is your school counselor?" She recalled the name from the referral note in the chart.

"Uh-huh."

Vanessa crossed her legs, locking her hands around her knee. "Well," she said, "when Mrs. Kirby referred you to us, she told us that you had worn a short-sleeved shirt to school. In the middle of winter. What that says to me is that you— very wisely—wanted to make this someone else's business."

"What do you mean, 'wisely'?"

"You knew you needed help, and you figured out a surefire way to get it. You might as well have spelled out 'help me' with those burns." She gestured toward Jennifer's arms.

"I don't need any help."

"Mrs. Kirby referred you to the program we have here for teenagers who were abused when they were younger. She must have had a good reason for doing that."

Jennifer looked away from her. Her cheeks had reddened, and there was the threat of tears in her eyes.

Vanessa stood up and moved in front of her. She took the girl's wrists in her hands and gently turned her arms until she could see the burns. Eight on her right arm, five on her left. Some of them were deep. They would leave ugly scars. Ugly reminders. Vanessa had a few of those reminders on her thighs.

Jennifer held her breath under Vanessa's scrutiny.

"Have you ever done anything like this to yourself before?" Vanessa looked into the girl's cloudy blue eyes.

Jennifer shook her head.

"Why now, Jennifer?"

"I don't know." Then, softly, "My boyfriend."

"Tell me about your boyfriend."

"He's not anymore. I mean, he stopped calling."

"How long had you been seeing him?"

"Six months."

"That's a long time." A lifetime when you were fifteen.

The girl nodded, blond hair glittering in the bright, overhead light.

"What happened?"

Jennifer shrugged, lowering her eyes, and Vanessa took a step away from her. She didn't want to crowd her.

"I don't know," Jennifer said quietly. "Something weird's been happening to me, and he couldn't take it."

"What do you mean?"

"I mean, suddenly I'm remembering these horrible things that I never knew happened to me."

Vanessa nodded. She would have to be careful. She was not one of those who questioned the existence of repressed memories; she'd seen too many examples of grotesque, credibility-straining, long-hidden memories that were later confirmed with proof of some sort. Yet the possibility of an overactive imagination could not be ruled out. First and foremost, though, Jennifer Lieber needed to know she'd be taken seriously here.

"Sometimes," Vanessa said, "when things are too painful for us to remember, we block them out." She'd always thought, actually, that repression was a wonderful trick of the psyche. She wished she'd had a little of it herself. "Did something happen that made you start remembering?"

Jennifer chewed on her lower lip. "Well, I had ... almost had sex with my boyfriend."

"Would that have been your first time?"

The girl nodded. "Only I couldn't do it, 'cause when he tried, I remembered ... something about my uncle." Jennifer turned her head away again, and Vanessa opted not to push her for details. There would be time later.

"Your uncle hurt you," she said simply.

"Yes, but I'd completely forgotten. Is that possible?" The words came out in a sudden rush.

"Yes. It's possible."

"He's dead now. He's been dead for two years, and I'd practically forgotten he ever existed."

"Did you explain to your boyfriend why you were upset?"

Jennifer nodded. "I was pretty hysterical, I guess, and he didn't believe me. He said I would never have forgotten something like that, that I must be making it up to get out of having sex. At first I thought maybe he was right, 'cause the memories were so fuzzy, but then they got clearer and clearer. I couldn't get them out of my mind." She pressed her fists to the sides of her head. "Josh and I were so close. I thought I could tell him anything. But when I tried to tell him more about what I was remembering, he said I was crazy and stopped calling me."

"I'm sorry."

"After a couple of weeks I couldn't stand it anymore. Every time I closed my eyes, more memories would come. I was afraid to go to bed at night. So finally, I tried to tell my mother, except I couldn't possibly say that I started remembering those things while I was having sex, 'cause she would've shit."

Vanessa smiled her sympathy at the dilemma.

"She got really pissed off when I told her. How could I say something like that about her dead brother, and I've been watching Oprah too much. She actually said that, and I've never even watched Oprah once in my life. I found a picture I could show her, but—"

"A picture?"

Jennifer nodded. "My uncle's old room is still pretty much like it was when he was living in our house, and I remembered about a shoe box in his closet. I went in there and found a picture he'd taken of me and him together."

She squeezed her eyes together, her cheeks flaming. "I nearly got sick when I found it."

Proof. Vanessa felt profound relief. It would make everything easier. No one would doubt this girl now, and she could stop doubting herself.

"Where is the picture now?"

"I put it back, though I think I should have burned it. I can't show it to my mother. She'd blame me for it. I know it. She hardly talks to me. Just shakes her head at me. And my boyfriend's gone. After he stopped calling, I went sort of numb." She held up her scabbed arms. "I did this to see if I could still feel anything, and you know what? I couldn't. It doesn't matter, though. Nobody believes me anyway."

"I believe you," Vanessa said. "And I'll listen to you. And there are other people who will listen and believe you, other people here who are trained to know how to help people who are going through what you're going through. And there's a group here of girls—and some boys, too—who are your age and who've had similar experiences, and they'll believe you. They'll let you know you're not alone, and you're not crazy."

She told Jennifer a little more about the program and used the examining room phone to make an appointment for her with the social worker. She was about to leave the room when the girl said, "I just couldn't talk to that other doctor."

Vanessa stopped, her hand on the doorknob. "Well, at least he knew that. We'll give him a few brownie points for knowing when to come get me, okay?"

"Okay."

Vanessa stepped back to the table to give the girl a hug,

then left the room and walked down the hall to her office. She understood Jennifer's fears. She no longer identified with every speck of these kids' pain; it had happened to her so long ago. Still, she understood.

And she had something to offer Jennifer. Before she'd created the AMC program, she could not have offered much. She dreaded returning to that state of professional helplessness.

Walking back to her office, she remembered the phone call she'd been about to make to Walter Patterson. She had spoken to the key members of the network and decided that she would contact Patterson while they would begin to pull together case histories and statistics they could use to make their case for funding. Very sympathetic-sounding guy, this Patterson. Terri Roos in Sacramento had heard that he particularly liked innovative programs, programs that helped people who weren't being reached in any other way. That fit their kids, all right.

Once inside her office, she closed the door, took a moment to collect her thoughts, then dialed Patterson's number on Capitol Hill. She did not even hear a ring before someone answered.

"Walter Patterson's office." The voice was male, surprising her.

"This is Dr. Vanessa Gray at Lassiter Children's Hospital in Seattle, Washington," she said. "I'd like to speak with Senator Patterson, please."

"What is this regarding?"

Vanessa sat up straighter in her chair. "I'm director of a program for adolescents who were abused as young children, and I understand he's the person to speak with about generating support for that type of program."

"Right. Hold on a second."

Vanessa heard the man ask someone else in the office, "Is Zed in yet?" and her heart froze.

"Excuse me." She spoke into the phone, but the man must have had the receiver away from his ear. "Excuse me!" She stood up, as if that could give her voice more power.

"Yes?" The voice was back on the line.

"Did I hear you say 'Zed'?"

"Oh, right. Walter Patterson. He goes by Zed."

Vanessa said nothing. She could not have spoken if she wanted to.

"He's in," the man said. "If you hold a moment, I'll see if he's free to pick up now."

"No," Vanessa said quickly. "No. I'll call back."

She hung up the phone, staring at it as if it were some futuristic contraption that had carried her into the twilight zone.

Zed Patterson.

Could there be more than one man with that name?

II

Vienna

It had been a week since Claire's meeting with Randy and nearly three weeks since the incident on the bridge, but she was still having trouble keeping thoughts of Margot at bay. Each time she caught herself recalling that night in Harpers Ferry, she tried to substitute some other thought—about work, or Jon, or Susan. But Margot kept creeping in.

She'd put the Chopin CD in its case and tucked it into the box of old records in the family-room closet. But just yesterday, while on hold during a phone call to a physician's office, the nocturne filled her ears. She thought of hanging up on the music but gave into it instead. She could hum along with it now. She knew the subtle shifts in the melody and could anticipate the parts that would make her throat tighten. There was a conspiracy afoot, she thought. Margot did not want to let her go.

She did not talk about Margot anymore, though, and she tried to be her old self around Jon. He didn't know that she occasionally woke up in the middle of the night with a start, imagining herself on the edge of the bridge. And she didn't tell him that once, before she'd gotten out of bed in the morning, she saw again that bizarre image of smooth white porcelain smeared with blood. There was pain accompanying the image this time, a searing pain deep in her gut. She lay very still until the pain passed and the vision faded, and within minutes she had convinced herself that she had dreamt them both.

And then the call came from Randy.

He reached her early in the morning at her office and began by thanking her for giving him the opportunity to talk about Margot. He'd found her very easy to open up to, he said, and meeting with her had helped him in a way he hadn't known he needed. Now he felt ready to hear about his sister's last moments on the bridge. Would Claire please have lunch with him?

She felt like screaming, *No! I want to be free of your damn sister.* Yet she had asked him to share so much painful, personal information. She could not possibly turn down his request for her to do the same.

Besides, there was a pull to see him she could not quite deny to herself. Listening to that rich, resonant voice over the phone made her remember the odd comfort she'd felt with him, the sense of knowing him well, when in truth she didn't know him at all.

She waited until that evening to tell Jon. They were eating pasta at the kitchen table when she finally dared to bring it up. "Randy Donovan called to ask if I'd meet him for lunch." She poured dressing on her salad, keeping her eyes on the task, but she could feel Jon watching her.

"Lunch?" he asked. "Why?"

"He wants to know what Margot said to me on the

bridge. I'd rather not have to talk to him again, but he was so nice to me that I feel an obligation."

Jon swirled a forkful of linguine in his spoon. "Wouldn't it be easier to tell him over the phone?" he asked.

"I don't know. It's not the kind of thing you dump on someone." She felt the eggshells beneath her feet. There was tension in the room, and she didn't know how to diffuse it. Jon was still swirling the pasta, trancelike. "Are you upset about this?" she asked.

He sighed and set down his fork. He reached across the corner of the table to hold her hand, and she folded her fingers around his. "I thought you were getting over this whole Margot thing," he said. "I'm afraid he's going to open it up for you all over again."

"I'm fine, Jon. I can handle it."

"I hope so." He squeezed her fingers before drawing his hand away.

Again, the tension fell between them, this time in the form of silence. Claire tried to eat but found it hard to swallow.

Finally, Jon spoke again. "When are you supposed to see him?"

"Tomorrow."

She and Jon usually spent their lunch breaks with each other, either in his office or hers. Occasionally they went out to a restaurant, sometimes alone, sometimes with colleagues. And every once in a while, she would meet Amelia or another friend for lunch and Jon would go out with Pat. But this was different. She felt as if she were breaking some unspoken covenant between them.

"We have a meeting with Tom Gardner at two tomorrow," Jon said.

"I'll be back in plenty of time."

Silence again. Jon took a sip of water, then said, "How about a vacation?"

She was caught by surprise. "What?"

He started swirling linguine again. "Someplace warm. Hawaii? The Caribbean? We could get away for a week or so."

She was amazed he would suggest going away when they were in the throes of planning the retreat. But the idea of escape was extremely seductive. Hawaii was thousands of miles from Harpers Ferry and Margot and the bridge.

"God, yes." She smiled. "I'll start packing."

Jon laughed, and the sound was warm and wonderful and all too rare these days. "Okay," he said. "Think about where you'd like to go and when we can carve out some time, and let's do it."

Traffic was heavy as she drove to the Chain Bridge Theater at noon the following day. She'd suggested they eat at a restaurant midway between her office and the Fishmonger, but Randy said he'd prefer meeting at the theater. No one used it during the day, he said, and he often took his lunch break there. "After working in a restaurant all day, I'd just as soon spend my time off someplace else," he said. "Tell you what. If you'll meet me at the theater, I'll provide the lunch."

She stopped at a red light about a mile from the theater and glanced in her sideview mirror to see it completely filled with green. Drawing in a sharp breath, she turned quickly to look out the window. She expected to see someone in a kelly green shirt leaning against her car, but all she could see was the white line in the road, the side of the red sedan stopped behind her, and the pale gray light of the midday sky.

She looked into the mirror again to see the rear end of a car traveling in the opposite direction. The green was gone. *You are losing it, Harte.* She checked her rearview mirror. The woman in the red sedan was applying lipstick.

The light changed, and when she stepped on the accelerator, the muscles in her legs were trembling.

Randy was in the pew where they had first met. The clear glass of the chapel's very tall, narrow, arched windows let in the only light. The small building seemed far more a church than a theater today, its stage hidden behind heavy, royal blue curtains.

Randy turned as she walked down the aisle. He smiled and stood up. "Thanks for meeting me here," he said, helping her off with her coat.

She sat down. "You're welcome."

He was wearing a sweater that matched the blue of the curtains. "As I was waiting for you, I realized I couldn't possibly talk about Margot in a restaurant," he said. "I need the peacefulness of this place. The privacy."

Again she had that sense of knowing him from somewhere else. She wanted to touch his arm, squeeze it, to let him know she understood, but she locked her hands in her lap, telling herself that the odd warmth and affection she felt for him made no sense in light of their one brief meeting.

"How about lunch?" He lifted a basket from the floor and set it between them on the pew. Claire smelled something smoky that made her mouth water.

"I have wine or club soda." Randy reached inside the basket. "Wasn't sure what you'd prefer."

"Wine," she said, although she never drank wine at lunch.

He poured them each a glass of wine, then drew two large, elegantly prepared plates from the basket. Each plate was weighted down with big clumps of tuna resting on leaves of romaine and nestled beside red grapes and sourdough rolls.

"Smoked tuna all right?" he asked, handing her one of the plates.

"That sounds wonderful."

He gave her a fork, along with a cream-colored linen napkin, and Claire pulled the plastic wrap from the plate and took a bite of tuna.

"This is delicious," she said. She thought guiltily of Jon eating his tuna salad at the desk in his office.

"Thanks." Randy leaned back against the pew and rested his plate on his knees. "Well, can you eat and talk at the same time?"

She nodded. "What is it you'd like to know?"

He took a sip of his wine. "I want to know exactly what happened that night in Harpers Ferry."

Claire looked across the theater at the heavy blue curtains, thinking back to the snowstorm on the bridge. She did not have to reach too deeply into her memory, despite the energy she had put into blocking that night from her mind. Every movement of Margot's body, every word she had spoken, was as clear as if it had occurred only minutes before.

She spoke quietly, telling him about her first glimpse of Margot. "Once I realized it was a person I was looking at—a woman who was undoubtedly in some sort of distress—I had to go out to her."

"Why didn't your husband go with you?"

"He uses a wheelchair. He wouldn't have been able to get out of the car with the snow and all."

"Oh," Randy said. "I didn't know."

Claire described walking across the bridge to reach Margot and not being able to make herself heard until she stepped out onto the platform.

"I still can't believe you did that." Randy shook his head. "I don't know anyone that brave."

Claire ate a few grapes before responding. "I didn't think about what I was doing," she said. "Besides, the platform was fairly wide. I knew that as long as I held on to the railing, I'd be fine."

"If you say so. Go on. How did she look? How was she dressed?"

Claire described the tattered clothing, the too-short pants, the wet tennis shoes, the coat suited more for spring than winter, and Randy grew agitated next to her, rubbing his hand back and forth across his beard.

"Damn." He looked away from her. "I never even thought of that. Of clothes. I should have gotten her things. It never crossed my mind. I'd bring her food when I'd go to visit. She wouldn't eat it, but that seems to be the only thing I know how to do—feed people. I never thought of clothes. Shit."

She felt the pain in him, as she had the last time they'd met. This time, though, he wasn't trying to hide from it. He was letting himself step into it, surround himself with it.

"Maybe she had more suitable things, but she just didn't care what she wore," Claire offered, wanting to relieve his suffering. "I'm sure they would have told you if her lack of clothing was a problem."

Randy looked unconvinced. "Go on, please. What did she say to you? "

"At first, nothing. She seemed to be in a world of her

own, although I'm certain she knew I was there." She remembered how Margot had reminded her of an ice sculpture, she had been so completely covered by snow. She could not tell him that. "There was a peacefulness to her," she said instead. "Really, there was."

He nodded but did not look at her.

"She kept asking me to leave her alone. At one point, she said she had died on that bridge years ago."

Randy looked at her sharply.

"After you told me about the accident, I realized that she must have been referring to that night. She must have felt like she died when Charles died."

Randy nodded. "Yes, I think she did. Margot's life—the life that had any quality to it—ended that day, too. After that, she might as well have been dead."

"She said she could hear music. Chopin, she said. Nocturne in C-sharp Minor, which is very beautiful. I listened to it for a few days after . . . I met her."

Randy said nothing.

"And she said something weird. Something about how he couldn't hear the music."

He frowned. "Who couldn't? Chopin?"

Claire shrugged.

"She must have her composers mixed up," Randy said. "Beethoven's the one that went deaf, wasn't he?"

"Yes, I think so."

"She must have really been losing it to get them mixed up."

"Or maybe she meant Charles? Since he was no longer alive to hear it?"

"Maybe," Randy agreed.

"I tried to hold on to her, and for a while, she let me."

"Hold on to her? How?"

"Just my hand on her arm." She circled her hand around Randy's arm, through his sweater, then let go quickly.

He leaned away from her, his eyes wide. "Christ, lady, you *are* nuts, you know it?"

"Jon called the police from the car. Maybe that was a mistake, because that's when she panicked. When she heard the sirens. Maybe I could have talked her out of it if the police hadn't come."

"Yeah, and maybe you'd have ended up in the river along with her."

She didn't try to argue the point with him. She thought about what had happened next and found that she didn't want to talk about those minutes of negotiation between herself and Margot. She didn't want to talk about letting go and not letting go.

"So, she got scared when the police came," she said, "and that's when she jumped."

The crystal angel, flying, in slow motion. Claire's stomach lurched. She grabbed for the back of the pew, knocking her fork and most of her grapes to the floor.

"Oh, I'm sorry!" She could not bend over to retrieve the fork. The chapel was spinning enough as it was.

"I've got it." Randy reached down and picked up the fork and three grapes. He set them on his own plate. "Are you okay?"

"Yes, just . . . embarrassed." She could feel the heat in her face. "I keep getting this dizziness," she admitted. "I know it's linked somehow to being on the bridge. I really didn't feel dizzy up there at the time, but now every once in a while, I remember being there, and suddenly I feel as though I'm falling."

There was sympathy in his eyes. "I'm sorry," he said. "I'm sorry I made you think about it."

She looked away from the warm blue of his eyes. She thought she might cry.

He took her empty plate from her lap and put it in the basket along with his own. Then he pulled out the thermos. "Are you ready to switch to some very weak coffee?"

"Yes," she said.

"I should have made it black and brought some milk along for myself," he said. "I wasn't thinking."

"I like it this way. Honest."

He poured the milky coffee from the thermos into a Styrofoam cup. "I fell down some stairs a few years ago," he said, handing the cup to her. "I missed the top step and—" He made a plane with his hand and sent it into a nosedive, and she shuddered. "Broke a couple of bones in one foot, and for weeks afterward, every time I'd close my eyes, I'd feel like I was falling again."

"Yes," she said. "That's exactly what it's like."

He smiled at her, a little sadly. "You were really very kind to talk with me about her when it shakes you up so much."

"I'm sure it wasn't easy for you to tell me about the night Charles fell from the bridge, either."

"No. It wasn't." Randy looked into his cup. There was a long silence. Somewhere outside the theater a car horn honked, and the sound seemed to float just below the beamed ceiling for a few seconds before fading away.

"All right," he said finally, drawing in a long breath. "She seemed to be at peace. That's what I'll try to remember."

"Good," Claire said. "That's what I'm trying to keep in my mind, too."

Randy stroked his meticulously trimmed beard again, his eyes on the high arched windows. "You mentioned your own sister last time," he said suddenly.

She was surprised he remembered her talking about Vanessa. He'd seemed so distracted at the time.

"Yes, and I wrote to her after we spoke." She had written Vanessa a short letter, telling her how much she wanted to talk with her. "I realized after you and I spoke that I wanted to try to get in touch with her. I haven't heard anything back, but it's really too soon to expect a response."

"When was the last time you saw her?"

"When I was ten."

"Wow. What do you remember about her?"

Claire smiled and took a sip of coffee. "I remember that we shared the most idyllic childhood imaginable."

"But you said something about your parents getting divorced and your father taking your sister away and you never getting to see her again."

Claire shrugged. "In spite of all that, it was wonderful." She saw the doubt in his eyes. "Honest. It was."

"Convince me." He blotted his clean lips with a corner of the napkin. "I'm a skeptic about the existence of happy childhoods."

"Well, my great-grandfather was Joseph Siparo," she said. "Have you ever heard of him?"

"No. Should I have?"

"He was one of the top carousel horse carvers in the country in the early nineteen hundreds." She could feel herself lighting up as she spoke, and she saw her smile reflected in Randy's eyes.

"Really?" He seemed intrigued.

"Uh-huh. He died long before I was born, but he taught his son—my grandfather, Vincent Siparo—how to carve, and my grandfather built a carousel in his backyard."

"No kidding! Wasn't the era of carousel horse carving over by the time your grandfather got into it?"

"Yes, but he was"—Claire hesitated, then smiled at the memory of her grandfather—"an eccentric. He'd been a farmer all his life, but the older he got, the more he wanted to carve, and finally he just stopped farming and started carving. People would come from all over to see his carousel. And that's what I grew up with. At least in the summers. During the school year, I lived here in Virginia. In Falls Church, with Vanessa and Mellie—that's my mother—and my father. But I barely remember those nine or ten months of the year. All I really remember is Pennsylvania and the farm and the carousel."

Blood on porcelain.

She ran her hand across her eyes as if to wipe away the image and was relieved when it quickly faded.

"That does sound like a pretty seductive way of life for a child," Randy said. "Cary—my son—is ten, and I can just picture how he'd feel having an amusement-park ride in his backyard. Not sure a carousel would do it for him. Sidewinder, maybe." Randy seemed lost in thought for a moment.

"You have a family," Claire said, surprised. For some reason, she'd pictured him single and was pleased to know he was taken care of, that after this difficult discussion he would have someone to go home to.

"I'm divorced," Randy said, quickly dashing her fantasy. "It's been almost a year now. My son lives with my ex-wife, but I see him quite a bit."

"Well, I'm glad you have some time with him."

"So." Randy was quick to change the subject. He brushed a crumb from his gray wool slacks, then stretched out, his back propped up against the end of the pew. "Did you ride on this carousel a lot?"

"Yes." Claire smiled. "My childhood was one long, wonderful carousel ride."

His own smile was slow in coming, and indulgent, she thought. "Well," he said, "if that's the case, then you've been very lucky. I'm glad for you, and I envy you. But I still don't believe you. The words 'happy' and 'childhood' don't belong in the same sentence."

She shook her head at him. "I think it's a matter of what you focus on," she said. "Of course there are bad times in a child's life, and if you limit your thinking to those times, the whole picture will be distorted. What about your own son? Can you honestly say he's having an unhappy childhood?"

"Oh, yes. I can say that with absolute certainty, and it tears me up inside. And your daughter?"

"Blissful," she said, although a knot formed in her stomach at the memory of the fights in those last few years before Susan left for school. Normal, though. Perfectly normal in adolescence.

"You called your mother 'Mellie'?"

"Yes. She said it made her feel too old to be called Mom."

He gave her one last dubious smile as he sat up straight again and put their empty cups in the basket. "Listen," he said, "how would you like to see *The Magician of Dassant*?"

"We'd *love* to," she answered, and then quickly realized that he might not have meant to include Jon in his invitation. She colored at the presumption, but before she could say anything, Randy spoke again.

"Fine. There'll be two tickets for you at the window on Sunday night—is Sunday okay? Saturday's sold out."

"Sunday's fine."

"And be sure to come backstage afterwards. I'd like to meet . . . Jon, is it?"

"Yes." *Jon*. She looked at her watch. One-forty-five! They were supposed to meet with Tom Gardner at two. She would never make it. She could call Jon from the theater, but that would put her even further behind. Better to simply drive to the foundation and be late. She could have sworn she'd been in the theater no longer than an hour.

"I've got to go," she said. "I'm late for a meeting."

She stood up slowly, alert for the dizziness. It was there, but short-lived this time, and she steadied herself easily with her hand on the pew.

Randy followed her up the aisle and into the foyer, where the sandwich-board poster beckoned her to come to the play. She pushed open the front door and stepped outside.

Randy caught her arm. "Thanks for this, Claire," he said. "For talking with me." He did not let go of her arm, and their bodies brushed against one another through their heavy wool coats. "How would you feel about having lunch together again sometime?" he asked.

The question surprised her, and she was tempted to say yes, but she couldn't. Shouldn't. How was she going to put Margot behind her if she continued a friendship with Randy?

Randy misread her hesitation. "Purely platonic," he said.

"I've become a hermit since my divorce. My life's been made up of work and isolation and some brief, lovely moments of theater when I can pretend to be someone else." He looked up at the spire jutting into the gray sky. "I've been living that way for more than a year. It feels good to talk to someone. To really talk. You're a nice person. Kind and brave." He smiled. "I'm only looking for friendship, though. I know you're married. And probably very busy, and I'd understand—"

"I'd like it," she said, the words coming out with a life of their own. She stood on her toes to buss his cheek. Muttering a good-bye, she turned away from him quickly and headed for her car. She'd rather he didn't see the mix of emotions in her face. Not until she'd had a chance to scrutinize them herself, a chance to understand why the comfort and safety she felt with Randy Donovan seemed somehow tinged with danger.

12

Mornings in the big upstairs bedroom of the farmhouse were blindingly bright and filled with the scent of coffee. The sun poured through the open windows, washing over the yellow flowered wallpaper and warming the oak floor. The two little girls slumbered in their beds, burrowed beneath airy patchwork comforters their grandmother had stitched together from a lifetime's collection of fabric scraps. Seven-year-old Claire was usually first to open her eyes, and she would stretch, reaching her arms behind her to touch the glossy brown wicker headboard as she breathed in the scent of coffee and sunshine. Her five-year-old sister, Vanessa, rarely woke up before Claire called to her across the room, and even then she would sometimes squirm down in the bed and wrap the comforter around her like a cocoon.

On one particular morning in July, Claire awakened later than usual. She woke up Vanessa, who was grumpy and sulky, as she always was in the morning until she'd had a chance to wash her face and brush her teeth. Claire helped the younger girl get dressed, although Vanessa was pretty good at it by then and insisted on buttoning the little round buttons on her shirt by herself. It was still early when they clattered down the wide staircase and ran into the kitchen.

"What beautiful daughters I have!" Mellie stood up from her seat at the table and, as she did every morning, pulled the girls into her arms, smothering them with noisy kisses. Tucker, the spotted dog, leaped around their feet. Mellie looked up from her daughters to her own mother, busy frying doughnuts at the stove. "Aren't they beautiful, Mother?"

Dora Siparo turned from the pan of oil to assess her grandchildren. "More beautiful every day," she said.

The girls plunked themselves down at the table. Claire folded her hands on the table's edge, and Vanessa clumsily followed suit.

"Coffee, please," Claire said.

"Coffee, please," Vanessa mimicked.

Mellie pushed Vanessa's chair closer to the table. "Yes, ma'am," she said. She poured them each a cup of coffee—or rather, she poured a splash of coffee into their big, wide cups, followed by a generous stream of milk. Their grandmother set plates in front of them, each bearing a doughnut coated with powdered sugar.

Mellie sat down at the table with them. Her long, wavy blond hair was the same color as Vanessa's, catching the sun like the facets on a diamond. Claire's dark hair was more like her father's, very thick and slightly coarse. It had little shine at all to it. Soon she would be at an age where that sort of thing mattered to her.

"You know what day it is, girls, don't you?" Mellie asked as she lit a cigarette.

Claire wrinkled her nose at the question. "*Mellie*," she protested. Claire had told her mother many times that she did not like to think about what day it was during the summer because counting the days would only bring her closer to September, when she would have to return to Virginia and school.

"Friday?" Vanessa asked. Vanessa did not yet attend school, and she was always willing to play her mother's guessing games.

"And you know who comes on Friday?" Mellie's blue eyes twinkled behind a curl of smoke.

"Daddy!" Vanessa gave a little jump in her chair.

Mellie leaned across the table to tap Vanessa's nose. "That's *right*, Angel. And you're going to have so much fun with him this weekend, you won't be able to stand it."

Vanessa beamed, her golden hair and tiny pearly teeth sparkling in the sunlight. Everyone knew that Len Harte liked to baby and spoil his youngest daughter. Everyone knew it, but nobody said a word about it.

Len was able to join his family at the farm only on weekends because he had to work during the week, selling insurance in Virginia. The girls missed him, but every night Mellie told them stories about what he was doing during the day and how much he was thinking about the three of them, and it was almost like having him with them at the farm.

When their father came on the weekends, he made up intriguing games to play with them and took them on exciting day trips. He seemed to know that it would take something really special to pull the girls away from their grandfather and his carousel.

After breakfast, Dora filled a thermos with coffee and put a couple of doughnuts in a paper bag for the girls to take to their grandfather out in the barn.

The barn stood alone on the far side of a broad green field. The girls ran toward it, Tucker yapping at their heels. Claire carried the thermos because she was older and the thermos was more dangerous to carry than the bag.

The barn seemed to grow impossibly large as they neared it. It was painted a bright and beautiful red, like Mellie's fingernails.

The front doors were enormous, but this summer, Claire had the height and strength necessary to pull them open. She tugged on the left door, and Vanessa darted past her into the barn, clutching the bag of doughnuts to her chest.

"Leave them open, Claire." Vincent Siparo's deep voice boomed from the workshop that sprouted from the side of the barn. "It's going to be a hot one today."

Claire had to set down the thermos to open both doors wide. The outstretched doors left a huge gaping hole in the barn, and the carousel nearly spilled into the field. Claire's favorite horse, the white, wild-maned Titan, was right in front, the gold of his serpentine mane glowing. If the carousel were to begin spinning, surely Titan and the other horses would simply leap off and gallop free into the field.

Inside the workshop, Vanessa climbed onto one of the heavy wooden chairs to hand her grandfather the doughnuts across his big worktable. The bag had grown a little oily, and Vincent set it carefully to the side of the table before pulling out one of the doughnuts. He liked to keep his work space clean.

The workshop smelled of wood shavings and of Vincent

himself. The scents had blended together over the years. There was the smell of the cream he combed through his thinning gray hair, and the soft, sweet smell of the pipe he slipped, unlit, into his mouth from time to time as he worked and that he smoked for real on the porch in the evenings. Sometimes the smell was of paint, or of the oil he used on the mechanism that made the carousel spin. They were comforting smells, all of them, and there was no place the girls would rather be than there in their grandfather's workshop.

Claire raced into the room and handed him the thermos. He opened it, and the aroma of coffee joined the other scents in the air. "You're on the late side this morning, ladies," he said. There was a white dusting of powdered sugar on his lips, and the light from the window sparkled in his blue eyes. "I couldn't figure out where to start on my work. Made me realize I don't know what I'd do without you two."

The girls giggled. He always said that. How did he ever get anything done during the part of the year they were not around?

The workshop was nearly as wide as the barn, but narrow. Long, thick, slablike tables lined one wall, and they were often covered with carved pieces of wood, unpainted and waiting to be glued together. A horse head here, a tail there. Against the short wall at the far end of the room stood shelves covered with paint and tools. Windows lined part of the other long wall. Any wall space not covered by shelves or windows was graced with large photographs, some in color, but most in black and white, of the carousel horses the girls' great-grandfather, Joseph Siparo, had carved. His horses were on carousels around the world. He had taught Vincent how to carve, and although no one was interested in buying handcarved horses for carousels these days, Vincent didn't care. He carved to his heart's delight, making a carousel for himself. And, of course, for his granddaughters.

"May I please have the clay, Grandpa?" Vanessa asked, her little teeth flashing, and Claire covered her own mouth with her hand. She had recently lost one of her front teeth. She didn't smile too widely these days.

In one corner of the workshop stood a cabinet filled with playthings for them. Jacks and pick-up-sticks and a jump rope and a ball and Candyland. And clay. That was their favorite, but it was on a shelf too high for them to reach.

"Yes, *you* may have the clay," Vincent said mysteriously to Vanessa, "but now that Claire is seven, I think it's time she had a piece of wood to work with."

Claire stared at him. "Wood?" She smiled. The gap in her teeth showed small and dark.

From beneath the table, Vincent pulled a brick-sized block of pale wood and a small knife.

"Come here, Claire." He scooted his chair back from the table to lift her onto his lap, and he rested the wood on her knees. "This is balsa wood," he said. "It's very soft and easy to carve. I'll teach you how, all right?"

Claire stared reverently at the block of wood. "Yes." From across the table, Vanessa watched and listened, her small mouth open and, in her eyes, a resigned jealousy. Claire shrugged at her.

Vincent spent nearly half an hour showing Claire how to use the knife. She leaned against his chest, his gray beard softly scratching her temple. When he spoke, she could feel his voice deep inside her ribcage. Vanessa looked up from her clay from time to time, studying her sister with quiet longing.

"You'll be able to do this someday, too, Vannie," Claire said to her after climbing off Vincent's lap to take a seat at the worktable. Vanessa nodded glumly and returned her attention to the clay. She was making something unrecognizable, as usual.

Vincent turned on the big window fan, slipped the unlit pipe into his mouth, and the three of them settled down with their projects. Tucker yipped as he dreamed, and every time he thumped his tail in his sleep, Vanessa giggled.

When they'd first arrived at the farm this summer, the girls had been confused by Tucker's appearance. He was smaller than he used to be. He had more dark patches on his short white coat. He licked their hands more than he used to and sometimes nipped annoyingly at their heels when they ran. As a matter of fact, he seemed like a completely different dog. But everyone was calling him Tucker.

"Where's the *real* Tucker?" Claire had asked Mellie.

Mellie had glanced at her own mother. "This dog is really named Tucker," she had said.

"I mean the *other* Tucker."

Mellie knelt down to stroke the impostor's too-small head. "They gave the other Tucker away, honey," she said. "You know how he loved being around you kids?"

Claire nodded.

"Well, Grandpa and Grandma knew he couldn't be very happy with just the two of them, so they gave him to a family with lots of children. And now he's the happiest dog in the world, right, Mother?"

Dora turned away, a small smile on her lips. "If you say so, dear."

So, Claire and Vanessa were getting used to this Tucker. He was skinny and yappy, and he licked too much, but he was a good fetcher and better than no dog at all.

After an hour or so of working with her clay, Vanessa went into the barn where she could lay down for a nap. Vincent had put some old blankets on a couple of crates, and the girls napped there every day. Today, though, Claire did not bother with a nap. She was working on her wood with extraordinary care, and she was still working on it when Vanessa appeared again in the doorway of the workshop.

"I think it's time for our ride now, please, Grandpa," she said.

Vincent smiled and set down the tool he was using. He took the pipe from his mouth and stroked his hand across his beard. "Think you two have worked hard enough to earn a ride?" he asked.

Claire nodded and held up her hand to show him the new blister forming on her thumb while Vanessa pointed to the clay blob she had made. Vincent lifted Vanessa into his arms and walked over to her project. He held the lump of clay into the light from the windows. "I see, Vanessa," he said. "This is not a horse. It's a giraffe, right?"

Vanessa broke into a grin. "Yes!"

"It's a giraffe with a very odd tail."

"Yes."

"Well, I can see that you've been working every bit as hard as Claire." He set her down on the floor again. "A ride for you both."

Claire raced to the carousel, hopping onto the platform

and running over to Titan. It took some effort, but this summer she could reach the horse's stirrup and pull herself onto his back without her grandfather's help. Meanwhile, Vincent lifted his blond granddaughter onto the back of a standing gray horse. Vanessa said it was her favorite, but she had a new favorite every day, while Claire had favored Titan for several years now, ever since Vincent had first set the white stallion in place on the carousel. Claire shivered with excitement as she waited for the ride to start. The music—"The Sidewalks of New York"—began to play, the carousel turned, and Vincent waved at the girls as they swept past him on his whimsical creations.

Each time Claire passed the brass ring chute, she held tight to Titan's pole and reached out to try to grasp a ring, usually succeeding once during a ride. Vanessa did not even bother trying. She didn't care, she said, but the look in her eyes was wistful each time she passed the chute. It was a long reach, though. Long and scary from the top of a horse. It didn't matter. Vincent always gave Vanessa an extra ride, too, brass ring or not.

As they did every afternoon, the girls and their grandfather ate a big lunch with Mellie and Dora in the kitchen of the farmhouse. Everyone knew what a sacrifice it was for Dora and Mellie to make it to the table: They were missing their "stories" on the television. Vanessa had actually been named after one of the glamorous soap opera stars while Claire was the namesake of Dora's sister, who had died many years earlier.

Mellie still wore her satin robe at the table, and she held her hands away from the food so as not to mess the barn-red manicure she'd just given herself. She'd curled her hair and put on makeup. The girls thought she was the most beautiful woman in the world.

The farm was surrounded by thick forest, and after lunch, as he always did, Vincent took his granddaughters on a long walk through the woods. He showed them jack-in-the-pulpits and fungus that he claimed lit up at night, and for the second time that summer, they saw a spotted fawn. He knew everything there was to know about the woods, and they loved holding his big hands as they walked. They stayed in the cool shelter of the forest until the heat of the day had worn off a bit before returning to the barn and the workshop.

Late in the afternoon, when the sun burned a deep bronze across the fields outside the workshop windows, they heard Len Harte's car pull up the long drive to the house. The girls ran out of the barn and across the field. When they reached the house, their father was standing in the yard, holding Mellie, kissing her, and the girls jumped around his legs until he finally bent down to pick them up—Vanessa first, then Claire—and the four of them snuggled and laughed and giggled together in the warm golden air in front of the sun-drenched farmhouse.

13

Vienna

Jon looked up from the phone to see Claire standing in the doorway of the study, wearing her red slip.

She pointed to the clock on his desk. "We should leave here in half an hour," she said.

He nodded and covered the mouthpiece of the phone. "Gil Clayton," he said, letting her know who the call was from, and he smiled at her look of amazement. For the past three years, he and Claire had been trying in vain to talk Gil into bringing his innovative fitness workshop to the SCI Retreat. The date for this year's retreat was clear on his calendar, Gil was telling him now, and he was looking forward to coming.

Claire gave Jon a thumbs-up sign before disappearing back into the hall.

"So," Gil was saying, "I'll be in the Washington area next Saturday. I can stop by the foundation to meet with you and Claire and firm up the arrangements then."

Jon opened his appointment book and grimaced. The

accessibility conference was next weekend, and he would be hard-pressed to say which event was more critical. He and Claire would have to split the tasks. Not their usual mode of operation, but necessary in this case. "We've got a conference in Baltimore next weekend," he said to Gil, "but one of us will be here to meet with you."

In the kitchen, he found Claire and Amelia leaning over the counter, studying a recipe card. Amelia looked up when he wheeled into the room.

"Hi, Jon." She grinned at him. Amelia's straight, chin-length hair had turned completely gray in the few years since Jake's death, but the color looked so natural on her and so perfectly matched the smoke of her eyes that he could barely remember its original shade. "Claire had given me her manicotti recipe, and it didn't turn out right, so she's changing it for me."

The thought made him hungry. "It's been a while since we've made that ourselves, Claire," he said. "How about when Susan gets here? She loves it." Susan was coming home later this week to pick up her car.

"Sure." Claire did not look up from the card. She was still in her slip. She stole a look at the clock on the microwave, and Jon could feel her agitation from across the room.

"I found the problem," she said. She walked over to the table and started rummaging around in her purse, pulling things out, littering the tabletop with keys and change and folded-up scraps of paper. "I can't find my good pen," she said. A rare line of irritation dissected the skin between her eyes. She turned on the overhead light and held the purse up to peer inside.

Amelia caught Jon's eye. She nodded her head in Claire's direction as if to say, "What's with your wife?" and he shrugged in response, although he knew. Claire had been talking about the play all day, talking about it as though they'd been invited to the White House for dinner. What should they wear? What time should they leave? Amelia was an interruption.

"Have you seen it?" Claire looked at him. "The good pen you gave me?"

"No." He reached into the basket they kept on the counter, pulling out a dime-store pen. "Use this one." He wheeled toward her and pressed the pen into her palm.

Claire closed her purse with a snap and jotted something down on the card before handing it to Amelia. "That should do it." She smiled, but it was not a Harte smile. Not by a long shot, and Amelia knew it.

"You all right, hon?" Amelia rested a hand on Claire's arm.

"We're just running so late." Claire lifted her hair from her shoulders as though it was making her too warm and let it drop again. "Sorry. I'm frazzled."

Jon looked at the clock himself. The performance was at eight. It was now six-thirty. They had plenty of time.

"Well, you guys enjoy yourselves," Amelia said. She patted Jon's hand, nodding again in Claire's direction. "Get this girl to relax, Jon," she said.

"I'll do my best," he promised.

Claire did seem more relaxed once she was dressed and putting on her makeup at the vanity dresser in their bedroom. She was wearing a red dress he had always liked but hadn't seen on her for a while.

He was in his closet, pulling a gray tweed jacket from its hanger, when he heard a car on the gravel driveway followed by the slamming of a car door.

Claire, lipstick in hand, looked at him as he wheeled out of the closet. "Who can that be?" she asked.

They heard the kitchen door open and then a female voice.

"I'm home!"

Susan. A couple of days early. He and Claire exchanged looks across the bedroom, and for the first time in what seemed like weeks, Claire flashed him a genuine smile.

"In here, Suse," she called, and a moment later Susan popped into the room.

"Hey, guys." She grinned. "I could get a ride home tonight instead of Tuesday, so I took it."

Claire was on her feet, pulling her daughter into a hug. "It's so good to see you, honey," she said.

Susan was dressed in black jeans, chunky black shoes, a green wool jacket and a blue baseball cap set low above her huge, nearly black eyes. Shiny dark hair fell in rivulets over the green hills and valleys of her jacket. She was the world's cutest kid. Jon grinned and held his hand out to her.

She bent down to hug him, pressing her lips to his cheek. "Where you guys going, all decked out?"

Claire reached out to straighten the collar of Susan's jacket. "To a play," she said.

Susan took a step back to study her mother. "That dress is so sexy on you, Mom."

Claire smoothed her hands over the skirt of her dress. "Sexy?" she repeated. "It's just a simple dress."

They were both right, he thought. The red fabric had a shine to it, but the dress buttoned up the front and was plainly cut, almost tailored. On most women, the dress would indeed look simple. But on Claire it was undeniably sexy—the red stood out in flaming contrast to her dark hair, the shimmery fabric clung to her breasts and the slender line of her hips.

"Susie's right," he said. "You look terrific."

Claire waved away the compliment. "Well, I wish we weren't going out, now that you're home," she said to her daughter. "You should have let us know you'd be getting in today. Don't you have classes tomorrow?"

"Yeah, I do. That's why I have to go back tonight."

"Tonight?" Claire's smile faded.

"You just got here," Jon said.

"'Cause I could get a ride, Dad."

"But we expected you to spend a few days with us," Claire said.

Susan shook her head, and the streaming hair changed course on her jacket. "Can't, Mom. Sorry. I'm just gonna grab something to eat and head back."

Claire looked at her watch. "But we won't be able to spend any time with you."

Just what she wants, Jon thought. Susan had planned this well.

"Look, Mom, I wouldn't have been home at all if I didn't have to leave my car here because of the storm and had to get it, so this is just like a bonus or something that I'm here at all, all right?"

Jon had to smile. Sometimes Susan's reasoning was so convoluted, so desperate, that it was nearly impossible to follow. He shared Claire's disappointment, though. He'd wanted Susan around for a few days this week, wanted the three of them to feel like a family. "Maybe we should skip the theater?" he suggested to Claire. He didn't share Claire's enthusiasm for seeing this play, not even after she read him the review from the local paper, in which the performance of the entire cast—and most notably, of Randy Donovan—was deemed "magnificent."

Claire gnawed her lower lip uncertainly, but Susan didn't give her a chance to answer.

"I'm only going to be here five seconds, Dad."

"Of course we'll skip the play," Claire said. "We'll go out to dinner instead—to Anita's, okay, Susie? Your favorite? Then we can—"

"*Mom*, please," Susan said. "I don't have time and you've already got plans, okay?"

Claire's shoulders sagged and she looked at Jon.

"What time's your first class tomorrow?" he asked.

"Not till eleven," Susan answered.

"Could you drive down in the morning, then? Not have to drive all that way tonight in the dark?"

"I have stuff to do at school in the morning."

"She'll be fine driving," Claire said as she ran a comb through her hair. "She's the best driver. Remember she won that award in high school?"

Susan rolled her lovely eyes. "I'm not the best, Mother. I'm an okay driver. A good one, maybe. That's all." She finally unzipped her jacket but still did not take it off. "I'm sorry I can't stay longer. Next time." She started toward the door. "I'm getting something to eat and then I'm out of here."

Claire wrinkled her nose at Jon once Susan had left the room. "Oh, well," she said. "At least she cares enough to not skip her classes tomorrow. And she is an exceptional driver."

He gave her a smile. "You about ready to go?" he asked, and she was on her feet before he'd finished the question.

He could see no logic whatsoever in the Sunday-night traffic jam that greeted them on Maple Avenue. They inched toward McLean, Maple giving way to Chain Bridge Road. They were still talking about Susan, but as the traffic thickened, Claire grew quiet, and he knew her attention had shifted from their conversation with their daughter to the evening ahead of them.

The cars came to a standstill, and Claire glanced at her watch for the third time.

"We'll make it," Jon said. It was only seven-thirty, and they were moving again.

"That must have been the problem." Claire pointed to a tow truck as it lumbered around the corner, dragging a dented gray BMW behind it. "Poor people," she said. "Hope no one was hurt."

After another half-mile or so, he noticed that Claire had raised her purse to the window and was holding it up against the glass.

"What are you doing?" he asked.

"The lights in the sideview mirror," she said. "Blinding."

Blinding? He glanced in the rearview mirror near his head. Lots of traffic, but nothing out of the ordinary. He looked at Claire again. She was pressing the purse to the window with her palm, and her eyes stared straight ahead. He said nothing. She was doing many things lately that made no sense to him.

She'd spent nearly two hours at lunch with Randy. She'd arrived late for the meeting they'd had scheduled with Tom Gardner, one of the foundation consultants, and she seemed completely unable to focus on their discussion. Even Tom had commented on it.

"Yoo-hoo, Claire," Tom had said. "You with us?"

Claire had blushed and apologized, but she did not lose the preoccupied furrow in her brow, the faraway glaze to her eyes, and in that moment Jon knew that her obsession with Margot St. Pierre had in some way shifted to Margot's brother.

They'd finally talked about her tardiness later that afternoon, sitting in her office. She apologized again, then told him about the play tickets and how much she wanted Jon to meet Randy. She added, with some hesitation, "I might like to have lunch with him again sometime." She was sitting behind her desk, doodling with a pencil on the edge of a memo pad. Long, sloping lines, backward Ss, covered the border of the paper. "I'd like to have him as a friend. I've never really had an opposite-sex friend, the way you have Pat."

He thought of Pat, of his friendship with her, a friendship tender, simple, and long-standing. And thoroughly platonic. The comparison gave him some comfort.

He'd worked out at the gym after leaving the office, and each time he thought of Claire having lunch with Randy, he made himself recall his lunches with Pat. Pat was a good listener, the kind of listener who made him feel as if every word he said was significant, who pressed him for details he simply could not believe anyone other than himself would find interesting. He pictured the dimples that made Pat look so young and vulnerable, and he began to imagine Randy looking like Pat—overweight, goofy grin, endearing. Of course Claire would want to spend time with him. And the fact that he enjoyed talking with Pat took nothing away from his feelings for Claire. They were two different people; he received different gifts from each of them. And so he told himself, as he studied the lines in his face in the locker-room mirror, that was the way it would be with Claire and Randy Donovan.

One of the two handicapped parking spaces at the theater was vacant, and Jon pulled the Jeep into it. There was one low step into the foyer of the chapel, which he negotiated easily with a wheelie. Claire picked up their tickets at the small window in the center of the cold foyer and hung up their coats before they made their way to their seats in the second row.

Jon transferred to the padded pew, and Claire wheeled his chair to the side of the aisle, parking it against the wall, out of the way.

The theater was filling quickly, and Jon was glad to have so many warm bodies around him to take the chill from the air. Claire sat next to him and began reading the program. Jon read the bio on Randy. Randy Donovan had been one of the founders of the Chain Bridge Theater ten years earlier, and there was a long list of productions that he had directed or in which he'd appeared. And he was the owner of the Fishmonger Restaurant, as Claire had mentioned. Theater? Restaurant? Was he gay, perhaps? Jon was disgusted with himself for stereotyping the man but comforted by the thought all the same.

He was holding Claire's hand as the play began. The first fifteen minutes established that the little French town of Dassant was suffering from famine and plague and a serious decline in moral standards. The group of women on the stage lamented their woes, at great length, and Jon found his attention wandering.

Suddenly, a tall, bearded man dressed in a dark suit appeared on the stage. The magician, no doubt. Jon felt the sharpening of tension in Claire's fingers.

Randy Donovan had total command of the stage. He would fit in no role other than the lead. He stood over six feet tall with a powerful build, his hair and beard jet black, and Jon tried to discern if his charismatic presence was part of the role or simply part of Randy himself. One thing was for certain: It was no longer possible to equate Randy Donovan with Pat Wykowski.

Claire leaned close to whisper to him. "They dyed his hair," she said. "It's not actually that dark."

The play was lost on him. Instead, during the next hour and a half, Jon found himself reevaluating his life, picking apart the world he'd made for himself. He'd built it with such confidence, with such a sense of comfort and ease. He'd thought it was solid. Right now, though, it seemed made of glass.

He was completely dependent on the woman at his side, wasn't he? She'd rescued him from his dungeon of self-pity when he was a teenager and taught him how to turn his gloomiest thoughts into creative ideas. She had been by his side through everything. Through the fun stuff—traveling, conferences—and through the terrible times as well. The illnesses he'd had. Infrequent, but incapacitating. Taking care of his intimate physical needs. Right now, that thought made him cringe.

He clutched Claire's hand more tightly, and she squeezed his in return, although her eyes remained fixed on the stage.

She had been his only lover, and he hers. She didn't know what it was like to make love to a man who could feel the touch of her fingers on his skin, who could achieve an erection with ease. A man for whom climax was not a small triumph.

Claire leaned over to whisper to him again. "Are you

enjoying it?" she asked, and Jon nodded absently, struggling to return his focus to the play. Randy was dancing, first with one woman, then another. Jon hunted for a word to describe him and came up with "debonair." Randy was no longer wearing his suit jacket, and the sleeves of his white shirt were rolled up to his elbows. He was broad in the chest, narrow at the waist, where the shirt was tucked into his pants. The bulk of his thighs was apparent beneath the dark fabric of his trousers.

Jon rested a hand on his thigh. The muscles in his own legs had long ago atrophied, and those low in his belly were undeniably flaccid. He wanted to glance down to see how apparent the bulge of his belly was.

What had they talked about at lunch, Randy and Claire? Margot, of course. But for nearly two hours?

Claire let go of his hand to turn a page in the program. She held the program into the light from the stage to read something, and when she rested it once more on her lap, she did not take his hand again. Jon felt the emptiness in his palm. She even leaned away from him slightly. He could feel her slipping away from him, feel his world slipping away, here, in this tiny converted chapel, as they watched the magnificent performance of the Magician of Dassant.

The play came to a close shortly after ten, and the curtain calls seemed to drag on forever. Randy received a standing ovation, during which Jon sat, clapping hands that felt stiff and wooden, while Claire applauded above him.

When the actors left the stage for the last time, Claire took her seat again.

"He said for us to come backstage afterwards," she said, looking around the small theater. "He wants to meet you. We'll wait until it clears out a little in here."

"All right." Jon nodded.

"Weren't the costumes wonderful?" she asked.

"Uh-huh."

"And that one young girl who played Emilie. She was terrific. And I never expected that twist at the end. Wow."

She talked on about the play, but he could not concentrate on her words.

Claire, my world just fell apart.

"I think we can maneuver well enough now." Claire stood up and retrieved his wheelchair from the aisle. Jon transferred into it, while Claire studied the exit leading backstage.

"Hmm," she said.

Jon looked toward the exit himself. There were five steps leading up to the door. "Oh."

"Maybe there's another route," Claire said. "You want to wait here while I check?"

"No, I'll come with you." The thought of sitting like a stranded duck in the middle of the emptying theater did not appeal to him, and he followed along behind her as she headed toward the side.

The exit led into a long hallway, and Claire broke through the crowd ahead of him to hunt for a more accessible route backstage. Jon wheeled to the side of the hall, trying to stay out of the way of the milling crowd.

Claire returned, a look of disappointment on her face. "There's one step through that rear door, but once you get over that one, there's a little landing and then a bunch more."

"Look, why don't you go say hi and then we'll head home," he suggested. "I'll wait here."

She rested her hand lightly on his shoulder. "I wanted

you to meet him, though." She looked around the hall, a frown on her face. "Well, I'll just let him know what happened so he's not waiting for us."

He watched her walk off down the hall, slim hips swaying slightly beneath the shiny red fabric of her dress.

She was gone for five minutes, during which Jon read the bio notes on every performer in the play as well as those of the lighting crew, the costume designer, and the stagehands. Only a few people remained milling in the hallway when Claire returned. She was not alone. Randy Donovan walked at her side. He was still in his fitted white shirt and dark trousers, still with the high color of his stage makeup staining his cheeks.

"Sorry you couldn't get backstage." Randy held out his hand, and Jon shook it, his eyes now on Claire. She looked extraordinary. What other forty-year-old woman could get away with wearing her hair that long? It was dark—nearly as dark as Randy's dyed hair—and very thick. The silver at her temples softened her, made her look vulnerable. Her cheekbones were prominent, her lips full. Green eyes big and smiling. He could detect few signs of age in her face. She was tall—five eight—yet she had to look up at Randy, and when she did so, her face was radiant.

"We really enjoyed the play," Jon said. "Thanks for the tickets."

"Glad you liked it."

It was rare for Jon to feel the indignity, the inequality, of his seated status. This, though, was one such occasion.

The two grown-ups smiled down at him.

"I'm sorry about your sister," Jon said.

"Thanks." Randy shook his head. "Weren't you

shocked when Claire went out on that bridge?" He sent Claire a look of admiration, which, Jon thought, made her blush.

"Not much she does shocks me anymore," he said.

"She's very courageous." Randy slipped his hand to Claire's back, the touch light and brief.

"Yes," he agreed. "She is." He could think of nothing more to say, and a few awkward beats of silence filled the hallway.

"Oh, by the way." Randy turned to Claire. "I found a fountain pen in the pew after you left on Monday. Could it be yours?"

"Yes. Oh, that's great. I couldn't imagine where I'd lost it."

"The pew?" Jon asked. "You mean you ate lunch here?" He had pictured them, stretching out their lunch breaks, in a restaurant. But they'd been here, most likely alone, in the intimate quarters of this dim little chapel.

"Yes," Claire said. "Randy brought smoked tuna from his restaurant. It was delicious."

He wondered why she hadn't told him that, why she hadn't told him that this was where they'd met. *So what?* he thought to himself. *It's not like they met in his bedroom.*

"I'll go get the pen," Randy said. "It's in my briefcase. Be right back." He walked away from them, and Claire folded her arms across her chest and leaned against the wall opposite Jon to wait.

She looked down at him. "You look tired, sweetheart," she said.

He wanted to turn his chair away from her scrutiny. "Not at all," he said, although he felt very tired. He felt as tired as he'd ever been in his life.

It was close to midnight by the time he got into bed. He watched Claire sitting in her blue robe, combing her hair at the dresser mirror.

"You're very beautiful," he said. "I think it's been a while since I've told you that."

She smiled at him in the mirror. "Thank you."

"Could we talk, please?" he asked.

She stopped the comb, and her smile was replaced with concern. "What about?"

"In bed?" He patted the mattress, and she nodded. He preferred talking to her there. Bed was the only place he could really hold her.

She slipped off her robe and climbed into the bed next to him, turning off the lamp on the night table. He could detect the scent of her skin cream, and the familiarity of the smell was soothing. He wrapped his arms around her, his hands on her bare skin, and held her as close to him as he could. Breathing deeply, he wondered how to begin. What should he say? In twenty years, he had never felt threatened by anyone, by anything. He knew she sensed his distress, because she held him tightly, too, pressing her cheek hard to his shoulder.

"I love you, Mathias," she said.

"I needed to hear that," he said.

She raised herself to her elbow. "Do you have some doubt?"

Drawing her head to his shoulder again, he said, "Let me talk, all right?"

She nodded, her hair brushing his chin.

"There's something . . . strange going on with me."

Her head jerked up, and he felt her alarm. She thought he meant something physical.

"Emotionally," he said quickly. "I'm feeling . . . I think I'm too dependent on you."

"That's crazy." She flopped her head onto his shoulder again. "It's *okay* for two people to be dependent on each other. Isn't that what we're always telling the couples we see?"

"But I'm *too* dependent. I don't know how I would manage if anything ever happened to you."

She sighed. "First of all, nothing is going to happen to me. Second of all, you've traveled all over the *world*. I've seen you do things that would make a walking man quake in his hiking boots."

She wasn't getting it.

"It's Randy." The words slipped out of his mouth, far too loudly.

The silence was sharp and tense. "What about Randy?" she asked finally.

"He's so slick. He seems fake to me, or—" This was not true. He had not for a moment doubted Randy Donovan's sincerity. He growled at his ineptitude to say what he meant. "Look, seeing him standing next to you and putting his hand on your back and talking about feeding you lunch made me want to punch his goddamned lights out."

He'd expected her to laugh. Instead, she lay perfectly still. He could not even feel her breathing.

"You're making way too much of this, Jon," she said finally. "You sound as if you're afraid I'd have an affair with him or something."

"I'm not sure . . ." He swallowed hard. "Maybe I am."

"God, Jon, don't you know me better than that?"

"Well, frankly, right now I don't know. He seems interested in you, and I think you're leading him on. Innocently, maybe. You look up at him with those green bedroom eyes of yours, and—"

She sat up, hugging her pillow to her chest. "I cannot believe what I'm hearing," she said. "Jon, I *love* you. You're my husband, and Randy is a friend. That's all there is to it."

"All right," he said quickly, touching her arm. She was right. He was blowing this entirely out of proportion.

She stroked her fingertips over his chest. "You know you're being ridiculous, don't you?" she asked.

"I hope so."

"*Jon*," she nearly wailed. "You're saying you don't trust me. After twenty years of being married to me, how can you say that?"

"I trust you. What I don't trust is ... I don't know. Being forty, I guess. I mean, you and I have seen it happen far too often. The midlife stuff. It creeps up on you. It eats up the healthiest-looking marriages before anyone knows what's hit them."

"It's never going to happen to us, though. Don't even think it."

She lay next to him again. The conversation did not satisfy him, but he didn't know how to turn it around. After a moment, she spoke again.

"I won't see him anymore, then," she said. "Not if it makes you this uncomfortable. It's not that important to me."

He sighed. "That's not what I want." It was, but he knew he was wrong to ask that of her. "If you say he's a friend, then he's a friend. I'll accept that."

She leaned on her elbow again, then lowered her head to kiss him, and her hair fell onto his chest. Grinning, she said, "Hey, Mathias, don't torment yourself over things that will never happen. You and I are going to float through midlife the way we've floated through everything else. Understood?"

He nodded and kissed her, and she settled back into his arms. In a few minutes, her breathing became deep and regular. He did not let go of her, though. Not for half the night, even though she felt edgy beneath his arms. Even though, at moments, her body felt like that of a stranger.

14

Seattle

"Patterson's going to be wonderful, Vanessa." Terri Roos sounded more enthusiastic than Vanessa had ever heard her, but it was an enthusiasm she couldn't possibly share.

"Well, go on," she said into her office phone. "Tell me what he said."

It had been over a week since her attempt to call Walter Patterson's office, and during that time she'd suffered two migraine headaches, innumerable vivid nightmares, and a stomach so queasy she had simply stopped trying to eat anything other than soup. She'd called Terri on Friday to ask if she might be able to make the first contact with Patterson, mumbling some weak excuse about being too busy. As if Terri had any more free time than she did. Yet Terri had agreed without complaint. Now Vanessa had to listen to the results of that call.

"He's gotten so many victims' rights bills through," Terri said. "And he's already sponsoring something he's calling the Aid to Adult Survivors Bill for adults who suffered childhood abuse. He admitted he hadn't thought specifi-cally of programs for adolescents, though. He's all for including their needs in the bill, but he said it's going to be a hard sell, and he doesn't want to screw up the chances of getting the rest of the bill passed by attaching something to it without a good sense that it will have support. So"—Terri stopped to draw in a breath—"we need to get to work. I told him about the network, and he thought we might be able to pull it off. We have to flood him with statistics showing the need for AMC programs. And get this: In May, in order to get support for his bill, they're planning to hear testimony on Capitol Hill from women who were abused as children. He said we might be able to piggyback on that hearing."

Vanessa frowned. "You mean, have teenagers testify?" She did not like the idea.

"Well, not necessarily. It could be adults who can talk about the difference a program like the AMC would have made in their lives."

Vanessa reached up to touch one of the roses in the vase on her desk. Brian had sent them two days earlier. He'd been gone for the past five days but would be home tonight. Thank God. "Is there some cosponsor of this adolescent bill?" she asked Terri. "Someone other than Patterson we can communicate through?"

There were a few seconds of silence on Terri's end of the line. "There's no cosponsor yet, but why would you want to talk with anyone else? Patterson's the best. There's no one who can help us more, Vanessa."

She felt the pressure starting in her temples. A few jagged lights, like sparks of lightning, flickered in the corner of her right eye. A migraine. Just what she needed.

Wedging the phone between her chin and shoulder, she reached into her top desk drawer for a prescription bottle and shook a couple of the pills into her hand while Terri continued.

"At some point, you and I and a few others from the network should make a little trek to D.C. to have a face-to-face with this guy," Terri said.

"No." Vanessa popped the pills into her mouth and swallowed them dry. "I mean, I doubt I'll be able to get away from the hospital anytime soon."

Terri was quiet for another second or two. "Are you okay, Vanessa?"

"Oh, yeah. Just battling migraines this week." She glanced up as Lauren Schenk, one of the nurses on the unit, appeared in her open doorway.

Terri continued talking. "You poor thing," she said. "I'm so sorry. Well, listen, give me a call when you're feeling more like yourself, all right?"

Lauren was motioning to Vanessa that she needed to talk. It looked like something that couldn't wait.

"I've got to go, Terri." Vanessa stood up. "Thanks for taking care of everything."

"It's Jordan Wiley," Lauren said before Vanessa had even set the receiver back in its cradle.

"What's wrong?" Vanessa followed Lauren out of the office, and they walked rapidly down the long hallway of the adolescent unit.

"Not sure. He's having trouble breathing. Chest pain. He's in a lot of distress. Pete Aldrich thinks he's fine. He thinks it's anxiety." Lauren tucked a strand of dark hair behind her ear, then glanced at Vanessa. "Pete doesn't know I came to get you," she said. "But you know Jordy.

He's not the type of kid who complains unless something's really wrong."

Pete Aldrich was standing in his green scrubs, leaning over the counter of the nurses' station, writing in a chart. He looked up as she and Lauren approached, and Vanessa could almost hear him groan. He gave Lauren a look of betrayal before speaking to Vanessa.

"The kid's fine," he said. "Nail beds are pink, lips are pink. He's had a normal blood study. I even did a rhythm strip."

He turned the chart so that she could read the results of the studies. Normal, as he had said.

"I think he should have a chest X ray," Lauren said, and Vanessa admired her courage for standing up to the resident.

Pete ran freckled hands through his red hair. "He's got a vicious cycle going," he said. "He has some trouble breathing, gets scared, the breathing gets worse, he gets more scared, and on and on." His tone was singsong; he nodded his head from side to side as he spoke.

Vanessa didn't utter a word. She closed the chart and walked across the hall to Jordy's room, Lauren following close behind.

Jordy was hunched over his pillow, breathing rapidly, obviously pulling for air. He looked up when she walked into the room.

"Dr. Gray! Something's wrong," he said. "I can't breathe."

"Let me take a listen." Vanessa pulled the stethoscope from the pocket of her white coat and leaned over the boy, setting the disk on his back. She was vaguely aware of Pete appearing in the doorway, leaning against the jamb, but she kept her attention on Jordy. At first his breath sounds did not strike her as unusual for him, but as she continued to listen, she thought she detected a subtle difference between his left lung and his right. The left was not aerating well.

Above Jordy's head, she tried to convey her concern to Lauren, who nodded. Pete Aldrich's arms were folded across his chest, and he looked smug, as if he was waiting for her to reach the same conclusion he had.

Vanessa stepped away from her patient. "Well, I can see you're having a genuine problem here, Jordan," she said. She did not want to alarm him, and so kept her suspicion to herself. After all, she might be wrong. "Let's get an X ray and see what's going on, all right?"

Within seconds, Lauren had procured a gurney, and she and Vanessa transferred Jordy onto it.

"Don't make me lie down," the boy said, panicked.

"No, sweetie, you can sit up," Lauren said. "Here's your pillow."

Jordy clutched his pillow to his chest as they wheeled the gurney out into the hall, past Pete, whose pale eyebrows were knitted together above his blue eyes.

"You come with us, Dr. Aldrich," Vanessa said as she passed him. If her hunch about this patient was right, she wanted Pete Aldrich to see what he'd missed in his cavalier dismissal of Jordy's complaints.

Pete fell in next to her, protesting, arms flailing. "I don't have time to humor this kid when there are—"

Vanessa stopped walking and stared at him. "You're coming with us." She kept her voice calm, quiet, but it was a major struggle. She walked toward the elevator without looking back.

Pete followed them into the elevator, angry smudges of red on his cheeks. He kept his eyes riveted on the door in a furious glare while Jordy gasped and wheezed on the gurney next to him. Lauren held an oxygen mask to the boy's face and uttered words of comfort.

"We'll be there in just a second." Vanessa leaned close to Jordy. "And in a matter of minutes, we'll know what's going on."

Jordy didn't acknowledge her in any way. All of his effort was focused on his breathing, and she felt increasingly certain of her diagnosis. She had never seen Jordan Wiley in this sort of distress.

After the X rays had been taken, Vanessa, Lauren, Pete, and the technician stared at the image of Jordan Wiley's lungs.

"*Shit*," Pete said. The X ray clearly showed that Jordy's left lung was 30 percent collapsed.

"Let's go." Vanessa pushed past him into the room where Jordy sat fighting for breath. No time to deal with Aldrich. They had a real emergency on their hands. She told Pete to call the cardiothoracic resident and have him meet them in the adolescent unit.

"We know what's wrong, Jordan," she said, motioning for Lauren to help her move the boy onto the gurney again. "We're going to take you back upstairs and fix it."

"What is it?" Jordy struggled to get the words out.

"I'll tell you as we're moving."

In the elevator, Jordy started to cry. "Suffocating," he said. A film of sweat covered his face, and his lips were now clearly blue.

Vanessa had never seen him cry. She put her arm lightly around his shoulders. "You have a pneumothorax," she said calmly. "That means your left lung is partly collapsed. A bubble in the wall of your lung broke, and the air is leaking out."

He looked at her with new panic in his eyes. "God, does that mean I—"

"It's treatable," she said quickly. "It's not all that uncommon. It can even happen to a healthy person, sometimes. We'll work fast and get you feeling better very soon."

He nodded, the overhead light winking in his little gold earring as he moved his head. She could see him struggling to pull himself together and stop the flow of tears, and she was touched by his bravery and his trust in her.

Back on the sixth floor, they wheeled him into the treatment room of the adolescent unit. If circumstances had been different, she would have used the opportunity to teach Pete Aldrich how to perform this procedure, but her fury with the resident had not yet subsided enough to even acknowledge his presence in the room. Quickly and carefully, she inserted the large-bore needle into Jordy's chest, attached a syringe, and pulled back on the stopper. The relief in Jordy's face was immediate, but his comfort was short-lived. By the time Vanessa had finished the procedure, the cardiothoracic surgery resident was next to her, ready to insert the wide, metal-tipped chest tube. Vanessa held Jordy's hand while the surgeon did his job, and the boy cried out in pain.

Only when Jordy was finally sedated, breathing more easily and, at least to some small extent, free of pain, did Vanessa become aware again of the throbbing in her head.

She walked out into the hall and saw Pete Aldrich at the nurses' station, and she marched toward him, her rage building with each step. She stopped at the counter and put her hands on her hips.

"Don't you *ever* make unilateral decisions like that again," she said. There were others around—nurses, medical students, a couple of patients. A few of them continued with their work, as if they hadn't heard her. Others turned to stare, startled by the irate tone of her voice. "Tests and studies are only part of medicine, Dr. Aldrich. You need to learn to listen to the patient as well, something you seem incapable of doing. And you need to listen to the nurses, who are with these kids twenty-four hours a day and know them better than you ever will. You have a nice little rhythm strip, nice blood work." She gestured toward the chart. "So nothing can be wrong. Meanwhile your patient is dying, and when he does finally succumb, you can take your lab reports with you to bed at night to comfort you."

Vanessa turned on her heel and walked down the hall, not slowing her pace until she'd reached her office. Inside, she shut the door and sat down at her desk. She felt sick to her stomach, and her skull was splitting in two. She could not recall another time when she'd publicly lambasted a colleague. She'd come close, but she'd always been able to summon up the last-minute control she'd needed to bite her tongue, at least until she could get him or her behind closed doors. This time, though, the thought of control had not even passed through her mind. Not until now. She'd really lost it out there.

Her eyes suddenly stung with tears that took her by surprise, and she fought them with a vengeance. Just two more hours to survive in the hospital, she told herself. Then she'd be home with Brian. Then she could let her defenses down.

Her tears didn't start in earnest until she pulled into the driveway and saw Brian in the garage, tinkering with one of his tennis rackets. They were tears of relief this time. Between her nightmares and agonizing over how to handle the Zed Patterson situation, the past five days had seemed like five months.

She blotted her eyes in her rearview mirror before getting out of the car, but Brian knew. His smile faded the second he saw her.

"Oh, baby," he said, pulling her into his arms. "What's the matter?"

For a moment, she didn't speak. She sank gratefully into the softness of his white cable-knit sweater.

"Just a shitty day," she said finally, her lips against his neck.

He drew back from her and looked hard into her eyes. "Forgive me, Van, but it looks like it's been a shitty *five* days."

She nodded and felt her lower lip begin to tremble. "I've missed you," she said huskily. "And my head hurts. And my stomach's upset. And Terri Roos spent half an hour on the phone with me this afternoon, telling me how godlike Zed Patterson is. And one of my kids got really sick. And I chewed out a resident in front of the world."

He was leaning against the painted garage wall, holding her, stroking her hair. "What can I do to make it better?"

She sighed. "Can we just sit for a while? Let me unwind?"

"Of course. I've already built a fire in the den."

He walked ahead of her into the house. She took a minute to wash her face in the powder room off the kitchen. By the time she reached the den, Brian was playing a Kenny G. disc on the stereo, and the sultry strains of a clarinet filled the room.

"The roses you sent were beautiful." She stopped to pick

up the stack of mail resting on the chair by the doorway, then sat next to him on the sofa.

He put his arm around her shoulders as she began sifting through the envelopes.

"Why don't you look at the mail later?" He tried to extract the stack from her hands, but she held tight.

"I need a good, mindless activity right now." She came to a postcard picturing a spectacular white castle and turned it over, smiling. "J.T.," she said. "In Germany."

"What does she say?"

Vanessa read the card out loud.

"'Frank and I are settling in. I'm very happy, although I don't think I'll ever get used to being a military wife. I'm not quite used to being a wife, period. The down comforter is great—a super wedding present. Thanks! We use it every night and it makes me miss you, 'Nessa. You and Brian have to visit us here. Pleeze! I love you, J.T.'"

Vanessa bit her lip. J.T. Only twenty-one. Born around the same time as Anna, and probably the closest thing she would ever have to a daughter she could know and love. "She's too young to be married and living so far from her family," she said.

"Frank's her family now," Brian pointed out.

Vanessa stroked her fingers over the picture of the castle. J.T. Gray had long ago changed Vanessa's life. Vanessa had even stolen the little girl's name—with the blessing of J.T. and her parents, of course. What a relief it had been to rid herself of the Harte surname.

"When can we visit them?" she asked.

"Summer?"

She nodded, tears welling once more in her eyes, and Brian hugged her with a laugh. "You really are in a misty mood tonight," he said. Once more he reached for the stack of mail on her lap, and once more she resisted him, suspicious now.

She sorted through the remaining pieces of mail until her hands froze on a lavender envelope with a silver return address sticker. *Claire Harte-Mathias.* Two forwarding addresses were pasted to the front of the envelope.

"Oh, crap," she said. "Just what I need." She stood up, struggling vainly to tear the envelope in two as she walked toward the fireplace. She pulled open the screen, but Brian was next to her in a few quick strides, and he caught her arm in his hand.

"Don't burn it," he said.

"Yes." She pulled free of him and reached again for the screen, but he grabbed the envelope from her hand.

"I won't let you, Van. You—"

"You don't have any right to tell me what I can or can't do with her fucking letter." She reached again for the envelope, but he held it behind his back.

"Please, Van. Just put it away somewhere. Or let me keep it in my office, if you don't want it around. Someday you might change your mind."

She held her hand out, palm up, and said coldly, "Give it to me."

He resisted another few seconds before handing it over. She drew back the screen, slipping the envelope into the fire, and together they watched the lavender paper blacken and disappear behind the tongues of flame.

The clarinet music filled the room, soft and bittersweet.

"Do you remember what Marianne said when you quit therapy?" Brian asked quietly.

"No," she said, although she remembered very well. She

wished now, though, that she had never shared Marianne's parting words with Brian.

"She said that—"

"I know what she said." Vanessa took her seat on the sofa again. Leaning back, she closed her eyes.

"You're not ready to terminate therapy." Marianne had spoken calmly, but she'd sat on the edge of her large brown leather chair, as she always did when she wanted to make a point.

"I'm fine, now," Vanessa had insisted. "Nothing really bothers me anymore. And I finally have a relationship I haven't screwed up."

"Yes, you've made very good progress. But I'm concerned your problems will reemerge when something happens to trigger those old feelings."

"But I've dealt with those old feelings." Vanessa had felt impatient, annoyed with Marianne for not acknowledging all the work she'd done.

"Yes," Marianne had said, "but you haven't confronted the people who hurt you. In your case, Vanessa, it's a necessary step."

Brian sat down next to her. "She said you needed to confront the—"

"Brian." Vanessa opened her eyes. "Not tonight. Please." She touched his cheek. His face was tight with worry. "I'm sorry," she said. "I just want to live my life *now*. In the present."

"All right, Van." He rested his cheek against her hair.

She drank in the smell of him, sinking her fingers into the softness of his sweater, and tried to forget about them all—Zed Patterson, Claire Harte, even J.T.—the conspiracy of reminders suddenly poised to attack.

15

Vienna

Amelia was propped up in her bed, reading a novel, when Claire brought in the tray laden with tomato soup, half a cheese sandwich, and a dish of applesauce. The late-morning sun played across the pink comforter and white flannel sheets. Amelia looked much better than she had the night before, when she'd been battling the flu. Claire had come over to nurse her through the fever and had been stunned by her friend's pale, weepy weakness.

"Want some more water?" Claire picked up the empty glass from Amelia's night table.

"Please." Amelia's damp gray hair was combed back from her face, and she'd taken the time to put on lipstick after her shower. She grinned at Claire. "God, I could really get used to being waited on."

Claire carried the glass into the bathroom and began filling it at the sink. She caught her reflection in the medicine cabinet mirror and was surprised by the tired, red look of her eyes. There was a small, round magnifying mirror jutting from the side of the cabinet, and she turned it toward her for a closer look, only to find the entire mirror filled with green.

She let out a shriek, dropping the glass on the edge of the sink, where it splintered into a thousand pieces.

"Are you all right?" Amelia called from the bedroom.

Claire could not answer right away. She sat down on the edge of the tub and closed her eyes. "Just broke the glass," she called back. "Sorry. I'll clean it up." But she made no move to get up. Instead, she slid sideways along the edge of the tub until she reached the wall, and she leaned against the cool tile, waiting for the panic to pass.

What was wrong with her? The mirrors were every-where. Small mirrors, usually filled entirely by the color green or, on a few occasions, by a mixture of colors that shifted in the glass until she averted her eyes—which she did quickly. The vision was invariably accompanied by a strong, sudden, incapacitating nausea, like the nausea hold-ing her captive right now in Amelia's bathroom.

It was minutes before she felt ready to get up from the tub. She hung a washcloth over the small mirror and care-fully picked up the larger shards of glass before leaving the room.

"Broom in the hall closet?" she asked Amelia as she passed through the bedroom.

"Uh-huh." Amelia looked up from her soup. "Sorry you have to do that."

"It'll teach me to be more careful next time." She got the broom from the closet, took it back into the bathroom, and began cleaning up the splinters of glass.

It was Saturday, and Jon was in Baltimore for the week-end, attending the Accessibility Conference. She had stayed behind, since one of them needed to meet with Gil Clayton to talk about the workshop he'd be presenting at the SCI Retreat. It felt odd to be separated from Jon and to imagine him handling a conference alone. Watching him drive off in the Jeep the day before, she'd felt an unfamiliar emptiness. She did not let herself sulk, though. She would have a good quiet weekend, she told herself, the meeting with Gil her only obligation. But then Amelia had called, achy and feverish. Usually, that would not have been enough to reduce Amelia to tears, but yesterday had also been her twenty-fifth wedding anniversary—or it would have been, had Jake lived. That, in combination with her illness, had been enough to flatten her.

So, Claire had spent the night with her. She'd listened to Amelia's grief over Jake's death. It had been three years, but Amelia's pain was still alive, and Claire could not bear to see her suffering through it. She tried to talk her into watching an old Steve Martin movie, something that would make her laugh, but Amelia was too lost in the past to concentrate on anything other than her own misery. Claire let her talk herself to sleep, then made up the bed in the guest room and fell asleep herself.

When she checked her home answering machine this morning, there was a message from Randy. She had spoken to him a few times on the phone since the night of the play. He'd invited her to lunch once, but she'd declined. Not yet. Let Jon get used to the idea of this friendship-over-the-phone first. She'd been surprised by Jon's jealousy, by an insecurity she'd never seen in him before. She told him about each of the phone calls, almost verbatim. She hoped that the more open she was about Randy, the more she could convince her husband that he had nothing to fear.

Jon would listen politely, then gradually shift the conversation to work and the foundation, subjects that, ever since that night on the bridge, could not hold her attention as securely as they once had.

She looked forward to Randy's calls. He talked about Cary, his ten-year-old son, and she talked about Susan. Randy seemed to be a devoted father, although he rejected that compliment vehemently.

"I haven't been the greatest dad to him," he'd said. "I'm trying to make up for it, though. I was a workaholic. I focused practically all my energy on myself and the restaurant and not enough on my family."

With each call, each conversation, Claire felt the closeness deepening between Randy and herself. She could listen to that rich, warm voice on the phone for hours. The attraction was not physical. Not sexual, at any rate. Yet she wanted him close to her. She wanted him in her life and had even considered fixing him up with Amelia. After last night, though, she knew it would be a while before Amelia was ready to let another man take Jake's place in her heart.

"The play's over," Randy had said that morning on her answering machine tape, "and Cary's got a bad cold this weekend, and LuAnne doesn't want to let him visit. So, looks like I have some time on my hands, and I woke up with a yearning to see a Siparo carousel horse. I was wondering if you—and Jon too, of course—would like to join me for a trek to the Smithsonian this afternoon."

She'd called him back, telling him that Jon was out of town and that she would not be able to go because she had to take care of Amelia. But now Amelia looked 100 percent better.

"You go home," Amelia said after Claire had gotten up the last of the glass. "I'm fine now."

Claire sat down on the bed, cross-legged. "You sure?" She was picturing the Museum of American History at the Smithsonian, the display of carousel horses. She wanted to go.

"My temperature's normal. I'm normal." Amelia laughed. "I was out of it last night, wasn't I?"

Claire reached out to stroke the back of Amelia's hand. "It was a hard night for you."

"Well, I think I m going to sleep away the afternoon, so there's no point at all to your being here."

Claire offered to go to the grocery store for her or to do a load of laundry, but Amelia wouldn't hear of it. Claire might have insisted had she not felt the pull of an afternoon with Randy and a herd of wooden horses. She called him again from Amelia's kitchen, and a few hours later, she was riding in his car on the way to the Smithsonian.

It was odd to stroll through a museum with a man at her side, a man whose arm occasionally brushed against hers, whose eyes were nearly at the level of her own. It was odd not to have to think about negotiating narrow doorways and locating elevators. It was freeing, and she felt a pinprick of guilt for noticing the difference at all.

There were several examples of carousel horses lining the walls, and Claire did not have to say a word to Randy for him to know which was the finest, the most striking, the most beautiful of them all. He went immediately to the prancing chestnut stallion, even before reading the plaque that identified it as a genuine Siparo.

"It's stunning." Randy ignored the sign admonishing him not to touch and rested his hand on the carved saddle.

He admired the wind-blown golden mane of the horse's tucked head. "Is this gold leaf?"

"Yes." She cupped her palm beneath the horse's muzzle, remembering what it was like to watch her grandfather painstakingly set the thin sheets of gold on the sticky varnished surface of a mane. "Butterfly wings," she said.

"What?"

"My grandfather said the gold was as thin as butterfly wings."

"Oh." Randy smiled. "Where are the rest of the horses your great-grandfather carved?"

"Some are in museums, some on carousels around the world. The closest is in New Jersey. Some of them belong to collectors." This was not her favorite topic. Her family had been shortsighted in not holding on to any of their treasures. Not one of Joseph Siparo's horses had been kept in the family.

"And the carousel your grandfather built in the barn? What happened to it?"

Claire moved to another horse, a heavily armored Stein and Goldstein. Beautiful in its own right, but not a Siparo. "After my grandparents died, my mother sold the farm and donated the carousel to Winchester Village Amusement Park in Pennsylvania. I haven't seen it since I was twelve."

"Really? Wouldn't you like to?"

"Yes, and I always planned to. Every year, when Susan was small, we would talk about going up there, but something always got in the way."

Randy ran his hand lightly over the smooth saddle of an Illion's Appaloosa. He was grinning.

"What are you thinking about?" she asked.

"Oh." He seemed surprised by the question. "Cary. I

was just remembering the last time I took him to King's Dominion. I went on practically every single ride with him. I was pretty sick by the end of the day, but he could have gone for another few hours, I think."

"You miss him," she said.

Randy nodded, dropping his hand to his side, slipping it into his pocket. "I've gotten used to having him with me on the weekends. I enjoy being with him more than I could have imagined. I just wish I'd taken advantage of those days when I was around him all the time. It's easy to take people for granted, you know?"

She nodded.

Randy walked slowly toward one of the other horses. "And I hate to think about what it was like for him during that last year or so before LuAnne and I separated," he said. "His mother was miserable, his father was at work during most of his waking hours. The only time the three of us were together, Cary would have to listen to LuAnne and me fighting."

Claire was walking toward the far wall, where black-and-white photographs of horse carvers were displayed, and without warning, the bloodstain filled her head. The image was clearer than she had ever seen it before. The white, porcelainlike surface was not flat, but gently rounded, curved. The stain itself was nearly rectangular in shape, dark at one end, blurring to almost nothing at the other. Claire leaned against the wall, a moan slipping involuntarily from her lips. She was almost certainly going to get sick, here in the middle of this exhibit.

"Claire?" Randy wrapped a hand around her arm.

"Can we get out of here?" she asked, pulling free of him, starting to walk. If she had fresh air, sunlight, she would be all right. She walked blindly through the hall, trying to push the image from her mind.

"Claire, wait a minute." Randy caught her elbow, but he could not slow her down. She was nearly running through the hall, as though she knew exactly where she was going and would disintegrate if she did not get there soon. Turning a corner, she came face-to-face with the dead end of the corridor and a door marked Personnel Only, and suddenly it was as if all the oxygen had been sucked from the air.

Gasping, she made an about-face, ready to flee in the opposite direction, but she found herself in Randy's arms instead. She sagged against him.

"Please," she said. "I need to go outside."

"In a minute."

"Now," she said, but her voice had lost its power, and she felt the solid comfort of his arms, the warmth of his chest. Locking her own arms around him, she held tight. Her cheek was pressed to the dark blue cotton of his sweater, and she did not budge. Once she moved, she would have to speak. How could she explain her preposterous behavior to him? How could she make sense of it to someone else when it made no sense to herself?

She felt shored up by his arms, and after a moment pulled herself away from him, embarrassed. The image was gone. Brushing her hair back from her face with her fingers, she looked down at the floor. "You must think I'm batty," she said.

"Was it the dizziness again?"

She shook her head. "No. Something else." She pressed her palm to her temple, smiled weakly at him. "I'm cracking up, I think."

He put his arm around her waist and walked her around the corner to a bench. She sat down without protest.

"Tell me what upset you," he said.

"I'm hallucinating or something." She laughed and felt the color rise to her cheeks. "I keep seeing what looks like a piece of porcelain stained with blood. At least, I guess it's blood. It's happening more often lately. And there are mirrors, too." She shuddered. She did not want to think about this. Turning to him, she grabbed his hand. "Do you have time for a movie?" she asked. "Is there anything really funny playing? I want to get all these weird pictures out of my mind. I want to spend a couple of hours laughing."

A man and woman passed by them. The woman stared at her, and Claire thought her desperation must be etched into her face.

"Where are you getting that picture from?" Randy asked. "The blood, I mean. Is it from something you read? Something you've seen?"

"Maybe. I don't know. I don't care. I just want it to go away." She looked down and was mortified to see that she had drawn his hand onto her knee, her fingers digging into the flesh. She let go quickly. "I saw it for the first time in the little theater," she added. "The first time I met you there."

"Really?" He looked upset, as though he might somehow be responsible for her discomfort.

Claire tried to stand up, but he caught her arm, held her down. She was finished with this conversation. If she thought about it any longer, the image might reappear and steal her sanity again.

"What did you mean about mirrors?" Randy asked.

"I don't want to talk about it anymore, Randy, please. Can we leave?"

"Not quite yet," he said. "First I want to tell you something." He shifted on the hard bench and waited for a line of small children to pass by them before he spoke again. "For the longest time, I would get this . . . picture in my head," he said. "Sometimes I'd go a month or so without it, but at other times I would see it a dozen times a week. This went on from my late teens until just a few years ago, and sometimes I still have it."

"What was it?" she asked. "Was it horrible, like the blood?"

"It was very strange. At least it was strange to me at the time. I would see this sort of gray blur in the lower field of my vision, with something pointed and silver jutting up from it."

Claire thought of saying "how bizarre," but caught herself. She was in no position to criticize the figments of someone else's imagination.

"The vision was always accompanied by a sick feeling. A horrible sense of doom."

"Yes." Claire studied him, completely alert.

"Then one day a few years ago, I chaperoned Cary's field trip to Harpers Ferry." He let out a mirthless laugh. "LuAnne was always helping out at the school, so I'd promised to chaperone the next trip. I wanted to back out when I found out where they were going. Once I left Harpers Ferry, I never intended to set foot in that place again. But I couldn't see a way out of it without disappointing Cary. So anyway, we're on this bus and going across that shitty bridge, and it's winter, and I'm on the right side of the bus, and I happen to look out the window toward the town and what do I see?"

Claire was sitting on the edge of the bench, eyes wide. "What?"

"A gray blur with something pointed and silver jutting up from it. It was the trees. The deciduous trees. Just a blurry mass of gray at that time of year. And there was a church steeple sticking up from the trees. That was the same view I'd had from the bridge the day Charles fell." Randy laughed again. "I couldn't stop staring at it. I wanted to shout and laugh and cry. All those years, that image had been locked in my mind, and I suddenly felt like I'd been set free."

"But you said it still comes some—"

"Yes, but I know what it is now, and I can tell it to take a hike. It has no power over me anymore." He leaned back against the wall, letting his words sink in.

"So you think that what I'm seeing might be some sort of . . . flashback to something that happened in the past?" she asked.

"Has it only been happening since the night you were with Margot?"

"Yes."

He frowned. "Maybe it's tied to that night somehow, then. But you didn't see any . . . any blood that night, did you?"

"No." She thought suddenly of Susan's horrendous bicycle accident. Susan had been ten or eleven, riding down the hill on Center Street when a car pulled out of a driveway, directly into her path. Susan had flipped over her handlebars onto the hood of the car. Claire had arrived on the scene as the paramedics were loading her stoic, bleeding daughter into the ambulance. She remembered that scene vividly, though, and it felt very much a finished part of the past. Nothing was hidden or haunting.

"Maybe it's something from very long ago," Randy suggested. "From your childhood."

"No." Claire shook her head. "There's an extremely unpleasant quality to it. Nothing that horrible ever happened in my childhood."

"Ah, I forgot," Randy said. "The long carousel ride."

She ignored the mocking tone. She was going to leave now, whether he came with her or not. She wanted to be done with this. "So," she said, "how about that movie?"

"Let's follow this through, Claire." Randy seemed to have no interest in leaving. "Think about the image, or flashback, or whatever it is. Let's try to figure out—"

"No." She stood up. "I just got rid of the damn thing. I'm not going to try to reproduce it."

"But it will come back. You said yourself that it's getting worse."

"I'll go to a movie by myself, then," she said.

Randy folded his arms across his chest. "I haven't known you very long," he said, "but one thing I figured out about you right off the bat is that you like to pretend everything is fine even when it isn't. Are you aware of that?"

She pursed her lips. "I have an optimistic view of things, if that's what you mean," she said.

"Like a childhood where your parents got divorced," Randy continued as if she hadn't spoken, "and your father took your sister away, never to be heard from again. That's not fine. That's not even tolerable."

Claire felt unexpected tears burn her eyes, and Randy reached up to lightly squeeze her hand. "Did you cry when your father took Vanessa away?" he asked. "Did your mother cry?"

She wanted to fight him, to turn and walk away, but she

felt drawn in by the questions. Had she cried? She had no memory at all of that day. Had Mellie? She could only picture Mellie laughing. Loving. She could not recall her parents arguing, could see no picture of them other than their embracing in the kitchen of the farmhouse, her father telling Mellie she was the most beautiful woman in the world. That picture warmed her, here in the cool corridor of the Smithsonian. Randy was wrong. She was grateful to him—for listening to her, for not making her feel like a lunatic—but he was wrong.

"I'd like to leave," she said again. Something in her voice must have told him she could not bear another second of his interrogation, because this time he simply shrugged, stood up, and slipped his arm lightly across her shoulders, and they walked down the hall toward the exit.

16

Vienna

Outside the museum, the air was blustery cold. It was only six o'clock but dark as midnight, and Claire would have sold her soul for another few hours of sun. She'd longed to step out of the museum into bright, fresh air and leave the memory of the last hour inside with the horses.

They were not going to a movie. She sensed Randy had no interest, and she did not push it, although she would have welcomed the escape. They walked the short distance to his car in silence. He opened the door for her, and she got inside, shivering. Randy took off his coat and laid it carefully across the backseat before getting in himself. She had the urge to touch him again, to crawl once more into that solid, warm embrace he'd offered her in the museum. She needed some of that warmth right now. She was freezing.

She folded her arms above the seat belt and looked out the window as the car pulled away from the curb, and soon they were on 66, heading toward Vienna. It was several minutes before Claire realized how carefully she was riveting her eyes on the cars ahead of them, avoiding any glimpse into the sideview mirror next to her.

She glanced over at Randy, drew in a breath. "Can I tell you about the mirrors?" she asked, surprising herself. Hadn't she said she didn't want to think about this any longer?

Randy nodded without taking his eyes from the road. "Of course."

"Well, right now I'm trying not to look in your sideview mirror, because when I look in small mirrors, I see them filled with green."

Two long frown lines cut across Randy's forehead. "This is new, too?" he asked. "Since the night with Margot?"

"Yes." She waited for him to speak again, hoping he had some simple explanation for this phenomenon.

"Weird," he said.

"This morning I was over at a friend's house and she had a small mirror in her bathroom. When I looked at it, it was filled with green. It shook me up so much, I dropped the glass I was holding."

He nodded toward the window next to her. "Take a look at the mirror," he said.

"No."

"What's the worst thing that could happen?"

"It could be green."

"And?"

"And I'll feel crazy and nauseated—it nauseates me, for some reason—and I'll get sick in your car."

He smiled, reached over to briefly lay his hand on hers, as if he could transfer some of his strength to her through his touch. "Look at it," he repeated.

She turned her head slowly until the mirror was in her line of vision and squinted at the glare of headlights from the cars behind them. She smiled. "It's just a mirror," she said.

"Well, damn, girl." He laughed. "I was hoping it would be green. How are we going to solve the puzzle if half the pieces are missing?"

She liked his willingness to take on her problem. She glanced in the mirror again. Headlights. "Maybe this morning was the last time I'll see the green."

"Right, Pollyanna." Randy turned onto the exit ramp for Vienna. "What's it like?" he asked. "Green as in trees? Or like paint on a wall? Cloth? Does it have a texture?"

She forced herself to think about it. "It's a kelly green," she said, pleased she could recreate the image in her mind without feeling the terror. "And it's smooth, I think. It moves, though. And sometimes there are other colors." She felt wonderfully free, saying all of this out loud. Randy nodded as she spoke, as if he heard this sort of thing every day.

"It must all be connected somehow," he said, his eyes on the traffic ahead of him. "The colors in the mirrors, the bloodstain, the dizziness. Don't you think?" He glanced over at her, and she shrugged. "Either they're all tied somehow to the situation with my sister, or else those few minutes on the bridge triggered something you experienced yourself or read about or saw somewhere."

"Maybe," she said. Right then she didn't care. She felt fine. The car had warmed up, the sideview mirror was just that, and she could say any damn crazy thing to Randy that popped into her mind.

As they drove through Vienna, she studied him openly.

His hands circling the steering wheel were large but well shaped. The streetlights and shop lights shone in the glassy blue of his eyes and outlined his profile with one perfect, unbroken white line.

"You're beautiful," she said impulsively, then colored when he looked at her with raised eyebrows. "I'm not trying to be ... provocative," she said. "I just think you're a wonderful person."

"Well, thank you." He grinned. "It means a lot to me to hear someone say that. You can't know how much."

He turned onto her street, and she continued watching him as he pulled into her driveway, where they were immediately surrounded by the dark shelter of the trees. Randy stopped the car in front of the garage and turned in his seat to look at her. "I'm very glad you went with me today, even though it was hard for you some of the time." He looked down at the steering wheel, ran a finger along its curve. "I've been lonely for a long time. It was great having some adult company for a change."

"You need to meet people," she said. "There are billions of organizations for singles. Lots of ways to meet potential friends. What have you tried so far?"

"So far?" There was sadness in his smile. "I've tried two things: work and avoidance. They're the safest ways I know of to cope with being single again."

"Cop-out," Claire said.

"Guilty." He nodded.

She thought again of Amelia but immediately discarded the idea. Even if Amelia could muster up the interest, Claire wasn't ready to share Randy with anyone yet.

She looked up at the dark windows of her house. She didn't want him to leave.

"Would you like to come in? I could scrape together something for dinner."

He did not hesitate. "I'd like that," he said, and he was out of the car before she could change her mind.

Inside the house, she hung up their coats and bustled around the family room, straightening things that were already straight, fighting an odd sense of guilt that she was doing something wrong by being alone in the house with the one person Jon would least like to be there. And she felt, too, an undeniable hint of danger—she was happier than she should be to have him there. She did not want him as a lover, true, but the closeness, the safety she felt with him had the potential to be equally as intimate.

In the kitchen, she opened the pantry door and stared at the shelves, then walked back to the door of the family room. "Pasta?" she asked.

Randy turned away from the bookshelf that was holding his attention. "You know"—he pointed to the fruit bowl on the dining-room table—"I would be very content with an apple."

She frowned at him. "That's it?"

He nodded, and she took two apples from the bowl, washed them, and walked over to where he stood next to the bookshelf. He was looking at a photograph of her and Jon and Susan. The three of them were sitting on a rock next to a creek. They had gone canoeing that day—the yellow bow of the canoe was visible in one corner of the picture. Susan could not have been more than twelve. Had it really been that long since they'd all canoed together? They used to do so many things as a family.

"Susan's really cute," Randy said, taking the fruit from her hand.

"Thanks." She bit into her own apple and sat down on the arm of the sofa.

Randy looked up from the photograph. "May I ask a rude question?"

She knew what he was going to say before he said it, and she smiled. "Yes, she's Jon's."

He laughed. "I guess that's not the first time you've been asked that." He lifted the picture from the shelf and held it toward the kitchen light. "I was trying to see if she looked like him at all."

"She looks more like him than she does me," she said. "She has those big moony eyes of his."

"I didn't realize ... I thought, you know, that if you were paralyzed from the waist down, that automatically meant you couldn't ... " He shrugged his shoulders, and she felt his discomfort.

"Well, Jon and I lucked out," she said. "Usually a man, if he can function sexually at all, still has problems with fertility. We weren't able to have a second child, but we felt very lucky to have Susan."

Randy gnawed his lip, not looking at her. "So, someone who is a paraplegic can still have sex?"

"Anyone can have sex," she said. "It just might not be the kind of sex *you're* thinking of. It all depends on the level of the injury—where the spinal cord was damaged—and whether the trauma was complete or not and a thousand other variables. In Jon's case, it wasn't complete. That doesn't mean he's home free, of course. It's difficult for him to—" She stopped herself. Jon would have no problem talking about this, but she felt the sharp knife of betrayal as keenly as if she were cutting herself with it. He would not want her discussing his sexual limitations with Randy

Donovan. "Well," she smiled weakly. "This is Jon's story to tell, not mine."

Randy nodded. His face was very serious.

"Anyhow, what we tell the couples we counsel is that you have to let go of your long-held concept of what 'having sex' means. There are plenty of other ways to give and receive pleasure."

Randy set the picture back on the shelf, shaking his head.

"What?" she asked.

"I don't know." He bit into the apple, and it was a moment before he spoke again. "I guess I'm just amazed by you."

"What do you mean?"

Randy studied the apple, running his thumb over the shiny red skin. "I think about you a lot," he said, glancing at her. "About your life. About what it must have been like for you to be married to Jon all these years. Obviously you two are really good together. And you've done so much for other people, with the foundation and all the projects you've taken on."

"And?" She did not know where he was going with this.

He studied her intently. "Are you really happy, Claire?"

"Of *course*."

He laughed. "I wouldn't expect you to say anything else. Glowing childhood, glowing marriage, right?"

She did not smile.

Randy pressed his lips together, studying the apple again as if the words he wanted to say were etched in the skin. "I admire you a great deal," he said. "And I don't know how to say this. It's going to come out crass, and you don't have to answer. But you're so attractive. So vibrant. And all your adult life, you've been with a man who . . . who's in a wheelchair, and you deal with that, I guess, and that's one thing, but then I think, you can never really hug or—"

"We hug." She laughed.

"No. I mean, you're saying he has problems sexually and—"

She drew in a sharp breath. "That's not what I said. He does just fine sexually."

"I don't mean that in a blaming way. I know the problems are related to his injury, but how have you lived with that all your adult life? How do you keep yourself from wanting more, or from wondering what more there is, or—"

"Randy," she said, "you're out of line." She spoke softly, with only enough force to put an end to the questioning but not so much that he would feel reprimanded. He was not the first person to ask her those questions. He would not be the last.

He sighed and nodded. "I guess I am." He gave her a sheepish look. "Forgive me."

"You're forgiven."

He walked into the kitchen, and she heard the *thunk* of his apple core as he tossed it into the trash can under the sink. Back in the family room, he sat down on one of the barstools. There was color in his cheeks, and she knew he regretted his probing.

"You know why my wife left me?" he asked.

"Because you were a workaholic?"

"Well, that was definitely part of it. That and the fact that she met someone she found more intriguing than me."

Claire grimaced. "I'm sorry."

"But the real reason, at least in my mind, was that I had a heart attack a few years ago."

"You?" She leaned forward, stunned. Randy looked so fit.

"Yes." He brushed a piece of lint, real or imagined, from the arm of his sweater. "I was thirty-two. A fluky sort of thing. I had surgery, and now I'm in pretty good shape. But to LuAnne, the writing was on the wall. She figured I would get sicker and sicker, that it was just a matter of time until the next heart attack, and the one after that. She even said as much. 'I love you, Randy, but I can't bear the thought of spending the best years of my life taking care of an invalid.'"

Claire shook her head. That sort of conditional love was beyond her comprehension. "What kind of mother is she?"

"Actually, she's a good mother to Cary. I can't fault her there. Cary's a good-looking, perfect, healthy child, and as long as he stays that way, LuAnne will be a great mom for him." He stretched his arms out with a sigh. "So, anyhow, you can see why I think you're something special for sticking by Jon all these years. For your loyalty to him."

"You make it sound like it's a sacrifice on my part. It's not. I love him."

"I know, but I just can't imagine how you deal with the . . . the physical limi—"

"Jon's not a cross to bear." She felt the stirrings of a familiar indignation. "He's the sexiest man I know."

Randy ran his hands through his thick hair. "I'm sorry, Claire," he said, the red blotches on his cheeks again. "I can't seem to shut myself up. We've talked about so much these past few weeks, and I guess I just kept talking without thinking I was going too far." He stood up from the barstool and stretched. "I think I should go," he said.

She wanted him to stop talking about Jon, but she did not want him to leave, as though her sense of security would walk out the door with him. Yet she could think of nothing to say to make him stay without sounding as though she needed him more than she should. So she stood as well and got his coat from the closet.

At the door, he drew her into a hug, but quickly let her go again. "Maybe Jon would have some idea of where those little flashbacks of yours are coming from," he suggested. "Maybe it's something you've forgotten that he would remember."

"Oh, I wouldn't tell Jon about them," she said.

"Why not?"

"I just wouldn't, that's all." She had not thought to analyze that automatic decision. "It would worry him."

Randy frowned. "He's your husband, and this is a problem you're having."

She shook her head. "Jon's had too many bad things happen in his life. I don't see the point in laying something else on him when this is probably going to go away on its own."

Her words sounded doltish to her ears, and she was not at all surprised by the mildly scornful look Randy gave her. But she was right. Jon had never been able to tolerate her suffering without suffering himself. He'd already shown his distress over her preoccupation with Margot. She couldn't ask any more of him.

"I enjoyed the museum." Randy slipped his pipe out of his coat pocket. "And I'm sorry if I upset you."

"I'm not upset," she said. But she was. Her chest was

heavy with he sudden realization that she found it easier to talk about her problems with a near stranger than with her husband. She doubted Jon would be able to listen to her the way Randy had in the museum today. Or rather, she would never give him the chance.

She watched Randy drive down the driveway, his car quickly disappearing in the trees, before closing the door against the cold air.

In the family room, she stood numbly for a moment before walking over to the bookshelf. She picked up the photograph of her family again. The three of them were smiling. Jon had his arm wrapped around Susan's slender shoulders. His hair was darker then, with very little gray, and his smile was wide. The three of them looked rosy from the sun. Tired and happy.

Jon was wearing shorts. His legs with their wasted muscles hung limply over the rock, and they were even slimmer, more shapeless, than Susan's preadolescent legs.

She ran her finger lightly over the glass. No, that had not been the first time she'd gotten those questions about Jon. She'd heard them from her girlfriends over the years, friends who should have known better. Girlfriends with supposedly whole husbands. They'd joke about sex in general, and occasionally about the limits they assumed Jon to have, and maybe because she laughed along with them, they never knew their words hurt. Sometimes, the conversations took a more serious turn. Intimate. Confidential. A caring friend—Amelia had often been guilty of this before Jake died—would try to elicit from her some dissatisfaction or tell her about something she was missing. Or they'd talk about their admiration for Claire. Always the admiration, as if Claire had sacrificed everything to devote her life to caring for a needy child. No matter how probing the questions, how condescending the advice, how great the insult, she would respond by defending Jon fiercely.

An idea began taking shape in her mind as she stood in the family room, staring at her husband's picture. Setting the photograph back on the bookshelf, she turned and headed for the bedroom.

She changed into her gray angora skirt and sweater—her sex-kitten outfit, Jon called it, although she knew it was conservative enough for her to get away with. Just. She crammed a few things into her overnight bag and within twenty minutes of Randy's departure left the house herself.

The drive to Baltimore took her just over an hour.

At the hotel, she let the valet park her car. Once inside the massive lobby, she studied the computerized sign to learn which meetings were in session, and she guessed that Jon would most likely be attending the wine-and-cheese reception in the Rosewood Ballroom. She stopped briefly in the restroom to freshen her makeup, fluff out her hair. Then she found the ballroom.

She studied the room from the doorway. It was large and high-ceilinged, loosely filled with men—and a few women—in austere business apparel. They milled between tables bearing hors d'oeuvres and punch bowls and bottles. Far across the room, she saw Jon, one of the few people in the crowd using a wheelchair. He was talking to a half-circle of men, and she started walking toward him.

Heads turned and conversations ceased as she walked through the ballroom, through the throng of businessmen, who seemed to be devouring her with their eyes. There was a sudden electric charge in the room, and she knew she was the cause of it. She fought her self-consciousness with a smile.

The eyes in the room followed her to the half-circle of men, where she tapped deliberately on Jon's shoulder. Let them eat their lecherous little hearts out, she thought. Let them envy the hell out of that guy in the wheelchair.

Jon looked up at her almost blankly for a moment before breaking into a grin. "What the hell are you doing here?"

"I missed you," she said, bending low to kiss him, and she felt the snugness of her skirt on her hips, felt the eyes in the room. She stood up again, holding out her hand. "Room key?"

Still grinning, Jon pulled the plastic card from his pocket and dropped it into her palm. "I'll be up very soon," he said, and she knew that among the eyes watching her as she left the ballroom were those of her surprised and ego-boosted husband.

"What's this all about, Harte?" he asked as he wheeled into the room half an hour later. She had taken a bath and now sat in the king-sized bed, wearing one of his shirts, half-buttoned.

"You're the most incredible man in the world, and I was afraid you might forget it if I wasn't here to tell you."

He transferred to the bed with a quick flick of his hands on the wheels of the chair and pulled himself close to her. "Well, you can bet every man in that room is having his own personal fantasy about what's going on up here right now," he said.

She kissed him and felt a tenderness mixed with a sudden, unexpected urge to cry. She shifted on the bed so that she could straddle him, grinding her hips against his.

"Well, they can imagine all they want, but they'll never be able to get an accurate fix on how obscenely good this is going to be, Mathias."

He reached up and drew her head down to his, kissing her fervently, but she caught his hands and held them down on his pillow as she began an unhurried, thorough, methodical tour of his eyes and ears and cheeks and mouth with her lips.

She knew his body nearly as well as he did. She knew where he could feel her touch, where to caress him with her fingers, where he would prefer her lips, her tongue. But after a few minutes she found herself kissing him, touching him, in places he would never feel a thing, as if she were unable to get enough of him tonight. And she did not dare stop, did not dare slow down, because her tears were so close to the surface, so close, and she was afraid that if she stopped touching him for an instant, they just might spring free.

17

Jeremy, Pennsylvania
1960

The farmhouse slept in the stormy darkness of the Pennsylvania countryside, and the rain beat a steady rhythm on the roof above the big upstairs bedroom. Tucker was hiding under Claire's bed, and Vanessa lay next to her sister, calm now. When the thunder had started, Claire had let Vanessa get into bed with her. She and Vanessa were not afraid of much. They would pick up spiders with their bare hands and climb so high in the oak tree they would not be able to see the ground. But Vanessa claimed to fear lightning. Many six-year-olds were afraid of lightning. She didn't want to be different.

Vanessa liked to sleep with Claire. It was a little ritual they went through when a thunderstorm hit at night. Vanessa would whimper under her comforter until Claire invited her into her own bed, which she always did, even though Vanessa would get so hot during the night that Claire would have to roll the blanket down to the foot of the bed. That little golden body burned like a furnace, and when she rolled over, her skin stuck to Claire's like iron to a magnet.

The thunder seemed to have stopped, and Claire had almost drifted off to sleep when a sudden clap cracked outside the window. Vanessa jerked awake. She made a whimpering sound and pulled the sheet over her blond head as the lightning filled the room, illuminating the furniture and stuffed animals and the pictures on the wall. Then all was quiet again. Even the pattering of the rain had stopped, and it was so still that the sound of voices coming from downstairs was impossible to miss. It was Friday night, and Len had arrived at the farm around dinnertime. The room he shared with Mellie was directly below Claire and Vanessa's room. Usually, the girls could not hear their parents talking. Tonight, though, their voices were loud.

"You and the kids are coming back to Virginia with me Monday morning," Len's voice boomed.

Vanessa pulled the sheet from her head and met Claire's eyes. They held their breath, waiting for a reply from their mother.

When Mellie answered him, she did not speak loudly enough for the girls to make out her words. But whatever she said made Len furious.

"You fucking whore!" he yelled.

"Not so loud!" Mellie said. "You'll wake the whole house."

"Do you think I care? Maybe your parents should know what kind of tramp they raised."

"Len, *listen* to me. You're jumping to ridiculous conclusions."

Len's voice deepened to a growl, and it was impossible

to understand what he said. The girls heard a sudden grunt from him, then a small scream from Mellie and the sound of a piece of furniture scraping the floor. Vanessa let out a gasp and grabbed Claire's arm with her small, damp hand.

"Shh," Claire said. But the voices were low and quiet now, too quiet to hear. She and Vanessa looked at each other, a deep sort of fear in their eyes that no spiders, no thunder or lightning, that nothing else in the world had ever been able to put there.

"Do we have to go back to Virginia?" Vanessa asked.

"Shh!" Claire elbowed her sharply. Vanessa was incapable of whispering. "Of course not. It's summer. We stay here in the summer."

The house grew still once more. No more terrible words rose from the downstairs bedroom. A gentle stream of cool air slipped through the barely open window, bringing with it the clean, rain-washed scent of the farm. Suddenly, Vanessa squeezed Claire's arm.

"Claire?" she asked.

"What?"

"What's a fucking whore?"

Claire thought about this for a minute. "I don't know," she said, and she didn't. She was old enough, though, to know it was not a good thing to be.

The sun poured through the windows in the morning, and the walls of the room looked like lemon custard. The white eyelet curtains billowed gently at the windows, and the aroma of coffee floated on the light breeze. Claire and Vanessa dressed quietly, solemnly, neither of them mentioning the night before, but the memory of those few minutes between their parents rested in their hearts like heavy stones.

"I'm not hungry," Claire said. "You want to skip eating with Mellie and Daddy and just go out to see Grandpa?"

Vanessa hesitated only a moment before nodding. It had been a terrible night, the sort of night that could only be forgotten in the safety of Vincent Siparo's workshop.

Downstairs, Mellie sat alone at the kitchen table, smoking a cigarette. She hadn't put on her makeup yet, and small lines were etched into the skin around her eyes and mouth. The whites of her eyes were pink; there were half-moons of gray on the skin beneath her lower lashes.

"Hi, babies," she said when the girls walked into the kitchen. Her smile did not look real.

"We're just going straight out to the barn," Claire announced.

"Oh, no." Sometimes Mellie could put on a whiny-little-girl voice, and she was doing it now. She stubbed out the cigarette. "Grandma's on the porch shelling peas and I'm all by myself. Have some breakfast with me. I've been waiting for you to come down."

Vanessa and Claire exchanged looks. They were trapped. They sat down at the table as Mellie hopped up to get the coffee.

"Is Daddy still sleeping?" Claire asked.

Mellie did not look at them as she splashed coffee into their cups. "Daddy had to go back to Virginia. He realized he had too much work to do to spend the whole weekend here," she said. She sounded as if she were rehearsing the lines in a play.

"Is he mad at you, Mommy?" Vanessa only called Mellie "Mommy" when she was upset about something.

"*Mad* at me?" Mellie laughed as if that was the craziest

thing she'd ever heard, and Vanessa actually smiled. "Why would you think a thing like that?"

Mellie plopped one of Dora's greasy doughnuts onto each of their plates.

"We could hear you yelling last night," Claire said.

Mellie sat down again and looked from daughter to daughter, a perplexed expression on her face. "Yelling? Last night?"

Claire nodded.

Mellie shook another cigarette from the box of Salems. "Well, we were *talking*, but we certainly weren't yelling."

"Daddy sounded mad," Vanessa said.

Mellie slipped the cigarette between her pale lips and lit it with a shaky hand. "He was tired," she said, blowing a stream of smoke into the air. "You know how grumpy he can sound when he's tired?"

The girls nodded.

"I think you completely misunderstood whatever you heard, punkins," Mellie said. Then she smiled. "That's what you get for snooping."

Vanessa lifted her doughnut to her mouth, pressing her tongue against the powdered sugar, her eyes never leaving her mother's face. Claire picked her own doughnut apart on her plate. "You two have these worried little frowns on your beautiful faces." Mellie smiled, and this time the smile looked real and reassuring. "I've never seen such silly little frowns."

Vanessa scrunched up her nose, trying to make her frown even sillier, and Mellie laughed with delight.

They ate their breakfast, chatting about one of Mellie's stories on TV as though the people in the soap opera were real—neighbors or relatives, perhaps—and as though this was just another Saturday on the farm, even though it would be the first Saturday that Len Harte was not with them.

When the girls got up to leave the table, Mellie rose, too, and gathered them into her arms, planting kisses on their cheeks and the tops of their heads.

"Nothing's wrong, darlings," she said. "All is right and safe and good in your world, and it will always be that way."

Len returned to the farm the following weekend, and the weekend after that as well. Only once did the girls think they heard another argument between their parents. Again, it occurred late at night, and when they asked Mellie about it the following morning, they were not at all surprised to hear they had been mistaken. Actually, Mellie told them, she and Daddy had been laughing together about one thing or another. She was sorry they had been loud enough to wake them.

But Len Harte did not seem like himself for the rest of that summer. He was grumpier than he used to be. Mellie said that was because he was working too much and too hard. He was absent-minded, too. Once he brought a doll for Vanessa and forgot to bring anything for Claire. It was not an intentional oversight. Anyone could see the stunned look on his face when he realized he had nothing for his oldest daughter. He said he'd inadvertently left his gift for Claire at home in Virginia. Claire tried very hard to believe him.

That night Len drove Claire into town and let her pick out a doll from the five-and-dime. The selection was limited, and the doll she chose—a pink-skinned baby doll with short brown curls—seemed plain to her. But Mellie and Dora and Vincent made such a fuss over it that by the time Claire climbed into bed that night, she had almost come to believe that her father had given her the prettiest doll of all.

18

Baltimore, Maryland

Jon opened his eyes in the morning to find Claire awake and watching him. Her head was on the hotel pillow, and there was a smile in her eyes. The crisp white sheet rested low on her breasts, and he reached out to slip one fingertip beneath its hem.

He remembered back to the night before, to seeing her in that crowded ballroom. He'd felt an instant of visceral attraction before he even recognized her as his wife, and a surge of pride once it all sank in. He'd had plans to get a drink with some of the conference attendees after the reception, but none of them questioned his change of heart once they'd seen Claire. It was rare for her to flaunt her looks that way. He'd forgotten how well she could do it when she wanted to.

Jon rested his palm on her cheek. "Do you know how much it means to me that you came up here?" he asked.

She curled her body closer to his, wrapping her arm

around his waist, and he sank his fingers into her hair. "I wanted to sleep with you."

"What a surprise to look up and see you in that room with all those stodgy suits. A sight for sore eyes, in that sweater. Mmm."

"Think I'm getting too old to wear that outfit?"

"Never." He drew away only far enough to lift her chin for a kiss, then held her close again. Sleeping with her last night, feeling so close to her, made him keenly aware of the distance that had crept between them this past month.

She had cried sometime during the night. He'd heard her, at first not placing the sound of her quiet sniffling because her tears were so rare. He had asked her what was wrong, and she'd simply requested that he hold her. She didn't seem to want to talk, and he didn't press her.

"What time's your first meeting this morning?" she asked.

"Not until ten, so we can goof off for a while. Shall I call room service? Do you feel like breakfast in bed?"

She nodded, and he made the call as she lay next to him, stroking his chest.

"I want to talk to you," she said when he had hung up the phone. "I want to tell you about my weekend so far." There was a strange tone to her voice. She sounded like Susan when she was testing the waters, trying to determine the safety of bringing up an inflammatory topic. Or maybe it was only his imagination.

He propped up his pillow and leaned back against it, wrapping his arms around her. Her hair was every-where—splayed over his arms and chest, pressing against his face where her temple met his cheek. "Go ahead," he said.

"Well, Amelia got sick Friday night."

"She did? What kind of sick?"

"Just some flu thing, but she was very upset because it would have been her and Jake's twenty-fifth anniversary."

"Oh, yeah. That's right." He coiled a strand of her hair around his finger.

"She was a mess, so I stayed with her Friday night and yesterday morning. By yesterday afternoon, though, she was feeling much better, so I—now, please don't be upset by this, Jon."

"Upset by what?"

In the hall outside their door, someone dropped something—a tray of dishes, perhaps—and Claire started. He held her tighter. "Well," she said, "I'd told Randy so much about the carousel that he wanted to see the Siparo horses, so he invited us—you and me—to go to the Smithsonian. You weren't there, of course, so I went with him alone."

His fingers balled into a fist around the strand of hair. "Yesterday afternoon?" he asked. "Before or after you met with Gil Clayton?"

Her hand froze on his chest.

"Claire?"

"Oh, my God, Jon. I completely forgot."

He pushed her away from him to look her in the eye. "Please tell me you're kidding."

She sat up, pulling the sheet to her breasts. "I guess I got confused by Amelia being sick. It threw off my plans, and it never occurred to me to check my appointment book because it was a weekend. So when Randy called I . . . I just completely forgot about Gil."

"How the hell could you forget?" He wanted to shake her. "Do you know how important that meeting was? That

was the whole reason you didn't come up to this conference with me, remember? The whole reason you stayed in
Vienna. Not to go out with Randy Donovan."

"I'm sorry."

"What the hell is happening to you?" He threw off the
sheets and reached for his chair.

Claire leaned forward quickly, curving her hand around
his arm, tugging at him, trying to keep him in the bed, but
he shook her off. The warmth of the night was gone.
Forgotten. He did not look at her as he transferred into his
chair, and he wheeled into the bathroom with a few quick
flicks of his wrists.

He closed the door behind him and sat still for a few
minutes, breathing deeply, trying to get control over an
anger that was alien to him. He pictured Gil Clayton arriv-
ing at the deserted foundation office, unable to get in.
Checking his watch. Freezing in yesterday's windy cold.
How the hell would they make this up to him? Damn
Claire.

She was wearing jeans and a white sweater by the time
he came out of the bathroom and had combed the tousled
look out of her hair as best she could. She must not have
taken the time the night before to remove her eye makeup,
and now there were faint dark circles beneath her eyes. On
the table by the window rested the two breakfast trays,
which must have arrived while he was in the bathroom.

She stood up. "I'm sorry, Jon," she said again. She was
wringing her hands. He had never seen her do that before.
"I really screwed up. I know that."

He did not look at her as he wheeled to the table. "I'm
done in the bathroom if you want it."

She squeezed his shoulder as she walked past him toward

the bathroom, and Jon sat stiffly, seething above his orange juice and fruit cup and muffin. Was there any time during their twenty-three years together that he'd felt this kind of anger toward her? He could think of none. But there had never been a Randy Donovan in her life before.

She came out of the bathroom and sat across from him at the circular table, making no move toward the food on her tray. "I'll call Gil when we're done with breakfast and apologize."

"It's too late for a simple apology. Maybe you've forgotten, but this is a man we've cajoled and begged and kissed up to for the past three years. We'll have to come up with something more inventive than 'I'm sorry.' I'll take care of it." He knew that the tone of his voice implied that he no longer trusted her with this. And he didn't. He glanced at her. She was staring down at her plate, and he saw her swallow hard.

He ate an orange section from the fruit bowl on his tray. "So," he asked. "Was it worth it?" He was appalled at the sarcasm in his voice. He knew how to fight fair. He trained people in those skills. Right now, though, there was greater satisfaction in fighting dirty.

"Was what worth it?" She raised her huge green eyes to him.

"Your little trek to the museum, which I might point out is the type of trek you and I haven't made together in what . . . a decade?"

"You always say we never have time."

"No, Claire. *You* always say that, but apparently you can find time when the magnificent Randy calls, even if it means shirking your responsibilities."

"Please don't talk that way. I said I'm sorry. I don't know

what else to do." There were tears in her eyes, but they did not spill onto her cheeks. "What can I do, Jon?"

He sighed and leaned back in the chair. "Can you make the old Claire come back?" he asked. "The Claire who was always dependable and who gave a shit about her work?"

Claire pressed her fingertips to her lips and stood up. She walked over to the window and pulled the wispy curtain aside to look out. "I wish I could," she said without turning around. "I miss her, too. I'm not intentionally trying to screw up. My life doesn't seem to be in my control anymore and I—"

"*Bullshit.*" He saw her start, the way she had when she'd heard the noise in the hallway. She didn't turn around, though. She remained a dark, featureless silhouette against the backdrop of the window. "Whose control is it in, then?" he asked. "Do you hear yourself? What would you say to one of your patients if they started talking that way, huh?"

She didn't speak and finally, Jon slit open his muffin, buttered it, and took a bite. He had nearly finished it when she returned to the table and sat down.

"I know this isn't the time," she said, her voice so soft he could barely hear her. Her eyes were lowered to her lap. "I know you're furious with me right now, but I want to tell you what's been happening to me lately."

Her voice chilled him, tested him. She was waiting to see if he would hold tight to his anger or let it go, at least for the moment, to give her something she seemed to need desperately. He remembered her crying last night, and the memory took the edge off his rage.

He rested his napkin on the table. "What do you mean?" he asked.

Claire picked up her own still-folded napkin and began playing with it, twisting one corner. "Well, these strange little images keep popping into my mind," she said. "Tiny little snippets. They're probably nothing, but they scare me."

What was she talking about? "What kind of images?"

He listened as she described a bloodstain on a piece of porcelain. The image would slip into her mind unexpectedly, she said, and it made her feel dizzy, sick. Then she told him about small mirrors filled with green.

"Remember when we were riding to the play and I held my purse against the window?"

He nodded. He remembered it vaguely.

"It was happening then. I put up my purse so I couldn't see the mirror." She looked down at the napkin she was twisting in her lap. "Weird, huh?" she said, and he saw her struggling to smile.

He leaned forward until his fingers touched her knee. "Why haven't you told me this was going on?" he asked.

She shrugged. "I was hoping they'd go away, but they haven't. Randy thinks it might be something from the past. I have no idea what it could be, but I do think I have some gaps in my memory, Jon." She looked at him as though this idea had just occurred to her, and he sat up straight, immediately alert.

"Why do you think that?" he asked.

"Well, you know how I always talk about the carousel and how wonderful my childhood was?"

He nodded. Yes, he knew.

"Well, Randy was asking me things like, how did I feel when Vanessa left? How did Mellie react? And I don't remember. I was ten when Vanessa left. I should remember *something* about it, but I don't. I only remember Mellie saying that we'd see her again soon, but—"

"Mellie was crazy," Jon interrupted her. He had never said those words to her before, although he'd thought them often enough.

"Well, she wasn't *crazy*. She just, you know, had her own way of handling things."

Yes, indeed she had. Mellie had lived with them during the last three months of her life, ten years ago. She'd been terminally ill with lung cancer, yet even then, even in those terrible last stages, she would not admit to being seriously ill. She had a chronic cough, she would tell visitors. A chronic cough, she would even tell herself. Mellie had a way of twisting the truth to keep everyone smiling. Jon realized back then that Claire had the same dubious skill, and that she'd come by it honestly. Probably unhealthy as hell. But now that she seemed to be losing that ability, he missed it.

"Well, anyhow, Randy doesn't buy it that only good things happened to me. He tried to push me to—"

"Don't let him push you into anything, Claire. Come on. You probably had a dream sometime that you don't remember and these are just little images from the dream. Nothing more than that."

She had twisted the napkin into a long pink snake, and she raised it to the table. He pried her hand from it, squeezed her fingers.

"Please listen to me," he said. "You were a happy, satisfied woman before this thing with Margot happened. At least I think you were, am I right?"

"Yes," she said. "Absolutely."

"And I know it takes time to get over that sort of

trauma, but it seems to me that by seeing Randy—Margot's brother, for heaven's sake—you can never really put the whole thing behind you." He recognized the self-serving element to this argument but forgave himself for it. Spending time with Randy was hurting her, he was certain of it. Those little snippets she was talking about shook him up. They were small things, simple things. Maybe they actually were from a dream. Or maybe they *were* from the gaps in Claire's memory, the existence of which she could only guess at but which he knew for a fact. He had long taken comfort in Claire's selective memory. "If you'd forget about Randy and Margot and put your energy into work or planning a vacation or *anything*, then maybe everything else would fall into place." He wondered if she heard the urgency in his voice.

She lowered her gaze to the table, nodding slowly. "You're probably right," she said. "When I'm not in the middle of one of those ... flashbacks ... it's easy for me to imagine they'll just disappear one of these days. Or that I'm making too much of them. I probably am." Her smile was very weak, and he felt a crack in the armor around his heart. He had to remind himself she had come *here* last night. She'd driven an hour to sleep with him. She could have spent the night with Randy, and he never would have known. But she hadn't. She'd wanted to be with him. Randy was a friend, as she'd said. A friend who did not seem afraid to challenge Claire's blindly optimistic attitude toward life. Randy would not have let the tears she'd cried in bed last night go unexamined.

He was sorting his papers for that morning's session as she was preparing to leave. He watched her pack her overnight case on the bed. There was a heaviness in her shoulders he had never seen before. He wheeled over to the bed as she zipped the case closed. He reached for her hand, and she sat down on the edge of the bed, facing him.

"I'm sorry we fought," he said.

"And I'm sorry about Gil. Really, I am."

"I know." He stroked his thumb across her palm. "I think we need to make some changes," he said. "Do you think we could do something fun together? Besides planning a vacation, I mean? We need to make it a point to get some fun back in our lives. When was the last time, Claire? I can't even remember."

She smiled wryly. "I thought last night was kinda fun."

He returned the smile, squeezed her knee. "Yes, it was. But you know what I mean. When you said you and Randy went to the museum, I felt—"

"Hurt."

"Yes. Left out."

"I'm sorry. I didn't think about that."

"So, could we do something like we used to?"

"Yes," she said. "We can each think about what we'd like to do, then compare lists and decide on something."

She was trying to put some cheer in her voice and failing badly. Her heart would not be in this, he thought.

"All right." He leaned forward to kiss her. "I love you, Harte."

"You too, Mathias."

She gathered up her overnight case and her purse and headed for the door. He watched her leave the room, then wheeled immediately to the phone.

He was relieved to find Pat Wykowski at home. "I want to run a hypothetical situation by you," he said.

"Shoot." Pat was cooking something. Pots and pans rattled in the background.

He ran his fingers over the keypad on the phone. "Let's say that Party A doesn't remember something that happened to him or her in the past—something bad—and Party B knows what happened. Should Party B tell Party A what he or she knows?"

"This does not sound like the sort of thing that would come up at an accessibility conference," Pat said.

"So what's the answer?"

Pat hesitated a moment. "Well, there are differing theories, but I'd say that Party A has blocked those things for a reason. It's probably a good healthy defense mechanism and Party B should keep his or her trap shut."

Jon looked out the window, wondering if he'd presented the situation accurately. "But what if Party A is beginning to have disturbing . . . flashes of memory seeping into his or her head which may or may not be related to what Party B knows?"

"If the memories are interfering with Party A's functioning, then Party A better get his butt into therapy—with someone *competent*—and figure out what's going on. But he has to uncover that sort of stuff on his own time frame. Party B needs to trust A's little psyche to feed the information to him at a pace he can tolerate."

Something fell, clattering, on Pat's end of the line, and she muttered to herself before speaking into the phone once more.

"Come on," she prodded, "who are we talking about? If it's one of our patients, I should know about—"

"It's not," he said. "Don't push me on it, Pat, okay?"

She sighed. "Okay. Well, I'm making low-fat spinach bran muffins. I'll bring you one tomorrow."

He grimaced at the thought. "Can't wait," he said. They talked about the conference for another minute or two before ending their conversation.

After hanging up the phone, Jon sat still for a minute, looking out the window, disappointed and at the same time relieved. He wanted to help Claire, yet he could not imagine hurting her with what he knew.

He stared out at the distant harbor, a quiet fury building inside him until it suddenly exploded. He pounded his fist on the wheel of his chair. *God damn you, Mellie*, he thought. *Now look what you've done.*

19

Seattle

The phone calls were getting to her.

Vanessa arrived in her office after rounds to find three message slips on her desk and the phone ringing. She did not pick it up. The receptionist would answer it and write out another message slip, which she would ignore for as long as possible.

When she'd put together the network years ago, she'd hand-selected the most motivated, dynamic, and committed people she knew in the adolescent medicine world. Yet even she could not have predicted the current level of energy and enthusiasm in that geographically scattered group. Once word had gotten out that help might be available in the sympathetic form of Senator Zed Patterson, members of the network, desperate to keep their programs alive, sprang into action.

And it seemed as though they'd all decided to begin with a phone call to her. She knew they viewed her as the leader of this fight, and she was trying to come up with a subtle way to shift the focus to Terri Roos, or to anyone willing to take it on. How obvious would it be if she were to take an entirely passive role in the battle? She simply had to extract herself from this mess as best she could for the sake of her health, both mental and physical. She was doing all right during her waking hours; the headaches were better, and her temper was under control at work. Once she was asleep, though, the control was snatched from her hands. The real Vanessa Gray—Vanessa *Harte*—emerged at night. The scared and helpless little girl on the carousel.

Her own AMC program would still reap the benefits of any positive change, whether she was active in the fight or not. She would have to come up with some logical-sounding excuse, though, and right now she couldn't imagine what that might be. She only knew that she could tell no one the truth behind her refusal to deal with Patterson.

She moved the message slips to one side of her desk and opened the chart she'd carried with her from rounds. Shelley Collier. The anorexic who, after four weeks in the eating disorders program, should have been ready for discharge by now. She studied the results of the girl's most recent tests, a frown on her face. The numbers were not good and made little sense. Pete Aldrich had reported that, despite the fact that they'd taken away her laxatives, forced her to eat, and did not allow her to exercise or use the bathroom after meals, Shelley continued to lose weight.

Vanessa leafed through the chart. Was there some other disease process at work here? Or were they missing something obvious?

She had a sudden hunch. She'd seen a case like this once

before. Getting up from her desk, she tucked the chart under her arm and left her office.

The housekeeper was emptying the trash basket in one of the private rooms when Vanessa found her.

"May I speak with you a minute?" She motioned the woman out into the hall.

The housekeeper pulled off one of her plastic gloves to brush a strand of dark hair from her forehead, then followed Vanessa out of the room. She stood next to her supply cart, waiting expectantly.

"This may seem like an odd question," Vanessa said, "but can you tell me how often you fill the soap dispenser in room six-oh-one?"

The housekeeper looked at her quizzically. "Funny you ask that," she said. "I've noticed that I have to fill that one three or four times more often than in the other kids' bathrooms."

Vanessa had to smile. Her hunch had been right. "Thank you," she said. She was about to turn away when she decided she owed the housekeeper an explanation. "The patient in that room is drinking the soap," she said simply. "Making herself a little laxative cocktail."

The housekeeper grimaced, then shook her head. "These kids." She turned to extract another glove from the box on her cart, muttering to herself. "Crazier every year."

At the nurses' station, Vanessa shared what she'd learned with Shelley's nurse, adding that the girl would need to be watched in the shower as well as after meals. They would help Shelley Collier in spite of herself.

She checked on a few other patients, including Jordan Wiley, who had received a second chest tube sometime during the night. It had been a week since the placement of the first tube, which was not working efficiently, and as

Vanessa examined the raw-looking incision in his side, Jordy fought tears of pain and, most likely, fear. Even with the second tube in place, his lungs did not sound good. She watched his face as she listened to his chest with her stethoscope. His eyes were squeezed tightly shut. The blue veins in his temples were visible beneath the pale skin.

"The pain meds aren't holding you, are they, Jordan?" she asked.

"No," he whispered without opening his eyes. "But if they give me more, I'll be asleep, and I don't want to be asleep."

Instinctively, she ran a hand over his frizzy dark hair. A rare gesture for her. What was it about this kid that tore at her heart?

"Hopefully, this second tube will start making you feel better very soon," she said.

He nodded, eyes still shut, his blue-tinged lips pressed tightly together, and she knew he didn't believe her optimistic words of comfort any more than she did.

By five o'clock, there were eight message slips dotting her desk, and she settled into her chair with a bottle of apple juice and an air of grim determination to begin returning the calls.

She tried directing the callers to Terri. "Terri's the one who's talked to Patterson," she said. "She's in a better position than I am to tell you how to proceed."

But her colleagues in the network were not that easy to get rid of. They were tenacious about engaging her in conversation, and all of them had an enthusiastically delivered story to tell her about Zed Patterson.

"He single-handedly kept abortion rights alive in Pennsylvania," one of them crowed.

"He helped an old coworker of mine start a victims' assistance program," said another. "She went to his office and talked to him about the people she wanted to help and he actually *shed tears*."

The man was quickly assuming legendary status, and as Vanessa listened to her smitten colleagues, sparks of lightning jerked their way into the corner of her vision.

She returned six of the calls before the urge to escape grew too strong to fight. She needed to run. It was the only solution to the mounting tension in her body.

She changed into her warm-up suit and running shoes and took the stairs down to Darcy's office, even though she doubted Darcy would want to join her. Darcy was in the twelfth week of her pregnancy, and her morning sickness was lasting well into the night. On their last run together, Darcy had stopped twice to throw up.

Darcy groaned when she saw Vanessa standing in the door of her office.

"Forget it," Darcy said. "No way."

Vanessa gave her a rueful smile. Darcy did look a little green. No point in badgering her. "Maybe next week," she said.

"Don't count on it." Darcy swiveled her desk chair to face her friend. "I know you can't really understand how this feels, but I spend seventy-five percent of my time these days wishing someone would shoot me and put me out of my misery."

Vanessa had to force her smile. "Sorry, Darce," she said, backing out of the room. "You take care of yourself, okay?"

She walked down the hall, pushed open the back door of the hospital, and started running.

The evening was remarkably warm for mid-February.

Vanessa tried to find her pace as she ran toward the park. Spiky-skinned creatures crawled beneath the surface of her skin, and she pounded the pavement hard to get rid of them. Without Darcy, she could run faster, harder, getting the steam from her system before going home to Brian, who did not deserve the secondhand wrath.

Darcy talked nonstop about her pregnancy these days. Vanessa didn't mind listening—as a matter of fact, she found Darcy's excitement contagious—but if Darcy said to her one more time, "I know you can't understand how I'm feeling," she was afraid she might slug her. But she bit her tongue each time. There was no point in telling Darcy she was wrong. No point in talking about Anna. She didn't need to open old wounds.

A stone lay on the sidewalk ahead of her, and she kicked it hard, sending it skittering across a nearby lawn. Turning the corner, she was startled to see a man running toward her. For an instant, her heart kicked into high gear, but then she saw that he was in a running suit. He was someone like herself, she thought, out for a run on a beautiful winter night.

She sidestepped toward the street to pass him, but he did the same, and she almost laughed at the inevitable collision until she saw the quick thrust of his arms toward her and felt his hands at her throat.

She did not have time to think. She dropped her chin to her chest and pulled hard with her left hand on his arm, drawing him even closer to her. His dark eyes widened with surprise. With the heel of her right hand, she used all her strength to snap his chin up and back, and he let out a grunt. She made a fist and brought it down as hard as she could on his collarbone, and the crack was unmistakable.

"Fucking bastard." She kneed him in the groin, and as he doubled over, she kneed him again in his face. In the faint light, she saw blood spurt across the fabric of her warm-up pants.

He was on his hands and knees on the sidewalk, but Vanessa was not through. The adrenaline pumping through her body made her feel like a coiled spring, and as the man collapsed on the ground, she kicked him, in the face, on his back, on his side. She screamed at him and kicked him until someone pulled her away, and even then she still kicked the air. A siren blared in the distance, and only then did she realize that a strange man was holding her in his arms, and she was crying and cursing and tearing at his coat collar with her bare fingers.

Her attacker was in surgery, the police told her as she sat next to Brian in a waiting room at the station. The man would live, but he would be very uncomfortable for a long time. Most likely he was the same man who had raped two women in the past three months, dressing as a runner, pulling them into the bushes. Now he had a broken nose, a broken collarbone, a broken knee, and kidney damage. She knew she had broken a bone in her own little finger during the fray, but she kept that information to herself. She would take care of that later.

She owed Zed Patterson, she thought. She owed her gullible colleagues in the network and the shortsighted hospital administrators. She owed everyone who was raising her ire, because that would-be rapist had gotten it all. The rage that should have been spread out among many had all been heaped on his unsuspecting body.

Word of his foiled attack had apparently spread quickly.

By the time she and Brian left the police station, TV vans and reporters crammed the parking lot. Vanessa leaned against Brian with a groan. He swept the reporters away with his arm as they crossed the lot to his car. She thought of saying a few words into those microphones, of telling women to get training in self-defense.

"I'm five five and one hundred and ten pounds," she imagined herself saying. "If I can do this, you can, too. Empower yourselves." Yet she was too drained to speak to anyone, and the words slipped from her mind as she settled into Brian's car.

She pressed her head back against the seat as they drove out of the lot.

"Straight home?" Brian asked.

She shook her head. "Hospital." She held up her throbbing hand. The finger was swollen now and turning purple. "Emergency room."

He stopped the car in the middle of the street and turned on the overhead light to study her hand. "Vanessa." He frowned at her. "They asked if you were hurt. Why didn't you say anything?"

"I wanted to get away from them and their questions." She started to cry, unexpected and irksome tears, and Brian reached over to hold her hand, ignoring the honking of the car behind them.

"Were you afraid?" he asked after a moment.

"No." She had not been. Only at first, when the man's sudden appearance had startled her. After that, even when she'd felt his thumbs against her windpipe, she had not felt fear. Only rage. "I think I saw him as Zed Patterson," she said. "If they hadn't pulled me away, I would have killed him. I couldn't stop." She cringed at the memory of the last few kicks she'd delivered, when his body had felt like a rag doll beneath her feet.

The car passed them, followed by another.

"Too bad they stopped you." Brian put his own car in gear again, and as they started to roll up the street, Vanessa reached for his hand and held it snugly in her lap. Brian was smiling. He glanced at her. "How long ago was that self-defense course you took?"

"Centuries," she said.

Twenty years, at any rate. Twenty-two years.

She'd been beaten up once in her life, when she was six-teen, a year before Anna was born. It happened shortly after she'd stopped going to school—she'd never officially "dropped out." She was still living with her father then. At least she had a room in his house where she kept most of her clothes. He was rarely there. He'd made his money by then and had adopted the flamboyant, always-on-the-move lifestyle of a jet-setter. He didn't particularly care where she was.

She'd been walking to a boyfriend's house when it hap-pened. The man appeared out of nowhere, and before she could force a scream from her throat, she lay beaten and bruised in the gutter. She'd crawled to her boyfriend's house. She could not remember the boy's name—she didn't remember any of their names. He talked her out of calling the police. He had a record, he told her, and they might think that he'd done it. Plus, they would probably make her go back to school, and they'd get her father involved. So, she slept for two days straight in her boyfriend's bed with a heating pad and cold compresses. Once she was feeling better, the boy spent an entire night teaching her how to defend herself, teaching her techniques he said he'd learned in prison. Then he took her to a self-defense class taught by an old friend of his. It didn't matter how small she was, the instructor said, or what sex she was. She could kill if she had to. She'd thought she'd forgotten all she'd learned back then, but in some sloppy yet effective form, it had come back to her on the street tonight.

Brian parked the car in front of the hospital. Vanessa reached for the door handle, but Brian stopped her with his hand on her arm.

"Marry me," he said.

She had to laugh. "Why are you bringing this up now?" she asked. "I'm a mess. I just almost killed someone. I wake up every damn night with bad dreams. You should be running in the opposite direction from me, not proposing."

"I'm asking you now because I want you to know that even at your angriest, saddest, most volatile, most screwed-up moments, I still love you." He leaned his head back against the seat, but his eyes never left her face. "I love you because you're the smartest woman I've ever known. And because when you talk about your patients, there's passion in your eyes, and your concern for them is so genuine, and you get such a thrill out of the challenge of figuring out ways to help them. And when we make love, you make me feel like no one ever has before. And I love you because, even though you're busy as hell, you take the time to make me chicken Kiev, and you tuck mushy cards in my suitcase when I have to travel."

She felt the tightness in her jaw as she tried to keep her tears from falling again. The Adam's apple bobbed in Brian's throat. He ran his finger lightly over her swollen hand. "And when something hurts you, I feel it too, Vanessa," he said. "If you choose never to marry me, I would still stay with you. But you won't ever convince me that's what you really want."

She wanted to believe he meant what he was saying. She *did* believe him. "I don't know how bad this is going to get," she said, "this mess with Patterson, and—"

"Van?"

She said nothing, waiting for him to continue.

"If I were diagnosed tomorrow with a terminal illness, and I had three years to live, and they were certain to be terrible years during which I could do nothing except lie in bed and drool, what would you do?"

The scenario was impossible to imagine, yet she felt herself tearing up at the thought of him wasting away like that. "I would take care of you," she said. "I'd try to make you comfortable and make you chicken Kiev every night and—"

"Or if my ex-wife suddenly sued me for who knows what and sent me death threats and I had to spend all my money—every last dime—on lawyers, what would you do?"

"I'd help you any way I could. I'd listen to you rant and rave about her." This made her smile—she had already done a few years' worth of that listening. "I'd give you my money to help you pay your legal fees."

"So, why do you think I would walk away from you when you have problems, huh? Do you think I'm less noble than you are?"

She smiled again. "I love you," she said.

"So, will you please marry me?"

She looked into her lap, where his hand formed a nest around her bruised and swollen finger. "Yeah," she said, heart thumping. "I will."

20

Jeremy, Pennsylvania
1960

At lunch one day, Vincent Siparo announced he was too tired to take an afternoon walk with his granddaughters. He was tired a lot toward the end of that summer, and he got out of breath easily, so Claire and Vanessa decided to go for their walk in the woods without him, Tucker tagging along at their heels.

They were smart girls, and they knew the woods well; it would not even occur to them to feel fear as they trudged through the trees.

"Let's explore," Claire said, turning off their usual path, and Vanessa followed dutifully. Soon, they were walking through an unfamiliar section of the woods, and the girls carefully twisted branches and dropped stones on the path as markers, the way Vincent had taught them to do, so they would always be able to find their way back.

Suddenly, Vanessa stopped walking, her eyes riveted on the ground near a gnarled old oak tree.

"What's the matter?" Claire asked.

Vanessa pointed to the ground in front of her. Claire walked toward her sister gingerly—in case it was a snake that had caught Vanessa's eye. But it was not a snake. In front of Vanessa, beneath some fallen limbs and dried leaves at the foot of the oak, a wooden cross jutted from the earth. Claire tugged away some of the dead limbs, and the two girls stared at the cross. Painted in white letters on the wood was the name TUCKER.

They knew a little about graves, but not much. Their grandpa Harte, Len's father, had died a year ago, and Mellie wouldn't let them go to the funeral, but they'd heard some-one talking about the grave where he was buried. When Claire asked Mellie if Grandpa Harte was under the ground, Mellie had laughed. "Of course not. He's in heaven. You know that. The grave is just a place for people to go to remember the person who's in heaven." It was hard to believe what Mellie said sometimes. Kids at school talked about people being buried. Perhaps some people were buried when they died, but not if they were a Harte or a Siparo.

Yet here was a grave. Both girls turned to look at Tucker, who sat nearby waiting for them. When they looked in his direction, he flapped his pointed tail on the leaves.

"Is this the other Tucker?" Vanessa asked.

"It can't be," Claire said. "Mellie said he lives with another family with a lot of children, remember?"

"Yes." They stared again at the cross. The lettering was perfect, white outlined with a line of gold, like the gold Vincent used on the horses.

"Maybe there was another Tucker before that Tucker," Claire suggested. "And *he's* in heaven and this is where

Grandma and Grandpa come to remember him."

Vanessa nodded solemnly. "Maybe there's been a million Tuckers," she said. "We could ask Mommy."

"No," Claire said. "I don't know why this grave is here, but if we ask Mellie, we'll never be able to figure it out."

They considered asking their grandfather, but even though Vincent was working in his shop by the time they got back to the barn, he seemed too tired to bother with their questions. He breathed hard every time he got up to get a paintbrush or a rag, and he grunted every time he lowered himself to his workbench again. The doctor had told him not to smoke his pipe any longer, but he still slipped it, unlit, into his mouth when he worked.

Claire and Vanessa sat down to play with their clay. Claire had quietly given up on the wood after last summer, and no one had said a word to her about it. Vincent never even mentioned the fact that she no longer picked up the wood and the carving knife. Perhaps he had seen her frustration when she worked with it. No matter how careful she was with the block of wood, she was always cutting off a piece she'd wanted to remain on the carving, and there was no way to fix that sort of mistake.

When Vincent announced it was time for their afternoon ride, the girls set their clay on the worktable and ran into the barn. Once they'd hopped onto the platform of the carousel, Vanessa ran straight to Titan.

"I want to ride on Titan today," she announced.

Claire stared at her younger sister in disbelief. "Titan's *mine*," she said.

"You *always* get to ride him. I should get a turn, too."

Claire's fists were knotted at her sides. "Grandpa!" she called.

Vincent started walking toward them from the workshop. "What's the problem, girls?" he asked, stepping onto the platform next to Titan. He stroked the horse's long white head lightly with his hand as he looked down at his granddaughters.

"Vanessa wants to ride Titan!" Claire said. "Tell her she can't."

"Ah," Vincent said. His blue eyes looked tired, but there was still a sparkle in them. "Well, how about giving her a turn?"

Vanessa nodded vigorously while Claire went red with rage. "He's mine!" She wrapped her arm possessively around the jumper's delicate leg. "He's always been mine. She can have all the other horses on the whole carousel."

Vanessa stomped her foot. "She always gets to ride him."

Vincent picked up his blond granddaughter, wheezing with the effort. "You know he's Claire's favorite, Angel?" he asked. "That she's always picked him to ride on?"

Claire nodded indignantly, her own nostrils flaring.

"And that even if you get to ride him every once in a while, he'll always be Claire's special horse, just like any of the others can be your special horse?"

Claire cocked her head at Vincent suspiciously.

Vincent knelt at her side, Vanessa still in his arms. "I know Titan's your horse, honey, but don't you think you could let Vanessa have a turn on him sometimes?"

Claire pouted at her younger sister, whose glittering blond curls spilled over her grandfather's arm. Strangers on the street could not resist running their hands over that golden hair. It was nearly the same color as Titan's mane.

"I hate you," Claire said to Vanessa.

Vincent reached out to touch Claire's arm. "Now, Claire," he said. "No, you don't."

"I do too. I don't even want to ride on this stupid carousel if she's on it."

But Vincent was firm. And so Claire sat sulking on the blanket-covered crate in the corner while her grandfather puttered with the hinges on one of the doors and Vanessa spun around, giggling, tossing back her head as she galloped through the barn on the proud white stallion.

In front of the farmhouse, a short distance from the barn, Len and Mellie were getting into their car. They started down the long driveway in the green Plymouth, and even though the carousel music was loud, the car could still be heard as it passed outside the barn. At least Claire could hear it from her perch on the crate. Behind the barn, the car engine stopped abruptly and a door slammed. Then the yelling began, mean and ugly and loud. Vincent raised his head from his work on the door, looking at the wall of the barn as if he could see through it to his daughter and son-in-law on the other side.

Claire watched her grandfather, her mouth open, waiting for him to acknowledge the fight, to do something about it.

Vincent walked over to the carousel. He grabbed hold of one of the poles and stepped onto the moving platform, making his way among the horses to get to the organ. He turned the music up, so loud that the floor of the barn trembled and no other sound could possibly be heard. Then he crossed the platform again and stepped off. Droplets of sweat poured down his cheeks, glistening in the gray of his beard, and he pulled a handkerchief from the pocket of his overalls to wipe his face.

He smiled at Claire then. "Vanessa's having a great ride there on Titan, isn't she?" He had to shout to be heard above the music.

Vanessa was leaning over, hugging Titan's neck as she rode up and down, up and down. It was impossible to tell where the horse's mane ended and the girl's hair began.

Vincent went back to the door and lifted his hammer to one of the hinges.

In the corner, Claire raised her feet to the crate, hugging her knees to her chest, pulling herself into a tight little knot against the wall.

The fighting was gone, if it had existed at all. It could have been laughter, some sort of game perhaps. If any memory remained of the shouting, or the anger, or the slamming of the car door, it would soon be swallowed by the loud, lilting music of the carousel.

21

McLean

She'd lied to Jon, for the first time in her life. It could not even be called a white lie, a simple fib she could shrug off. She'd called him from home, leaving a message on his voice mail at the foundation. Her hand had trembled as she clutched the receiver, but her voice was cheerful and even. She thought, with some disgust, that she sounded remarkably believable, as if she were a liar with plenty of practice. And she had been practicing lately, if omission could be considered a lie. It had been nearly a week and a half since that abysmal morning in the hotel in Baltimore, and she hadn't told Jon any more about the flashbacks, although they certainly had not stopped. He thought she should be able to control them; she wished that were the case. While doing paperwork in her office the other day, she'd seen a drawing of a robin on the forms and memos instead of the words actually printed on the paper. A child's drawing, as if from a coloring book. The robin's breast was outlined in a deep, waxy red. She found the drawing curious and was annoyed that it stole her attention from her work, yet it didn't frighten her as the other images did.

But then there was the music box. She'd been shopping after work yesterday with Amelia. They were at the mall, in a shop filled with music boxes. Amelia was hunting for a birthday gift for her niece. Claire walked among the boxes, studying the dancers or skaters or, in a few cases, carousel horses that adorned their lids. She opened one with a horse and carriage on the top, and the melody that drifted out into the store was "Let Me Call You Sweetheart." Innocent enough, but with the first few notes, Claire began trembling. She slammed the lid closed so sharply that the saleswoman looked up from her seat behind the counter.

"Please be careful," the woman said, "they're very delicate."

The vertigo was immediate, and the nausea followed quickly. Claire leaned against the glass counter, breathing deeply through her mouth.

"I'm not feeling well," she said to the woman. It was a struggle to get the words out. "May I use your restroom, please?" She was only vaguely aware that Amelia had stepped to her side and was resting a hand on her back.

The saleswoman shook her head. "I'm sorry. We don't have a restroom for the public, but there's one at Bloomie's. That's just—"

"Please," Claire said. The room was beginning to spin.

"Claire." Amelia smoothed a strand of Claire's hair away from her face. "You're so pale. What's the matter?"

Claire started to cry. She was still lucid enough to know her public tears should embarrass her, yet she was not lucid enough to care.

"You *must* let her use your restroom," Amelia said. The strength in her voice was wonderful, and Claire leaned against her friend, weeping freely. She felt the eyes of other customers on her. They could all go to hell.

The saleswoman relented, leading Claire and Amelia into a corridor behind the shop where there was a small bathroom cluttered with boxes.

"Will you be all right alone?" Amelia asked, and Claire managed to nod before stepping into the room and locking the door behind her. She sat down on the toilet, fully clothed, and leaned back against the tank. She shut her eyes but immediately saw her hand lifting the lid on the music box, the small horse and its miniature buggy tilting into the air. She opened her eyes again quickly and began reading the handwritten signs on the wall and door of her little cubicle. *A Satisfied Customer is a Repeat Customer. Salesgirl of the Month: Ginny Axelrod*. There were at least a dozen of the signs, and reading them calmed her, numbed her.

"Claire?" Amelia knocked on the door. "You all right, hon?"

"Fine," she said. She was breathing normally again. She wet a tissue at the sink and, without looking into the small wall mirror, dabbed at the skin below her eyes, hoping to wipe away any trace of her tears.

Amelia, white-lipped and worried, was waiting for her when she opened the bathroom door. Claire gave her a big smile.

"Sorry," she said. "I don't know what happened to me. Just felt like I was going to be violently ill for a moment, but it passed."

Amelia put an arm around her shoulders, hugging her. "You scared me, girl. You sure you're all right?"

"I'm perfect," she said. But once they'd stepped back into the shop and Amelia announced she wanted to look at more of the music boxes, Claire felt the panic boiling up again.

"I'll wait for you out in the mall." She pointed to the bench outside the door of the shop, and Amelia nodded.

It was not enough to escape from the store, she thought as she waited on the bench. She needed to escape from her skin. Glancing at her watch, she wondered if she would have time to call Randy before Jon got home that night. She wanted to tell him what had happened. She hadn't seen him since their visit to the Smithsonian, but she'd spoken to him every day on the phone. She was no longer telling Jon about those phone calls.

When she finally did reach Randy that evening, he pushed her as she'd known he would, in a way she both dreaded and welcomed. He would not stay on the surface of her thoughts any longer. Where might she have heard that particular melody before? he asked. Could she imagine how it would sound played with different instruments? What did she hear if she gave her imagination free rein? She had no answers to his questions, but she endured them anyway until the discomfort got too great and she begged for a change of topic.

She heard Jon pull into the garage while she was still talking with Randy, and she hung up the phone before he got to the back door, angry with herself for her deception. If Jon asked her who she'd been talking to, she would tell him. But he did not ask, and she did not volunteer.

The lie she'd told him tonight, though, was deliberate. Calculated. Unforgivable.

"I know you're working late," she'd said in her message

on his voice mail, "so I hope you don't mind if I take in a movie with Amelia." *Take in a movie?* She'd never used that expression before. It had just popped out. "I'll see you tonight."

The truth was, she and Randy were going dancing.

She thought about the lie as she put on her violet dress, which was too dressy for the office, but nothing special, really. She should have at least told Jon she was seeing Randy tonight, simply omitting the part about dancing. That's what would hurt Jon, the dancing, because that was one thing they'd never been able to do together.

She'd loved to dance as a teenager, before meeting Jon, and she remembered the sadness with which she'd given up that pleasure. She'd lost a lot of friends back then. It wasn't that they disliked Jon, although he had sometimes pushed people away with his bitterness during those early months after he'd transferred into her high school. She'd lost her friends simply because she gave them up for him. He was new to his wheelchair back then, and the activities of her friends seemed out of his reach. Claire didn't mind. She was in love. She never let herself think about what she'd given up for him. There was danger in thinking too much.

She was still squirming over the lie as she got into her car and drove down the driveway to the main road. She should not have involved Amelia. By tossing Amelia into the story, she was making it seem as though being with Randy was wrong in and of itself.

And it could not be wrong. She wished she could tell Jon that Randy was not the cause of her problems. Rather, in a way she could not explain, she felt certain that he was the cure. This sort of clandestine meeting, though, could not become the norm. She would have to find a way to occasionally spend time with Randy without hurting Jon in the process.

Randy had asked her if she could drive tonight; his car was in the shop. She followed his directions to the row of town houses in McLean, a few blocks from the little theater, and pulled into the space in front of number 167. The parking lot was well lit, and she could see that the town houses were quite stunning. Randy had told her they were only five years old, but their weathered-brick exteriors gave them a soft, mellowed appearance. Number 167 stood fully in the glow of one of the parking lot lights. It was built of faded white brick. The shutters were black and the door, red. Wintergreen azalea bushes graced the small front yard, and she wondered what color they would bloom in the spring.

She was at the top of his brick steps, about to lift the brass knocker, when Randy opened the door.

"Almost ready." He smiled. "Come in."

She stepped into the small living room, which was filled cozily with heavy, dark antique furniture.

She took off her coat, and he slipped his arm around her for a brief hug. His beard softly brushed her cheek. "Haven't seen you in too long," he said. "You look good."

"Thanks." She smiled with a sense of safety she had not felt since the last time she'd stood in his arms.

"I'll be back in a second," he said, heading for the stairs. "Make yourself at home."

She sat down on the plush, pillow-laden sofa and studied the room. A black-and-beige Oriental carpet nearly covered the hardwood floor. The corner near the fireplace was dominated by a huge, dark, rolltop desk, open to expose dozens of drawers and shelves and compartments. Any visible papers were neatly arranged. In fact, despite the riot of furniture and fabric, a sense of order enveloped the room.

The walls were thick with paintings, all Hudson River Valley-style with their dark and haunting images of thick trees and black water. On the mantel, though, were a few decidedly contemporary framed photographs. Claire walked over to the hearth. Two of the pictures were of the same boy—Cary, no doubt. One had been taken at the age of six or seven, the other at nine or ten. He had Randy's blue eyes and a tentative smile. The third photograph was the family portrait she had given him from Margot's room. It was in a different frame, however, a brass frame warmed by the sepia tone of the photograph. The image of the gawky-looking, dark-haired boy who stood apart from his family made her smile with a tenderness she had not felt the last time she'd seen the picture.

They talked about dancing as they drove to The Castle, a club he said he and LuAnne had one visited in Rosslyn. He loved to dance, he said. It was the performer in him. LuAnne, though, would have preferred almost any other activity, and so they hadn't gone dancing very often.

The dance floor was large and uncrowded, and the music was provided by a DJ who played an eclectic mix of Glen Miller, Eric Clapton, Billy Ray Cyrus, and some loud and unrecognizable disco music. Randy taught her the Texas two-step and a few other dances that had either been invented or reincarnated during her last twenty danceless years.

He had not lied about enjoying the performance aspect of dancing. Randy had no inhibitions whatsoever, and after a few shy, stiff moments, Claire let herself be swept into the freedom he offered her on the dance floor.

As the evening wore on, the music grew progressively slower. The lights dimmed, and the dancers paid less attention to the steps and more attention to one another. Randy held her as they moved smoothly around the floor, but there was nothing suggestive in his touch, nothing insistent in the press of his thigh against hers, and that relieved her, let her relax. He held her hand on his chest, but he did not stroke her fingers, nor did he shift his other hand from the small of her back. He didn't nuzzle her temple, like other dancers were doing. It felt so good to be holding a man this way, though. Standing. Moving. She did not want to let go, ever, and she was disappointed when he broke the spell by talking.

"Let's see if the DJ has 'Let Me Call You Sweetheart,'" he said.

She could not tell if he was teasing. "No, thanks," she said. "And I'm sure he doesn't."

"Seriously. What if he does? It might—"

She shook her head. "Forget it."

"It'd be perfect if he did. You could flow with the feelings, Claire. See where they lead. You ran away from them too quickly in the store."

"I was going to pass out."

"Well, if you pass out, I'll be right here to pick you up."

She felt hot tears. "You don't know how bad it feels," she said.

He tightened his arm around her. "All right," he said. "You win."

She was almost disappointed that he let it go. She longed to know the source of her discomfort, but she did not yet have the courage to let him push her without pushing back.

"Well, whether he has your favorite little ditty or not, the DJ's done a great job with the music selection tonight," Randy said.

"Yes," she said, breathing more easily now that the danger had passed. "A little bit of everything." She thought of all the Chopin she'd listened to after Margot's death. "Except classical."

"Perfect. I loathe classical."

She cocked her head to look at him. "That's ironic, isn't it? That you had two siblings who were classical pianists, and you hate the stuff?"

He groaned. "I used to think that if I heard Chopin played one more time, I'd explode. Margot and Charles would listen to that stuff *ad nauseam*, and when I'd complain, they'd look at each other as if they couldn't understand how I could possibly be related to them. They'd say, 'Can't you hear how beautiful it is?' and they'd play it louder, as though I was missing the point because I couldn't hear it well enough. It sounded like nails on a chalkboard to me."

Claire rested her cheek against his shoulder, thinking back, remembering Margot on the bridge. "Was it you?" she asked.

"What are you talking about?"

"Margot said, 'He could never hear the music.' Could she have been talking about you?"

Randy missed a step. She felt his toe under her foot. "It's possible," he said.

"But why? Why at that moment would she have been thinking about you?"

"I don't know."

"She said—"

"Claire." He stopped dancing and looked down at her, squeezing her shoulders so tightly it hurt. "Could we talk about something else, please? Or better yet, not talk at all?"

He averted his eyes, and she knew better than to continue her questioning.

"All right." It was her turn to let it go.

They started dancing again, but Claire felt the change in him. He moved stiffly; his hands had lost their tenderness.

When the music ended, he asked her, "Can we get out of here? Do you mind leaving now?"

They got their coats and walked to her car in silence. He slipped his pipe into his mouth but did not light it.

"What time do you need to be home?" he asked once they were sitting inside the car.

She turned on the heat, shivering, as she calculated how long it would have taken for a movie and a quick bite to eat with Amelia.

"I have an hour," she said, and somehow she was not surprised when he suggested she drive to the deserted little theater in McLean.

It was dark inside the theater, cool and still. Randy lit the balcony lights but left the others off, and he and Claire moved to the middle of the chapel, sliding into the pew that had begun to feel as if it belonged to them.

Randy leaned forward, elbows on knees. He had not spoken since asking her when she needed to be home. "I've never told a soul what I'm about to tell you," he said.

She rested her hand lightly on his back. The balcony lights hit her fingers, making them glow against the dark cloth of his suit.

"I was jealous of Margot and Charles," Randy said. "There were plenty of times when I was a kid that I wished they would disappear." He glanced at her. "I told you about my father, right?"

Claire nodded.

"According to my mother, I'd inherited all his loser qualities. I swear, I think I was basically a normal kid, but next to the 'angels,' as my mother called them, I looked like a juvenile delinquent who was tone deaf and all thumbs and nothing but trouble. If she and my stepfather, Guy, could have found a legal way of getting me out of their hair, I'm sure they would have done it without batting an eye."

"I'm sorry, Randy."

"I did love Margot and Charles, though," Randy continued. "It's amazing that any of that feeling could survive, but on some level I know I did."

"That bond between siblings is hard to break," she said, although she did not know that for sure. She thought of Vanessa. She must have loved her sister, but she could not recall that emotion. It came with the territory, though, didn't it?

Randy didn't seem to hear her. "I didn't tell you the complete truth about what happened that night on the bridge."

"You didn't?" She wondered what part he had altered.

"No. The truth is that my younger brother Charles was no dare-devil. He was not the kind of kid to go running out on the platform outside the guardrail. As a matter of fact, both of them were terrified of crossing the bridge at all. I don't think they'd ever done it on foot before. If they needed to go across, they'd always get a ride. But with the snow, that was impossible, which was why I was supposed to walk them."

Claire could see once again that pristine blanket of snow, and her curiosity was piqued. "What happened?"

"Margot was doing okay with it," Randy said. "She walked right in the middle of the road and was singing something to keep from thinking about how high up she was. She was doing pretty well. But Charles was really in a panic. I guess I felt—I don't know—a lot of things. Embarrassed that I had such a wimp for a brother. Sorry for him that he was so scared. Angry that I'd had to go fetch the two little angels when I could have been building snowforts with my friends."

Randy turned his head from her, and the balcony lights caught his temple, his cheek, the long eyelashes she had not noticed before. She did not like the pain she saw in his face. She thought of stopping his story, of telling him it didn't matter. It happened so long ago; why think about it now? But he continued before she could speak.

"I wanted to help Charles. I mean, I think my intentions were noble. I don't think I'm kidding myself on that. I wanted to help him get over being such a wimpy little pantywaist. So I held his hand as we walked, and I told him there was nothing to be afraid of. It was just a bridge, for Christ's sake. Charles looked up to me. He wanted my approval, and I know he was trying to be brave, but I remember looking at him once, and his face was absolutely white. I remember thinking that he looked like a mime. Anyhow, he was hanging on to my hand, and I kept walking closer and closer to the edge of the bridge, telling him, 'It's okay. It's just a bridge. It can't hurt you.'"

He ran a hand across his beard and closed his eyes, and Claire put her arm more fully around him.

"It's all right," she said, although she was not certain what she was alluding to. She was always good with those empty words of comfort. Her forte.

His voice was thick when he spoke again. "As we got closer to the edge, he really started getting scared. I could feel him shaking all over. I started saying things to him to shame him into bravery. I told him my friends thought he was a . . . a pansy. I think that's the word I used. That they would ask me about my two little sisters." Randy shook his head. "God, that must have hurt that little kid, hearing that. He was only ten. Cary's age." Randy grimaced at that realization, then drew in a heavy breath.

"The bridge was different then," he continued. "The guardrail isn't much to speak of now, but it was essentially nothing then. It was just a metal railing, and that was all that separated the bridge from the platform, where you were with Margot. So, I got Charles all the way over to the railing, and he held on to it as we walked, and I was telling him he was really great to be walking right next to the edge of the bridge like that. But he was crying. Trying not to let me see, but I could tell he was scared shitless. He wouldn't let go of my hand for anything. One hand on the railing, the other hanging on to me."

Claire could see the scene, could feel the cold railing in her hand. She did not want to hear any more.

"And I got this great idea to show him how there was nothing to be afraid of," Randy said. "I told him I was going to go out on the platform. It was icy out there, and my plan was to hang on to the railing and skate along while Charles walked on the bridge side of the railing. I'd done it before with my friends. It seemed like no big deal to me, but Charles started crying in earnest, because it meant he would have to let go of my hand. Margot stood in the center of the bridge, screaming at me not to do it."

"Randy," she said softly. "I can see where this is going. You don't have to—"

"Yes, I do," he said, his voice feverish. "I wrenched my hand out of Charles's and . . . " He stopped speaking, covering his eyes with his fingers. Claire tightened her hand on his shoulder. "Oh, shit," Randy said, "I can see his face. He was just frozen there, too afraid to move. Clutching the railing with one hand, the other reaching for me. He was crying. Margot was yelling something at me. I don't remember what. I kept saying, 'I do this all the time. Don't be such a baby.' I ducked under the railing and started skating—sliding on the ice, leaning back. I kept calling to Charles to come on, telling him to hang on to the railing with both hands if he had to, but to start walking, and I was getting further and further away from him, and he couldn't budge. I moved back toward him and tried to coax him, and he kept begging me to come back onto the bridge and take his hand. I was within a yard of him, and I promised I would walk right next to him, me on the platform, him on the bridge with the railing between us. 'Come on,' I said. 'You're not a pansy, are you?'"

Suddenly, Randy sat up straight, throwing off her arm. "God, if any kid ever taunted Cary that way, I'd kill him."

Claire nodded. "I know, but you were just being a—"

"I promised to stay close to him on the other side of the railing," Randy interrupted her. "He finally mustered up all his courage and took a step, and then I darted away from him. Teasing him. I just wanted him to see that he could do it on his own." He made a wry face. "Or maybe I wanted to torment him."

"Or maybe you were just being a fifteen-year-old boy." She wanted to soothe him. Save him.

"And then," Randy said, "I swear I don't know how it happened." He raised his hands, palms open, before tightening them into fists. "There must have been ice beneath the snow right there. It was as though something sucked him under the metal railing, out onto the icy platform. He was wearing mittens, and couldn't get a good grip on the railing, and in an instant he was gone. There was this fucking horrible look of terror on his face. Then he disappeared. If he screamed, I don't remember it. Maybe because I was screaming so loud myself." Randy leaned back against the pew. His face was very pale.

"I'm so sorry." Claire had taken her shoes off, and she drew her feet up to the padded seat of the pew, the skirt of her violet dress covering her legs. "But it was long ago. So long ago. You can't fix it."

"No, I certainly can't." He shook off her attempt to comfort him. "Anyhow, the rest of the story is the same as I told you. Margot tried to go after him, and fell herself, and I did carry her, unconscious and bleeding, all the way home. Of course I lied to my mother and stepfather about what happened, and Margot was in no shape to talk. Once she was better, I lived in terror that she'd tell them the truth, but she never did. I'm not even sure she remembered it. As we got older, I wanted to ask her why she kept it to herself, but she was so strange by then. I always wondered if she would have developed those psychiatric problems if she hadn't gotten that head injury." He sighed. "I like to think it was inevitable, but I don't really believe it. I guess what I do believe is that I killed both my brother and my sister that night."

What a burden to live with, Claire thought. What terrible guilt to carry around. "You were just a kid yourself, though," she said. "Kids aren't great at thinking through consequences. And they don't think in terms of danger. Or mortality. If you'd known your brother could get hurt, I'm sure you would have done everything possible to prevent it."

Randy looked at her. "Do you know I never even told LuAnne the truth about what happened that night?"

"Why me?" she asked. "Why now?"

"Because I knew you wouldn't run away. You try too hard and too fast to fix people, but you don't run away from them, no matter how messed up they are." He shook his head. "I guess I always thought that LuAnne only needed one little excuse to walk out the door. I could never have told her what I just told you."

Claire rested her chin on her knees. "I'm so glad you could tell me," she said. The score was somehow evened. They had each shared something private. Painful. She wanted to hold him, to make him feel the way she had the week before, when he'd held her in the museum. Safe and warm and accepted. She settled for resting her hand on his arm. The stillness of the chapel surrounded them, and she closed her eyes.

Angel. Hadn't people called Vanessa "Angel," with her golden curls, her innocent little perfect-toothed smile? Hadn't that been Mellie's nickname for her?

"What are you thinking?" Randy asked after a few quiet minutes had passed.

"Vanessa. I'm not sure why. Something you said."

"What did I say?"

She shook her head. "I don't know. Maybe it was the

'angel' bit. My mother called Vanessa 'Angel.' She had this golden, sort of glittery, ethereal hair." For some reason, the thought of that little blond girl irritated her. "It doesn't matter," she said. "I don't want to remember."

"I think you need to remember."

"I doubt there's anything to *be* remembered."

"I think the lady doth protest too much." He turned his head to smile at her. "You look like you're about ten years old yourself right now," he said. "With your feet up, hugging your knees."

She hesitated before speaking. "That's how old I was then," she said. "The summer Vanessa left." She felt herself tiptoeing toward something. What, she wasn't sure. "I know that's the age I was. I just don't remember anything else about it."

"Okay," Randy said. "You were ten. What do you remember from age ten?"

She shrugged, unable to pluck that age from any other. "Nothing," she said.

"Well, what grade were you in?"

"Fifth, I guess."

"And who was your fifth-grade teacher?"

"Um . . . " She tried to remember, came up blank. "I don't remember any of my elementary-school teachers."

"How old would Vanessa have been when you were ten?"

"Eight."

"And why did your father take her with him rather than you?"

She shrugged again, uncomfortable now. She did not want to think about it.

"Sounds like you were a little jealous of her, huh? The way I was jealous of Margot and Charles? Vanessa was beautiful, had this great hair."

"I wasn't jealous of her." Maybe she had been. She did not remember.

"You were probably glad to see her go."

"I was not."

"Of *course* not, Randy," Randy mimicked her. "How could you even imagine that such a negative thought could exist in this bowl-of-cherries head of mine?" He tousled her hair.

"Well, even if I had been jealous," she said, "that's normal in kids. The way you envied your siblings. Perfectly normal. All I know is that, for whatever reason, my father took Vanessa to Washington State with him, and I never saw either of them again."

"*Let me call you sweetheart,*" Randy began to sing. "*I'm in—*"

"Stop it!" She pushed him away from her and felt the heat in her face.

"I'm sorry." Randy lost his smile. His fingers crept under her palm until he was holding her hand. "I'm sorry."

She let him hold her hand. "Mellie told me I would see Vanessa and my father again very soon," she said quietly. "She always said that. Whenever I would ask when I'd see them again, she'd say, 'Very soon, darling.'"

"Your mother was a liar."

"In a way, I guess she was, but it was only to make things easier on me. She lied to protect me. To help me get over something painful."

"The truth is the only thing that can help you get over something painful. It's out in the open. You deal with it, and you're done with it. Secrets and half-truths live on forever."

She was barely listening. She lifted her wrist into the

light from the balcony to see her watch. As usual, she had stayed far too long with Randy. "I need to get home," she said.

They put on their coats in silence and walked toward the door. In the foyer, Randy turned off the heat and the balcony lights, leaving them in complete darkness as he pulled her toward him for a hug.

"Well," he said, holding her, "this was quite an evening. The dancing was fun. This last hour was hell, though."

"Yes." She tightened her arms around him and knew by the way his body melted against hers that he felt the warmth and safety she was offering him. What *she* felt was love, deep and pure and whole. She felt closer to Randy than she'd felt to Jon—to *anyone*—in a very long time. Still, when he shifted his head, when he lowered his mouth to hers, it was unexpected and dishonest and wrong, and she quickly turned her face away from him.

"I'm sorry," he said into her hair. "Out of line again. Please consider that a mere thank-you kiss for making me feel as though I have a life again."

She trembled as she pulled away from him.

"You have an unusual marriage," Randy said after a minute. "I shouldn't take advantage of Jon's tolerance by"—he hunted for the words, then laughed—"by getting too familiar with you. I don't know how I'd feel about my wife going dancing with another man, no matter how platonic their relationship was."

Claire hesitated a moment. "He doesn't know," she said. "I told him I was going to a movie."

Reaching for the door, Randy turned to look at her. "With me?" he asked.

"No. I said I was going with a girlfriend." Hearing the

lie from her own lips sickened her. She should have told Jon the truth. She would, as soon as she got home.

Randy dropped his hand to his side. "Why did you lie to him?" he asked.

"Because I didn't want to upset him."

He sighed with a shake of his head, reaching past her again to push open the door. "You're your mother's daughter," he said.

"What do you mean?" She stepped out into the night.

He turned her toward him, his hand on her arm. "I don't like being part of a lie, Claire."

"Neither do I," she said. "It was a mistake. I didn't think it through carefully."

He looked down the street, in the direction of his house. He pulled his pipe from his coat pocket, tapped it against his palm. "I'm going to walk home," he said.

"Are you sure?"

"Yeah. It'll feel good." He lit the pipe, and the smoke rose into the cold air in small, fragrant puffs. He took the pipe from his mouth and touched her lightly on the arm. "Good-night, Claire," he said.

She watched him set off down the street, and she made no move toward her car in the parking lot. She did not take her eyes from him until he'd been swallowed by the darkness, and she knew then that she was in trouble. She did not want to go home, or see Jon, or feel the weight of her lie hanging over her. She would not confess it to him. What was the point? Confession would only ease her soul and hurt his. Besides, if she had to lie to see Randy the next time, she would do so all over again.

22

Vienna

The call from Amelia came at nine o'clock, just as Jon was wheeling in the back door of the house. She wanted to speak to Claire.

Jon hesitated for a moment, mentally replaying the message Claire had left on his voice mail. "Isn't she with you?" he asked. "She said you two were going to a movie."

"That's news to me. You're sure she said Amelia?"

"Yes. Absolutely. Maybe a later movie?"

"I'd know about it by now, Jon, don't you think? Look, tell her I called, okay?" She laughed. "And tell her that next time she uses me as a cover she'd better let me know so we can get our stories straight."

He didn't smile.

"Jon? Is everything all right?"

"Yes. Fine. I'll tell her you called."

He hung up the phone and sat in the middle of the kitchen for several minutes, thinking. Somewhere there lurked a logical explanation for this. He would not spend his energy hunting for it, though. She could tell him when she got home.

He built a fire in the fireplace and sat in the recliner, sifting through a stack of articles he'd collected over the years. There were magazine and newspaper pieces on museums and day trips and restaurants and parks, and a batch of pamphlets on wheelchair accessible events. He'd gone through this file of articles twice since their talk in Baltimore, putting together a partial list of things they could do for fun. As far as he knew, Claire had not even begun her own list. He felt like a nag each time he brought it up and so had not mentioned it in several days. He would present her with his list this weekend. If she did not make one of her own, he supposed that was her choice.

He lost himself so thoroughly in the brochure on wilderness adventures that he was only vaguely aware of the knot in his stomach, the tension in his arms. When he next looked at the clock on the mantel, it was after ten.

She was with Randy. He leaned his head back against the recliner, shutting his eyes. She was with Randy, and she had lied to him about it. And why would she lie unless something more was going on there than friendship? What had happened to him and Claire, to their marriage? He could not believe he'd reached the point of suspecting—no, of *knowing*—that she was betraying him. Was this the first time? She hadn't mentioned Randy more than once or twice since that weekend in Baltimore, and he'd hoped that their argument in the hotel had shaken her up sufficiently to put her back on track.

An hour later, Jon was in the kitchen, taking his medication before going to bed, when Claire walked in the door.

"I'm sorry I'm so late," she said, setting down her purse.

"We were talking, and I didn't realize what time it was." She was rosy-cheeked, and she kept her coat on as she opened the dishwasher and began unloading the dishes. Not long ago, she would have walked in the door and kissed him before she did anything else. Now she was not even looking at him.

"Who was talking?" he asked.

She didn't answer. She pulled a frying pan from the dishwasher and set it on the counter.

He stiffened his spine, girding for battle. "Amelia called here at nine, looking for you."

Holding a glass in her hand, she turned to stare at him, mouth open, and he felt something like hatred toward her. He wheeled his chair toward the hallway door.

"Get whatever you need from the bedroom," he said. "Because you're not sleeping with me tonight."

She set the glass on the counter. "Jon, wait. Listen to me."

"Go to hell! I don't want you anywhere near me. You've got a choice. Susan's room or the guest room. Or you can go back to Randy."

He heard her start to speak, but she quickly stopped herself, and he turned to face her again.

"What? You're going to try to tell me you weren't with him tonight?"

She drew the lapels of her coat together, like armor. "I was with him, but it's not what you think."

His heart contracted painfully in his chest. He wished he'd been wrong about them being together.

"You lied to me about being with him," he said, "and I'm supposed to assume there's nothing between the two of you?"

"There *is* something between us. A friendship. And it's important to me. I didn't want to lie to you, but I know you're . . . uncomfortable about him, and I don't know how to see him without upsetting you."

"Where were you tonight?"

She swallowed hard. "Dancing," she said.

"*Dancing*. You always said you didn't care about dancing."

She sat down at the table and, with a tired gesture, swept her hair back from her cheek. Her coat fell open, and he could see that she was wearing the violet dress he'd bought her the year before.

"I *don't* care about dancing," she said. "It's not that important to me." She shut her eyes and drew in a breath. "That's not exactly true," she said. "It's not a big deal, Jon, but I've always said I don't care about it so you wouldn't think it mattered to me that we couldn't do it."

He had an urge to pick up the glass from the counter and throw it at her, hard. "And what else have you lied to me about over the years?" he asked. "What else can't I do that you're yearning to do, that you want to do so much you'd do it behind my back?"

"Oh, Jon." She knelt down next to him, her hand on his arm. "Please, please, let's stop this. I'm sorry."

He could see the soft, inviting place where her breasts met under her dress, and he recoiled at the thought of Randy having that same view of her. Worse, of touching her there. He brushed her hand from his arm.

"Your apologies are starting to have an empty ring to them," he said.

Claire stood again, then said softly, "I'll sleep in Susan's room."

Sometime during the night, he felt her slip into the bed

beside him. She lay next to him, weeping softly, those tears as rare as diamonds, and there was no way he could cast her out again. Almost reflexively, his arms moved to encircle her, to draw her to him, and her body shaped itself to his as he pulled her closer.

"I'm scared," she whispered. "What's happening to us, Jon?"

He shut his eyes. "What's happening is that you seem to be getting involved with someone else."

She didn't speak for a moment. "I know it must seem that way to you," she said finally, "but my interest in him is not romantic. I swear it."

"What is it then?"

She hesitated. "It's . . . remember I told you about those little flashbacks?"

"Yes."

"Well, I'm sorry, but I'm still having them. They're worse, actually."

"Oh, Claire." He buried his face in her hair. She was apologizing the way a sick person might for being a burden. "Why haven't you told me?" he asked.

"I think you'd rather not hear about them."

He ran his hand over her hair. "Why do you say that?"

"Because you want me to be cheerful and happy, and right now that's impossible for me."

It was true that he would give anything to have his beautiful, effervescent wife back. But he pulled this scared, sad woman closer to him. He took in a long breath, let it out. "And so, you and Randy talk about the flashbacks?"

"Yes. For some reason, he brings them out in me, and I don't feel so afraid of them when I'm talking to him. He tries to get me to think about what they mean. Where they're coming from."

You asshole, Donovan. The man had no idea what he was getting into.

"Try telling *me* about them, Claire," he said bravely. "Give me a chance to listen."

For a long time, she said nothing. When she finally spoke, her voice was halting, not her own. "Well, there are the ones I told you about. The bloodstain and the mirrors. And at work the other day, I kept seeing a robin. A *drawing* of a robin, like from a coloring book, and ... Oh! 'Let Me Call You Sweetheart.' I heard it in a music box and I—"

"You mean, from the carousel?"

"The carousel?"

"That was one of the songs your grandfather had on the carousel, wasn't it? Didn't you tell me that, or maybe Mellie—"

"Yes, you're right. But why should that upset me?"

"Oh, Claire, hon, I don't know." He hugged her. "All this is tangled up in your head, and somehow it's gotten linked to Margot and the bridge and Randy."

She said nothing.

"Why open the past?" he asked. "I've heard you say that to people more times than I can count." Claire had no tolerance for therapists who mucked around in their patients' childhoods. He did not completely share her philosophy, but right now, he felt desperate to have her heed her own message. "Focus on the here and now," he said. "That's what you always say, isn't it? Leave the past alone."

"But it won't leave *me* alone." She pulled away from him, punching the mattress as she spoke. "I mean, I don't remember any of it, but if you look at the facts—Vanessa getting dragged away from her mother and sister forever—if you look at that one fact alone, it's enough to make my childhood look hideous."

He stared at the ceiling as he stroked her hair. He wished he could pull her back from the path she was on, but already it seemed too late. She'd started a journey—one he knew in his heart she needed to make—and it had no shortcut. If she wanted to see it through to the end, there was nothing he could do to put a stop to it. Nor did he have that right. But couldn't she continue the journey without Randy Donovan?

"Is it platonic, Claire?" he asked.

She seemed to catch her breath. "How could you think anything else?"

"Well, to start with, you lied to me."

"I shouldn't have lied. It's just that I knew you'd be upset."

He sighed. "You and I are in trouble here. Our marriage is in trouble, and—"

"Don't talk that way. Please. We'll be fine."

He pressed his lips to her hair. He wanted to believe her, but these days, Claire's assurances had lost the ring of truth.

"I have to ask you for something," he said. "I don't ask a lot of you, Claire, but this is very important to me."

She raised herself up on her elbow to look at him, and he was relieved when he saw the love in her eyes. "Anything," she said. "You know that."

"I want you to stop seeing Randy."

She didn't respond, but lowered her head to his shoulder again, slowly.

"Claire?"

"It's not fair to ask me to do that." She was sniffling. "Please, Jon. Please don't give me ultimatums."

He lay very still for a moment. He could think of nothing more to say. He was gentle as he let go of her, even managed to brush his lips across her cheek before he turned on his side, away from her.

She touched his shoulder. "Don't pull away," she said. "Please. Talk to me."

But he shut his eyes, and after a moment, her hand slipped from his shoulder.

So, she would spend her time with Randy Donovan. She would slip further from her marriage, further from him. And she would chip away at the memories of a childhood that, Jon knew, was far more hideous than she could ever imagine.

23

Seattle

Vanessa spent the evening in the library, surrounded by congressional directories and microfilm reels of newspaper articles. She had to make some sense of this. How did Zed Patterson go from being the deputy sheriff of a little farming community in Pennsylvania to a state senator? And how did he come to have an interest in victims' rights, of all things?

The network was gleefully courting him. Terri Roos was no longer the only one in regular contact with his office. Everyone seemed to be taking delight in their stimulating chats with the compassionate Mr. Patterson.

"But he really wants to talk to *you*, Vanessa," Terri had told her the day before. "Your name keeps popping up in his conversations with other people, so he's figured out that you're our guiding force. Do you have time to give him a call?"

Vanessa forced herself to consider it. Patterson wouldn't know, she thought. He couldn't possibly figure out that

Vanessa Gray was, in reality, Vanessa Harte. And even if he heard her childhood name, she doubted he would make the connection. He probably didn't remember her at all.

But she begged out of calling him once again, and this time she sensed Terri's impatience. "Some people are upset that you're not being a team player on this, Vanessa," Terri said. "They're saying we should proceed without you."

Vanessa bit her lower lip, hurt. She was hungry to join her colleagues, hungry to *lead* them in this fight. She wanted to see this thing through, but that was impossible. Not as long as Zed Patterson was going to walk with them every step of the way.

"Terri, please don't leave me out," she said. "I can't give you my reasons for not being more fully involved right now, but my heart's still where it's always been. I'm committed to the AMC programs, you know that. I just can't work through Patterson. It's . . . it's political."

She could almost hear Terri's brain cells swirling, trying to make sense of Vanessa's words. "You mean, you'll get in hot water with the hospital or something?" Terri asked.

"Something like that. You can consult with me. You can use me any way you want. But I can't deal directly with Patterson's office. All right?"

Terri had accepted her refusal to participate with reluctance. She was sure to pass Vanessa's cryptic message on to other members of the network, and they would concoct theories to explain her unwillingness to deal with Patterson. But even the most inventive among them would never come near the truth.

Brian was her balm, her shelter in the midst of the storm surrounding her. In three weeks, they would be married. She had told no one because it seemed unreal to her. Until the justice of the peace pronounced them husband and wife, she would not believe it. She wanted it, though. She wanted that bond with Brian and felt very certain that he wanted it, too. She would be safe; he wouldn't leave her.

She'd stopped taking her pills, hesitant about it at first. It was the wrong time for her to get pregnant, she'd said. She was still having nightmares, and her days were filled with anxiety over the AMC program and the dilemma she was in—the person who could best help her and the program was someone whose name she could not utter without an attack of nausea.

Brian shot her arguments down, one by one, and she secretly welcomed the loving words of persuasion coming from his lips. She'd cried after they made love last night, the first time since she'd stopped the pills. She'd cried not out of regret or fear but because he would be leaving again this morning, and for the first time she felt as if she couldn't bear the separation. That was when he suggested she spend her evenings researching Zed Patterson's personal and professional life. Make sense of it, Brian had said. Get control over it.

She started with the *Congressional Directory*. Walter Zedekiah Patterson had been born in Harrisburg, Pennsylvania, on June 3, 1935. He'd been president of a social fraternity in college, then served two years as deputy sheriff of Jeremy before being elected to the office of mayor. He had a law degree from the University of Kentucky and was first elected to the Senate in 1977. He married Elizabeth Gregg on April 7, 1963, and was divorced from her in 1965, with no children. He married Penelope Carter in 1985 and had a son, Kevin, born 1987 and a daughter, Kasey, born 1989.

She had not pictured him with children. The thought disturbed her, and she stared at their names for a long time.

She scrolled through a series of newspaper articles about him. The articles covered legislation but gave her little insight into the man. There was one photograph, gritty and in profile, and she scrolled through it quickly. She had no interest in seeing Zed Patterson's face.

It was nearly closing time in the library, and she was so tired that she almost missed the headline in the Seattle paper: *Molestation Charge Filed Against Senator*. Sitting up straight in her chair, suddenly wide-awake, she hunted for a date on the paper. The article was from this past December, just two months ago.

She scanned it quickly the first time through.

The Patterson family had taken a baby-sitter along with them on their vacation to a Delaware beach the previous summer. The baby-sitter was a thirty-year-old woman who was accompanied by her eleven-year-old daughter. The girl was claiming that, on two occasions when she was not feeling well and had stayed home from the beach, Senator Patterson had come into her bedroom, sat on the edge of the bed, and fondled her. On a third occasion, he kissed her on the mouth when she was going to bed and no one else was around. The girl apparently told her mother about the incidents only the week before, after the mother had complained about the senator not paying her on time.

There was a direct quote from Patterson as he swept aside the girl's allegations: "This is a disturbed young girl who, already at the age of eleven, has been in trouble with the police for shoplifting as well as with the school system for truancy. My wife and I knew she had problems when we allowed our sitter to bring her with us to the beach, but her mother is an excellent child-care provider—beloved by, and very responsible with, our children—and we felt that perhaps by allowing this young girl to spend time with our family, we could help her. We all had an excellent week together at the beach. I'm perplexed and saddened by her allegations."

Acid rose in the back of Vanessa's throat. She read the article three more times, then hunted through other papers for more information on the girl and her accusations but found nothing. She made a copy of the article, ignoring the librarian who was telling her the library was closed and she would have to leave.

The instant she got home, she called Terri Roos, not even bothering to sit down or unbutton her coat.

"Are you aware that molestation charges were filed against Zed Patterson?" she asked Terri, pacing back and forth across the kitchen floor.

Terri yawned. "Yeah. By a very screwed-up-sounding kid."

"*Terri.*" She was appalled that Terri would use those words to describe a child. Terri's devotion to Zed Patterson was blinding her. "You knew this and didn't mention it to me?" she asked.

"He didn't do it, for Christ's sake."

"You mean, they cleared him?"

"Not yet. They had a preliminary hearing, and the trial's next month. But it's cut-and-dried, Vanessa. The kid is a very disturbed little girl he was trying to help."

Vanessa was squeezing the receiver in her hand. "Listen to yourself," she said. "You run a program for kids who were abused. You know, better than ninety-nine percent of the population, how kids can be discounted when they report this stuff. And you're willing to say he's innocent without even—"

"The man is a champion of victims' rights, Vanessa. He breaks his back for kids who have suffered real abuse. There's no way he could ever—"

"You don't know anything about him. You've seen ministers and teachers and lawyers and doctors who've done it." She waved her arm through the air. "For heaven's sake, Terri, wake up."

Terri was quiet for a long time. "Vanessa," she said finally, "listen to me. First, I don't appreciate being screamed at over the phone. Second, while you've been an incredibly hard worker and a driving force behind the network for a long time, the truth is that you've done jack-shit to help us out with the lobbying and other critical work that needs to be done now."

Vanessa leaned against the wall, eyes closed, while Terri continued.

"Now, I don't believe for half an instant that this man who breaks his back every day to protect the rights of women and kids could be guilty of hurting a child. But Vanessa—forgive me for this—even if he is guilty, he's a powerful force in the Senate, and we need him. Got that? I mean, what do you expect us to do? Let go of the one true advocate we have because some fucked-up kid said something negative about him?"

"Actually, yes," Vanessa said. "At least, I would hope you'd care enough to uncover the truth."

She hung up without waiting for Terri's reply and stood staring down at the phone. How many bridges had she burned with that call?

She glanced at the clock on the microwave. Ten-thirty. It was time for bed, but she made herself a cup of tea instead and carried it into the living room, where she settled down on the sofa with a stack of journals. She would not go to bed. Sleep would only bring her the carousel, and she knew she would fare better tonight if she didn't sleep at all.

24

Jeremy, Pennsylvania
1962

The big doors of the barn were closed much of the summer because Vincent was ill. Every once in a while, he'd manage to get out to the workshop, and Claire and Vanessa would join him there. But despite the coziness and the warm, familiar smells, the workshop was not quite the same as it used to be. Vincent didn't seem to want to talk, and the sound of his breathing often filled the air as he whittled or painted or glued pieces of wood together. He kept his pipe in his mouth, but he never smoked it anymore.

The young deputy sheriff was around a good part of the summer, helping Vincent with the mechanical workings of the carousel. Zed Patterson. "He's a genius at making that thing go," Vincent would say, and then he'd laugh. "He doesn't understand the meaning of a carousel, though, that boy. Says I should put some prettier music on the organ. What's he expect—a little Mozart? Chopin? Not on *my* carousel."

One day—it was not a Friday—Len Harte showed up unannounced. He walked into the kitchen where Claire and Mellie sat at the table hulling strawberries while Dora rolled pie dough on the kitchen counter.

Len walked straight across the kitchen floor to where Mellie sat and slapped her hard across the face. Mellie's head snapped to the side, and his hand left a mark on her cheek as red as the berries.

Dora gasped, and Claire dropped the strawberry she'd been hulling to the floor. She had never seen her father hit a person before. He did not even hit her or Vanessa when they deserved it. "My God, Len." Mellie stood up, her pale hand with its pink nails pressed against her cheek. "What's—"

"Where's Vanessa?" Len boomed. He looked directly at Claire, who drew her feet onto the chair and hugged her knees close to her body.

"Upstairs," Claire said, the word barely audible. Vanessa had been upstairs most of the morning. She'd said she wasn't feeling well.

Len stomped through the kitchen and pounded up the stairs. Mellie looked at her mother. "Why is he acting like this?" Mellie asked.

Dora was trying to press a wet cloth to Mellie's cheek, but Mellie brushed her hand away and started up the stairs after her husband, with Claire not far behind her.

From the stairwell, they could hear Vanessa crying in little hiccupy sobs.

"Now!" Len yelled at Vanessa. "You have three minutes."

At the top of the stairs, Mellie turned to Claire. "Go downstairs, darling. Everything's going to be all right. You just go down and wait with Grandma, and I'll get everything straightened out up here."

Mellie's cheek was still red, but she was smiling. She would fix whatever was wrong.

Claire walked slowly down the stairs. She sat at the table again while Dora ran the rolling pin this way and that over the dough on the counter. The dough was so flat that from where Claire was sitting, it looked as though Dora was rolling the pin on the counter itself. Dora talked about the state fair while Claire poked at the strawberries in the bowl. Dora spoke very loudly, as though she could overpower the screaming and shouting from upstairs and somehow prevent Claire from hearing it.

After pressing the paper-thin dough into the bottom of a pie plate, Dora pulled a coloring book and a box of crayons from the cupboard by the back door and set them on the table in front of Claire.

"Let me see you color something pretty," she said, and Claire obediently opened the book to a picture of two robins and a worm.

It wasn't long before footsteps thundered on the stairs and Len came flying through the kitchen. Claire looked up from her coloring only long enough to see that he was dragging Vanessa by the arm and carrying a suitcase with his free hand. Vanessa was crying so hard she was choking on her tears as her legs scrambled to keep up with his. Then Claire returned to her coloring, carefully staying inside the lines. She did not look up at her sister again. And she kept coloring as Mellie ran, screaming, after Len and Vanessa into the yard. That was not like Mellie. Claire squeezed the red crayon as she worked it around the robin's fat breast. Dora talked even louder. There would be a lot of strawberry pies entered in the state fair this year, she said. The weather had been just right for strawberries. And Claire colored, and as the screaming and yelling and little sobs grew to a crescendo, she held the picture up for her grandmother to see.

Len's car screeched away from the house and sped down the long driveway. It was a while before Mellie came back into the house. Her eyes were red, but she was no longer crying. Dora and Claire looked at her.

Mellie pulled one of the kitchen chairs close to Claire and sat down. She took both of Claire's hands in hers. "Your daddy and I have decided to live apart for a while," she said calmly.

What did that mean? "Are you divorced now?" Claire asked. She had a friend named Barbara whose parents were divorced. Barbara saw her father every weekend.

"Divorced!" Mellie laughed as though Claire had said something wildly amusing, and Claire smiled uncertainly. "Of course not. Sometimes a married couple needs to have some time apart. That's all. And Daddy wanted to take Vanessa with him so he wouldn't be too lonely. And you'll stay with me so I won't be lonely either."

Mellie stood up and lit a cigarette. She walked to the counter where Dora was laying strips of dough on top of the strawberries in the pie tin.

"I believe that's the most delicate pie crust I've ever seen you make, Mama," Mellie said. "You'll win first prize this year for sure."

25

Vienna

Each time Claire raised her eyes from the papers on her desk, the office swirled around her and the windows danced momentarily on the wall before snapping into place again. She could not shake this grogginess. Sleep had been fitful the night before, for both her and Jon, and they had spoken little on the drive into work. Were they both simply exhausted, or did he feel as she did—that once she'd told him she wanted to continue her friendship with Randy, there was little else to be said? He'd stroked her shoulder in the car this morning and rested his hand on hers, and she'd felt the sadness in his quiet touch, a strange sense of resignation that brought tears to her eyes. Jon was in pain, and she could not bear that she was the cause of it.

At ten o'clock, she had her third cup of coffee and met with two of the rehab therapists, Kelley Fielding and Ann Short, to talk about a problematic patient they shared. Kelley was much improved in dealing with her male patients. Her new sense of confidence was evident, and she practically carried the meeting by herself, which was just as well, since Claire's concentration was nonexistent.

Claire spent much of the meeting pondering her choices. She tried to imagine her life without Randy in it. It would be like cutting off her air supply. *Cut the theatrics*, she told herself. You have a wonderful husband and an incredible life and no financial problems and what the hell more do you want? Maybe Jon was right, and the memories would die a natural death if Randy were no longer around to stir them up in her. Maybe she could go back to the woman she used to be—the pre-Margot woman who could turn every problem into a challenge, every tense situation into a festival. Then again, maybe not. It was hard to imagine feeling good again. She never felt happy anymore, never content or at ease with herself. It was as if she were passing through a long hallway, and she had seen too much behind the doors to go back again unchanged. Randy held the key to the last door, but Jon sat in the center of the hall, his chair too big for her to circumvent without injury to herself or to him.

And what would her life be like without Jon in it? Unthinkable. Unbearable.

At noon, she carried their lunches into Jon's office. He looked surprised to see her as he raised his eyes from his work.

"Can I come in?" she asked.

"Of course." He moved his papers to the side of the desk and took the bag she held out to him. They were quiet as they poured bottles of apple juice into Styrofoam cups and opened their bowls of salad.

Jon squeezed a packet of dressing onto his salad and

glanced at her. "Margaret's accepted our invitation to be keynote speaker at the retreat," he said.

"Fantastic." She did not care who spoke. She didn't care if anyone spoke at all. In years past, the SCI Retreat had consumed them both. This year, it seemed like an event in someone else's tiresome dream.

"I've made a decision," she said.

Jon raised his eyebrows. "About?"

"I won't see Randy anymore." She looked at him. "I'll go to his restaurant this afternoon to tell him in person, but that will be it. I'll try very hard to put this past month or so behind me, and I'll think of some things we can do for fun. And plan a vacation, if you still want to do that. I love you, Jon. I'm sorry I've been so difficult lately."

Jon set down his fork. He wheeled his chair over to the door and shut it, then reached toward her. "Come here," he said.

She stood up and let him pull her onto his lap. Silently, he buried his head against her shoulder, and she felt his relief and his love. She held him close, struggling to share those emotions with him, but a numbness quickly settled over her.

Finally, he spoke. "How can I help you?" he asked.

"Be patient with me," she said. "I'm hoping the crazy little flashbacks will go away when Randy goes away, like you said."

"And if they don't, Claire, you could see a therapist."

"Maybe." She supposed that would be the next logical step, but she could not imagine trying to sift through those images with anyone other than Randy.

Jon rested his hand on her knee, above the wool of her skirt. "You know," he said slowly, "you're supposed to be a professional counselor, but I don't think you've ever really looked at yourself."

His words made her prickly. She got off his lap and took her seat by his desk again. "I've been in therapy before," she said.

"Yes, I know. But that was to learn how to deal with a disabled husband or cope with an adolescent daughter. You've never really looked at Claire."

She replaced the lid on her uneaten salad as he spoke, and by the time he was finished, she'd stood up. "I don't think I want to look at Claire right now." The alien angry tone in her voice startled her. Jon shouldn't want her to look at Claire, either. She might just discover that Claire was a little resentful, that she felt coerced into giving up something she wanted because Jon couldn't handle it. "I'm going to put on my happy face again—I've always been great at that, right? And then we can both pretend that none of this ever happened."

There was a red blotch on Jon's neck, and his hands were tight, white-knuckled, on the wheels of his chair. Claire slipped past him and pulled open the door. She walked through the maze of hallways, quickly, so that no one would think she had time to talk.

In her own office, she sat down and rested her head and arms on her desk. Well, that had not gone quite the way she'd planned. Jon was right. The times she'd been in therapy, she'd made sure to let the therapist know that she was all right—it was the people around her who merited her concern. *I am very happy. I have a wonderful, perfect marriage. My husband is sweet and generous and loving; my child is bright and beautiful. A little on the feisty side, but I'm glad she has that spirit. My childhood? I was surrounded by love and laughter.* Two different therapists had bought it. That's how convincing she had been, how deeply she'd believed the words herself at the time. She did not believe them any longer.

She had plenty of work to do, but she left the foundation without finishing her lunch and drove to the Fishmonger in Arlington.

The small parking lot was full, and she had to leave her car two blocks away. She unbuttoned her coat as she walked toward the restaurant, trying not to think too much about what she would say when she got there. She would let her words come out unrehearsed. Inside the crowded restaurant, she was greeted by the smell of fresh fish and lemon and mesquite. Knowing Randy and his taste for antiques and order, she was surprised by the rustic trappings of his restaurant. The wood ceiling was crossed with thick beams, and the tables were made of heavy rough-hewn wood. She could not picture him selecting the colorful paintings of tropical fish that hung on the walls.

The hostess, an attractive, dark-haired woman in her thirties, greeted Claire with a smile. "One?" she asked.

"I'm not here to eat," Claire said. "I'm looking for Randy Donovan."

"He's in his office. Who shall I say is looking for him?"

"Claire Harte-Mathias."

"Oh, *you're* Claire." The hostess set down the menus and shook Claire's hand with a grin. "We owe you."

"What do you mean?"

With her hand on Claire's arm, the hostess gently guided her away from the door, out of hearing range of other customers.

"Randy's been depressed ever since his marriage broke up. He'd come into work and mope around and not talk to anyone," she said. "He was so miserable that we all worried about him. Since he's been seeing you, he's been a different guy. He actually seems happier than he did when his marriage was okay. He's a lot more fun to work with now."

Claire forced a smile, taken aback by the phrase "since he's been seeing you," as though they were dating. "Could you tell him I'm here, please?"

"Sure will." The hostess walked to the rear of the restaurant and disappeared through a doorway. In a moment, she stepped back into the room, waving for Claire to join her. "Right through there." She pointed down the short hall.

Randy appeared at a door on the left, wearing a surprised smile. "Come in," he said.

Claire walked into a small cubicle and was suddenly surrounded by the dark antiques and paintings Randy loved. An enormous mahogany desk dominated the little office. Bookshelves lined two of the walls, and three Windsor chairs filled the remaining space. A thin spiral of steam rose from the cup of beige coffee on his desk. His unlit pipe rested next to the cup, and the soft, sweet smell of his tobacco enveloped her. She felt quick tears form in her eyes. It had been a mistake to come here. She should have told him by phone.

Randy shut the door and sat down behind the broad, gleaming desk, gesturing toward one of the chairs opposite him. She sat down herself, and he gave her a grin. "What a nice surprise," he said.

She drew in a breath. "I had to talk to you and didn't want to do it over the phone." She clutched her purse on her lap. "I can't see you anymore, Randy."

His smile faded, and he leaned toward her. "*Why?* Was it the kiss? I knew that was a mistake the minute I—"

She shook her head to stop him. "That's not it," she said. "It's Jon. And it's me. You were right to be upset that I lied to him. And I would have to keep lying to him to see you, because he feels threatened by you." She grimaced, lowering her eyes. She didn't want to make Jon look small, petty.

"Oh." Randy pressed his lips together. Then suddenly, he leaned forward in his chair, speaking quickly. "Well, first, let me say that you're right. I mean, you're making the right decision here. I admire you for it. But I sure as hell don't like it. And I . . ." He gave his coffee cup a little shove with the tips of his fingers, shaking his head. "I was getting in a little too deep, I think. Christ, I told you something I've never told anyone, something horrible, and . . . That's not it, is it?" He interrupted himself. "Is that why you don't want to see me? Because of what I did on the bridge?"

"Oh, no." She felt a wave of guilt. He had taken a risk by telling her his secret, and now she was discarding him. "I was happy you could tell me what really happened."

Randy ran the tips of his fingers up the side of the cup. "For the last few days or so, I knew that what I was feeling for you wasn't what I should be feeling." There was color in his cheeks above his beard, as if he'd just stepped in from the cold, and he seemed unable to look at her directly. "When LuAnne ran off with . . . her boyfriend, I made a deal with myself that I'd never get into that position," he said. "I'd never do to some other guy what that bastard was doing to me. And as I started . . . caring about you, I tried not to think about Jon. Or maybe I did think about him—about what I could give you that he couldn't."

Yes, she thought, remembering Randy's patient questioning about her memories. But Randy was probably referring to activities of a more physical nature. Like dancing. Or sex.

"You're right," she said. "And I'd be doing to Jon what LuAnne did to you."

He shook his head again. "I hadn't reached out to anyone in so long," he said. "You made it so easy. And you're right to pull back, because the truth is, it doesn't feel like a simple friendship to me anymore. When I kissed you last night ... Well, that was an accident. But if we're together, it would happen again, or at least I would want it to. I don't think I could be with you and not touch you, Claire. All I could think about after I left you last night was having you in my bed, making love to you."

His words took her by surprise. She knotted her hands together above her purse, pressing her fingers against one another until they hurt. She could feel the keen edge of her own need, although it was not the sort of physical desire he was referring to. Her need went deeper than that. She wanted to hold him, to be held, safe and warm and shielded from the rest of the world while she talked about the things that haunted her.

"I think I was falling in love with you," he said.

She studied his handsome face, the color still mottling his cheeks. "Well," she said softly, "I think our relationship was very important to both of us, but for different reasons. I loved you practically from the moment I met you. I don't mean a romantic sort of love. But you felt so comfortable and ... somehow familiar to me. It was as though I'd discovered a brother I'd never known I had."

"Oh." Randy's smile was rueful. "I guess it's best we part

ways then, Claire, 'cause I sure wasn't thinking of you as a sister."

She looked down at her purse, played with the clasp.

"What about the flashbacks you've been having?" Randy asked. "The memories?"

"I'm going to try to put them behind me," she said. "Go back to being the person I used to be."

"Ah, right." He suddenly broke into song. "*Life is a carousel, old chum*," he sang, his deep voice filling the room with the altered lyrics.

"Oh, Randy." Claire leaned on his desk, frustrated. "I felt like I was getting close to something important. It scared the shit out of me, but I think I was really gaining on it."

"I think you were, too. And maybe someday you'll be ready to meet it head-on and kick it in the teeth."

There was a knock on his door. The hostess opened it enough to peek inside.

"Sorry to interrupt, Randy," she said, "but you're needed in the kitchen."

Randy nodded, and Claire stood up reluctantly as the hostess closed the door again.

Randy stood too but remained behind his desk. "I'll miss you," he said.

"And I'll miss you." She reached for the doorknob.

"Jon is a lucky son of a bitch."

She gave him a lifeless smile. "Thanks," she said, then turned to leave the office.

Outside the restaurant, she walked toward her car, the cool air nipping at her face.

Mrs. Rustadt.

She stopped in the middle of the sidewalk. The image

was startlingly vivid. The woman was bending over a desk, helping a child with his work. Her fifth-grade teacher. Gray hair. Thick glasses. She'd wear the same dress for five days in a row. And she'd gotten angry—*furious* at Claire once for sharpening her pencils during quiet time.

Claire wanted to run back to the restaurant to tell Randy she'd remembered one of her teachers. He would be pleased, ask her questions, draw her out. But it would not be fair to him—not fair to either of them—and so she forced the memory to the back of her mind and continued walking toward her car.

26

Those first few days in the car, traveling across the country with her father, Vanessa could not stop crying. Even in the small hotel rooms in the strange towns that quickly began to blur together, she clung to her edge of the bed and wept until sleep freed her from pain. The pain, both physical and emotional, was raw and tender and new to her. Nothing in her life had prepared her for it. Len, preoccupied with his own suffering, could not even guess at the depth of his daughter's anguish. If he'd known, he would have cared. He was not an unkind man. He was simply caught in the circle of his own dreams and disappointments.

When they were on the road, Vanessa waited for the police to stop them. Surely Mellie had alerted them to the fact that she was missing. But police cars passed them by as if her father were simply another parent out with his child. In the hotels at night, she waited for Mellie herself to show up and reclaim her daughter. No one came, though, and Vanessa struggled with the hurt and confusion. A good mother would try to find her daughter if she cared enough about her.

Len talked almost nonstop during those early days on the road, mainly about his fury toward Mellie. He said things about Mellie that Vanessa did not understand or believe or want to hear. He smoked cigarette after cigarette and punched the buttons on the radio, crying at times himself, almost like a child. And he was as helpless as a newborn on those nights when Vanessa awakened from sleep in their hotel room, wild-eyed and screaming in the throes of a nightmare. He would try to hold her, to talk her through it, but she would throw off his arms, leap from the bed, and race into the bathroom, where she would remain for the rest of the night. It might have been a mistake to bring her with him. He adored this little girl, but his decision to take her had been rooted more in revenge than in love.

They both grew calmer as the days and the miles put Jeremy far behind them. Vanessa gradually stopped crying. She tried not to think about Mellie, and she tried to forget what Claire had done. A few times she even sang along with the music on the radio, and Len talked about how he was going to "make a killing" on the West Coast. He talked about "investments" and meeting up with friends who had "big ideas." He and she would have money, he told his daughter. Toys and clothes for her, cars and women for him. When he said the word "women," he wore a smile Vanessa had never seen on his face before.

It wasn't until they reached Seattle that he finally apologized to her. Seattle was in the midst of the World's Fair, and Len took her up in the new revolving tower that stood high above the city. From there they could look down at the world below and practically map out their new life.

"I needed some of my family with me," he said. "I would have taken both you and Claire, but the truth is, your sister—" he shook his head. "She's too much like your mother. You got your mother's looks, but Claire got her . . . " He threw up his hands, as though he could think of no words to describe what Claire had inherited from Mellie. "You've always been easier for me to get along with," he continued. "I feel bad, though, that I pulled you and Claire apart."

Far in the distance, Vanessa could see the hazy shape of mountains. "That's all right, Daddy," she said. She kept her eyes on the peaks so she wouldn't see her father's look of surprise. He thought he had stolen her from her family and the farm. He didn't know that he had rescued her. And she would never tell him.

27

Charlottesville, Virginia

Jon turned off the highway onto the road leading to Monticello. Beside him, Claire was singing along with the tape player. "Mr. Tambourine Man."

She was singing loudly, badly. It was hard to say who had the worse voice—Claire or Dylan. Didn't matter. She drowned Dylan out, reciting every obscure verse, and Jon reveled in the unbridled happiness in her voice.

Monticello was on Claire's list of things to do. They'd been alternating between his list and hers during the past week and a half, starting with a weekend in Ocean City, where they'd encountered a hail-storm on the boardwalk and spent most of their time in their hotel room eating and making love. Next, they visited the aquarium in Baltimore, then attended a play at the Kennedy Center. He had to admit that some of their fun had a forced air about it. Their relationship had taken a hit in the past couple of months, and it was bound to be a while before they settled back into their old, comfortable ease with one another. Almost two weeks had passed since she'd announced she would no longer see Randy, and they had packed those weeks so full of activity that there was little time left over to wallow in sadness or regret. They'd even taken a couple of days off from work, which, whenever he stopped to think about it, would throw him into a panic. There was so much to be done before the retreat.

Claire was really trying. A casual observer would probably think she was back to her old self. Touched by her resolve, Jon tried to ignore the heaviness in her gait and her lackluster appetite. He did not comment on her uncharacteristic teariness after they made love or the fact that major portions of the play they'd seen had gone over her head. She was not carrying her share of the work at the foundation, either. He hadn't said anything to her about it, but he knew that she was far behind schedule on her retreat responsibilities.

Sometimes, lately, she'd get up in the middle of the night. She never used to do that—she'd always been a sound sleeper. He would ask her if she was okay. She would say she was fine, and he would accept her answer. Should he challenge her on it? Good old Randy would have. Screw Randy. Jon blamed him for this whole mess. That was easiest. Neatest. As far as he knew, none of the people who were truly responsible were still alive to blame.

But Claire was better in other ways. A bit better every day. He didn't know if she was still experiencing the odd visual images she'd discussed with Randy, and he was not about to ask her. If she was no longer having those intrusive flashbacks and he mentioned them, they might start up again.

She was still singing "Mr. Tambourine Man" as she held

his chair steady for him while he transferred into it from the car. She was even dancing a little, and she bent down to hug him from behind, kissing the top of his head.

They joined a small tour group inside the foyer of Thomas Jefferson's home. Their guide was a graceful woman with a wealth of knowledge, and Jon was quickly absorbed by tales of Jefferson's intellect, wide-ranging interests, and a genius that bordered on the eccentric. They passed through his library and parlor and dining room, finally reaching his peculiar bedroom. The room was divided in two by a bed squeezed between two walls. An intriguing clock hung on the wall at the foot of the bed. Jon started to point it out to Claire, but she was staring at something, her chin tilted upward, her hand pressed to her mouth. He followed her gaze to the high wall above the bed, where three glassless oval windows opened into darkness. A storage closet was behind the windows, the guide was saying, looking up at the odd openings herself. Jefferson had stored his out-of-season clothing there.

Claire's face had turned gray, and Jon felt sweat break out on his chest. There were a few people between them, and he could not easily get to her with his chair. She glanced at him, nothing short of terror in her eyes, then quickly passed behind the guide and out of the room.

The guide stopped her lecture midsentence. "Ma'am?" she called after Claire, but they could hear Claire's footsteps hurrying down the hall.

Jon wheeled out of the room after her. From behind him, he could hear the guide opening a door, telling someone that a member of her group needed to be escorted from the building.

Claire had made it only as far as the library before getting sick. She was leaning against the wall, tears running freely down her cheeks. Another guide, this one a middle-aged, gray-haired man, was already at her side by the time Jon reached her. Claire gave Jon a look of stark humiliation, then grabbed the guide's arm. "I'm so sorry," she said. "I can't believe I . . . I couldn't find my way—"

"That's all right." The guide looked down at Jon. "You're her husband?"

Jon nodded, his eyes on Claire. "Are you okay?" he asked.

Claire nodded, swallowing hard. She was breathing rapidly. She did not look okay at all, and he hoped the guide could get her out of the house before she was sick again.

The man took Claire's elbow and led her toward the foyer, Jon following behind them. "These things happen," the guide said kindly. "And it's just one of those sturdy carpets used for foot traffic. Not an antique. Nothing we can't clean."

They had reached the front door. There were steps leading down into the yard. Jon would not be able to get out that way.

"I have to go around to the lift, Claire. Will you be all right out there?"

Claire nodded, then headed for the stairs, the door swinging closed behind her. The guide looked down at Jon. "Stomach flu?" he asked.

"No. No, I think it's something else."

The man studied him quizzically. He should have said it was the flu and left it at that.

It took him a few minutes to find the lift and wheel himself around the outside of the house to the bench where Claire was sitting. She looked at him sheepishly. "I feel like an imbecile." Her voice was weak. Jon wanted to turn back the clock to those hours in the car when she'd been singing merrily along with Bob Dylan.

"What happened back there?" he asked.

She shrugged. "I made a fool out of myself, that's what."

He leaned forward to hold her hand. "It was warm in there," he said. "Stuffy. Was that it? Do you feel better now?"

She pulled her coat tighter across her chest with her free hand. There were tears in her eyes as she stared out across the grounds.

Jon sighed, giving in to the inevitable. "It wasn't just the stuffiness, huh?"

She shook her head. "No."

"I love you, Claire," he said. "Talk to me." He sounded remarkably strong, but his bravado was a facade. As false as her good cheer had been these past couple of weeks.

"The same stuff," she mumbled.

"You mean, you had some sort of . . . flashback in there?"

She nodded, gnawing her lower lip, tightening her grip on his hand. "Those oval windows," she said.

"What about them?"

"I don't know. They just . . . freaked me out."

"I'm sorry," he said. "This is the first time in a while, though, isn't it? I mean, you haven't had those flashbacks since . . . for a couple of weeks, right?"

She looked directly at him. "I have them all the time," she said softly.

"You do?" he asked. "Are they still those bits of memory that don't make any sense?"

She nodded, and he knew she was waiting for him to ask her more. What did she see, what did she feel when those memories cut her down? She *wanted* him to ask. She was begging for it with her eyes, with the coiled stiffness in her hand beneath his. But he was not equipped to ask those questions. Or perhaps he was too well equipped. Maybe that was the problem.

"Will you see a therapist, Claire? Please?"

For a moment, she simply stared at him. "All right," she said finally, and he could see the disappointment in her face as she turned away from him, as she pulled her hand from under his and slipped it into her pocket.

She stood up and they moved in silence down the path toward the car. He couldn't blame her for her disappointment. She had given him the chance not only to recapture their old intimacy but to build on it, lift it higher.

And he had let her down.

28

Vienna

"So, you're used to fixing things," Debra Parlow said to Claire, "and this woman on the bridge was one of the few things you've encountered in your life that you simply couldn't fix."

Claire nodded from her seat on the edge of the sofa in Debra's office. She'd been talking to the therapist for ten minutes, and her anxiety was mounting rather than abating. She had her eye on the office door. She had asked Pat Wykowski for the name of a therapist without telling her who the referral was for, and Pat had recommended Debra highly. "She's very skillful and warm," she'd said. Claire did not doubt Pat's assessment, but it didn't matter. She could not talk easily about this topic to anyone. With one exception.

"And ever since that night, you haven't been able to concentrate on your work?"

"That's right," Claire said. If she were not half the team of Harte-Mathias, she would have been fired by now. She was of no greater value at home, either. The laundry was piling up, and she could not remember the last time she'd cooked a meal or made more than a quick run through the grocery store.

"And you mentioned vertigo?" Debra said.

"Yes. Ever since that night. It's not constant. Not too bad. Sometimes I feel like I'm falling, but it doesn't last very long. That's not the worst part."

"What is the worst part?"

"I've been having these little flashbacks—at least that's what I call them. A friend suggested they might be memories from my past. But maybe they're a fabrication, I don't know." She looked at Debra for confirmation of that theory, which did not come.

"What are they like?" Debra asked.

Claire shook her head quickly. "I don't think I can talk about them. Not yet. Not specifically."

"All right. How about generally?"

"Well, they're odd. Sometimes they pop up out of the blue. Other times they're triggered by something. The worst happened the other day at Monticello. I saw something there—just an architectural feature that disturbed me for some reason—and I actually threw up in the house."

Debra wore a frown. "That must have been very embarrassing."

"Well, yes, but it's over and done with."

"Is it?"

Claire started to nod, then made a face. "Well, though, now I feel nervous it will happen again. It's unpredictable, and what if I'm in a meeting or the grocery store or—?"

"Or in this office?"

She felt her cheeks redden. This was so childish. "Yes," she said.

Debra offered a sympathetic smile. "The restroom is right outside my door. The trash can is inches from your right leg."

"Okay. Thank you." Claire tried sitting back more fully in the sofa but succeeded only for a second before returning to her perch on the edge of the cushion. She wished she could relax.

"So, do these memories seem tied in some way to events from your past?"

"'Memories' is really the wrong word for them," Claire said. "They're more like little visual fragments, and I can't seem to connect them to anything that's ever happened to me." She looked out the window. There was a large, full weeping willow in her line of vision. "At first I wished they would go away. Just stop. But it's obvious they're not going to, and now I really want to understand them. To pursue them, wherever they want to take me. It terrifies me, though. The unknown. I want to know and I don't want to know." She doubted she would ever be able to pursue those images with Debra Parlow. She was digging her fingers into the seat cushion, ready to push herself up and out of the room.

"It makes sense that you feel that way." Debra shifted position in her chair. "But memories we've blocked for one reason or another don't usually come to us until we're ready for them."

"Well, I'm not sure I'm ready." Claire described the dream she'd had the night before. She'd been standing in her kitchen, and all the cupboard doors were open, the space inside black, like the black behind the oval windows in Thomas Jefferson's bedroom. She'd walked around the kitchen with a determined stride, slamming the cupboard doors shut, one by one, saying, *no, no, no.*

Debra looked intrigued. "What are you afraid you'll learn if you really take a look at those flashbacks?"

Claire studied her hands in her lap. What was she afraid of learning? That her life was not what it seemed? That her childhood had been bad? Her marriage was bad? "I'm not sure," she said.

"Was there any abuse in your past, Claire? Anything you recall from your childhood?"

She raised her eyebrows in surprise. "Sexual, you mean?"

Debra shrugged.

"No. Not sexual or physical or verbal. Nothing. And the flashbacks are not at all abusive in nature."

Blood on white porcelain.

Claire jerked on the sofa, raising her hand as if to bat the image away. She quickly composed herself, lowering her hand to her lap. "I just saw . . . " She shook her head.

"An image?"

"Yes. I don't want to talk about it. Sorry. I don't mean to be evasive." If Randy were here, she could talk.

"That's all right." Debra was studying her closely. "What do you remember about growing up?" she asked.

Claire looked out the window again. "That it was pretty wonderful," she said. "I spent a lot of time on my grandparents' farm, and it was great. Although"—she looked at Debra—"there are things that happened to me, and I know from a factual standpoint they must have been unpleasant—like my parents divorcing—but I have no memory of them."

"Are your parents still living?"

"No."

"How long ago did they die?"

"Both of them died around ten years ago, I guess."

"And how did they die?"

"I don't know how my father died. We were estranged at the time. My mother had lung cancer."

"And you were close to your grandparents?"

"Very. Especially my grandfather. He was a carousel horse carver and fun to be around."

"Wow, I can imagine." Debra's eyes lit up. She asked some questions about the carousel and her grandfather, and Claire answered them matter-of-factly. She knew that Debra was using the topic to put her at ease, to gain rapport. She wished the ploy were working.

"How old were you when your grandparents died?" Debra asked.

"I was ... " Claire was suddenly aware of a hole in her memory. She pressed her fingers to her temples, eyes closed, struggling to pull an answer from the void. Finally she looked up at Debra. "I have absolutely no idea," she admitted.

Debra wore a puzzled expression. "Can you remember *how* they died?"

Again, Claire searched the void, and this time found a small particle of truth. "My grandmother died in her sleep," she announced.

"Of?"

Claire shrugged. "Old age? I don't know. Wait. We stopped going to the farm when I was ... thirteenish? So she must have died around then."

"And your grandfather? Do you recall when and how he died?"

"He . . ." She made her visit to the void brief this time. She shrugged. "Sorry."

"Any siblings?"

She told her about Vanessa, and Debra's frown deepened as she listened to Claire talk about their father's stealing Vanessa away. Debra asked several questions about Len Harte, and Claire answered them as best she could. It was true, though, that there was a great deal she didn't know.

"And how about your husband," Debra asked. "Can you talk to him about the flashbacks?"

Claire hesitated. Slowly, she shook her head. "I'm not comfortable talking about them to him, and he's not comfortable hearing about them. But . . ." Claire gnawed on her lip. "There's a man. He's the brother of the woman on the bridge." She described her connection to Randy. "For some reason, he's the only person I feel I can talk to about what's going on. I feel completely safe with him."

Debra shifted in her seat again, this time with a complete change in posture that suggested she was thinking: "Aha! So *that's* what's really going on!"

"It's not romantic." Claire tried to nip the therapist's specious theory in the bud.

"I see." Debra asked a few questions about Randy, questions about Jon. Claire tried to describe her love for her husband and the tender sense of security she felt with Randy, but she soon realized that nothing she said was going to change the therapist's new course of reasoning.

This was useless, she thought, sinking low into the couch. If she could not make Debra understand her feelings, if she could not even imagine letting one of her flashback images leak into this room without the need to bat it away, what good was this going to do? She remembered her dream. Slamming shut the cupboard doors. *No, no, no.*

"It would probably be best if you had a couple of sessions a week," Debra said. "I know it's frightening right now, Claire, but we'll make this office a safe place for you to let your memories out."

Claire could think of nothing Debra could do to make this office feel safe. "How about once a week?" she countered, and it took her more than a few minutes to convince the therapist to accept her proposal.

She told Jon the truth that night: She had felt extreme discomfort in Debra Parlow's office. She would go back, she said, but she had serious doubts that she would ever be able to solve her problems there.

"If it doesn't work out with her, then we'll find you another therapist," Jon said with the simple optimism that she herself had once possessed in grand measure.

The morning after her session with Debra, Claire awakened to the sound of sirens and hammering and shouting and the throbbing, persistent strains of an organ.

Let me call you sweetheart.

She tried to scream, but the sound was locked in her throat. She grabbed Jon's arm, shaking him, and when he did not wake up, she bolted from the bed in a panic. The room spun as she ran across the floor and into the hallway.

In the family room, she pulled the afghan from the sofa, wrapping it around herself as she sat down and reached for the phone. She dialed Randy's number, the sirens still in her head. Her heart pounded against her ribcage, and she leaned back on the couch, hoping she would not get sick.

"Hello?" Randy's voice was muffled by sleep. What time was it? She had no idea.

"I woke you. I'm sorry, but I had a nightmare, or maybe a memory. I don't know." She was crying, and only then realized she'd been crying from the moment she'd opened her eyes that morning. Maybe she'd even been crying in her sleep. "It's terrible, Randy. I can still—"

"Slow down," Randy said. "Take a deep breath." His voice was low and calm and warm, and she clutched the phone with both hands and tried to settle her breathing. Her heart was going to leap from her chest.

"There were ambulance sirens," she said. "First they were in the distance, then coming closer and closer. And 'Let Me Call You Sweetheart' was playing. It was organ music, like on the carousel. And they were hammering crates closed—big wooden crates, and—"

"Who's 'they'?"

Claire closed her eyes to try to recapture the image, but instead she saw a towel hanging on a towel rack, the wall behind it tiled in white. The towel was also white, but stained with blood. Claire leaped from the couch as if she could run from the picture in her mind.

"Oh, God, Randy," she said, "make them go away! The flashbacks just keep coming. Or maybe I'm making them up. They're too crazy to be real. But if I'm making them up, then I must be crazy."

"Whoa, Claire." Again the calm, deep voice filled her head, and she stood still in the middle of the room. "Did you figure out who was hammering the crates?"

"No." She pressed one hand to her forehead. "It was just a sound. The hammering."

"How do you know it was a crate?"

"I just do."

"What else?"

"Someone was screaming."

"Male or female?"

"Female, I think." The vertigo struck suddenly, and she sat down on the couch again, swallowing hard. "I can't think about it anymore. I have to stop."

"What makes you think the sirens were from an ambulance? Not a fire truck or the police?"

"Randy, I can't now! I'm so dizzy, and Jon could wake up any second." She was shaking. She stretched the afghan to cover her feet. "I wish you were right here next to me," she said. "I think I could do it then—think about the dream."

There was a long silence. Her heart thudded dully in her ears.

"What do you want me to say, Claire?" Randy asked finally. "I would love to be right there next to you. I haven't been able to stop thinking about you. But we can't see each other without feeling guilty, and I don't want that."

"I know," she said softly, glad he was willing to provide the voice of reason she seemed to have lost.

"I'm sorry you're still going through all of this," he said. "I was hoping Jon was right and that once I was out of your life, you'd feel better."

"I don't think I'm ever going to feel better until I know why this is happening to me. I started seeing a therapist, but I'm afraid to talk to her about the flashbacks. I feel like something terrible will happen if I start talking about them without you around. Like I may completely lose any grip I still have on my sanity, which isn't much anymore. Oh Randy, how can I see you? I don't want to lie, but Jon will never understand."

"Does he know what you're going through?"

"A little. Jon wants to help me, but he just isn't capable of it. Maybe if I begged him to listen to me, he would, but the truth is, I only feel able to really get into the details with you."

She drew in a breath. Her heartbeat had finally slowed down. The trembling had stopped, and she didn't think she could conjure up the sound of sirens or hammering or music if she tried. "I'm better now," she said. "I should go. Jon will be up soon."

Randy didn't speak right away. "I don't want to let you off the phone," he said finally.

And she didn't want him to. "If I can come up with a way to see you, would you be willing?"

"Of course. But not if it involves a lie."

"No, I won't lie anymore." She thought she heard a sound in the hallway. "I have to go."

"All right, Claire. Please take care of yourself."

She hung up the phone but stayed on the sofa, wrapped in the afghan, clinging to the small sense of calm Randy had given her, wondering how she could hold on to it for the rest of the day.

Jon had awakened abruptly as Claire fled from the bedroom. She had not taken the time to pull on a robe, and the gray morning light washed over her bare skin as she ran. She was crying, gasping for breath, as if something were chasing her. He'd called her name, but she didn't seem to hear him, and he'd gotten out of bed and into his chair to follow her.

From the hall, he'd heard her on the phone and knew immediately whom she had called. He'd sat and listened, eavesdropping shamelessly. The sound of her crying cut through him. He had never heard such desperation in her voice before, such panic. The fear she had allowed him to see these past couple of months was nothing compared to the real terror churning inside her. She was pouring it out to Randy Donovan, though. Talking to Randy, her guard was down; she held nothing back. *Jon wants to help me, but he isn't capable of it.*

She was right. He sat quietly in the hallway, waiting for her to hang up. He was steeling himself, trying to find a sort of courage he'd never needed before. He was going to help Claire the only way he could.

She hung up the phone, and Jon wheeled into the family room. Claire was wrapped in the afghan, her legs folded beneath her on the couch, one shoulder bare. Her face was pale and pinched with the guilty look of a child caught in some forbidden act. He felt a painful rush of love for her, and although he wanted to pull his chair close, he stayed in the doorway. It would be easier that way.

He could almost see her mind racing as she tried to create an explanation for why she was up so early, wrapped in a blanket on the sofa.

"I had a terrible dream," she said. "I panicked and called Randy before I stopped to think about it. I'm sorry." She had obviously meant what she'd said about not lying anymore.

"I heard the call," he said.

"You did?" Alarm sharpened her features.

"Yes. All of it."

Her tears started again, and she pressed a fist to her mouth. Still, he made no move toward her.

"Claire," he said, his voice strong, "I want you to leave."

"Leave? What do you mean?"

"I mean, I want you to leave the house. Leave me."

"*What?*"

"Then you can see Randy as often as you like without—"

"No!" She put her bare feet on the floor and leaned forward. "That's not what I want."

"Apparently that's what you need, though. You just said that. I heard you."

"Jon—"

"You're right. I haven't been able to help you with this. I'm very sorry . . . " He felt the threat of tears and struggled to hold them back. "I'm too close to it to help you."

"You've helped me, Jon. You've—"

"I want you out." He cut her off, suddenly sick of the way she always changed reality to make problems disappear.

Claire sat back. She licked her lips. The crease between her eyebrows was deep. "You can't be serious."

"Yes, I am. You cannot stay here." His hands were tight on the wheels of his chair. "I don't want you here."

"But you . . . how would you manage?"

He drew in a sharp breath. Her words made him angry, and the anger felt good. "I'm not a child!" he said. "I need a wife, not a fucking caretaker!"

"Don't yell!" She lifted one hand from the afghan to tug anxiously at her hair. "Please don't be angry. I didn't mean anything. I just . . . I can't leave you. It doesn't make any sense for me to—"

"It makes more sense than going on the way we have been, with you wanting to be with someone else."

She opened her mouth to protest, but he cut her off again.

"Don't deny it, Claire. You want him; I'm giving you permission to have him."

"It's not like that," she snapped. "It's not what you think. It's *never* been what you think." Her anger was raw and unfamiliar. "I had the first real male friend in my adult life and you took him away from me."

"So, now I'm giving him back to you." He started to turn his chair around. "And I'm getting dressed for work. You've got all day to pack up and get out, but please be gone by the time I get home."

"What do you mean, I've got all day? I have to work, too."

"Forget work. You haven't been doing any anyhow. I've done ninety-five percent of the work on the retreat."

She looked down at the floor. He knew she could not argue with him on that.

"I know I haven't been able to concentrate very well at the office," she said, "but I still want to come in and—"

"*No*, Claire," he said, unnerved by the thought of her there. "I don't want to see you, all right? Get it? I don't want to have to look at you in the morning after you've been sleeping with Randy all night." His voice broke then, and the tears he'd been fighting spilled over his cheeks.

Claire was instantly on her feet. "Jon, please!" She grabbed his arm, but he pushed her away. His fingers caught in the weave of the afghan, accidentally pulling it from her breasts, and he let go quickly. He pressed his palms hard on his thighs.

She sat back on her heels, clutching the afghan across her chest. "Sleeping with Randy is not what I want." Her voice was tiny, defeated. He could barely hear her. "I only want to feel better. I want to feel happy, like I used to."

He wished she would yell at him again. Her sadness made this harder, and he had to force himself to turn his chair around and wheel back into the bedroom.

Once in the bedroom, he stared at the closed door for several minutes before starting to get dressed. The useless muscles in his thighs began to spasm as he pulled on his pants, and once or twice he had to blink to clear his vision. He thought of Claire in the family room. Maybe she was calling Randy. Or maybe she was crying, still struggling to make some sense of his order to leave. That had been the hardest thing he'd ever done. Hard and painful and filled with risk. But as he brushed his teeth and combed his hair and studied the lines around his eyes in the mirror, he felt a growing certainty that he'd been right to do it.

29

McLean

It was raining, a cold rain that matched the chill in her heart. She drove through the dark streets of McLean toward Randy's town house, her suitcase in the backseat. What were you supposed to pack when you had no idea where you were going? She'd taken only enough for a few days, enough to keep her afloat until she had a clearer sense of what she would do next.

She figured she could stay at Randy's for a night or two, then she would have to find a place of her own. What that meant, she couldn't say. She could not think beyond the moment.

Randy had sounded stunned when she'd called him late that morning to tell him Jon had asked her to leave. She heard him trying to contain his pleasure, worried he might be gaining something at the expense of someone else. He asked concerned and sincere questions about Jon. Had he been thinking clearly or simply acting on the emotion of the moment? Did he seem terribly distraught? Would he be all right without her?

She shared his concern and even called Jon around noon to ask him if he had reconsidered.

"Absolutely not," Jon had said. "I want you out. And please don't call me again today."

She'd hung up the phone with a sense of freedom edged with fear, and with tearful gratitude toward her husband. This was a gift he was giving her. She knew it, and she was certain he knew it as well.

Still she worried about leaving him alone. She bought groceries, stocking the pantry and refrigerator. She made and froze two casseroles and a huge pan of lasagna. A long note was waiting for him on the kitchen table, reminding him to take his medication, telling him where she kept the emergency numbers, the spare keys. She vacuumed the entire house and changed the sheets on the bed.

The flashbacks had been constant while she worked in the house, but she blocked them, shutting the cupboard door on them over and over again. Soon. Soon she would be with Randy and could let those images take her wherever they pleased.

"I'll have to find a place to stay," she'd said to Randy on the phone. She'd thought of saying "a place to live," but that sounded too permanent, too final.

"You can stay here tonight," Randy offered. "I have a guest room. I'll help you think about what to do after that."

Her car skidded as she turned into the parking lot of his town house. Not thinking, she pressed the brake, and the rear of the car fishtailed behind her. She lifted her hands from the wheel, abdicating control, and was almost surprised when the car came to rest safely in the center of the lot. She took a deep breath and resumed driving, parking close to 167.

The rain had stopped. It was after seven, and the parking lot light illuminated the white brick as it had on her last visit to the town house. She took her suitcase from the seat and marched toward the house and up the front steps, where she lifted the heavy brass knocker and let it fall.

After a moment, Randy opened the door. He was wearing a red flannel shirt and khaki pants. His smile was tentative.

"Well," she said. "I'm here."

He hesitated a moment before wordlessly pulling the door open, and she stepped inside to feel the dark warmth of the room embrace her. Randy set her bag on the floor next to the staircase, then, without saying a word, moved forward to hold her. She closed her eyes, wrapping her arms around him, breathing in his scent. His heart beat against her breast. It was a strong, solid beat, and she could almost feel it pick up speed as he pressed his hands to her back, his touch a little fevered. She pulled away gently, and his hands fell to his sides.

"I've made dinner," he said. His cheeks were flushed. "You haven't eaten yet, have you?"

"No, though I'm not sure I can." Other than the scraps she'd nibbled on as she put together the casseroles, she had not eaten all day.

His kitchen surprised her with its bright white cabinets, but in all other ways it reflected Randy's taste. Gleaming copper pots and utensils hung suspended from the ceiling; the spice racks ran the length of one counter, and the spices were arranged alphabetically. The floor was hardwood—dark oak—and a massive butcher block island rested in the exact center of the room. Everything was in order. Not a crumb on the counter.

The copper glow of the pots and pans filled the room with a soft light. Randy had made chicken in wine sauce. She surprised herself by having two servings, and she smiled at him across the table as she ate, aware of the comfort she felt with him, comfort that had been missing in her life during the two weeks she'd cut herself off from him.

"I made the bed in the guest room," he said when they were nearly finished eating. "I'd much prefer that you spent the night with me, but I seem to recall a comment about me being your long-lost brother, or whatever." He gave her a rueful smile. "I don't think sleeping with me is what you're after, unfortunately."

"The guest room will be perfect," she said.

Climbing the stairs to the second floor, she felt a wave of homesickness, which she quickly swept from her mind. She got a glimpse of Randy's bedroom as she walked through the upstairs hall toward the guest room. His room was dimly lit from some unseen source. A sleigh bed, unmade but not disheveled, curved gracefully along the far wall. The sheets and comforter were a green paisley print that seemed to fit both the room and Randy. Dark. So dark she could barely see the pattern in the fabric from the distance of the hallway.

The guest room was also bathed in pale light from the yellow-shaded lamp on the night table. The bed here was brass; the spread, a patchwork of creams and peaches. She set her suitcase on a trunk in the corner.

"Do you need anything?" Randy asked from the doorway.

"No," she said. "This is great."

She felt sleepy as she climbed into the high bed, but the

moment her head touched the pillow, the sirens and hammering and screaming filled her ears again. She sat up, startled, and the sounds began to fade. Drawing back the gauzy curtain at the window next to the bed, she stared out at the parking lot. The wet macadam was shiny with moonlight.

Once her breathing had returned to normal, she lowered herself beneath the covers again. Thoughts of Jon tried to slip into her consciousness, but she fought them off by naming the states in alphabetical order, then the capitals. She had nearly bored herself to sleep when the sound of hammering struck again. The bloody towel blew across her vision like the sail of an ill-fated ship. This time, she jumped out of bed, the strange room twirling around her as she pulled on her robe, and she shivered as she slipped down the hall to Randy's room.

His door was open, his room lit now by moonlight. She knocked on the open door, feeling foolish, childish.

Randy rolled onto his back. "Claire?" he asked.

She hugged her arms across her chest. "Who else would bug you in the middle of the night because she's seeing things that aren't there. And hearing things. The sirens and—"

Randy threw back the comforter. He got out of bed, reaching for the robe draped over the footboard. He had nothing on, and the moonlight captured the lines of his body in sharp detail. Claire turned her head away.

He was wearing a blue robe as he walked from the room. "Come on." He nodded toward the end of the hall, and she followed him into a small dark room where she could just make out a sofa and some large piece of exercise equipment.

They sat down on the sofa together, and he put his arm around her.

"Tell me," he said.

She raised her feet to the sofa, covered them with her robe. "I keep hearing those sounds from that dream this morning," she said. "And seeing this bloody towel."

"What bloody towel?" The day's growth of beard on his chin lightly scratched her temple.

"I don't know. It's white. It's hanging on a towel rack and it's . . ." For some reason, the towel made her think of Italy. "You know, I don't think this fits into the other flashbacks. I think maybe this is something I saw when I was in Italy one time. I have no memory of ever seeing it there, but I don't have a memory of anything else either, so why should that be any different?"

"What makes you think you saw it in Italy?"

"I don't know. Just a feeling."

"Maybe it's tomato sauce and not blood."

That made her laugh; it was such a wondrously hopeful thought. Perhaps all her fragments of memory were no more than the distorted creations of a mind that had suffered too much excitement on the Harpers Ferry bridge.

"I'm still curious about the hammering," he said. "Who's doing it? And how do you know it's a crate they're hammering?" He questioned her for a while, and she tried to let the sounds slip into her mind again, but they were subtle, barely there, as if they had run their course for the night. They offered her little in the way of answers.

"I'm not hiding from the sounds," she said, more to herself than to Randy. "But I don't think I can force them."

She closed her eyes as silence filled the room. The scent of pipe tobacco was mixed with something else in here, something pleasing. A scented candle, perhaps. Or pot-pourri.

"Claire." Randy spoke quietly, and she turned her head so she could see him.

"Yes?"

He ran his hand slowly across her face, then lifted her chin with his fingers as he kissed her. The kiss was slow. Dizzyingly slow, and it stopped only to start again. Claire barely felt it, though. Her mind burned with confusion. Should she allow this or not? She did not want it, but he did. So badly. Yet she couldn't lead him to think that she shared that need.

"Randy." She lifted her fingers to his lips, shifted her head away from his.

He nodded. "Right. Sorry."

"I know I'm asking a lot of you," she said. "I like it when you hold me and comfort me. I seem to need that. But I don't want more than that, and I know I'm being unfair to—"

"I'm a big boy, Claire," he said. "Let it be my problem."

"All right." She lowered her feet to the floor and stood up slowly. Bending over, she hugged him lightly. "Thank you."

"I'm glad you're here," he said as she left the room, and she turned to smile at him.

"So am I," she said.

It was cold in the guest room. She had not noticed the temperature before, but now the chill made her pull the blanket and spread up to her chin.

Jon.

Alone with her thoughts, defenses down, he was there. She squeezed her eyes closed, thinking back to that morning when he'd told her to leave, his voice firm, absolute. Would he be able to sleep tonight, alone in the bed they'd shared for so long? Was he thinking about her, here with Randy? He probably thought she was sleeping with Randy. She touched her lips where Randy had kissed her, and her eyes filled.

Oh Jon, don't think about this. Don't. Take a sleeping pill. Lose yourself in sleep, sweetheart, please.

She crawled as far beneath the covers as she could get, but no matter how closely she wrapped the blanket around herself, she could still feel the cool air of the room against her skin.

In the morning, she found a container of egg substitute in Randy's refrigerator, along with green and red peppers and an onion, and while he showered, she made him an omelette. His heart would not suffer at her hands.

She was pouring a bowl of cereal for herself when he walked into the kitchen. He was wearing the blue terry-cloth robe he'd had on the night before and carrying the *Washington Post* in its plastic bag. Wet from a shower, his brown hair looked very dark, and he had combed it back from his face. She was struck by his handsomeness.

"Good morning." She smiled. "I've made you a fantastic breakfast."

He glanced at the frying pan. "Looks good." Sitting down at the small oak table in the corner, he rested the paper on the broad window ledge. There was a quiet restraint to him, something she could not quite read.

She transferred the omelette to a plate and set it on the table in front of him, wincing as he automatically reached for the pepper without even tasting the eggs first.

"I was thinking about your living situation," he said, looking up at her. "The guest room is yours whenever you want it, except when Cary's here. And he's coming this afternoon, I'm afraid. It's my weekend to have him, and I don't want him to meet you. Not yet, anyhow. It would confuse him."

She sat down across from him with her bowl of cereal. "You could just introduce me as a friend," she suggested.

Randy shook his head. "No." He set down his fork and reached across the table for her hand. "Listen to me, please. I'm very"—he looked away from her, struggling to find a word—"very uptight about all of this. I feel like I'm the cause of you and Jon splitting up."

"You're not the cause. *I* am."

"And I feel like I'm taking a big risk with you. Letting myself care about you, get close to you, when I don't know that you'll ever want the same sort of relationship with me that I want with you. Whether you do or not, I'm willing to take that risk for myself, but I'm not willing to put Cary in that position. All right?"

She was touched by his concern for his son. "All right." She picked at her cereal. "Will I ever get to meet him?" she asked.

He cut into the omelette with the side of his fork. "I hope so. Once I feel as though I can explain your existence to him clearly."

"Kids are more resilient than you think." She smiled at him. "He'll be fine. Does he like museums? Maybe some-day we could—"

Randy suddenly grabbed her wrist, and she dropped her spoon into the bowl.

"You're not listening to me," he said, his voice more

gentle than his actions would suggest. "I'm *upset*, Claire. Please stop talking as though there's nothing wrong. Please don't wear your fake smile when you're with me. Everything is *not* fine. Things are screwed up, and that's just the way life is sometimes and you have to deal with it. If you pretend things are fine, nothing ever gets fixed."

She drew her hand away from him and lowered it to her lap. A cold fear swept over her like a blanket of snow, and she knew she had wanted something from Randy she had no right to ask for. She wanted to be taken care of, to take care of him, to move into a new life without concern for the old. She was good at turning a messy situation into one that sparkled with possibilities. It was, perhaps, her one real skill.

"This is the only way I know how to be." She felt the tremor in her lower lip and struggled to still it. She would not be needy with him. She would not be pathetic. "If you take away my optimism, I won't have anything left. I'll just be a scared, crazy woman with a bunch of scary, crazy memories."

"That's crap. You're courageous as hell."

"No, I—"

"Hey, Claire." He cut her off, his fingers touching her hand again. "Remember the woman who went out on the bridge with my sister? She was a real chickenshit, wasn't she?"

She smiled, shrugging. Then she straightened her spine with determination. "Okay," she said. "So how do I find a place to live?"

Randy pulled the newspaper from its plastic bag and handed her the classified section. She felt teary again as she opened the paper to Rentals, and the print blurred on the page. She read him the ads, and by the time they were through with breakfast, she had circled several—small apartments in private homes, mostly, where she wouldn't have to sign a year's lease.

Randy had commented on the ads as she read them— "good part of town," "too far from me," "a lot of traffic noise"—but it was apparent that, with Cary's imminent visit, he would not be able to accompany her when she went to look at the apartments.

"What are you doing?" he asked, wearing a half-smile, half-frown as he pointed to the paper.

She looked down. She had covered the margins of the paper with that strange, reverse-S doodle she'd been drawing for weeks. Every blank piece of paper on or around her desk at the foundation had been graced by it.

She shrugged. "It's a new compulsion," she said as she shifted her eyes back to the ads, where the tiny print taunted her with enticing descriptions of things she did not want. She watched Randy as he stood up and began loading the dishwasher. His back was broad. She would not recognize him from this angle on the street. What was she doing here?

It would all fall into place, she told herself, folding the newspaper carefully in half. Everything would fall, neatly and comfortably, into place.

30

Vienna

Claire sat on the lumpy sofa in the small efficiency apartment, eyeing her surroundings. She'd been sitting there for thirty minutes, possibly an hour, although the entire contents of the apartment could have been memorized in a few seconds' time.

The apartment was charmless, although it was attached to a lovely old, noble white colonial on a quiet street no more than a mile from her own house in Vienna. The woman who owned the colonial had been surprised that Claire wanted to move into the apartment that very day, that very minute. She'd eyed her with such suspicion that Claire went to the bank in order to give the woman the first month's rent in cash. Money was not a problem; she had access to all the accounts she shared with Jon. There was a part of her, though, that felt as if she were playing a game when she turned the rent over to her new landlady. A month? In these two little rooms? Who was she trying to kid?

The rooms were furnished, barely. Besides the sofa, there was a small wrought-iron, glass-topped table and three matching chairs, which looked as if they'd been purloined from an ice cream parlor. Folding doors opened to reveal a stove, microwave, refrigerator, and sink. The second room, separated from the first by louvered doors, held a double bed with an ancient but pretty rattan headboard and a matching rattan dresser. The closet was surprisingly large, but the bathroom had barely enough room in which to turn around. Everything was spotlessly clean, though. That's what sold her on the apartment. No sign of previous tenants. She did not feel as though she was following in the footsteps of a string of miserable, displaced people who had no more than these two lifeless rooms to call their own.

She thought of Randy and Cary at the town house together, and she felt a loneliness unlike any she'd ever experienced before. She had never been alone. Never in her life. How did people tolerate this feeling? And she had no phone. Getting one, though, would imply a commitment to living in the apartment for more than a few days. She shuddered.

She wished she could talk to Amelia. How would she ever make Amelia understand what she had done? What Jon had done for her? Amelia would be horrified. Claire Harte-Mathias leaving her husband, her home, her job? Unbelievable.

She drove to the store and bought groceries and paper goods, dropping things into her cart without appetite or interest. She brought her purchases back to the apartment and put them into the empty cupboards and the refrigerator. Then she drove to Amelia's, but her knock was unanswered, and Amelia's car was not in the garage. She left a note on the back door. *I've moved. My new address is 507 Chesterwood. No phone. Please visit.* The note would blow Amelia's mind.

Then, finally, she did what she knew she had to do, what she'd been both dreading and looking forward to all day. She drove to her house.

Jon had burned himself the night before in the tub. A truly stupid mistake, one he hadn't made since he was a teenager. It was a testimony to how distracted he was. Claire had long ago etched a mark into the metal around the faucet control knob to prevent him from accidentally using water hot enough to burn. He'd filled the tub, carefully turning the knob only as far as the mark. He had even tested the water in the tub before getting in. But apparently he bumped the knob at some point, and a trickle of hot water had been left on, falling over his left foot while he soaked in the tub. He'd felt nothing, of course, and only when he got out of the tub did he see the angry red welt that had formed on the top of his foot. His heart rate had escalated. How bad was it? The last thing he felt like doing was spending the night, alone, in the emergency room. He held ice to the burn most of the evening, but while he slept, it rose into a long, crescent-shaped blister. Today he was leaving it open to the air, wheeling around with one shoe and sock on, the other foot bare.

It was Friday night, and the house seemed to vibrate with emptiness. Every sound he made—pushing in a dresser drawer, opening the refrigerator—echoed in the air around him. What a wimp he was. You've been alone before, he told himself. Just pretend she's gone shopping or over to Amelia's. He tried to immerse himself in the schedule for the retreat, but his mind seemed capable of concentration for only a fraction of a second before reality crept in again.

She was with Randy.

She had slept with Randy.

Perhaps she was even in love with Randy. And he had set the whole damn thing up.

Dusk was falling outside the study window that evening when he heard her car pull into the driveway. He looked up from his work on the desk. He had not expected to see her. Oh, eventually she would have to come home for more of her clothes or whatever, but he figured she would not even be thinking about home for the duration of this weekend.

He hated her to see him working on a Friday night. He didn't want to remind her that he was obsessed with work. Or worse, to see him looking so alone without her, a lost soul in his own house. He quickly wheeled out of the study into the family room and then remembered his exposed left foot. At least in the study it would have been hidden behind the desk. He transferred himself to the sofa, his foot hidden partly behind the coffee table, and turned the TV to the movie channel.

He heard her come in the back door and walk through the kitchen to the family room.

"Hi," she said from the doorway. "I hope you don't mind that I stopped by. I need to pick up some things." She looked wan and tired and drawn, but he could take no pleasure in her haggard appearance.

"Go ahead." He felt stiff. Awkward. He didn't know what to do with his hands.

She glanced toward the TV. "What am I interrupting?"

"Nothing." He hit the power switch on the remote control and set it next to him on the sofa. He tried to look at her but couldn't.

For the first time in his life, he felt embarrassed near her, embarrassed by his disability. She had almost certainly made love to a walking, feeling, and—most likely—sexually whole man last night.

She sat down on the edge of the rocker. "I want to give you the address where I'm staying."

"He lives in those town homes off Dolley Madison, right?"

"Yes, but I'm not staying there."

Jon stole a surprised glance at her. "Where else would—?"

She waved a hand through the air. "I might use his guest room sometime, but it's not what you think with Randy and me. I don't know how to make you believe that."

"Your actions lately make it pretty hard to believe."

She looked at him for a moment, a deep frown on her forehead. Then she pulled a scrap of paper from her purse and jotted down the address. Resting the paper on the coffee table, she looked up at him, green eyes wide. "I'm very scared," she said.

He nodded solemnly. "Me too." He wished she would leave. He didn't want her looking at him any longer.

She pressed her hands together, her fingers white, and he saw the subtle trembling in her lower lip. She seemed to compose herself quickly, though. "I love you, Jon," she said, "but I need Randy right now. I don't quite understand it. It's a very strong feeling. A very powerful need. I can't explain it."

Jon didn't look at her. He idly pressed the buttons on the

remote control. "You know, Claire," he said, "I really don't want to hear about you and Randy. Do you mind?"

"I'm sorry." Her voice was a whisper.

Neither of them spoke for a moment, the only sound the soft clicking of the keys on the remote.

"So, where are you staying?" He glanced at the piece of paper on the table but couldn't make out the address from where he sat.

"I found a little apartment in a private house on Chesterwood. It's really tiny, but I don't need much space. There's no phone, though. I don't know about getting one."

It was impossible to picture. He could see other people living that way, perhaps, but not someone like Claire, accustomed to a house like this one and a life of relative ease.

"Oh, Claire, I don't want you living like that," he said, his resolve instantly gone. "You can live here. Take one of the other bedrooms, but—"

"No." She was shaking her head, and he was surprised by the strength in her response. "That won't work."

Of course it wouldn't work. Randy would pick her up, or she'd stay out all night, and he'd live through the pain of last night all over again whenever she was gone.

"I'm going to pack some things," she said. "Would you mind very much if I took the toaster? You never use it." She stood up, and he saw her gaze drop to his feet. "What did you do to your—you burned your foot!"

Immediately, she was on her knees next to him, lifting his foot, holding it into the light. "How did you do this?" she asked.

He wished he had the ability to pull his leg away from her. "Hot water dripping in the tub. I must have bumped the knob."

"Oh, Jon. God. This isn't good. Let me take you to the emergency room."

He leaned forward to bat her away from him. "It's fine. It's nothing major."

She lowered his foot and sat back on her heels, but her eyes were still on the burn, her forehead furrowed. She spoke quietly. "Please let me take you," she said. "It really should be looked at."

He shook his head, and she sighed like a tired mother dealing with a stubborn child.

She stood up again. "I'd like to stop in from time to time," she said, "just to check on you. Unless—"

Jon threw the remote onto the table, making her jump. "Goddamn it, Claire!" he said. "I'm a grown man. Stop treating me like I'm something less than that."

She took a step backward. "I'm sorry," she said. She rubbed her forehead with shaky fingers. "I need to talk to you about ... Can I take some work home from the foundation? My not being there will leave a lot of projects up in the air, and I—"

"Forget work."

She turned her head toward the window and stared out into the darkness for a moment before speaking again. "All right," she said. "I'll be out of here in a few minutes."

He watched her walk into the hallway and listened to the sound of her packing, straining to hear her. As bad as it was to hear the zipper being pulled closed on the suitcase, it was better than the silence that would follow once she had left the house again, once she was back with Randy.

31

Darcy was on the phone when Vanessa walked into her office late that Monday afternoon. She motioned toward a chair in the corner, and Vanessa sat down and tightened the laces on her running shoes, her wedding band catching the glow of the overhead light. She and Brian had gotten married on Saturday, quietly, in the office of a justice of the peace, and spent the night at an inn near Vancouver. She had told Darcy and a few of her coworkers, and throughout the day people had been stopping by her office with surprised congratulations that made her beam and blush uncharacteristically.

She hadn't told a soul before the wedding, though, still unable to believe it would actually take place. And it almost hadn't. A few hours before she and Brian were to leave for the courthouse, Jordan Wiley's lung collapsed again, and she came into the hospital to see him receive his third chest tube. The tube helped; he was breathing more easily. But this two-month hospitalization was clearly wearing Jordy down. He'd looked exhausted when she saw him in his room that morning. Subdued and withdrawn. She'd been checking the placement of the torturous third tube when he asked her, "Do you believe in God, Dr. Gray?" She'd lied and told him that she did.

At rounds tomorrow, she would make certain that she and her young colleagues talked about death, about the fairness of letting Jordy know what lay ahead of him so he could say his good-byes if he wanted to. Yet, she was sure that Jordy knew better than any of them that this miserable hospitalization was probably his last.

Darcy hung up the phone and grinned at her. "You look so *different*," she said. "You look so married."

"Right." Vanessa brushed away the comment. "Put on your shoes."

"Can't go." Darcy stood up and started transferring a stack of books from her desk to the bookcase, one by one. "The nausea's finally gone, but now I have to pee every thirty seconds."

Vanessa rolled her eyes. "So, we'll pick a route near some bathrooms. Come on."

Darcy slipped a book into the case. "You don't understand," she said. "I mean, this is *major* discomfort. You can't possibly know—"

"Darcy."

"What?"

"I *do* understand. I was pregnant once."

Darcy's blue eyes widened and she stopped her hand midway to the bookshelf. "I . . . when? I mean—"

"When I was a teenager."

Darcy dropped back into her chair, the book still in her hand. "Shit, Vanessa. Why didn't you ever tell me?"

"Because I don't particularly like to remember it. But every time you say I don't know what this or that feels like, I—"

"I'm sorry." Darcy set the book on her desk, then leaned forward to squeeze both of Vanessa's hands, carefully avoiding the little finger of her right hand, which was still in its cast. "I didn't know."

Vanessa shrugged uncomfortably. "It's all right." She knew more of an explanation was necessary, and she doubted Darcy would ask. "I was seventeen," she said.

"And you gave the baby up for adoption?"

"No." Vanessa shook her head vigorously. "At least not voluntarily. They took her from me."

Darcy frowned. "Why?"

Vanessa folded her arms across her chest. How much was she going to tell? "They said I couldn't take care of her. And they were right. I was self-destructive. I was an alcoholic and using drugs."

Darcy stared at her. If she made the connection between Vanessa's description of her younger self and the way she often described the teenagers in the AMC program, she didn't say.

"You?" she asked. "That's so impossible to believe."

"But it was me," Vanessa said.

Darcy shook her head, then asked softly, "Do you have any idea what happened to the baby? Where she is?"

"None." Vanessa stood up as if Darcy had flicked a switch in her. She picked up Darcy's gym bag from the floor. "Come on," she said. "Let's run."

Darcy sunk lower in her chair. "Really, Van, I can't."

"Well," Vanessa shrugged again, "I'll see you tomorrow, then."

Before Vanessa reached the door, though, Darcy stood up and drew her into a hug. "I'm so sorry about your baby," she said, and Vanessa was surprised by the comfort she took in her friend's embrace. She had told Darcy the truth about herself and received nothing but good in return.

Once on the street, Vanessa was glad Darcy hadn't joined her after all. She did not feel like talking. Heading east past the post office, she started an easy jog. She'd changed her route since the night of the attack. Maybe someday she would run down that street again, but not now.

She hadn't told her father about her pregnancy. Secretly, she'd wondered how long it would take him to notice. He paid so little attention to her to begin with. She was nearly seven months along before he caught on. He was also ignorant of the fact that she had long ago quit school, and that she spent more nights at the homes of various boyfriends than under his own roof.

He made her see a doctor, and he and the doctor told her she would have to put the baby up for adoption. They didn't listen to her protests, and so she didn't keep her future appointments. Even now she was angry with that doctor. He'd had a chance to educate her, and he let it slip by. If he'd told her that drugs and alcohol could hurt her baby, she would have listened. At least in retrospect, she thought she would have.

She drank—she'd been drinking heavily since she was fourteen—and smoked marijuana and cigarettes. On some level she must have known there was a connection between what she ingested and the baby's health, because she took huge quantities of vitamins. But in her mind, the connection never extended to the drugs. Not until many years later, when it was far too late to make a difference.

Waiting for the birth of her baby, she was happier than she'd been in her life. Finally, she would have something that was hers alone, someone she could love who was guaranteed to love her back and who wouldn't—couldn't—leave her.

She stole baby clothes and blankets and a diaper bag. Pacifiers were easy to steal, and she had a collection of different colors and designs. Her layette was rounded out through the shoplifting efforts of her friends, especially the two young men who thought they might be the father of her baby. Vanessa's best guess at paternity, though, was a third boy who had passed briefly through Seattle on his way somewhere else.

She could only imagine herself having a girl, and she'd lie awake at night thinking of names. Anna was her favorite. An old-fashioned name that made her envision fields of wildflowers and butterflies and the safety and security that seemed a part of those images.

A girlfriend had dropped her off at the hospital entrance when her labor started. Alone and frightened and in worse pain than she'd thought a person could bear, she let the hospital staff call her father. He was there in the waiting room when Anna was born by cesarean section. Anna. Full-term, but only five and a half pounds. A pale, bony, round-eyed little baby with a dusting of pale silk on her head.

Anna had trouble breathing, they said, and they kept her in the nursery. Every chance she could, Vanessa would shuffle down the long corridor to the nursery to hold her daughter. She'd sit on a hard wooden chair and rock her, hum to her, ignoring the sideways glances the nurses would give her, the whispering that went on behind her back.

The nurses did not like her. They wore pleased expressions on their faces when they told her it was time to go back to her room. They would have to pry Anna from her hands, though, to get her to leave.

Her friends visited her in the hospital, sneaking her beer and cigarettes, and on a couple of occasions, making so much noise that the staff threatened to kick them out.

On Vanessa's fourth day in the hospital, a social worker from the county appeared in her room and told her she would not be able to keep Anna. "You can't take care of her," the social worker said. "You can't even take care of yourself."

At first Vanessa did not believe her. Could they do that, take a baby from her mother? She felt desperate. She promised to stop drinking, stop smoking. Return to school. She would change friends, move back with her father. Anything, if they would not take Anna from her. But the social worker's decision was firm, and the nurses looked at Vanessa with a smug sense of vindication. She wondered which of them had made the call to have her baby stolen from her. On one occasion, when she'd cursed at her night nurse and thrown her empty emesis basin at her, the nurse retorted, "You just about killed that baby when she was inside of you. Did you expect us to let you finish the job?"

Or maybe it had been her father who had arranged to have Anna taken away from her. A baby in his house certainly would have put a damper on his jet-setting lifestyle. Her indifference toward him turned to hatred.

It was many, many years before she realized they had all been right. The nurses, the social worker, her father. The situation had been poorly handled—cruelly and stupidly handled—but Anna had needed their protection from her.

At the age of seventeen, Vanessa Harte would have made a dangerous mother.

Long after Anna's birth, Vanessa studied fetal alcohol syndrome in medical school. During that time, she suffered a bout of anxiety and sleeplessness, and her hair, which had always glistened with curls and waves, began to grow in straight. She was haunted by fuzzy images of Anna as she struggled to remember her baby's tiny features. Hadn't Anna had the small head, the upturned nose, the elongated upper lip of an infant suffering from FAS? Or had the baby's face changed in her memory over the years to taunt her?

The day they transferred Anna to another, unnamed, hospital was the day Vanessa first cut herself. She had accidentally broken her water glass by dropping it on the edge of her bed tray, and she stared at the jagged pieces for a long time before picking one of them up and running it, slowly and smoothly, in a long line down the length of her thigh. There was no pain. Only a fascination as she watched the invisible line bead up into a slender thread of red. She made the second and third lines thicker. Then she left the hospital without the permission of her doctor to avoid the wounds being discovered. And, also, because she was desperate for a drink.

For two years, she lived with friends, occasionally returning home to beg for money, which her father would reluctantly provide. She hated asking him and would only do so when she'd exhausted all other avenues for generating income, including selling drugs and herself.

On her nineteenth birthday, though, everything changed.

She was driving a boyfriend's car when she ran a stoplight and broadsided a Volkswagen Beetle. She herself was uninjured, but through a drunken haze, she watched as a little girl—about Anna's age—was pulled unconscious from the crumpled VW and loaded into an ambulance. Vanessa stared after the ambulance as it sped off down the street, sirens blaring. She had nearly killed a little girl like Anna. The accident sobered her in a way nothing else could.

The court ordered her into a residential alcohol treatment program, and she went willingly, her nightmares of Anna, of the carousel, mingling now with nightmares of the accident. With a new subdued determination, she endured the symptoms of withdrawal and the seductive taunting of her friends, who called or wrote or visited her in the hospital. She found strength, though, in her thoughts of the little girl. J.T. Gray.

After two weeks in the program—and with the permission of J.T.'s parents—she was given a pass to visit the child in her room at Lassiter Children's Hospital.

She visited J.T. daily. The child was still in traction but was recovering well from her injuries, although she would always—*always*—walk with a limp. Vanessa spent hours entertaining J.T. in that hospital room and quickly fell in love with her. J.T., with her child's ignorance of Vanessa's role in her misfortune, fell for her young visitor even more swiftly. Ned and Sara, the girl's parents, seemed to see in Vanessa something everyone else had missed. Her intelligence. Her compassion. Or perhaps they were the first people to see her sober and real in a very long time. They could see the good parts of her beginning to break through.

When J.T. was released from the hospital, Ned and Sara hired Vanessa to help them with her at home. They didn't have much money, but they provided Vanessa with a room and meals and more of a family life than she'd known since before her father had taken her to Seattle. Ned took her to an AA meeting, and only then did she realize that he, too, had wrestled with the bottle. Her loneliness began to disappear. She'd spend her days with J.T. and her evenings with the entire family, reading or talking or working around the house. Sometimes she would go a week or more without a nightmare.

Sara was a teacher's aide, and she persuaded Vanessa to take the high school equivalency exam, which she passed easily. After that, she attended community college for two years at night, taking care of J.T. during the day.

The Grays moved away then, and Vanessa was left feeling as though she'd had little angels flutter into her life, do their good work, then flutter out again when she was capable of taking care of herself. And she was indeed capable. She had new friends through school and AA, new strength in the face of alcohol, and a goal for herself. She wanted to be a doctor.

Her father seemed relieved to provide her with the necessary funds for school. Her relationship with him had softened into one of mutual tolerance, which seemed to suit them both. Len Harte had never learned how to be a good father, how to shift the focus of his existence from himself to his child. Giving Vanessa money was the best he could do, and at that point in her life, it was what she needed most.

Vanessa slowed her pace as she ran along the sidewalk next to the cemetery wall. She would have to write to J.T. and her new husband, and to Ned and Sara, to tell them that she and Brian had finally gotten married. The Grays would be thrilled for her, if a little annoyed that she hadn't told them before the wedding. But they would understand.

She turned down an alley to take a shortcut back to the hospital. She felt a sudden yearning to get home to the life she had now. And to her husband, the man who knew everything there was to know about her and had still taken a vow never to leave.

32

Vienna

Jon looked up as Pat Wykowski wheeled into his office and dropped a manila folder on his desk.

"I was talking with Margaret Sulley this morning," she said, "and she's changed her mind. She wants to talk about the social aspects of rehab instead of independent living for her keynote address at the retreat."

"What a surprise." He smiled at Pat. Margaret would probably change her mind four or five more times before September. She was notoriously disorganized but a dynamic speaker once she'd settled on her topic. "And Tom Ferry's going to do the skin-care seminar," he added.

He had spoken with Tom an hour ago and had come close to asking him for advice about the burn on his foot. Tom had clearly been in a rush to get off the phone, and so Jon had swallowed his question. He'd taped a bandage over the burn that morning, barely looking at the still-red skin. If it was not healing properly, he did not want to know.

"So, what's so important it couldn't wait until this afternoon?" Pat asked.

It was ten o'clock Tuesday morning, and he'd called Pat to ask if she had time to meet with him. He would have insisted if she'd said no. He had to get this over with.

He'd told Jill, Claire's secretary, that Claire was out sick, but now he was about to tell the truth, for the first time. How much of the truth, he wasn't sure. Enough to give Pat a clear view of the situation, but not enough to humiliate himself.

"Could you close the door, please?" he asked.

Pat registered a flash of surprise at the request, raising her eyebrows, the dimpled smile temporarily in abeyance. She shut the door, then wheeled around to face him in her chair, hands folded in her lap.

"Claire and I have separated," he said. The words sounded so ridiculous that he almost laughed.

Pat looked at him uncertainly for a moment, then let out a laugh herself. "This is a joke, right?"

He shook his head. "I'm afraid not."

"*Jon*. You and Claire?"

'We've been having some problems for a while."

"You and Claire?" she repeated. "But you two work *everything* out. I've never known another couple who could handle adversity with such . . . such *sanity* and always come out on top, every time."

"Not this time."

"Was it a mutual decision?"

He drew in a breath, leaning forward on his desk. "I'm practicing on you, Pat," he said. "I don't know how to tell people about this, so maybe you can help me figure out what to say."

She brushed a thick strand of blond hair from her temple, revealing deep lines in her forehead. He had never seen those lines before. He wanted to erase them, and he longed to see her wacky grin. Pat Wykowski looking serious was almost too much to bear.

"What happened?" Pat rested an arm on his desk.

"I asked her to leave," he said.

"You *what*? Why?"

"She's been different lately, ever since she saw that woman jump off the bridge. It changed her." He wouldn't tell Pat about the flashbacks. She would ask too many questions.

Pat put on the even-featured face she reserved for those patients who did or said something she found abominable.

"But Jon," she said carefully, "enduring that sort of trauma would change anyone. Claire probably needs you more than ever. Can't you be patient with her? It hasn't been that long."

He was briefly confused before realizing that Pat thought that *he* was the partner pulling away. In a way, he supposed he was.

"She wanted to go." He ran his hand over the folder she had dropped on his desk. "See, she met the brother of the woman who jumped," he said, "and she's gotten ... attached to him. He's helping her make sense of what happened."

"Oh, my God." Pat shook her head. "Is she ... is this some kind of affair?"

He shrugged uncomfortably. "I'm not sure what to call it."

Pat stiffened in her chair, a flare of anger in her eyes. "I can't believe she would leave you for some other guy," she said.

Oh, that sounded ugly, and he had to look away. He fingered the edge of the folder. "It wasn't her idea. As I said, I offered her her freedom. All she did was take it."

"But she's so *devoted* to you."

He didn't like her choice of words. Devotion was different from love. Devotion didn't imply a relationship between equals.

"Maybe devotion's not the best foundation for a marriage," he said.

Pat was quiet. She wore her shrink-in-thought expression. "You and Claire never fought, did you?" It was more of a statement than a question. Almost an accusation.

"No. There was never anything to fight about."

"Maybe the two of you simply didn't deal with your problems."

"Well, you know Claire. Everything was always rosy in her eyes."

"And you liked it that way."

A wave of sadness filled his chest. "Yeah," he said, "I guess I did. And I miss it."

"Oh, Jonny." Pat wheeled her chair next to his so that she could lean over to hug him. In the warmth of her arms, he felt her love and strength and found he could not easily let go of her. When she drew away, he hoped the tears in his eyes were not visible.

"How are you doing?" she asked. "Do you need anything?"

"I need to know how to tell everyone else."

"Why should it all be on your shoulders?"

"Because Claire's taking some time off. I need to offer some explanation for her absence."

"Just tell them the truth," she said. "You're among friends here, Jon."

They sat together awhile longer. He did not want to talk much about the separation. She had questions about Randy but quickly dropped them when she encountered his resistance to answering them. He wanted her company, though, and she seemed to sense that. They talked about skiing and a little about the retreat, and when she finally wheeled to the door, it was close to noon. She looked back at him.

"Call me anytime, Jon," she said. "You've never lived alone before. Call me. I'm an expert at it."

He took her advice about telling the other foundation personnel, and by the time he'd left the office for the day, he had spoken to all eight full-time employees. He tried not to paint too black a picture of Claire. He tried to share responsibility for what had happened. At some point, he hoped they would be working with Claire again.

Their reactions amazed him. There was that initial sense of shock and sympathy, which he'd expected, followed by a perverse sort of relief, which he had not. "The team of Harte-Mathias is human after all," one of the physical therapists said.

After work, he went to the gym and spent nearly two hours working out, putting off the time he'd have to go home to his empty house. Changing his clothes in the locker room afterward, he forced himself to study the burn on his foot. There was no denying that it was worse. The blisters were oozing now. Ignoring the burn did not appear to be the treatment of choice. He would have to take himself to the emergency room after all.

Driving toward the hospital, he felt like an abandoned

child attempting to take care of himself without a grown-up around. Over the years, he'd had to go to the hospital numerous times, but always with Claire at his side. This felt like his first act as an adult.

He turned the car into the parking lot of the hospital, heart thumping. What would he say when they shook their heads at him and asked why he'd waited so long to come in? He practiced his response as he pulled into a handicapped-parking space. "I didn't think it looked that bad." Or, "It seemed to be getting better on its own." Or perhaps he would just tell them the truth: "It's easy to ignore a problem when there isn't any pain."

33

Billy Goat Trail, Maryland

Claire was glad she'd worn her hiking boots. Randy had warned her that the Billy Goat Trail would live up to its name, but she had not expected the entire two miles to be made up of rocks.

"Are you coming?" Randy teased from his perch on a boulder high above her. She looked up at him, winded. He and Cary hiked this trail at least once a month. She was at a severe disadvantage.

Claire studied the network of rocks between herself and Randy and started picking her way up to him. Once she'd reached him, they began walking and jumping over a long string of boulders. They moved quietly, occasionally stopping to look across the Potomac River to the Virginia side, where barely detectable rock climbers nudged their way up the cliffs near Great Falls.

It had been two weeks since she'd moved out of her house, and her life had slipped into a pattern. She slept in Randy's guest room more nights than she probably should, although she was careful to wait for his invitation. He seemed to want her there. They were intensely close in all ways but one, and she worried that she was keeping him from developing a more gratifying social life. He made light of her concern. There was a new, boyish happiness in him she had not noticed before. He was still protective of his privacy and his time with his son, though. That was fine. She could keep busy. She spent her days either helping him in the restaurant or painting scenery for the upcoming play at the little theater. Often she was alone in the chapel, working on the huge canvas flats. The painting offered her the long, quiet days she seemed to need so badly. She was grateful to Jon for freeing her from the foundation. She would have been useless in the office, and there was no way she could have allowed herself this time with Randy if she were seeing Jon every day.

She did talk to him, though. She called him every few days to see how he was doing. He would ask if she was having any more flashbacks, and she would give him a brief response. She figured his questions were borne primarily of politeness. Or perhaps he was simply looking for something to say.

They had discussed how to tell Susan about the separation. Claire could not get used to that word.

"Couldn't we just say we're living apart?" she asked him.

"I believe that's the definition of a separation, Claire," Jon had replied dryly.

They could come to no agreement on who should tell or what words should be used. Susan would be home for spring break in a few weeks, so they would have to decide how the telling should be done before then.

"Tell her the truth," Randy said to her more than once,

but Claire would still lie awake at night, trying to think of how she could possibly make her daughter understand what was going on.

She had failed in that attempt with Amelia. She'd had lunch with Amelia last week, and it had not gone well. Amelia did not understand what Claire could not explain. She had merely picked at her food as she listened to Claire talk about Jon, about Randy, about the flashbacks the incident on the bridge had jarred loose in her. Occasionally, Amelia's eyes filled with tears, but then suddenly, she would lash out, dry-eyed, fuming with anger. "You've always taken Jon for granted," she'd say, or "I don't even know you anymore," and Claire decided she would not see her old friend again for a while.

Ironically, she found her greatest support in Debra Parlow. She had canceled her second appointment with the therapist but forced herself to go to the third. Debra reassured her that she didn't have to talk about the flashbacks if she didn't want to.

She encouraged Claire to talk about Jon and Randy, though, and Claire struggled to make sense of the situation to the therapist.

"Why is it you can talk so easily with Randy?" Debra asked.

"I don't know. But I felt that way right from the start, as though I'd known him forever."

"Does he remind you of someone else you know? Someone you feel that secure around?"

Claire thought for a moment, then shook her head.

"Well," Debra said. "I think you're brave to be trying to figure out what's disturbing you, when it's obviously so uncomfortable for you. And you're right to do it, any way you can. You have to take care of *yourself* right now. You won't be of much use to anyone else until you've done that."

Claire certainly was not without guilt, but it was faint and transitory. She did not wallow in it. She was not without fear, either. She had no idea where she was going—not in her life, nor in the perilous unraveling of her memories. For once she was looking at what lay behind her and not at what was ahead. She continued to wonder if she might be fabricating the wispy fragments of memory. She spent an afternoon in the library, reading about "false memory syndrome." Given some prompting, people could make up images and flashbacks and highly detailed memories that even they believed actually occurred. Was that what she was doing? The theory offered her some relief. "It's just my overactive imagination," she announced to Randy one night, and Randy started humming "Let Me Call You Sweetheart," making her stomach leap into her throat.

If she were merely inventing the flashbacks, then she could choose their content, couldn't she? She could choose when and where they would occur. But she had no control over them, and although she certainly didn't welcome the strange, sometimes scary images, she no longer ran from them. She was not alone with them anymore. Randy was never more than a phone call away, and the safety she felt with him astonished her. He had no fear of anything she might tell him. Unlike Jon. Jon had quaked under the weight of the small and senseless scraps of memory. She could never have gone through this while living with him. His suffering would have been worse than her own.

She was remembering much, much more from her

childhood. She could now recall nearly all her elementary-school teachers and could even remember a handful of kids from her kindergarten class. Occasionally, a memory would come to her full-blown and highly detailed. None of them seemed very important, yet Randy treated each one like a milestone.

The only image she refused to pursue was the most tenacious—the smear of blood on white porcelain. Each time it occurred, she would back away from it, and the picture in her mind would put up a good fight before fading to black.

The images were expanding and multiplying, often prompted by Randy's relentless questioning. He was tireless, as though he'd taken her on as a project. But when he hugged her good-night, when he kissed her forehead tenderly in the morning, Claire knew she meant far more to him than a mere puzzle to be solved.

The trail suddenly grew rough and craggy, and Claire had to give it all her concentration. She and Randy rounded a bend, losing sight of the cliffs across the river. With a burst of energy, Claire raced up the side of a rock and waited there for her hiking partner. Randy pulled himself onto the ridge a few seconds later, and they stood looking out over the river as they labored to catch their breath.

"You're doing pretty well," Randy said, slapping her lightly on the back. "I know you haven't had much of a chance to hike in the past twenty years."

Claire shook her head. She knew Randy liked to feel as though he was giving her things Jon could not. "I didn't hike before I met Jon, either," she said. "Although, during the summers when I was a kid, Vanessa and I would go for long walks through the forest with our grandfather. He'd teach us how to mark the trail. Which is impossible up here." She turned away from the river. Boulders as far as she could see. Not a twig in sight. "I sure hope you know where we're going."

Randy leaped to an adjacent rock, and she followed. "So your grandfather was a woodsman," he said.

"He knew everything about the forest." She was picturing the lush green of the woods in Jeremy. The plants that seemed magical when described by her grandfather. Jack-in-the-pulpits. She could remember the comical name but not what they looked like. "Do you know what a jack—" She stopped walking suddenly as an image appeared in her head. "We found a cross in the woods one day," she said. "A grave."

Randy looked at her quizzically. "Whose?"

"Tucker's." She could see the name painted in white. "My grandparents' dog. Only that doesn't make sense, because . . . " She had the quick realization that none of this memory would make sense. Too hazy. Unimportant. "It probably doesn't matter." She started walking again, but Randy caught her arm.

"Whoa," he said. "I want to hear more. Why doesn't it make sense?"

"I don't know. I don't remember. Except that Grandpa wasn't with us that day. I don't think we were supposed to know the grave was there."

"Sit." Randy pointed to the ground and sat down right where he'd been standing, on the smooth rounded rim of a boulder. Claire sat next to him. The cold stone bit through the denim of her jeans.

Randy put an arm around her. "Okay. So you found this

grave, you and Vanessa. How did you know it was your grandparents' dog?"

"His name was on it. But see . . ." The memory was very foggy, and she struggled to bring it into focus. "My mother had told us that my grandparents had given the dog away."

"You mean she lied."

"Well, yes, to protect us. As usual. We were really small."

"Right." Randy's voice was cynical. "Cary's pet fish died when Cary was six and we talked about it and had a funeral, and Cary cried and said a prayer over the grave. I can't help but think that was a much healthier way to teach a child about death than if I'd lied to him about it."

"Of course you're right," Claire agreed. "My mother's intentions were good. Except that she told me that no one in our family was ever buried." She frowned, remembering the mixture of fear and sympathy she'd felt when she'd talk about death with other children. "For the longest time, I thought my family was different. In a good way. Special. I felt sorry for other kids. Their dead relatives had to lay in the ground. Mine would go to heaven. I don't remember how old I was before I realized that my family wasn't charmed."

Randy gave her shoulders a squeeze. "Your mother did not prepare you well for growing up."

"I'm sure she thought she was doing the right thing."

"Was your father the same way?"

"I don't think so."

"What was their marriage like?"

"It was good." She felt the weakness in the word and braced herself for Randy's inevitable retort.

"Then why did it end?" he asked.

"Good marriages can end," she said. "I'm a perfect example of it. Look at my marriage." Her words shocked her. Hot tears burned her eyes. Had her marriage ended? Was it over? She leaped to her feet. "We need to get going or we won't make the end of the trail before dark."

Randy stood up and suddenly wrapped his arms around her from behind. He pressed his cheek against her neck. He was not going to let her go.

"Did they ever fight? Your parents."

"No. At least I have no memory of them fighting."

"But you know in your heart their marriage could not have been good, don't you?" Randy prodded. "Assuming a good marriage could fall apart, the father wouldn't kidnap his daughter and never let the mother know where she was."

"I know you're right," she said tiredly. "But I still don't remember it being bad."

"Why did he take Vanessa and not you?"

"Because she was his favorite." The words slipped unexpectedly from her mouth, and before she could stop herself, she began crying in earnest. Pulling from his arms, she started walking across the rocks. She was relieved when Randy didn't follow her.

Angel. Vanessa *had* been her father's favorite. Mellie's too. Had she never realized that before, or had she simply never admitted it to herself?

The boulders dipped down to the water, and she picked her way among them, her vision blurred by tears. Randy caught up to her, helping her over a wide break in the rocks by taking her hand.

"Are you okay?" he asked.

"He gave her presents," Claire said. "Or when he'd have

a gift for each of us, she'd get the better of the two. I pretended it didn't bother me. If you'd asked me a few months ago, I would have denied that it bothered me at all. I don't think I ever admitted it to myself until right now." She wiped her eyes with the back of her hand. "I'm sorry." She grinned sheepishly at him. "This is ridiculous—a forty-year-old woman crying over her daddy. Don't listen to me."

"No one ever let you cry over him when you were a kid. It's about time, I'd say."

"He just . . . he loved Vanessa more than he loved me." She shrugged. "She was beautiful. She looked like my mother. It makes sense."

Randy put his arms around her and held her tightly. "Yeah," he said. "And it makes sense you would have resented the hell out of her for it, too."

"But I didn't. I was a little jealous, maybe. She was so pretty, and—"

"Do you have any pictures of her?"

Claire started to shake her head, but caught herself. Where were they, those pictures? In the attic somewhere?

She leaned away from Randy. "Yes," she said, "I do. I have pictures of everyone."

34

Jeremy, Pennsylvania
1964

Claire and Mellie arrived at the farm shortly after ten on a mild March morning. They'd sung songs the entire four-hour drive from Virginia, but Mellie's usual energy was lacking. She couldn't remember the words to "I Want to Hold Your Hand," for example, and she made Claire come up with nearly every one of the songs they sang.

Mellie had insisted that Claire come with her, even though it meant missing her best friend's twelfth birthday party. There would be other parties, Mellie had said, and that was certainly true. Claire was invited everywhere. She had many friends, and the parents of her friends adored her. "She's such a positive girl," they'd say. "So agreeable all the time."

It was strange to see the farm in March. Although the air was on the warm side, patches of white still dotted the field, and snow lay in a blanket on the shaded side of the big white house. Claire only glanced at the barn as she and

Mellie pulled their suitcases from the trunk of the car. She did not want to think about the barn. She had to keep reminding herself that they would never be here again in the summer. In fact, this was probably the last time she would ever see the farm at all.

As odd as it was to be at the farm in winter, it was stranger still to be inside the house without Dora Siparo's chatter to greet them. Claire had gotten used to not having her grandfather around, but she'd thought her grandmother would live forever. Dora had only been fifty-eight years old and had never been sick a day in her life.

Claire had stared at her mother in utter disbelief when Mellie told her what had happened. "Grandma passed peacefully in her sleep," Mellie had said. "Wasn't she lucky to go that way, precious? If I ever die, that's certainly how I'd like to go."

Mellie stood in the big farmhouse kitchen and looked around the room, hands on her hips. The table where Claire and Vanessa had drunk so many cups of weak coffee was littered with recipe cards and baking pans, as if Dora had been struck down in the midst of planning her baking for the day. Mellie let out a long sigh, then smiled at her daughter. "We have quite a job ahead of us this weekend, sunshine. And we're going to simply throw everything away, except the furniture, of course. That way we don't have to look at every little object and wonder, do we keep it or give it away or toss it out? We'll just toss everything. What do you say?"

Claire nodded. She had cramps. Two months earlier, on her own twelfth birthday, she'd gotten her first period. Mellie had responded with great joy and revelry, baking a cake to celebrate her "entry into womanhood." Claire was not yet certain this was something worth celebrating. It was messy, and it made her ache.

They began in Dora's bedroom. Mellie carried a few empty boxes upstairs and set them on the floor. Then she looked around the room.

"We'll start on the bed," she said.

The bed looked as though it had been hastily made, the quilt drawn up in a lumpy, wrinkled fashion to barely cover the pillow. Mellie pulled back the quilt, revealing blood-stains on the pillowcase and sheet. Claire glanced at her mother's face, but it was as if Mellie could not see the dark red splotches.

"Help me with this, darling?" Mellie asked.

Claire stared at the stains. Her grandmother had not died peacefully. She could ask Mellie what had really happened, but her mother's answer was sure to be full of twists and evasions and not worth hearing. Mellie needed to believe her own lie even more than she needed Claire to believe it.

Numbly, Claire pulled the corner of the sheet from the mattress.

The stain on the pillowcase reminded her of the map of Italy she'd seen in her geography book the week before, complete with little Sicily at the toe of the boot. Mellie shook the pillow out of the case, and Italy collapsed into the white folds of the cloth. Mellie bundled up the linens and threw them into one of the boxes. Then she began emptying drawers, dropping armloads of her mother's clothing on top of the soiled sheets. She had meant what she said. She was not taking the time to look at anything.

Until she got to the vanity dresser. Then she sat back in the flimsy little chair and lit a cigarette, and Claire followed her gaze to the framed picture on the dresser top. It was of her and Vanessa, sitting with Mellie and Len on the porch of their old house in Falls Church. After a moment, Mellie picked up the picture to study it more closely, and Claire braved the question she had stopped asking sometime during the last two years.

"When are we going to see Vanessa and Daddy again?" she asked.

She waited for her mother's encouraging response, but it was long in coming this time. Mellie let out another of her deep sighs. She ran a finger over her lower lip, took a drag of her cigarette, then nodded to herself. "We have to believe it will be soon," she said. "I feel it in my heart."

Claire had that familiar, funny mix of longing and trepidation she always felt at the thought of seeing her sister again.

Mellie set the picture on the floor, propping it up against the wall, and Claire realized with a surge of happiness that she did not intend to throw it away. Then Mellie picked up a small, delicate crystal angel from the collection of knickknacks on the vanity. It was a Christmas ornament; a tiny wire jutted from its halo. Mellie balanced the angel on her palm, and all the light in the room seemed to catch in the folds of the little angel's robe. It was beautiful. Claire watched her mother, hoping they could keep it.

"Mother always let me hang this one on the tree myself when I was little," Mellie said. She sounded as if she was speaking to herself.

Claire reached out to take the angel from Mellie's hand, but Mellie didn't seem to see her. She dropped the angel into the box, where it landed on a perfume bottle and splintered into tiny shards of light. Then Claire watched as

Mellie brushed the rest of the knickknacks from the top of the dresser with a sweep of her arm.

Claire stared at the jumble of broken glass and ceramic for a minute before walking into the bathroom, where she began emptying the medicine cabinet. It was full of ancient prescription bottles, some of them dating back to before she was born. She threw them into an old shoe box, along with glass bottles of thick liquid and oozing tubes of ointment. The towel hanging over the rack behind the door also bore a bloodstain. She folded the towel so the stain was not visible, so that when she walked past Mellie to throw it in the box with the linens, Mellie would not have to see it.

In the living room after lunch, Mellie plucked a book from one of the massive bookcases. "I suppose we should box up these books and try to sell them," she said. "Heaven knows, we can use the money, right? Once we sell the furniture and the house, though, we should be able to buy a little place of our own."

"I like where we live now." They were renting a small, two-bedroom house near the junior high school in Falls Church. Most of Claire's friends lived close by.

"It's better to own." Mellie pulled the big, broad photograph album with its dark brown leather cover from the lower bookshelf, and Claire's eyes widened as she watched her mother throw the album in the trash box. How many hours had she sat with her grandparents, looking at those old pictures? There were small, brown-toned photographs of Joseph Siparo carving horses. Pictures of Mellie when she was a baby. Mellie and Len's wedding. Claire and Vanessa riding the carousel.

"Can we save that, Mellie?" She pointed to the trash box.

Mellie looked up at her distractedly. Then she stubbed out her cigarette and patted the floor in front of her. "Come here, Claire," she said.

Claire sat down, and Mellie looked at her squarely, her blue eyes dry and cool. "You must always look forward," she said. "Remember that. Everything in this room is from the past. The past can only make you sad, and is that what you want?"

Claire shook her head.

"Of course not. The future is full of promise." Mellie smiled and lifted her hands up to the heavens. "It's wide open for you, darling. The past can only hold you back from moving forward. All right?"

Claire nodded, but she could almost feel the pull of the aged and love-filled pictures from where they rested in the box of trash.

Around one-thirty, the truck arrived. It rumbled and creaked up the long driveway. Claire looked out the upstairs window of her room—the room she had once shared with Vanessa—to see the truck pull into the field and come to a stop not far from the barn. Three men climbed out of the cab. Three burly, hateful men. She flew down the stairs, grabbing her jacket from the chair by the kitchen table, and ran outside. The ground was sodden as she raced across the field. The men were pulling open the broad barn doors as she neared them. She was breathless. They stood back, hands on hips, shaking their heads in awe at the unexpected beauty of the carousel in front of them. Before he died, Vincent had completed the carousel except for one horse. Someone from the park that was taking the carousel had told Mellie they would get an original Siparo for that spot.

"My grandpa made all of them," Claire said loudly.

The men turned to look at her, then at each other, chuckling to themselves. "He did a real fine job, missy," one of them said. Another of the men winked at her. "And we're going to be real careful moving them," he said, "so don't you worry about that."

She pulled a small crate from the corner of the barn and set it on the ground a few yards outside the open doors. She sat on the crate and watched them dismantle the horses from the carousel. It was a slow process, with the quiet working of screwdrivers and wrenches and little real action until it was time to actually remove one of the uncoupled horses from its roost. It would take two men, then, to carry the horse to a crate. Claire could not see inside the crates, but she hoped they were thickly padded. She felt relatively calm as she watched the men. Until they started working on Titan.

"He's my favorite," she said, hoping her words would make them take extra caution. But they were talking among themselves, trying to determine the best way to detach him or whatever, and they barely glanced in her direction. She said it again, this time only loud enough for herself to hear.

She blinked hard as they lowered Titan into the crate, and her chest hurt from the effort not to cry. The gold of his mane shone in the sunlight, then disappeared into darkness as they set the lid on top of the huge wooden box.

She had not heard Mellie approaching, but suddenly felt her mother's hand on her shoulder. "We deserve a break, don't we?" Mellie asked.

Claire did not turn around. She did not take her eyes from the barn.

"Let's go into town for an ice cream sundae," her mother suggested.

Claire didn't want to go. She wanted to stay right where she was until the carousel had been completely dismantled. She was an overseer. Her grandfather wasn't here to do it. Someone had to.

But she looked up at Mellie's face. There was a fragility there she had never seen before, or maybe it was the way the March sun fell on Mellie's pale features. Without protest, Claire stood up and followed her mother to the car, turning back only once to watch the men hammering shut the top of Titan's crate.

At the diner, Mellie dropped a bunch of coins into the little juke-box that rested on their table, and they took turns selecting songs. Over their sundaes, Mellie asked her a dozen questions about school and her friends, and Claire threw herself into the conversation, not thinking—and certainly not saying—anything about what was happening back at the farm, anything that might make Mellie lose her smile.

By the time they got back, the truck was gone. Claire walked into the barn. The carousel itself stood empty of the horses. The men would come again to take apart the platform and crate up the organ, and in another day or so, when she and Mellie were back in Falls Church, the barn would become nothing more than a barn. She walked around the platform for a while, but it was too eerie, too sad, and so she went outside again and walked slowly across the field to the house.

By the side door, the boxes she and Mellie had dragged from the house awaited the trash truck. She sauntered around the boxes, almost casually, until she found the one she was looking for. The photograph album jutted from one corner, and she carefully freed it and carried it into the house.

"Mellie?" she called once she was in the kitchen.

"In here!" Mellie sang from the dining room, and Claire tiptoed up the stairs to her bedroom, where she took her clothes from her suitcase and set the album deep inside.

35

Slim Valley Ski Resort, Pennsylvania

Why had he let Pat talk him into this?

Jon drove his Jeep toward Slim Valley, Pat riding next to him in the passenger seat. They passed through one small farming community after another, the gently rolling terrain still lifeless under its winter brown blanket. It was hard to believe that somewhere nearby existed a snow-covered mountain.

Pat was talking about plans for the retreat, but Jon only half listened, consumed by a mounting, multifaceted anxiety he was struggling to bring under control.

He'd tried to get out of the trip with complaints about his burned foot, but the burn was nearly healed, despite the dire predictions and chiding of the physician he'd seen in the emergency room. Pat had ignored his protestations anyway. Jon was too ashamed of the honest reason for his resistance to talk with her about it. Today, he would be lifted into a mono-ski by strangers, who would not know him as anything more than a mass of defective body parts.

He was accustomed to pursuing activities with Claire or other able-bodied friends. Always, he had held himself above the masses. It was not intentional, not a snobbishness, but merely a function of the fact that he was the guy at the top, the guy responsible for developing and financing the programs, including this particular program, Mountain Access. Pat was chattering about this person or that— friends of hers who would be skiing today. Unlike Jon, Pat belonged to dozens of these activity-oriented organizations. She was off on some adventure nearly every weekend.

Ski season was technically over, but an early-spring snowstorm had given Slim Valley a bonus weekend. "The weather god created that storm just for *you*, Jon," Pat had said to him the day before. "Come on. I know it's only been a couple of weeks since Claire left. I know you're grieving but I think it would do you a world of good to get out. Weekends are hard when you're alone."

That argument was probably her strongest. He dreaded the weekends and had already decided to spend this one in the office. "I have plenty of work to do," he said.

"All you do is work, Jon. It's not healthy."

The work kept his mind off Claire. Most of the time, anyhow. One night this past week, the pain of losing her, of imagining her with Randy, was so bad that he drank himself into a mindless stupor.

So he had let himself be persuaded. He and Pat had come close to blows over transportation to the mountain. Pat had wanted to ride in the car pool with the other members of Mountain Access; he'd wanted to take his Jeep, preserving the time he felt in control. Pat had finally relented and agreed to ride with him. She probably figured it was the only way she'd get him to go.

"There's the mountain." Pat pointed to an outcropping of white in the distance, a mere bump in the horizon covered by bare trees, and Jon thought she must be mistaken.

"What mountain?" he asked.

Pat laughed. "You'll see."

The Jeep began a gradual ascent, and piles of dirty, crusty snow appeared in clumps at the side of the narrowing road. Jon felt his ears pop.

"Make a left here," Pat directed after a few miles.

He turned the Jeep into the parking lot of the ski lodge. The handicapped spaces were filled, and they had to park a distance from the other cars in order to have room to fully open their doors. Jon got out of the car first, then steadied Pat's chair as she transferred from the Jeep's high seat. She muttered under her breath the whole time, and although he couldn't make out her words, he was certain she was cursing him for insisting they take his car. She was accustomed to a lift.

The air was crisp and cold as they wheeled to the front door of the lodge.

"Watch it." Pat pointed to the grate in front of the door. Jon angled his chair as he crossed over it, wondering how many wheelchairs had lost a caster in those grooves. Someone opened the door for them, and suddenly they were in the warmth of the lodge. Across the room, the mountain—it was not the Alps, but it would certainly do—shot up behind a glass wall, and Jon was mesmerized. A surge of excitement began edging out his apprehension.

There were wheelchairs everywhere. People turned to look at him and Pat, and he heard whispers of "Jon Mathias" coming from all directions at once.

"Hey, Jon!" someone called.

"Never thought we'd see *you* on the slopes, bro'," someone else shouted across the room.

"About time you saw what your money's buying, Mathias."

He and Pat were quickly surrounded. Many of the faces were familiar, others were not, but all were welcoming and friendly.

A member of the resort staff—a blond, tanned man in his thirties—walked over to Jon and pumped his hand.

"Come on," he said. "You and Pat come to the front of the line."

Only then did Jon realize there was a registration line to his right. He swallowed his discomfort as the blond man ushered them to the front, but the people they passed seemed unperturbed. They wheeled out of his way as though a red carpet marked his path, and within minutes he and Pat were registered and ready to ski.

Once outside, Pat went off with a group while Jon waited for the appearance of his instructor. Not far from him, he could see a few skiers transferring into the mono-skis. He'd never seen one of those contraptions up close before. They looked pretty simple from where he sat—a seat mounted above a single ski—and the skiers seemed to have little problem getting into them without help. For some reason he'd imagined having to be lifted into the ski like a sack of flour. He smiled as he watched.

"Are you Jon Mathias?"

The voice came from behind him, and he turned to see a young woman walking toward him. "I'm Evie," she said, holding out her hand. "I'll be working with you today."

She was tall and very attractive. Twenty-six or -seven. Her snug ski pants and jacket were a brilliant blue that matched her eyes, and wisps of blond hair fell from beneath her hat.

She sat down on a bench near him. She was a physical therapist, she explained in a sunny voice that distracted him from the little nervousness he had left. She asked him appropriate questions about his injury and abilities, listened carefully to his answers, then led him over to a mono-ski.

Suddenly, a young black man appeared next to them.

"This is Lou," Evie said. "He'll be your buddy."

"You look like you work out," Lou said to Jon. Despite the bulk of Lou's skiwear, it was evident that he spent a good deal of time in the gym himself. "Think you need any help getting into the ski?"

"I think I can do it," Jon said.

Lou pushed the ski next to his chair, and he and Evie guided Jon into it without incident. Evie strapped him in, and the fit was tight but comfortable. He was a little wobbly, though, until Lou attached the outriggers to his arms. The two small skis helped keep him upright.

"Hold your arms out to the side," Evie said. "Let's check your balance."

He did as he was told, and Evie and Lou applauded.

"He's not gonna have any trouble out there," Lou said. He explained the mechanics of the ski for getting on and off the lift, and when Jon had no problem mastering the lever, Lou looked at Evie and said, "I'm gonna find me a skier who needs my help."

Evie nodded as Lou walked away from them, and Jon grinned. If he was being patronized, he didn't care. He had this ski down pat. At least on level ground.

His first run was on the beginners' slope. Evie skied backwards in front of him, giving him directions the entire distance down the hill. "Turn your head to the right," she'd call out. "Great! Now the left. Now do a series of turns."

He was quickly gaining control of the ski. It felt like an extension of his body, and he longed to pick up speed, to really fly down the mountain, but Evie was methodical. "Got to learn the basics," she said when he complained about the slow pace, and he promptly took a spill on a turn, proving her point.

They took the lift up together, and he felt the rush of being carried into the air, mono-ski and all.

"You're doing incredibly well," Evie said as they rode in the air above the slope. "You must have skied before your accident."

"My parents bought me skis before they bought me shoes, I think," he said. "But it's been a long time. This feels terrific."

"Well, you're going to feel even more terrific in another few minutes," Evie said.

And she was right. The moment Jon pushed off from the top of the big slope, he felt whole. Able-bodied. The sensation, at first alarming, quickly thrilled him. What a total escape from reality! Bare trees flew past him, and he was carried back to the thrill of skiing as a teenager, before the accident. It felt no different. Maybe better. His euphoria stole his caution, and he took another spill—at high speed this time—near the bottom of the slope, but he was laughing when Evie arrived to help him up.

He pushed himself to the lift with his outriggers. Evie sat next to him again, and she teased him about his cockiness. He loved the lilt in her voice. He loved the view of the mountain from his seat on the lift and the bite of the cold air on his face.

He asked Evie questions about herself. Where she'd gone to school, where she was from. He liked looking at her. He watched as she drew a stick of lip balm across her full pink lips. Her goggles had fogged up, and when she opened her jacket to find a tissue, he could see the shape of her small breasts beneath the textured blue cloth of her long johns.

She's barely older than Susan. Don't be an idiot. But he was happy. Drugged happy. Crazy happy. Slipping off the lift, he was grinning to himself. *I don't need you, Harte.*

When he'd pictured how this outing would unfold, he'd seen himself—and Pat if he could tear her away—driving home early while the rest of the Mountain Access group put up in a nearby motel. But the sky was dark before he was ready to surrender the mountain. Pat had long since retired to the lodge, where he imagined she was warming herself by the fire, talking with other skiers. As he transferred back into his chair from the mono-ski for the last time that day, a wave of melancholy washed over him, and he felt the loss of the mountain and the loss of freedom, from both his chair and his thoughts.

Halfway home, he and Pat stopped for dinner. Over thick chowder and corn bread, they decided that it made no sense to drive the rest of the way home that night. They were tired. They could get a couple of rooms in the motel next door.

There was a moment of quiet awkwardness between them as they drove into the motel parking lot.

"We can get one room, if you're comfortable with that," Pat said in an offhanded way. He glanced at her, and she quickly added, "It'd be cheaper, and the rooms probably have two beds. Unless you'd rather not."

He did not care about the money, but the idea of sharing a room appealed to him. He wanted Pat's chatter surrounding him tonight. He was afraid of the void, of the crash that seemed inevitable after so full and glorious a day. He did not want to think about the nasty twist his life had taken.

"But if you'd rather get two rooms," Pat stammered on, "that's fine. I didn't mean to imply anything untoward." She was positively squirming in her seat, and he laughed.

"One room sounds good," he said. "I don't particularly relish the thought of being alone tonight."

The room was spartan but large, and it was indeed furnished with two queen-sized beds. He and Pat took turns in the bathroom. He would have to sleep in his T-shirt and boxers, but Pat emerged from the bathroom in an enormous pink nightshirt, an evil-looking black cat painted on the front, the fabric stretched across her large breasts. Obviously, she had been prepared to spend the night away from home. She must have known he would enjoy the slopes in spite of himself.

They got into their respective beds and turned off the lamps on their night tables. Jon stared at the ceiling, marveling at the oddity of the situation. Here he was, lying alone in a strange bed, while a woman he'd worked with for years—and whom he loved dearly—lay alone a few feet from him. Their wheelchairs stood like barriers on the floor between them.

In the darkness, they talked about skiing. Every time Jon closed his eyes, he saw the white ground falling away in front of him and felt the sensation of speed, smooth and freeing. Even after he and Pat stopped talking, images of the mountain continued to draw him, careening and weightless, into the valley below.

"How is Susan handling the separation?" Pat asked suddenly, jerking him miserably back to reality.

"Not well," he said. He and Claire had spoken with Susan two days earlier. As planned, Claire made the initial phone call, and Susan had reacted with a stunned, shocked silence, quickly followed by anger—anger that masked hurt or confusion or fear. It was clear that she blamed Claire for the separation, and Claire shouldered the blame with grace. He'd been surprised by her honesty with Susan. For once she didn't try to submerge the truth under a sea of wishful thoughts. Claire was changing.

"Susan's pretty confused," Jon said to Pat.

"Yeah, well, so's your wife, if you ask me." Pat's voice was uncharacteristically icy. "I mean, I understand that she's suffering some sort of posttraumatic stress because of the incident on the bridge, but she should be working it out with her husband at her side, not some other guy. She's in therapy, I hope."

"Yes, though I don't know how well that's going."

Neither of them spoke for a few minutes. All Jon could hear was the soft, steady hum of the traffic on the highway.

"I'm going to tell you something, Jon." Pat's voice cut across the dark room.

"What's that?"

"I could never say this to you in the light of day, but right now we're in ... well, strange circumstances."

He smiled. "Yes."

"I think you're an incredible person. I would much rather be next to you in that bed than over here. And I know at least six or seven other women who feel the same way."

He grinned at the ceiling. "Yeah? Who?"

"Never mind. Just remember that if Claire is crazy enough to actually end her marriage to you—and once you feel ready to move on, of course—there will be a string of women waiting to help you do the moving."

He looked over at his longtime friend, her face barely visible in the darkness. "Thanks," he said.

"You're welcome."

Another moment of silence passed between them, and Jon became aware of the broad emptiness of his bed. What the hell, he thought.

"Pat?"

"Yes?"

"Is there a chance you'd like to share my bed tonight in a non-consummatory fashion?"

It seemed to take her a minute to understand his choice of words, but then she laughed. "I'd love to."

He switched on the night table lamp and watched her sit up in bed. The cat's hindquarters were painted on the back of her pink nightshirt, and they swelled and shrank as she got into her chair. Moving his chair out of the way, Pat wheeled the few feet to his bed, where she transferred deftly in beside him. She lay on her side, her back to his chest, and he hugged her against him. Her breasts rested heavily on his arms. She was a much larger, much softer woman than Claire. Her hair smelled like summer sunshine.

"This feels good," she said.

"Yes," he said. And it did. "That's one of the hardest things for me to get used to. No physical contact. I don't mean sex. I mean touching. Hugging."

"At least you've had it for twenty years," she said, and he realized that Pat was one of those people who never had it, who went to bed night after night without the touch of another human being's hand on their skin.

He pulled her close and breathed in her sun-smelling hair. He had a pleasant sense of exhaustion and had nearly drifted off to sleep when Pat suddenly asked him, "Have you met the man?"

Jon drew in a long breath, fully awake. "I met him briefly," he said. "He's this big, good-looking dude who walks on two legs. I hate his fucking guts."

Pat shook her head, her hair brushing against his cheek. "I just don't understand Claire," she said. "I mean, she and I talked sometimes, Jon. Girl talk. And she'd rave about you. About how wonderful you are. It just blows my mind that she—"

"Claire raves about how wonderful everyone is, haven't you ever noticed that?"

"No, this was different. She thought she was so lucky to have you. It didn't matter one speck that you were in a chair. I mean, you know as well as I do that it's not that this other guy's able-bodied. You believe that, Jon, don't you?"

He sighed, wondering how much to say. "It's hard for me to feel as though he and I are on equal footing. Forgive the pun. But I *do* think the attraction goes beyond the physical. Way beyond. She claims it's not physical at all. Even if that were true, it doesn't make me feel any better. Maybe worse, in a way."

"What do you mean?"

He thought of his conversations with Claire over the past few weeks. She was still having flashbacks, she said. He tried to get her to tell him about them, determined to listen, but she gave him only the briefest description, and he knew it was Randy who was hearing her recollections in detail.

He squeezed Pat's arm. "Do you remember when I asked you about that hypothetical situation? Party A and Party B?"

"The blocked memories. Right."

"Well, I'm B and Claire's A."

"What on earth are you talking about?"

He pressed his cheek to her hair. "Claire doesn't remember a whole lot about her childhood," he said. "She's repressed a lot of it. I swear, I didn't believe in repression until I realized she was the master of it. She has completely blocked whole chunks of time. She only remembers the good times."

"Wow," Pat said. "That fits Claire, doesn't it? I always wondered how anyone could have such a perpetually bright outlook on the world."

"Well, she doesn't anymore. Not since she saw that woman jump off the bridge. She couldn't come up with any nice little clichés to make that experience go away. To change what happened. And then she started getting these little flashbacks, which I'm afraid might be some of the missing pieces from her childhood. The bad things that she's blocked. When she's with Randy—well, he seems able and willing to help her try to remember those things."

"Does he have the professional background to do that?" Pat switched to her shrink voice.

"No. At least I don't think so. He owns a restaurant."

"Asshole. He's playing with fire. She's forgotten those things for a reason. To protect herself. If he's forcing her to dredge up parts of her past she's not ready to remember, it could have a disastrous outcome. Even well-trained, well-meaning therapists have fallen into the trap of eliciting false memories from vulnerable patients."

"These memories are real."

"How do you know?"

"I know."

"Well, I still think this guy's out of his league."

Much as he would have loved to join her in bashing Randy, he knew it was unmerited.

"I don't think he's forcing her to remember stuff. Encouraging her, maybe, but not forcing. The flashbacks or whatever they are seem to be coming naturally. And slowly. But she's preoccupied with them. They're her world right now. There's no room for me in it."

Pat did not speak again right away. "Jon ... " She sounded hesitant. "These flashbacks of hers. Are they? ... You don't need to tell me the specifics, but how bad are we talking about?"

"Well, like I told you, I know something that happened to Claire that she doesn't remember. And it was bad, and I—"

"I don't understand how you could know something she doesn't."

He waved her question away. "Doesn't matter. Just trust that I do. So, do I tell her or not? I think maybe if I told her, it might put an end to this whole mess. She wouldn't need Randy anymore. At least not for the purpose of jarring her memory." He did not want to think about other purposes she might have for Randy.

Pat was thoughtful for a moment. "I'm afraid I still feel like I did back when you guys were A and B. It sounds like she's uncovering things at her own pace, Jon. I think it would be a real mistake to push her."

He nodded. "I hope you're right," he said. He would have loved to force an end to Claire's painstaking excursion into the past, yet he was still terrified of sharing what he knew with her.

"And *I* hope she's working with her therapist on this stuff and not just with the charlatan," Pat said. "This sounds like serious business."

"I know."

Pat let out a long sigh. "I'm glad you told me all of this, though," she said. "I've been feeling so much anger at Claire. Understanding the situation eases the fury a little."

"Don't let it ease too much, all right? I like having you to share my rage with."

The room fell quiet again. The muscles in Jon's arms were heavy and warm, and the scent of Pat's hair surrounded him like a summer day. This time when he closed his eyes, he fell asleep in the arms of a friend.

36

Seattle

The nearest newsstand that carried the *Washington Post* was a half-mile from the hospital, so Vanessa took a walk on her lunch break each day to buy a paper. Zed Patterson's molestation trial had started, and the Seattle papers did not cover it in the sort of detail she craved. Of course, there were no pictures of Patterson's young accuser, but Vanessa had a clear image of the girl. She was slight and scrappy, her body still that of a child. Her legs and arms were long, her knees knobby and covered with scrapes from one adventure or another. Her nearly white-blond hair was cut boyishly short. Her nose was upturned, her eyelashes so pale as to be nearly undetectable. Where this image came from, Vanessa could not have said. Yet from the moment she'd read the original article detailing the allegations against Patterson, the girl had appeared to her in this form.

Even when Friday's paper stated that the girl and her mother had immigrated to the United States from El

Salvador five years earlier, Vanessa could not lose the image of her mischievous blond waif.

And the waif was not being believed. By the second week of the hearing, the girl's own mother reluctantly testified to the trouble she'd had with her daughter. She'd been caught stealing, the mother admitted, and she lied frequently. The girl's aunt went so far as to pronounce her niece "evil." "She's not like the other kids in the family," the aunt said.

Vanessa read the testimony of the mother and the aunt and was convinced that this was not the first time the girl had been abused. She did not believe for an instant that kids were born bad.

Women's rights groups were conspicuously silent, and Vanessa guessed they felt as Terri Roos did—it would be a mistake to topple Zed Patterson from his throne of power. In the long run, women could only suffer from his downfall. The articles in the paper brimmed with his work on victims' rights and with his compassion for his accuser.

"This is a young girl clearly in need of counseling and guidance," Patterson was quoted as saying, "and our first priority must be to see that she receives the help she needs."

Pictures of him in the paper showed him smiling with an easy self-confidence. "I have complete faith in this country's system of justice," he stated on at least three separate occasions. Vanessa could only glance at the photographs. Any lingering over that face made her head throb and her stomach churn.

Apparently she was not alone in having that reaction to the senator from Pennsylvania. On day ten of the hearing—the day she was to take the stand herself and face Zed Patterson across the courtroom—the girl had to be hospitalized with gastritis. A hospital spokesman said she was reacting to the stress of the hearing, but it was clear that those in Patterson's camp read her sudden illness as backpedaling on the girl's part. She had not known what she was getting into when she made her accusation.

In other articles in the paper, Vanessa would see Patterson's name bantered about on this bill or that as though he were simply another senator with nothing else going on in his life. Innocent until proven guilty. Vanessa wondered if she were the only person in the country who was taking this hearing seriously. Why did no one seem to be helping this kid? Why was everyone wishing she would simply go away?

The paper printed the article about the girl's illness on a Tuesday. That Wednesday, Vanessa found herself sitting in one of the payphone booths of the hospital lobby, dialing the number of the girl's Washington, D.C., attorney, Jacqueline King. Her hands shook as she pressed the cool square keys on the phone. She was able to reach a partner of the attorney, who was in court that morning. Vanessa did not identify herself but got right to the point of her call.

"If I had information on an old case regarding Walter Patterson, would it help?"

The woman on the other end of the line did not respond right away. "What do you mean, 'an old case'?" she asked finally.

"I mean, if someone who had once been molested by the senator were to come forward now, would it do any good?"

Again the hesitancy on the other end of the phone line. "Are you saying this happened to you?"

Vanessa closed her eyes. "Yes."

"Jesus. Hold on."

Vanessa felt perspiration break out on her forehead. She gripped the phone in a panic. "You're not going to tape this, are you?"

"No. Just needed to get something to write with. Can I have your name?"

"No. I have to understand—"

"How long ago are we talking about?"

"Thirty years."

She could feel the woman's disappointment. "You're kidding." Her voice was flat.

"Are you saying it's too long ago to be of any help?" Vanessa heard the hope in her own voice. *Please tell me there is nothing I can do.*

"Jesus. Thirty years? How old were you? What did he do to you?"

"Are you saying you can't use the information?"

"Look, I have to talk to Jackie," the woman said. "We'll use it somehow. The truth is, we need something to save this case. No one believes this kid, except Jackie and me. And you just made me a whole lot more certain. Please give me a number where I can reach you once we figure out how to use this."

"No. I'll have to call *you* back."

"Jackie's working late tonight, but she's going to be tied up with a client till about nine. Could you call back at nine-thirty, our time? I'll be sure she picks up then."

"Yes, all right."

"Good. We'll talk to you later then."

"Wait!" Vanessa was not finished. "How's the girl doing?"

"She's terrified. You wouldn't believe how tough this kid is, ordinarily. Not afraid to walk by herself through the streets of D.C. at night. But every time she thinks about having to look Patterson in the eye and talk about what he did to her, she throws up. Every time. I'm not sure we'll ever be able to get her on the stand."

"What does she look like?"

If the woman was surprised by the question, she didn't let on. "Not like a kid who's going to win the hearts of the jurors, that's for sure. She's grossly overweight for her age. Never smiles. One eye doesn't track properly, and you can never be sure if she's looking at you or not."

Tears welled up in Vanessa's eyes. She wanted to hold this child. Probably no one ever held her.

"You might be her only hope," the attorney said. "You'll call at nine-thirty?"

"Yes."

Brian was off from work for two days, and by the time Vanessa got home that evening, he'd built an enormous fire in the fireplace, and a pot of stew was simmering on the stove. It was 5:30, 8:30 East Coast time. She'd called him earlier to tell him about her conversation with the lawyer. He knew what was on her mind when she walked in the door.

She dropped her briefcase on one of the kitchen chairs, checked her watch—although she'd checked it only seconds earlier—and grimaced at her husband.

"What should I do?" she asked.

"No one can answer that question for you."

"You could try." She smiled wryly.

He rested the mixing spoon on the stove and wrapped

Vanessa in a hug. "I think you're a gutsy, compassionate woman. You'll do what feels right to you."

She glanced without interest at the stew. "Can dinner wait a bit? I have some work to do at my desk first."

He looked at her, an unasked question in his eyes. "Sure," he said.

She sat down at her desk in the corner of the family room, sorting through a stack of bills and writing checks until 6:35. Brian sat on the sofa, reading the paper. He kept the fire going, rising wordlessly once or twice to add a log, and the heat of the flames warmed her. At 6:40, she tried to balance her checkbook, hunting for an elusive thirty-seven cents the bank said she had but that did not appear in her check register. Her chair faced the window, and she could see Brian's reflection in the glass. Occasionally, he looked up at her, but neither of them spoke. They had forgotten to turn on the stereo tonight; the crackling of the fire was the only sound in the room, and Vanessa could feel the slow passage of minutes, seconds.

The rich, tomato-heavy scent of the stew drifted into the room. A wave of nausea passed through her, and only then did she let herself think of the girl no one would believe. She looked at her watch again. Seven-ten.

Setting down her pen, she turned to face Brian.

"What could they possibly do with my thirty-year-old allegations?"

He folded the paper slowly and rested it on the coffee table. "I don't know, Van."

"Are you disappointed in me?"

He shook his head. "No."

"It's behind me. I have to leave it behind me."

He said nothing, and she was relieved when he patted

the sofa cushion next to him, inviting her to join him. She walked over to the couch. He slipped his arm around her shoulders as she sat down, and she got another whiff of the stew.

"I don't think I can eat tonight. I'm sorry. It looked delicious. Can we save it for tomorrow?"

"Of course."

Again the silence. She wished she had turned on the stereo on her way to the sofa.

Brian softly ran his thumb back and forth over her shoulder. After several minutes, he took in a long breath.

"It's only a little after ten now, their time," he said. "I bet that lawyer's still waiting there in the hope you'll muster up your courage and—"

"Brian, don't!" She pulled away from him. "I'm through with it, okay? I shouldn't have called in the first place. Please let it go."

He drew her back again by the shoulder. "Sorry," he said.

She felt restless and wired. She could go for a run. Or read. Rent a movie. She could not get a firm grasp on what she wanted to do tonight. The only thing she knew for certain was that she would not allow herself to sleep. Sleep would only invite a ride on the carousel. And next to her would be an unsmiling girl, so plump she would have to grip the pole to stay upright on the horse. Her one good eye would be focused hard on Vanessa as their horses galloped around and around, far too fast, in a circle that had no end.

37

Vienna

The bedroom smelled like Jon, like his aftershave, that warm and subtly masculine scent Claire had long associated with him. For a moment, she felt immobilized by the unexpected pain of longing. She had to force herself to walk into her closet and gather up the clothes and shoes she had come for.

Jon had been reluctant to have her come to the house at all, finally agreeing that she could stop by if she did so when he wouldn't be there. It had only been three weeks, but already the house felt as if it belonged to someone else. Things had been rearranged: The suitcases were no longer in the laundry room but had been lined up in the hall closet. The bread box was now on the counter closest to the sink. The coffeemaker had been moved next to the refrigerator. She received her biggest surprise, though, when she opened the cupboards to put away the food she'd bought in anticipation of Susan's arrival for spring break. She'd spent seventy dollars on Susan's favorite cookies and crackers and soups and frozen pizza, only to discover that Jon had already stocked the kitchen with the same items. She'd simply stared at the full shelves in the open cupboards, stunned that he had even known what to buy. He was doing okay. He was in control of his life. The house was clean, orderly. He'd even gone skiing, he'd told her. He was doing perfectly fine without her.

He'd asked her not to call so often. She didn't think she'd been calling him that much—every couple of days or so—but he said it made it harder for him when she called. So she'd stopped, and now there were days when she found herself missing his voice. She zipped up her packed suitcase and carried it into the kitchen, setting it by the back door. Then she went into Jon's bedroom closet, opened the trapdoor leading to the attic, and pulled down the stairs.

It took her twenty minutes to find the old photograph album. It was at the bottom of a trunk filled with Susan's ragged stuffed animals and lying beneath—ironically—two old hand mirrors, which Claire quickly turned facedown on the floor.

"I'm a danger on the road," she'd joked to Randy the night before, when she'd looked in her sideview mirror to check her blind spot and saw it filled with a shifting sea of green.

The album felt fragile in her hands as she carefully lifted it from the trunk. Randy wanted to see pictures of the barn, he said. He wanted to see her grandparents and parents, and Claire-the-child and her sister Vanessa. Claire had told Randy she didn't want to disturb Jon by coming to the house to pick up the album, but the truth was, she was afraid of the memories those pictures might elicit from her.

She had enough elusive thoughts floating in and out of her head as it was.

She stood up, feeling the weight of the album in her hands, and had a sudden recollection. She had rescued this album at one time. Someone—who?—had thrown it away, and she'd saved it from the trash pile. She looked down at the smooth brown leather, ran her hand across it, and for a moment considered sitting down at the top of the folding stairs to look through it. No. Not here in the cold dark of the attic. Not until she was with Randy.

She left a note for Jon on the kitchen table. *I took some clothes, my old Harte family photo album, and a few books.* She thought of other things she might say. She wanted to ask him if he recalled ever seeing a bloody towel on one of their trips to Italy, but she suddenly remembered the guarded, apprehensive look that would come into his eyes when she'd mention one of her flashbacks. That made her miss him less. Good. Being here, surrounded by Jon's things, Jon's scent, she needed a reminder as to why she was no longer with him.

There's enough food to keep Susan happy for several spring breaks. You did a good job grocery shopping. Was that condescending? She wished she could erase the line, but she'd written it in ink.

She stared at her daughter's name. Tomorrow Susan and Jon would be together in this house while she would be in her cubbyhole of an apartment. It seemed unnatural, unreal, and for the first time during this entire ordeal, she felt pure guilt: She was terribly selfish to put her daughter through this.

An hour later, Jon picked up Claire's note from the table. He smiled at her allusion to the food he'd bought for

Susan. Of course he'd taken care of that. What did she think?

She'd taken the photograph album. The words sent a chill through him.

He wheeled over to the refrigerator and took a plastic container of leftover macaroni and cheese from the shelf. He put it inside the microwave, then poured himself a beer, taking a sip as he waited for the oven to heat his dinner.

A decade ago, he had looked through that album with Mellie.

Mellie had been living with them a little over a month by then, suffering through the final stages of her lung cancer. Jon had been home from work with a urinary tract infection. Mellie was bedridden, but at least Jon could get around. He would make her lunch, change the television channels for her. Their odd bond of illness lasted close to a week. Claire would come home from work and ask how the two invalids were doing, and Susan, who was nine at the time, made them dual get-well cards, which they hung on the wall in the guest room, temporarily transformed into a room for Mellie.

Jon had never liked his mother-in-law. It was hard to like someone who kept a wall around herself, who answered questions with whatever she thought her questioner would like to hear, who never let people know who she really was. Something changed during their week together, though. Mellie began talking, saying things he knew she would never say to Claire. Perhaps not to anyone. "You're the strongest man I've ever met, Jon," she told him. "I can tell you anything, and you won't fall apart."

They sat together in her room one day—Mellie in the hospital bed they had rented for her, Jon beside her in his wheelchair—and looked through the old album, dusty from the attic. He loved seeing those pictures of Claire when she was small. So tiny and big-eyed and innocent. The pictures made him ache with love for her.

The album seemed to draw confidences from Mellie's lips. She told Jon that her husband used to beat her late at night after Claire and Vanessa had gone to sleep. She told him how her mother, whom Claire thought had died peacefully in her sleep, had actually died an undoubtedly frightening death of a hemorrhage, entirely alone there in the farmhouse in the middle of the night. She told him many things she'd never told anyone before.

One cold, rainy day, when his infection was much better and Mellie's cough was much worse, she told him that she knew where Vanessa was. Vanessa and Claire's father had died the year before, and he had left a letter to be delivered to Mellie at the time of his death. Vanessa was just graduating from college—at the age of twenty-eight—and planning to start medical school, he had written. She was extremely bright, but it had taken her a while to get her feet on the ground. And he'd enclosed an address for her.

Jon was repelled by the man who would keep his daughter separate from her sister and mother, and even more angry with Mellie for keeping her knowledge of Vanessa's whereabouts to herself.

"Claire has a right to know where her sister is," he'd argued.

"Why? They don't even know each other now. And it would only wake up the past." Mellie clutched his hand. "Claire's got a good life with you, Jon. Let the past rest."

She told him that she had traveled to Seattle herself after receiving the letter from her ex-husband, showing up at

Vanessa's rundown apartment building only to have her daughter tell her to "get the fuck off my porch."

Jon continued to argue with her until Mellie reluctantly gave Vanessa's address to Claire. Claire wrote a letter to her sister, the first of several that never received a reply.

Jon grew to like Mellie, if not love her. He grew to understand that although her secrecy might be misguided and harmful in the long run, it was borne of her intense love for the people around her. She simply didn't know how to be any different. In those last days before her death, though, she learned to open up, if only with her son-in-law.

After a particularly gruesome attack of coughing one day, she told him, "I'm going to die soon." His first impulse had been to say, "Of course you're not," or "Don't think that way," but he caught himself. She thought he was strong, and so he would be strong for her. He'd held Mellie's hand and looked her right in the eye.

"Yes," he said. "I know."

And she had smiled at him.

And then she told him something that took all his strength to endure.

38

Vienna

It was nearly midnight by the time Susan arrived home from William and Mary, but Jon had waited up for her.

"Hi, Dad." She walked through the kitchen door and breezed past him, stopping only long enough to bend down and whisk her lips across his cheek on her way to her bedroom. He heard her toss her things on the bed as he poured himself a glass of milk. After a minute or two, she reemerged.

"How was the drive?" he asked.

"Fine." She looked past him toward the refrigerator. "Is there any pizza or anything in the freezer?"

He nodded. "Plenty. Help yourself to whatever you can find."

He watched her walk across the room, struck by her thinness. She had always been slender, but now her jeans seemed to hang from her hipbones and bag around her thighs. "You eating enough at school?" he asked as she pulled the plastic wrapper from the pizza.

She shrugged. "I don't think about it much." She put the

pizza in the microwave. "When I get around to it, I guess. I've got so much work to do."

"You look like you're wasting away." He himself had lost ten pounds since Claire left. He could see it in his face when he shaved in the morning. "What are your plans while you're home?" he asked.

"See everybody." The microwave beeped, and Susan pulled out the pizza, tested the center with the tip of her finger, and put it back in.

"Who's home?" he asked.

"Everyone."

"Can you be more specific?"

"You know, *every*one." She rattled off a string of names as she slid the pizza from the oven to a plate. Then she sat down at the table and began eating in silence.

Jon watched the shimmering top of her head for a moment and let out a sigh. *Talk to me, Susie.* When had she changed? Where was the little girl who had bubbled around him, who wanted to talk about everything under the stars? Sometime in high school, that child had disappeared and left this uncommunicative kid in her place. And there was so much they should be talking about. In the past, both he and Claire would have been waiting to greet Susan when she arrived home from school. Neither he nor Susan was acknowledging what was different now.

Maybe midnight, though, was not the time to press her.

He took a long swallow from his glass of milk. "How's Lisa?" he asked, referring to the friend with whom she'd driven home.

"Good." She nodded, her mouth full, then looked up at him with her big, dark eyes. "You want some of this?"

"No, thanks." And then he couldn't help himself. "Your mother is anxious to see you," he said.

"Well, she can stay anxious." She answered quickly, as though she'd been waiting for him to raise the subject. "I'm not going to see her while I'm home."

"Susan, you have to. She's your mother."

She stood up, swallowing the last of the pizza and rinsing off the plate at the sink.

"I'm really tired, Dad," she said. "Good-night."

She escaped quickly to her bedroom, leaving him alone again, the air of the kitchen charged with his frustration.

Susan was true to her word. She was out day and night with friends. Jon rarely saw her. On the few occasions they were in the house together, she was steadfast about avoiding any topic of significance. She didn't return her mother's phone calls. The one time Claire managed to reach the house when Susan was there, Susan said abruptly into the phone, "I don't want to talk with you, Mother," and hung up.

One night, Jon came home from the gym to find his steel-hearted daughter in tears. He came in the back door and wheeled into the family room, where he saw her sitting on the sofa, facing the fireplace, head in her hands. Obviously, she thought she was alone, and he vacillated between interrupting her and ducking into his bedroom to give her privacy.

"Susan?"

She swung around to face him, her face a heartbreaking, tear-streaked red.

He wheeled toward her. "What is it, honey?"

Her lower lip trembled. "I don't understand how she could do this to you."

"She hasn't done anything *to* me. She's doing something for herself."

"I can't believe she's being so selfish."

He wondered how he could respond without shutting her up in the process. That was the last thing he wanted to do right now.

"You know," he said, "you've kept to yourself so much this week that it's been hard for me to know how the separation is affecting you. It's hard to know if you care or—"

"Of course I care. What do you think? I mean, suddenly my parents are totally fucked up, and my mother's screwing this total stranger. At least I assume that's what she's doing." She looked at him as if he might be able to banish the thought from her mind.

Caught off guard, he shrugged in discomfort. "I don't know the exact nature of their relationship," he said.

Susan's look asked him how he could be so naive. "She told me she needs him to help her sort out stuff from her past," she said, her voice edged with cynicism. "I thought that's what her shrink is for."

"Please see her," he said. "There's so much going on with her. I can't possibly explain her point of view to you. Let her try to—"

"If I see her, it's only going to be to yell at her. To talk her into coming home and being a normal wife and mother again."

"I don't want you to do that," Jon said with such force that he surprised himself.

"Why not?"

He didn't know how to make her understand something he was only coming to understand himself. "Because I need this time alone," he said. "I didn't realize it at first.

Believe me, Suse, the last thing I want is for Mom and me to split up. But I'm discovering things about myself."

Susan wiped her red nose with a ragged tissue. "What do you mean?" she asked.

"Well, didn't you wonder, when you went off to school, if you'd actually be able to take care of yourself?"

She frowned. "Well, yeah, but—"

"And then you found that you could, and it felt pretty terrific, right?"

She nodded again. "Yeah, but you're an adult. And you're my *father*. You've always taken care of everything. You can do anything, Daddy. I always think of you as"— she dropped her eyes to her lap, where she was tearing the tissue apart with her long fingers—"just as someone who can handle any problem, can fix anything. If you're not really like that, I don't think I want to know."

He laughed. "I'm not like that, Suse. Face it. Do you realize I've been with your mother since I was seventeen? Two years younger than you are now. The truth is, maybe I *could* handle just about anything, but I honestly didn't know that until she left. It's been good for me that way, sweetheart. Painful as hell, yes, but good for me."

"You could've figured that out without her dumping you."

He tried not to react to her choice of words. "She didn't dump me. I asked her to go. I knew she needed time to herself, too. You could just as easily say I kicked her out."

"Right, Dad." Susan crumpled her tissue in her fist. "Then she could have gone to . . . I don't know, a resort somewhere—by herself—if it's just that you need time to be apart or whatever. But I don't get why she needs to see someone else."

Jon straightened up with a sigh. "The truth is, Susan, that the man Mom is . . . involved with is seducing her in a way I never could."

Susan drew in her breath, her mouth a little O. "Daddy, don't *say* that," she said. There was a fresh torrent of tears, and she leaped from the couch to bend down and hug him. "Just because you can't walk doesn't mean you haven't been the best husband and father anyone could ever ask for."

He realized she had misunderstood his meaning, but he was so touched by her sudden, rare display of affection that for a moment he couldn't speak.

"Hon." He freed himself gently from her arms. "Sit down again."

She did so, but she still clung to the arm of his chair, sniffling quietly, looking for all the world like the little girl she'd once been. Jon rested his hand on hers, speaking softly. "I don't mean what you think. I don't mean that he's seducing her sexually." He felt odd saying that to her. "Not like a man seduces a woman. I mean he's seducing your mother with the *truth*. No one's ever done that with her before." He shook his head. "You know what she's like, how she always makes like everything's okay even when it's not."

"God, I *hate* that."

"Right. And it's hard to explain what's going on with her right now. You really need to talk to her to understand. Randy's giving her something I never had the guts to give her." He knew as the words left his mouth that they were no longer accurate. He could do it now, he thought. He could listen to her, maybe even draw her out. These last few weeks, he'd found a strength inside himself that he'd never known was there.

Susan shook her head, pulling her hand away, and he could see the teenage irritation beginning to replace the childlike sweetness again. "I just don't get what you're talking about," she said.

"Then you need to talk to her about it."

"No. I don't want to see her. I'm *embarrassed* by her. She's not acting like a mother."

She stood up, and Jon knew she'd reached the limit of her ability to endure this sort of conversation. It had been good though. Amazingly good.

"When are you heading back?" he asked.

"Tomorrow sometime." She picked up a textbook from the coffee table and headed toward the door.

"Susan?"

She turned to face him again.

"I love you," he said.

"I love you, too, Dad." She slipped quickly from the room, as if those words might burn her if she stayed a moment too long.

"I want to see the carousel in person," Randy said. It was Sunday, and he and Claire were sitting on the small sofa in Claire's minuscule living/dining room, looking through the photograph album for the third time and nibbling on the coffee cake Claire had baked in her small, temperamental oven. "The pictures are great, but I'm sure the black and white doesn't do it justice."

"I'd like to see it, too," Claire agreed. "Maybe we could drive up to the park one of these days?"

"Soon," he said.

Claire looked down at a picture of her mother. Mellie sat in a rocker on the front porch of the farmhouse. She was smoking a cigarette. During her first perusal of the album with Randy, Claire had suddenly remembered that it was Mellie who had thrown the pictures away.

"Why in God's name would she do that?" Randy had asked.

"We were cleaning out my grandmother's house after her death, and my mother said the album represented the past and should be tossed. She only wanted to think about the future." Claire remembered the little lecture Mellie had given her as they sat together on her grandmother's living-room floor.

Randy shook his head. "Your mother was a sick woman."

For once she said nothing to defend Mellie. "They moved the carousel the same day," she added.

"Really? How do you move a carousel?"

"They put the horses in big crates, and—"

"And they hammered them shut, I bet." Randy smiled at her, and it took her a minute to catch on.

"Yes!" She felt the skin of her arms prickle with goosebumps. She could even see Titan disappearing into one of the crates, but it was as if she were seeing it happen from a great distance. "It must have been terrible for me," she said, "but I don't remember feeling anything."

Randy squeezed her shoulders. He turned the page in the album to the picture that intrigued Claire most. It was of her grandfather, sitting at his workbench, the unlit pipe in his mouth. The picture had immediately reminded her of Randy. The beard, the pipe. The tender affection in the clear eyes. Randy failed to see the resemblance. He had even been a little insulted that she'd seen his face in that of a man nearly thirty years his senior.

All of the pictures were fascinating, but Claire was disappointed—and a little relieved—that they were nothing more than old reminders of a happy childhood. Small freeze-frames of a long-ago time and place. Little in the album had stirred new memories, and few of the photographs triggered emotions in her, good or bad. Except for the pictures of Vanessa. Each time the little blond girl appeared, Claire wanted to turn the page. She felt a weight in her chest and a restless urge to leap from the sofa and busy herself with something. Anything.

"Maybe you're worried about her," Randy suggested. "She was torn from your family. You probably feel guilty that she suffered such a terrible fate while you didn't."

She was certain that was not it, but she could offer no other explanation for her discomfort.

"You know." Randy traced circles on the album with his fingertips. "Maybe she remembers some of the things you've forgotten. She might be able to help you figure out what your flashbacks are all about."

The weight grew heavier in her chest, and she got up, suddenly consumed by a need to move the album from her lap to the table. The thought of Vanessa—of *anyone*—dumping a lifetime of memories on her all at once was frightening. A certain pace was unfolding as she worked backwards through the images of her past. It was tedious work, painstaking, but it felt right to her. She was one of those people who got into a cold pool slowly, cell by cell, as if she would die if she were submerged all at once. This seemed like the same thing.

"She won't answer my letters." Claire straightened the place mats on the table. "So it's not even worth thinking about."

"If you say so." He yawned, stretching his long arms above his head before standing up. "Be back in a sec." He disappeared into her bedroom, and she heard the closing of the bathroom door. She was carrying the coffee cake toward the kitchenette when she heard the knock on the front door. Setting the plate down on the end table, she opened the door to find her daughter standing on the step.

Claire caught her breath, then broke into a smile. Susan was too thin, but beautiful, her brown hair shining in the sunlight. She saw Jon in her face and was surprised by the sudden, sharp sting of tears.

"Oh, Susan." She reached for her daughter. "I'm so happy to see you."

Susan evaded the hug and stepped into the room, and Claire lowered her arms to her sides.

"I'm just here to say good-bye before I go back to school."

Claire nodded. "Yes." She wiped her eyes with her fingers. "I'm so glad. I was afraid I wasn't going to get to see you at all this visit. Please, honey, have a seat." She motioned toward the sofa, wishing that she could magically make Randy disappear from the apartment. "I have some homemade coffee cake."

Susan did not sit down. "I'm not staying that long." She leaned awkwardly against the glass-topped table and looked around the little room—at the coffee cake, the kitchenette, the African violet on the windowsill—anywhere but at her mother's eyes. She shook her head. "I just can't believe you're living like this," she said.

"Oh, it's not so—"

Randy suddenly appeared in the doorway from the bedroom.

"Oh." He looked at Claire uncertainly for a moment, then smiled. "Is this Susan?"

"Yes." That weight in her chest again. What did a heart attack feel like? "Susan, this is Randy."

Susan's eyes were like daggers; Randy had to feel them cutting him in two. She turned suddenly toward the door, but Claire quickly blocked her path.

"Please, don't go. Not yet."

Randy held up his hands submissively. "You two visit awhile," he said, his eyes on Claire. "I'll read in here." He backed into the bedroom, closing the louvered doors between the two rooms.

Claire looked imploringly at her daughter. "Please stay awhile."

Susan raised a trembling hand to her mouth. "God, Mother, what are you doing?"

Claire bit her lip. "It's so hard to explain."

Susan let out a sound of exasperation. "That's what Daddy says, too. I guess it's always hard to come up with a good reason for acting like a self-absorbed bitch."

Claire jerked as if she'd been struck. She wished Randy could not hear what they were saying through the louvered doors.

"Sorry." Susan lowered her eyes, cheeks flushed.

Claire touched her arm. "Please sit down and let me talk to you."

Tears suddenly appeared in Susan's eyes, spilling over, spilling down her cheeks. "I hate you right now, do you know that?" she asked. "I really do."

Claire reached for Susan's shoulder, her own tears falling at the sight of her wounded daughter. "Oh, honey, you don't mean that. You—"

"Yes, Mother, I *do* mean it." Susan jerked away from her mother's grasp. "You've always been like that. Daddy thinks you're changing, but you're the same as ever."

"What do you mean?"

"I'd say I hated someone, and you'd say, 'Oh, honey, no, you don't.' I'd say my teacher wasn't fair to me, and you'd say, 'Oh, honey, of *course* she is.' I'd say I was sick and you'd say, 'No, you're not.' I'd say my arm is broken, and you'd say, 'Oh, Susie, it's just a sprain.'"

Claire winced at that one. She'd waited so long to take Susan to the hospital that they'd had to rebreak the arm to make it heal properly. And Susan was right. In every example, she could hear herself saying those words. Worse, they suddenly sounded like something *Mellie* might say.

"You know"—Susan hugged her arms across her chest—"I thought I was crazy. According to you, what I felt, I wasn't really feeling. What I was thinking was all wrong. Well, somewhere along the way I figured out it was *you* who was crazy. I knew I had to get away from you or you'd make me just as nuts as you are. You know why I graduated early, why I worked my butt off to get out of high school? So I could get away from *you*. I couldn't get away soon enough."

Claire could not let that pass without argument. "No, that wasn't it. You were really so anxious to get to college, that—"

"Mother! Are you listening to me?" Susan glared at her, then laughed, throwing her arms up in a gesture of defeat. "Yeah, all right, Mom. That was it. I wanted to get to college. That was it. Good-bye."

She reached for the doorknob again, turning to look at her mother one last time. Her eyes were so mean and dark that Claire could almost believe she'd meant it when she said she hated her.

"Daddy's doing just fine without you, by the way, in case you care," Susan said. "I'm going to keep my eyes open for someone to fix him up with. Someone who'll appreciate him."

She walked out the door, slamming it hard behind her, and Claire watched her run down the driveway toward her car.

Randy opened the louvered doors. "I'd like to talk with her," he said.

She shook her head. "It'll just make things worse."

"Please let me, Claire."

She glanced out the window. Susan had her hand on the car door. "All right," she said.

Randy walked past her and out the door, and from the window she watched him approach the car. She was surprised that Susan didn't gun the engine and drive off. Randy squatted down on the curb, and for several minutes he and Susan spoke through the open window while Claire watched, still trembling from her daughter's tirade.

When he came into the apartment again, he wrapped his arms around her wordlessly and held her close.

"What did you say to her?" she asked.

Randy spoke softly against her hair. "I told her she was right," he said.

Claire leaned back to look at him. "You what?"

"I told her she was brave to lay all that on you. That it was important for you to hear it."

For a moment Claire said nothing, trying to absorb his words. "And what did she say?" she asked finally.

He laughed. "She told me to go to hell."

39

Seattle

"We're up shit creek, Vanessa." Terri Roos did not even say hello, and Vanessa wished she hadn't bothered to pick up the phone. She lowered herself into the chair behind her desk.

"What do you mean?" she asked.

"Do you remember what I told you about the Senate Victims' Assistance Committee? That they're having a hearing on Zed's Aid to Adult Survivors Bill next month?" Terri's tone was condescending, as if the matter were of such small import to Vanessa that she would have forgotten.

"Yes," Vanessa said. "I remember."

"Well, we've been trying to find witnesses willing to testify to the impact that childhood abuse had on them as teenagers."

"Right. And?"

"And the committee has this attorney screening the witnesses. We finally dug up five women willing to testify, but only one of them passed the screening. And one is not enough. Zed said we can forget about getting our funding this year unless we find more witnesses. He was very apologetic but said he hasn't been able to give the whole adolescent issue the focus it deserves. Even though he's going to be cleared on this molestation charge, it's sapped his time and energy." There was anger in Terri's voice. "He said we should—"

"What makes you so sure he's going to be cleared?" Vanessa interrupted her.

"Do you have any doubt?"

"The case isn't closed yet." She hadn't given up hope that the jury would see through the girl's anxiety to the facts. There had been inconsistencies in her story, true, and she had cried uncontrollably once she finally took the stand. She'd retracted some statements while embellishing others, but she had not retracted the main thrust of her accusations. Somehow, the jury would discern the truth.

"Well, anyhow," Terri continued, "Zed said that we should try again next year. That way we can—"

"My AMC program will be dead by then. Yours too."

"I know, but right now we have exactly one witness to testify to the need, and she's going to be lost in the shuffle."

"Why were the other witnesses screened out?"

"Not credible enough. Not professional enough in their presentation. Their problems during adolescence weren't compelling enough—the attorney's word, not mine," Terri added quickly. "A couple of them said they had repressed the memories of their abuse until adulthood, and that went over like a lead balloon. The lawyer said we'd be opening up a whole debate on repressed memories, that we're not going to be able to get a bunch of male politicians to buy into that right now."

A jagged flash of light appeared in the corner of Vanessa's vision. She reached in her drawer for the migraine pills, but the bottle was empty. She'd have to call in a prescription for herself. She was popping medication left and right these days. Head. Stomach. What if she got pregnant while she was taking all this stuff? She leaned her elbows on the desk and rubbed her temples.

"And now," Terri said, "the one witness we *do* have is starting to chicken out. She doesn't want to be up there alone. So Zed says if we spend this year trying to find decent witnesses and put together a good case for funding, we might stand a chance next year."

"We can't just give up, though."

Terri was silent. "Excuse me, Vanessa," she said after a moment, "but I really have to take issue with your use of the word 'we' here. I know you've got your reasons, whatever they may be, but you've really let the rest of the network do the lion's share on this. I'm only calling you in case, by some miracle, you happen to have a few sterling witnesses tucked away in your back pocket. And also, I thought you might appreciate an update on what's going on. You've been completely out of the loop on this."

"I know." Vanessa pressed the palm of her hand hard against her forehead. "I know, Terri, and I'm sorry."

She had not seen Jane Dietz in a year, not since her last annual examination. Sitting in Jane's waiting room, it was hard to believe it had been that long. Jane felt more like an old family friend than her gynecologist. Vanessa had seen her for the first time at Sara Gray's insistence when she was twenty years old. "You need to take better care of your health," Sara had said. Even then Jane had seemed old, with her gray hair and out-of-date horn-rimmed glasses. Now she was in her mid-sixties. Sometime over the years Vanessa had stopped calling her "Dr. Dietz" and started calling her "Jane." Whether that switch had occurred spontaneously or through invitation, she could not recall. It didn't matter. She felt a bond with Jane she had never experienced with another physician outside of her colleagues. She supposed that was why she had made the appointment today. Yes, it was time for her annual checkup, but it was more than that: She needed a dose of Jane Dietz.

Jane spotted her in the waiting room and nodded to her with a smile. From that brief exchange, Jane must have intuited that Vanessa needed to talk, because she had her receptionist usher her into her office rather than one of the examining rooms.

"It's good to see you, Jane." Vanessa sat down in one of the three leather chairs and looked across the desk at the doctor. What an anachronism this little woman was, with her steel gray hair pulled back into a bun and her harsh navy blue suit beneath the white coat. This year she was wearing wide tortoiseshell eyeglass frames.

"Good to see you, too," Jane said. "And I heard through the grapevine that you and Brian finally got married."

Vanessa smiled. "We did."

"I am enormously pleased, dear. Enormously."

"And," Vanessa felt her smile widen, "I'm hoping to get pregnant."

Jane's look of surprise was quickly replaced by a grin, out of place and endearing on her pale and wrinkled face. "That's good news, Vanessa. I have to say I never thought I'd see you pregnant, although I know you always wanted a baby."

"I do. And I want a *healthy* baby. I'm a little concerned about my age being a factor, and—"

Jane shook her head. "It shouldn't be. Not if you're healthy and we take the proper precautions to minimize the risks."

"Well, I've also been under a lot of stress lately, and the migraines are back." Her words sounded almost apologetic. Confessional. "And my GI tract's been ... overactive. I've been medicating myself, but I need to figure out what I can take safely, since I may get pregnant while I'm taking it."

Jane drew in a long breath and sat back in her chair, lips pursed. "And the nightmares?" she asked. "Are they back, too?"

Jane had never known the source of Vanessa's night-mares, only that she had them. She did know, of course, about Anna. Or at least that Anna had once existed. It had been Jane who'd persuaded Vanessa to go into therapy, who had given her Marianne's name.

"The nightmares are back," Vanessa admitted, "but certainly not like before."

"Are you seeing Marianne Sellers again?"

"No. I don't think it's necessary. Really, Jane, it's nothing like before. This is just some ... I don't know, residue from the old stuff. It'll pass."

Jane pursed her lips again. "All right," she said. "Let's do some blood work, and we'll talk about medication for your head and your gut. We'll get you ready to be a mom. But I urge you, Vanessa"—she leaned forward on her desk, her small dark eyes riveting behind the thick glasses—"you've come to see me because you want a healthy start on this new part of your life. A clean, fresh start. I've known you a long time. I know you don't get migraines unless something is seriously disturbing you. And I know it's not just work. You've dealt with insane amounts of stress on your job without so much as a tension headache, let alone a migraine. It's the old stuff, as you call it. You don't want to be carrying this load of stress around while you're trying to start a family, do you?"

Vanessa shook her head. Something about Jane made her feel like a child in desperate need of mothering. A child who welcomed a stern but caring hand.

"Please, Vanessa. Do what you need to do to clean that slate before you have a baby. For the baby's sake, if not for yours and Brian's."

"All right," she said, although she didn't know if she had the reserve it would take to clean that slate. More hours of talking about the past. Her eyes filled. She couldn't go through that again. The thought brought fresh, stabbing pain to her head.

"Vanessa?"

She looked at Jane through the blur of tears. "Yes?"

"I know you're hearing your biological clock ticking away, dear, but it will wait," Jane said. "It will simply have to wait."

That night, Vanessa called Marianne's office, only to learn that her former therapist was on a monthlong trip to England. Vanessa had to smile. Marianne had talked about taking that trip, always in the abstract, always with a wistful look in her eyes. Good for her, she thought. But lousy timing.

Marianne's answering service gave her the name and number of the therapist covering for her. Vanessa wrote the information down on a notepad, sloppily, almost illegibly. She knew she would never use it.

40

McLean

When she awakened, Claire felt hot and groggy and undeniably aroused. She vaguely remembered stretching out with Randy on his carefully made bed, talking over the events of the day. They had done that a dozen times before—lay on his bed to talk after a day of work—and so it had not occurred to her that it might be a mistake to do it again. It had been barely five o'clock then, and they were still in their work clothes. But they must have fallen asleep, and now the room was dark and the air felt thick with desire.

Randy's face was close to hers, his lips light against her cheek. His hand slowly kneaded the flannel of her shirt, just below her breasts. Through the fog of half-sleep, Claire moved closer to him, running her hand across his chest. He kissed her, and she felt the stirring in her body, a stirring borne of deprivation and a longing to please him. As he slowly worked the buttons on her shirt, she made a decision, not only to allow what was about to occur, but to embrace it.

She lay quite still as he undressed her, letting her need build with the eager pressure of his fingers against her skin. When she lay naked and bathed in moonglow on his bed, he straddled her, still clothed himself, and ran his hands in long, light waves over the hills and valleys of her body.

"Am I taking advantage of you?" he asked.

She rolled her head from side to side, not bothering to open her eyes. Then she pulled him toward her, and he balanced himself above her as she unbuttoned his shirt, unzipped his pants. He stood up to finish undressing, and she watched him, mesmerized by the way his erection stretched taut the fabric of his shorts. He was hard as steel already, and she had not even touched him.

He disappeared into the bathroom for a few minutes while she lifted the comforter and slipped under the sheets. When he returned, he was unwrapping a condom, and she could not help but recall the only time she and Jon had ever made love using one. They'd been teenagers then, young and green, and that scrap of latex had nearly driven Jon to tears of frustration as he tried to make it function with his temperamental erection. Randy, though, was having no such problem. The moon caught him fully in its light as he stood next to the bed, rolling the sheath over his penis. His thighs were thick and dark and muscular, and by the time he was in the bed again, kissing her, touching her, rubbing against her, Claire could think of nothing other than having him inside her.

He thrust into her slowly at first, but quickly picked up his pace, and she struggled vainly to capture the familiar sensations, the rising and falling and fullness she usually experienced with lovemaking. She was barely aware of her hand slipping between their bodies, her fingertips finding their place. The building up, the electric tension, was instantaneous as he thrust against the back of her fingers. She heard the ragged edge to her breathing. The light on the ceiling began to blur before she squeezed her eyes shut to focus on the fire as it spread through her body.

Randy came shortly after she did, although she was not at first certain that he had. He was so quiet, so contained. He lay still above her, breathing hard. After a moment, he rolled onto his side and slipped an arm around her shoulders. Claire felt sudden tears in the back of her throat, regret she did not want to feel.

"How are you?" Randy asked.

"Okay." She was not sure how she was.

"Just okay?" he asked.

"Give me time," she said. "I don't know how I feel about what just happened."

"Fair enough," he said. "I feel great about it, though." He kissed her lightly, then caught her hand and lifted it to his lips. When he spoke again, his voice was tentative. "Do you need to have your hand between us when we're making love?" he asked.

"Oh." Should she feel embarrassed? "I did that all the time with Jon. It was the only way I could have an orgasm during intercourse."

"But . . . I'm not disabled." He was speaking with great caution.

"It's a habit," she said. "Did it bother you?"

He shook his head. "It feels sort of . . . unnatural, but if that's what works for you, I guess it's all right with me."

Again, she could think of nothing to say. He did not seem bothered by her silence, and she gradually became aware of the even rhythm of his breathing, the rise and fall of his head on her shoulder.

It was far too early for sleep, but she continued lying there, eyes wide open, the knot of sadness still tight in her throat. In an instant, she had allowed the nature of their relationship to change, and she knew she had lost something in the process. Honor. Self-respect. She had crossed a line she had never intended to cross.

At breakfast the following morning, Randy touched her hand across the table, the tips of his fingers resting lightly on her gold wedding band. "Are you going to leave this on?" he asked.

She looked at the ring. She could not remember the last time she'd removed it, but she did so now, tugging at it, twisting it. She slipped the ring into the pocket of her robe, then looked across the table at the man who had suddenly become her lover.

"I don't know what I want, Randy," she said. "Please don't have expectations of me that I—"

"Shh." He leaned across the table to kiss her. "I don't. I'm just very happy you're here right now."

They talked awhile longer, and she studied him, reminding herself that she had felt the undeniable heat of desire the night before. But had it been desire for Randy or merely the desire of the moment? She couldn't say.

After breakfast, she put her dishes in the dishwasher and then climbed the stairs to the second floor, and only when she reached the guest room did she realize that her hand was wrapped, tight as a fist, around the abandoned gold ring in her pocket.

They made love in his bed again the following night. Claire did not even bother with the pretense of the guest room. She hadn't been able to sort out her feelings yet. They were snarled together in a tangle of guilt and need. She was making Randy happy, though. That in itself was worth something.

She lay awake after he'd fallen asleep, thinking back over the past week. She'd finished painting the scenery and was now spending her time either working with Randy at the restaurant or helping the seamstress with the costumes for the upcoming play. She was actually sewing. She *despised* sewing.

She missed her house. She missed Amelia and the foundation. She'd thought of asking Jon if she could return to work on a part-time basis. She'd talked to Debra Parlow about that idea, and Debra had agreed she needed the stimulation her old job would offer. But would that be fair to Jon? Especially now. How could she ask him to work with her when she was practically living with another man? And she could no longer say to him, with any honest indignation, that she was not sleeping with Randy.

She had called Jon's voice mail a few times, telling him thoughts she was having about the retreat, offering suggestions. Her mind-numbing activities during the day seemed conducive to the generation of creative ideas as well as to the regeneration of memories.

The memories often came to her these days in complete, detailed form, and they were no longer merely the pretty remembrances of a happy childhood. She saw her father slapping Mellie in the farmhouse kitchen; she heard her parents arguing loudly after she and Vanessa had gone to bed. Each new image surprised her, and she was still not convinced of their authenticity. She felt such distance from the memories that it seemed as if they'd been stolen from someone else's life.

"They're yours," Randy would say quietly, and she knew he was right.

She snuggled against him now, and he pulled her closer in his sleep, mumbling something she could not make out.

"Randy?" she asked. "Are you awake?"

"Yes." His eyelids fluttered open for a second before closing.

"Can we talk for a minute?"

"Mmm." He rolled onto his back. "Sure."

"I'm thinking of going back to work at the foundation," she said.

"Oh." He sighed, tightening his arm on her shoulders. "I didn't think painting scenery and sewing costumes would hold your interest very long."

"I miss my work," she said. "I think I can concentrate on it now. Part-time, anyhow."

He wrapped his other arm around her, too, squeezing her to his chest. "You miss Jon," he said.

She was surprised. "No, I don't. Not really."

Randy stroked her hair. "Oh, I think so."

Neither of them spoke for a moment.

"You never talk about him." Randy broke the silence.

"Well, no. My mind's been filled with other things lately." She stared at the ceiling. "Actually, I try not to think too much about him. It's too . . . difficult."

He ran a hand down her arm. "Tell me how you met him," he said.

"Why?"

"I'd like to hear about it."

She hesitated. "I'd feel strange talking to you about him."

"Tell me."

He was insistent, and she began to talk. She was accustomed to sharing her memories with him, and so slipping into this one was easy, so easy she was afraid she might forget to censor it for the tender ears of a lover.

She had met Jon on a clear, brisk day in October of her senior year. He wheeled himself into her homeroom for the first time, and Claire was immediately intrigued. She had never seen a wheelchair-bound student in her high school, with the exception of one of the football players who had broken his leg the year before and did a brief stint in a chair. But Jon Mathias did not look like a football player. Everyone's eyes fell immediately to his legs. Was this a kid with a temporary disability or something more? They needed to know quickly, as one did in high school, how to categorize the newcomer.

But it was more than the wheelchair that fascinated Claire. It was his face. His demeanor. He was unsmiling, almost angry looking, and he did not so much as glance at his prospective classmates as he wheeled himself to the front of the room with a note for Mrs. Wexler. Claire could almost see the chip on his shoulder.

The rumors spread at a furious pace. By lunch she knew that he was from California and that his back had been broken in a plane crash. He was—or at least, had been— very wealthy, attending only private schools. Most likely, he was accustomed to a very different type of student than those who now surrounded him.

Listening to other students talk about him, Claire felt a pain in her heart that grew as each new fact was revealed.

He'd spent six months in a rehabilitation hospital and was now living with an aunt in Falls Church. His parents and sister had died in the accident. In the space of six months, he had lost his family, had nearly lost his life, and had gone from being rich to not rich. Where was the money? If his parents had died, wouldn't he still have it? She knew the neighborhood where his aunt lived. The houses were small and poorly maintained. Maybe the money was nothing more than an embellishment to the story.

On that day in October, she was eating lunch with her boyfriend of six months, Ned Barrett, when Jon wheeled into the cafeteria. He stopped for a moment, looking dazed and daunted by the sea of tables. Then he wheeled himself forward again, toward the end of the food line.

"I can't believe they let him into this school," Ned said, his eyes following the chair. "Why didn't they stick him in Garrett?"

Jon had reached the tail end of the food line and sat staring at the waistband of the tall boy in front of him.

"Because Garrett is where the retarded kids go," Claire said. "Just because he's handicapped doesn't mean he's not smart."

"How do you know he's smart?"

"I don't know that. But you're assuming he's not just because he can't walk."

"Paralyzed from the waist down," Ned said with a snicker. "Walking's not all he can't do."

Claire threw her empty milk carton at him, and he laughed. Ned was a big, good-looking boy, with white-blond hair and pale eyelashes. He was vice-president of the class and quarterback of the football team. Claire thought she was in love with him and had recently contemplated losing her virginity to him. Sometimes, though, Ned's thick-headed insensitivity bothered her.

"It's not right." Ned's eyes were on Jon. "I mean, nothing against him—I'm sure he's a great guy and all—but how's he ever going to fit in here? I'm talking about what's fair to *him*. He should be with people like himself. You know, handicapped or retarded or whatever."

Claire was barely paying attention to Ned. She watched as another of the football players deftly cut in line in front of Jon, who actually backed his chair up a bit, doing nothing to regain his advantage.

"Did you see that?" Claire asked. "Stu cut in front of him."

Ned shook his head. "Yeah, well, that just proves my point. No one's going to treat him like he's human or—"

She was already out of her seat and walking toward the food line. She tapped on Stu's arm. The big blue-eyed halfback looked down at her, draping an arm across her shoulders. "Hey, babe, what's up?"

"Maybe you didn't realize it, Stu, but Jon was ahead of you in line."

"Who's Jon?" Stu looked down at Jon, who stared straight in front of him. "Oh, are *you* Jon?"

Jon said nothing. Claire saw blotches of color forming on his cheeks.

"Get behind him, Stu, come on."

Stu laughed but did not put up an argument. He stepped behind Jon's chair. "There, bleeding Harte, you satisfied now? No wonder Ned's so pussywhipped these days."

She touched Jon's arm. "Please excuse his rudeness. Not everyone here is like him. Most people are really nice."

Jon looked up at her, his big brown eyes stormy. "Thank

you," he said, and even in those two small words she could not miss his sarcasm. "You just made me look ten times more helpless than I already am."

She watched him numbly as he wheeled past her, and Stu chuckled. "Nice going, Claire," he said.

She returned to her table, where Ned was engrossed in conversation with a couple of other students about next week's game against Mount Vernon, and watched Jon make his way toward the food. Someone else cut in front of him, and two boys had a brief food fight in an arc above his head, but she didn't budge from her chair.

After school that day, she asked Mrs. Wexler to assign him to her.

"Assign him to you?" Her gray-haired homeroom teacher looked confused by the request.

"Yes. Pretend we do it all the time. Pretend like, whenever there's a new student coming in midyear, you assign someone to help them get a feel for the place. Not a bad idea, anyhow, right?"

"I suppose—"

"Great! Thanks." And she was off. She had cheerleading practice.

The following day, she told Jon he had been assigned to her and that they would have to eat lunch together. He did not seem pleased. Neither was Ned, who looked at her with sympathy when she told him why she couldn't eat with him that day. She tried to talk to Jon in the food line, but it was awkward, him being so much lower than she was. Besides, he wouldn't look at her and seemed to have nothing to say.

"You know, I'm sorry about yesterday," she tried. "About the food line. Stu made me so furious, and I thought I was helping you."

Jon gave a slight nod of his head. "You meant well," he said. "But that sort of thing is my problem to figure out, all right?"

There was no hostility in his voice, and for the first time he was looking directly at her. She wondered if it hurt his neck to look up that way.

"All right," she said.

Over the next few days, she barely left him alone. She knew she was forcing herself on him. It was hard for him to retreat from her because of his chair, and because he had no other friends to turn to. She told herself that he needed her to persevere. Besides, she had decided that he was the most beautiful boy she had ever laid eyes on. When she reported her infatuation to her two best friends, they looked at each other incredulously. "Better than Ned Barrett?" one of them asked.

Claire nodded. She didn't understand her reaction herself. Ned was Adonis perfect. Girls lost their concentration when they walked past him in the hall. Claire had seen more than one of them trip over her own feet while staring at him and trying to walk at the same time. But there was something about Jon's soulful eyes, those sexy, gaunt cheeks, and that slender, battered body that held enormous appeal for her.

At first, she had to badger him with questions. After a week, though, he seemed to loosen up and started talking on his own. He didn't want to be there, he told her one day in the cafeteria. He hadn't wanted to leave his rehab program, where he'd attended school with other kids like himself. Here, he felt like a freak. He had to use the service elevator in the rear of the school to get from floor to floor. And there were two steps between the hall and the cafeteria that seemed an insurmountable obstacle to him.

She strained her neck to see the entrance to the cafeteria without success. She could not picture the steps.

"You've never noticed them because they're not an obstacle to you. Try being in a chair for a day. The security guard has to help me up the steps. It's humiliating." He shook his head. "God, I want out of this place!"

He told her that he'd played tennis before his accident, that he'd been pretty good at it.

"I was supposed to play for UCLA next year," he said, and it hit her suddenly how his well-ordered, well-planned future had been snatched from him. It made her reach across the table to rest her hand briefly, lightly, on his, and he did not pull his own hand away.

He'd skied, too, he said. His family had flown to a resort in Colorado several times a year. He had loved skiing. She caught the tears in his eyes when he talked about it, even though he quickly turned his head away from her.

They fell into a pattern of eating lunch together, Jon talking about his past and complaining bitterly over what fate had handed him for the future.

"Why, that boy is spending all his energy feeling sorry for himself," Mellie said when Claire told her about her conversations with Jon. "You should start telling him about *you*. Let him think about someone other than himself for a while."

It seemed almost rude to talk about her own perfectly wonderful life when his was such a disaster, but she tried it.

Over lunch, she told him about cheerleading and Mellie and Ned.

He smiled at her. "Life's a bowl of cherries for you, huh?"

She shrugged, embarrassed. "It's pretty good."

He lifted the bun on his thin, dry hamburger and seemed to be studying the meat as he asked, "So, tell me more about Ned."

She told him about the various scholarships Ned had been offered, his skill on the football field, and his landslide victory in the vice-presidential election. Jon appeared bored by this information. She was bored herself.

One snowy day in late November, Jon did not come to school. Claire collected his homework assignments for him and drove to his aunt's house after school. Seeing the shabby-looking house from the street, she felt certain that his wealth had somehow died with his parents.

His dour-faced aunt let her in. Jon was sitting in front of the TV in the den, and he did not look sick. Perhaps he hadn't been able to get to school in the snow? He seemed embarrassed to see her there. She should have called first, but she'd been afraid he would tell her not to come.

"Are you sick?" she asked.

"Not really. It's just a . . . uh, a problem I have every once in a while. I'm fine now. Just needed to get it taken care of this morning."

Whatever it was made him blush wildly, and she didn't push for details.

"And you're really feeling all right now?" she asked.

"Yes."

"Then let's go out."

He looked surprised by the suggestion but followed her to the door, where he reached into a closet for his coat and gloves and hat.

She helped him into her car and wrestled the seventy-pound chair into her trunk. Then she drove to a nearby park, pulling her car into the small lot at the top of a snow-covered hill. She freed the chair from her trunk, bruising her right arm and left leg in the process, and then lifted out the two enormous metal trays that had been beneath it. Ned had stolen the trays from the cafeteria the year before.

"You used to love skiing, right?" she asked as he transferred from the car to his chair. It was getting dark out, but the moon was full and very bright, reflected off the white ground and trees. She and Jon had the hill—the entire park—to themselves.

Jon looked at the trays, wide-eyed. "What are you getting at?"

"Well, this will be more like sledding, but it's the best I can do."

Jon pointed to one of the trays. "You expect me to go down the hill on that thing?"

She could tell that he wanted to do it. There was excitement in his eyes. He had done nothing fun for so long.

She put her hands on her hips and looked down at him. "Chicken?"

"Bring the damn thing over here." He was almost trembling with anticipation, and she laughed as she helped him from the chair to the tray. She was worried about his legs and had to help him bend them into place. Then she sat down on her own tray and grinned at him.

"Ready?"

He nodded.

"Go!" They pushed off with their hands and went careening wildly down the long hill, their screams cutting through the moonlit darkness. The trays spun, and Claire felt the ice-flecked wind nipping at her cheeks. Jon spilled out of his tray near the bottom of the hill, rolling like a rag doll the rest of the way down, and Claire was relieved to hear his laughter as she came to a slippery stop next to him. He pushed himself to a sitting position in the cold snow and grinned at her. The moonlight glinted on his white teeth and carved triangular shadows into his beautiful cheeks, and she thought of kissing him. No. It was better to simply laugh together. Have fun. Take it slow.

She flopped back into the snow and spread her arms out to make a snow angel.

"Uh, Claire?" Jon was still chuckling.

"Yes?"

"How am I going to get back to the car?"

Claire stared up at the stars. "Hmm." She had not thought of that. She hopped to her feet. "I'll figure it out. Wait here."

At the top of the hill, she lugged the monstrous chair back into the trunk, then drove the car onto a service road and down to the bottom of the hill, maneuvering it as close to Jon as she could get without leaving the pavement. She got the chair out again, dragging it across the snow to him. Getting him into it took muscles she had never used in her life, and neither of them seemed able to check their laughter. They sounded like a couple of drunks, she thought. She finally managed to get Jon and the chair back to the car, where she helped him transfer into the front seat. Then she lifted the chair and the trays into the trunk once again. Muscles trembling and lungs burning, she got into the car herself.

Jon turned to face her, still wearing his grin. "Can we do it again?" he asked, and she laughed. She was exhausted, but she would have done it all night long if that's what it would take to keep that grin on his face.

She drove him home two hours later, and they sat in her car in his driveway. Claire looked at his house, small and crumbling in the unkind light of the moon.

"The rumor is that you were wealthy," she said.

He looked at the house himself, but she could not read his face. "I was."

"What happened?"

"There's still a ton of money, but it's all put away for me until I'm twenty-five. Right now, there's enough for me to use for college, but that's it." He made a wry face. "I don't think my parents planned too well."

"Oh, they planned very well, don't you see?" Claire folded her legs beneath her on the car seat, turning to face him. "If they'd left you a ton of money it would be just like having someone always around to beat up the guy who cuts in front of you in the food line. You'd never have to figure out anything on your own."

Jon smiled at her. "Is there any cloud you can't find the silver lining to, Claire?"

It was the first time she'd heard him use her name, and she was struck by the sound of it coming from his lips.

"No," she said. "I don't think there is."

He traced the outline of the glove compartment with his finger. "How serious is it with you and Ned?" he asked.

She wrapped her arms across her chest. It was getting cold in the car. "Well," she said, struggling with the answer, "my feelings about him are changing. Sometimes lately he seems pretty immature."

Jon turned his head away from her, then rested it on the back of the seat, his lips pressed into a tight line. "I don't know how to do this anymore," he said.

"Do what?"

"You know, start something. Ask a girl out. It used to be so easy. I saw someone I liked, I asked her, she said yes."

"Just ask."

He rolled his head on the seat back to look at her. "But Ned—"

"Forget Ned."

"But . . ." He waved his hand toward his legs, and she shook her head.

"I don't care," she said.

"But, a girl like you . . . You're probably used to having, you know, a physical kind of relationship with—"

Claire laughed. "Thanks a lot! Why don't you just say, 'Well, Claire, you look pretty fast to me.'"

"I just assumed that you and—"

"I'm a virgin."

"Oh. Sorry. I mean, I'm not sorry that you're a virgin, just that I made you say it." He laughed, but quickly lost his smile. "Wish I was one too. I mean, I wish I'd never had sex. I was just, you know, *mastering* it"—he laughed again—"when this happened."

For some reason, the word "mastering" sent a charge through her body.

"I'm sorry," she said.

"I mean, not being able to walk is one thing, but not being able . . . Shit. I'm preoccupied with it, with wondering if I can ever do it again or if I should become a priest or what."

She could not believe he was saying all this to her. "You're a seventeen-year-old boy," she said. "I think you're supposed to be preoccupied with it."

*

She stopped telling her tale to Randy there, abruptly. She had probably told him much more than he wanted to hear. Certainly he didn't need to know that it was Jon with whom she'd lost her virginity, in her mother's bed, while Mellie worked late at her waitressing job. Yet after Randy fell asleep, she couldn't stop herself from remembering that night. Through the combination of her inexperience and Jon's fear, their lovemaking was careful and stumbling, giggling and solemn, and ultimately, they agreed, perfect. If she hadn't loved Jon before that night in Mellie's bed, she did afterward, and she loved him with an intensity that swept all others from her heart.

4I

Seattle

Jordan Wiley died in the early-morning hours of the fourteenth of April, suddenly but not unexpectedly. When Vanessa arrived at the hospital, she found the unit quiet, the nurses teary and subdued. She kept her own tears in check, offering words of consolation to Jordy's family, praise to the nurses, and hugs to the devastated young female intern who had grown attached to the boy. Even Pete Aldrich was reticent and red-eyed at rounds, and she knew he would never forget Jordan Wiley. Jordy had taught him a few lessons about the human side of medicine.

She moved woodenly through her day, thinking of Jordy only when her defenses were down. She'd remember his fear and his courage but would quickly brush the thoughts aside before they could interfere with her work.

The tears found her that night after she'd gotten into bed. She lay close to Brian. The small TV on the dresser was tuned to the news on the chance there might be something about Zed Patterson's trial—the case was in the hands of the jurors now—but she was not listening. Her eyes were closed, her cheeks wet, and she relished the warmth of Brian's arms around her.

"Think of all the good you do," Brian said, attempting to comfort her. She knew that her crying upset him. He didn't understand that after a day of fighting the tears, they were welcome. She knew she did a lot of good, but she never wanted to lose her ability to respond to a loss.

She had nearly fallen asleep when he jostled her.

"The verdict," he said, and she bolted up in the bed and hit the volume control on the remote.

She had missed the commentary of the newscaster but caught the words "not guilty." Then Zed Patterson's grinning face was on the camera. He stood outside the Capitol building, surrounded by reporters and microphones. Vanessa forced herself to look at him. Oh, he was smooth. He was a thin man, his graying blond hair receding, and there was a slick handsomeness about him that made the hair rise on the back of her neck. She squinted at the TV screen, wondering if she would have recognized him if she had not known who he was. She wasn't sure. Yet if she bumped into this man on the street, she would still be frightened by his burning blue eyes. She'd seen them often enough in her nightmares.

Zed Patterson half smiled to the camera. "We must have compassion for her," he said, "and I hope you folks from the media will keep that in mind. It does no good to tear a young girl like that apart and ruin her future any more than she's ruined it for herself. Justice has been well served in my case, and I want to move on with my life knowing this girl will get help, not harm, from those around her."

The news program moved onto another story, and

Vanessa lay down again, closing her eyes. Brian slipped an arm across her stomach, and she felt his lips on her shoulder.

"He can talk a good line," Brian said.

"He's slick, all right. Bastard." She tried to mimic his voice. "'We mustn't hurt the poor child. She's already hurt herself so much, poor dear.' God, what a prick!"

"I'm sorry, Van," he said.

"I wanted her to win. What the hell was I thinking—that an eleven-year-old child could do it on her own? I couldn't possibly have done it at that age. I can't even do it now. I failed her. I could have done something and I didn't. And now I'm going to fail the AMC program because I'm not doing anything to save that either."

"What can you possibly do?"

Vanessa looked at the cathedral ceiling above her. The TV screen shot bands of changing color across the length of it. She could feel the lightness of Brian's breath on her neck. Inside her was a mixture of growing resolve and mounting terror. They came hand in hand.

"I can testify before the Senate committee on Capitol Hill. I can tell them about my own abuse and how it affected me as a teenager and—"

"Van!" Brian sat up. "Patterson heads that committee, for Christ's sake. They'll never use you."

"I won't name names. I'll just describe the experience."

"But he'll be there!" Brian's eyes were wild.

"And if he figures out who I am, then he does. And if he doesn't, he doesn't. I don't care. My purpose will be to make a plea for the AMC programs. They need witnesses with compelling adolescent traumas. They need responsible, credible professionals. I'm, unfortunately, perfect. And if I do it, the other witness won't be afraid to do it. Then maybe other women will speak up. And maybe that little girl won't become just another statistic. Maybe by the time she's a teenager and totally screwed up, there'll be a program in place to take care of her."

Brian held her hand, and she watched him struggle to absorb all she was saying.

"You know, I used to want you to 'confront your abuser,' as Marianne would say, but this is different," he said. "This is not what she meant. Maybe you need to talk to that therapist who's covering for her before you do anything. Don't rush into this, Van. You're scaring me."

"I'm sick of talking, and I want to do this. I want to testify." Vanessa sat up herself and squeezed both his hands. "I'm going to clean my slate, Brian. You once said that I should use Patterson. That's just what I'm going to do."

"But you've always been so careful to keep your past to yourself. You're in an important position at an important hospital, and—"

"You sound like I have something to be ashamed of."

"You know that's not it. Don't put words in my mouth."

"My position gives me credibility."

Brian looked down at the bed, where his hands were locked fast around hers. When he raised his eyes again, his face was lined with worry. "I'm afraid for you," he said. "On the surface you seem so strong, but I know better. I'm the one who wakes up with you in the middle of the night. I'm afraid of what it'll do to you to go public with something you've kept private all your life. And how can you possibly describe what he did to you when he's sitting right there in front of you?"

"I don't know," she said. "But I have to do it, Brian. The last thing I want to do is talk about my past publicly, but I can't live with myself if I don't." She raised her hands to his shoulders. "I'm going to need you to be there with me in Washington. All right?"

He nodded slowly. "All right."

She would call Terri Roos first thing in the morning and get the name of the attorney screening the witnesses. Wouldn't Terri be surprised? She smiled at the thought.

Brian suggested they turn on the night-light to ward off the bad dreams that were sure to come that night. But she left the light off and fell asleep easily, and she wasn't surprised to wake up in the morning from the first dream-free sleep she'd had in weeks.

42

Washington, D.C.

The closest parking space Claire could find was three blocks from the Marvin Center. There were puddles on the sidewalk, and she walked carefully, checking her watch every minute or so. She was distressed that she was going to miss the beginning of Jon's speech.

She had completely forgotten about this symposium at George Washington University. She had phoned Jon the day before to ask if she could work at the foundation again part-time—a proposal to which he had readily agreed. He'd thanked her for her suggestions on the retreat, saying he planned to use most of them. During their conversation, he mentioned the symposium, casually, and it was as if she'd been struck by a train. She and Jon were supposed to be the keynote speakers at the opening session. It had been arranged months earlier. Obviously, Jon was planning to do it alone. She felt as if she'd deserted him. They'd always spoken as a team. How was he going to pull this off on his own?

"I'm so sorry, Jon. I'd forgotten all about it, and you didn't say any—"

"No problem," he'd said, sounding far less concerned than she felt.

She hadn't made a conscious decision to attend the keynote address, but as she sat in Randy's kitchen this morning after he'd left for work, she knew that was what she wanted to do. She'd awakened with Jon on her mind after talking about him so much with Randy last night. It had been intentional on Randy's part; she was certain of it. He didn't want her under false pretenses. He wanted her to think about Jon and still choose to be with him. Randy didn't understand that it had never felt like a matter of choice to her.

Usually the drive from McLean to the university would take about twenty minutes, but an accident had slowed things to a crawl on the highway. Jon was scheduled to speak at nine, and it was nine-fifteen by the time she stepped through the main door of the Marvin Center. She was in the hallway outside the auditorium. Three women— a blonde and two brunettes—sat behind a long table covered with flyers and the dozen or so attendee name tags that had not yet been picked up.

Claire stood uncertainly a few feet from the table, shaking out her umbrella. The women looked at her, waiting. How was she going to get in? She was not a presenter. Not even an attendee. This was a predicament she had never before experienced.

She glanced at the double doors to the auditorium and stepped toward the women. "I'm not registered, but I would like to hear the keynote address," she said as she unbuttoned her raincoat. It was warm in the hallway.

The blond woman at the center of the table shook her head. "I'm sorry. You can't get in without a ticket."

"Just for half an hour? I'm unable to attend the rest of the day."

The woman was steadfast. She shook her head. "Sorry."

A burst of laughter from the audience sifted through the cracks in the double doors. Jon was already well into his talk, no doubt. "My husband's giving the keynote address," Claire said. "I would just like to hear him, then I'll leave, all right?"

One of the dark-haired women caught her breath. "You're Claire Harte-Mathias!" she exclaimed.

Claire smiled. "That's right."

The blond woman stood up and reached out to shake Claire's hand, suddenly meek. "Oh, I'm so sorry," she said. "I had no idea. Please, go in."

Claire nodded her thanks and walked past the table toward the auditorium doors.

The auditorium was very nearly filled. The walls were lined with wheelchairs, some of them occupied, others collapsed, waiting to be returned to their owners, who were sitting in the auditorium seats. The symposium was aimed at disabled individuals and their families, and a quick glance around the room told her that the audience was not limited to spinal cord injuries. She spotted a few white canes, and on the two large TV monitors that hung above the crowd, a young woman signed the words that Jon was speaking from the stage.

There were a few empty seats in the rear of the auditorium, and Claire slipped into one of them. Jon would never know she was there. Good.

He sat in his wheelchair on the broad, empty stage.

There was no dais in front of him, nothing between him and his audience. He had no notes, of course. He never used them. A handheld microphone was his only prop.

He was wearing a pink shirt she had never seen before, gray pants, and his gray tweed sports jacket. No tie. Even from this distance, she could see that he had lost weight. He looked relaxed, as he always did in front of a group.

He was okay. Better than okay. He was truly in his element. She looked around the audience. All eyes were riveted on the beautiful man in front of them. They were with him, nodding and smiling. Although he was alone on the stage, he did not look small. He was in total command of this auditorium.

She'd missed a good portion of his talk, but she knew what he would be saying. With this sort of group, he would talk about the different aspects of being disabled or of living with a person who was disabled. Usually, he and Claire would play off each other as they spoke, shifting easily back and forth between his perspective and hers.

He would probably describe the crash that had taken his family from him and left him damaged at such a young age. He'd talk about the loss of his identity during adolescence, when his identity had been fragile enough to begin with. And he would talk about Claire. Would he still do that even though she was not sharing the stage with him? Even though they were living apart? And would it make a difference to him one way or the other if he knew she was sitting in this audience?

She didn't have to wonder long.

"Often you hear a disabled person say that another person—or perhaps an event—was a catalyst for them," Jon said. "Someone or something that turned them around, that set them on the road to renewal. For me, it was my wife, Claire, who lifted me out of the self-pitying funk I was in and got me to look at what I *could* do instead of what I couldn't."

Claire had heard him talk about her in these terms many times before, but this was the first time she'd felt her eyes burn at his words.

"But you can love someone too much," Jon said suddenly, and Claire leaned forward in her seat. She had never heard him say that before in a lecture. She had never heard him say it at all.

"This is true, of course, whether your loved one is physically challenged or not," Jon said, "but it's particularly hard to avoid when the person you care about has such special needs. You love someone, so you want to do all you can for that person. They've suffered terribly, and you want to do everything in your power to protect them from further suffering."

There were nods of recognition in the room, and Claire wondered where this had come from, where he was going with it.

"Those of you who are able-bodied know what I'm talking about, don't you? You see a person you love struggling to cross the room to turn down the TV. What's the temptation? You could be at the TV in two seconds, while it might take them ten minutes. Think of the time and energy you can save them. But there's a cost involved. If you always help them, they'll never learn to do it for themselves, and they'll never have the pride and satisfaction of being *able* to do it for themselves. And they'll never know *how* to do it if, some day, you're not around. And it goes way beyond helping them with physical things. You try to protect them from emotional pain as well. We don't want our loved ones to feel any more pain than they have to. They already feel so much! But it's pain that makes us grow."

Jon leaned forward himself, as if he could get inside his audience. "Let us have that pain." The passion in his voice sent a chill up Claire's arms. "Let us own it. Give us room to grow as people." He drew in a breath. "And those of you who are disabled, or handicapped, or physically challenged, or whatever term, if any, you prefer for yourself. I bet you do it too, don't you? Try to protect those you love from suffering? I would be willing to bet that this room is full of highly skilled, experienced, and overzealous caretakers. Sometimes we take care of each other so well that we end up hurting each other in the process."

He had hit a nerve in his audience; Claire could see that. They buzzed and nodded and reached out for one another. In front of her, a man put his arm around the woman next to him and pulled her head gently to his shoulder. The interpreter signing on the monitor wore a bittersweet expression on her face as her hands came to a halt.

Jon was wrapping up now, but Claire was no longer listening to his words. She felt an overwhelming need to touch him, and she thought of walking to the front of the auditorium when he was finished to compliment him, to rest her hand on his shoulder. Perhaps she could call Randy and cancel her plans to meet him for lunch, then stay here and help with the symposium.

But she would do none of those things. She watched the applauding audience converge on the stage. She had no right to Jon anymore. Besides, he no longer seemed to need her. That was good, wasn't it? Then why did it feel so bad?

She wanted to turn back the calendar. She wanted to go back to that January snowstorm, put up for the night in the High Water Hotel, and never lay eyes on Margot, never meet Randy. She wanted freedom from the torment of her memories, and she wanted the smart, softhearted man on the stage. She wished he could have been the one to help her through these last couple of months.

Tears filled her eyes as she slipped quickly through the crowd toward the exit. She walked the few blocks to her car in the light rain, not bothering to open her umbrella. Once in the car, she turned on the engine, shivering as she waited for heat to fill the air.

She blew her nose, touched up her eye makeup in the rearview mirror. She would drive to the restaurant, she thought. She would spend the day with Randy, with the man who didn't love her enough to protect her from her pain.

43

Seattle

Starla Garvey. That was the name of the Washington, D.C. attorney who was screening witnesses for the Capitol Hill hearing on the Aid to Adult Survivors Bill. Her job was to select several women—and a couple of men—whose stories were compelling and convincing and to prepare them to testify before the Senate subcommittee headed by Senator Walter Patterson.

Starla. The name did not invite confidence, and Vanessa fought a sense of discouragement as she placed a call to the woman from her office phone. She got through to the attorney fairly easily, but Starla Garvey sounded rushed and harried on the other end of the line. Vanessa quickly got to the point of her call: She wanted to testify to the impact that childhood abuse had had on her as a teenager. She could also speak from a professional perspective, she suggested, offering anecdotes about the kids she was seeing in the AMC program. Ms. Garvey interrupted her.

"It's too late," she said. She had the faintest trace of a southern accent. "I already have the witnesses lined up."

"But you only have one witness who will be focusing on her problems as an adolescent."

"True, but that's not the major concern of this committee."

"But it should be. It *could* be if they'd hear something to make them prick up their ears. Please. Let me meet with you."

There was a sigh from Starla's end of the phone line, a rustling of papers. "No promises," she said. "I'll see you, but you have to be prepared for the fact that I might not use you after all. Can you come in this Tuesday at ten o'clock? The hearing's Wednesday, so we don't have much time."

"I'll be there," Vanessa said, and she hung up, marveling at the fact that she'd begged someone to let her do the last thing in the world she wanted to do.

She met Brian at a downtown restaurant for dinner that night. He was already sitting at a corner table when she arrived, nursing a glass of Perrier. He'd spent the afternoon playing tennis, and he was wet-haired from a shower and ruddy-cheeked from the game.

She told him about her call to Starla Garvey, and he listened carefully, his face sober.

"God, that's so soon," he said, putting into words what she'd been thinking all afternoon.

"I know. Can you get off?"

"One way or another." He smiled at her and squeezed her knee under the table.

She ordered salmon, but by the time it arrived, she'd lost her appetite. Each time she thought about putting her story into words for a stranger's ears, her stomach tightened. It was more than that, though. She was coming—slowly—to another decision. She looked across the table at her husband.

"I can't confront Zed Patterson directly," she said, "but I can confront my sister."

Brian's eyes widened, and he set down his fork. "Yes, you can," he said, nodding. "Do it, Vanessa. Please, do it."

She swept her hair back from her cheek. "It seems like the right time," she said. "I think I need to talk to her if I ever want to get it all behind me. It's now or never."

"Yes. And we'll be close to where she lives, right? Isn't she just outside Washington? I'll go with you, if you—"

"No." She shook her head quickly. "I don't want to actually see her face-to-face. I'll call her. Maybe even tonight." She glanced at her watch. "I'll say my piece, then say good-bye and good riddance, and that will be it." She clapped her hands together in a gesture of finality. "God, Brian, I don't know if I can do it. I don't know if I can do any of this."

"Think of the kids you work with," he said. Once he'd gotten over his initial panic about her testifying, Brian had been unwavering in his support. "Think of the kids who'll need an AMC program and won't have it. At least you'll know you've done all you can to help them."

She nodded, although she knew that Brian himself wasn't thinking about the kids. He was thinking about her, about both of them. He was thinking that although she had fought this stumbling block from her past as fiercely as she possibly could, it remained something that interfered in all she did. It was always with her, in her waking hours, and in her hours of supposed rest as well. She knew he was hoping that the next few weeks could somehow erase the past and clear a path for their future together. She was hoping for that same miracle herself.

Jon could hear the phone ringing from the garage. He'd just arrived home after working out in the gym, and his arms felt tight and tired and terrific as he wheeled into the house. He picked up the cordless phone from the kitchen counter.

"Hello?"

"May I speak with Claire Harte-Mathias, please?" The voice was curt, and he assumed the woman who owned it was selling something.

"I'm sorry, she's not here," he said. "Who's calling, please?"

There was a long moment of hesitation on the other end of the line, and Jon frowned. This was not a phone solicitor. "Hello?" he prompted.

"My name is Vanessa Gray," the woman said.

"Vanessa?" Jon asked. "Claire's sister?"

Silence filled the line again, as if the question required some thought. "Yes," she answered finally.

"Well, hello, Vanessa. I'm Jon Mathias, your brother-in-law."

"Can you tell me when Claire will be home?"

He was taken aback by her abruptness, and he pondered how to respond.

"We're separated," he said. "I know that the last time she wrote to you, we were still together, but we've been through some changes since then. Why don't I take your number and have her call you?"

"No." She nearly barked her reply. God, she sounded cold. "Can you give me a number where I can reach her?"

"She doesn't have a phone where she's staying." He could give her Randy's number, he supposed, but he would have to look it up. It might not even be listed. He had certainly never tried to call her there. "Or you could call her next week at the foundation. At work." It was going to be strange having Claire back in the office again. He'd told her she was welcome to come back, but now he had mixed feelings about having her that close to him when she would be returning to Randy every evening. "Would you like the number there?"

The hesitancy again. "All right."

He gave her the work number as well as the address of the small apartment Claire was living in on Chesterwood. "Thank you," Vanessa said. "Good—"

"Vanessa?"

"Yes?"

"Claire really needs to hear from you. I mean that. More than you can know. Your timing couldn't be more perfect."

44

Vienna

Claire was going to be late for her first day back at the
foundation, her first day of work in over a month. Randy
had delayed her at his town house with waffles and conversation; he was not happy about her return to work.
She'd rushed home to change into clothes appropriate for
the office, and she kept one eye on the clock as she tugged
on her gray skirt and red cardigan.

She was anxious about seeing everyone who knew, to
varying degrees, her role in what had happened to her
marriage. She was anxious, too, about seeing Jon, about
how the two of them would work together when their
etched-in-granite team approach had been so thoroughly
blown apart.

Grabbing her keys from the table, she raced out the front
door and almost crashed head-on into a woman coming up
her walk.

"Oh!" Claire said, startled. "Can I help you?"

The woman's straight blond hair was shoulder-length

and swept to the side above large blue eyes. At first Claire guessed her to be about thirty, but then she noticed the faint lines at the corners of her eyes and mouth.

The woman simply stared at her, and Claire felt a chill of recognition.

"Vanessa?"

"That's right."

Claire broke into a smile. "Vanessa!" She moved forward to embrace her sister, but Vanessa stiffened visibly, and Claire quickly drew back.

She glanced at her watch. Jon and the foundation would have to wait. "Come in," she said.

Vanessa followed her the few steps toward her door, and Claire's hand shook as she fit the key into the lock. It was obvious that her sister was not here to rekindle a relationship with her. She stepped through the door and motioned for Vanessa to join her inside.

"Would you like some tea?" she offered. "Something warm? The cherry blossoms are out, but the weather doesn't seem to know it's spring yet."

Vanessa shook her head. "All I want is a few minutes of your time."

Claire shivered at the ice in her sister's voice. "All right," she said. "But I'm late for work. Let me run next door to my landlord and call my office to let them know I'll be late. I don't have a phone here." She opened the front door again, but Vanessa stopped her.

"Don't bother, Claire," she said. "I'm only going to be a minute."

Claire reluctantly shut the door again, realizing as she did so that she had wanted to escape from this stranger with the riveting eyes and chilly voice.

She gestured toward the sofa. Vanessa slipped her purse from her shoulder and took a seat on the sofa's edge, hands folded over her knees. She was wearing a peach-colored linen dress, beautifully fitted over her slender figure, and Claire felt a stab of long-forgotten envy.

Pulling one of the wrought-iron chairs from beneath the table, she sat down herself. "I'm very glad to see you, Vanessa," she said. "I barely recognized you. Your curls are gone. It looks good, though, your hair. I—"

"Please." Vanessa held up a hand to put an end to her rambling. "I can't deal with the small talk. I'm only here because I have to be." She raised her head in the air like a racehorse. "I'm here to cleanse myself, to get rid of all the garbage I've been carrying around most of my life."

Claire felt a sudden jolt of fear, something close to panic. "I'm not sure I understand," she said.

"Then I'll get right to the point." Vanessa leaned forward. "I know what you did back then, when we were kids. I know you betrayed me, in the worst way a sister could betray a sister."

Claire shook her head. "I don't know what you're talking about." She didn't know, did she? Then why did she feel this urge to leap up and run from the room? Her skin felt itchy beneath her sweater, and she rubbed her arms.

"Zed Patterson," Vanessa said. "Is it coming back to you now?"

Claire frowned. "Zed Patterson? Was he the sheriff in Jeremy?"

Vanessa cocked her head to one side, narrowed her eyes. "You really don't remember this, do you?" she asked.

"I'm sorry, I don't have any idea—"

"Well, *I* remember it very clearly, because I still have nightmares about it. I still have the scars. Want me to refresh your memory?"

Claire saw a silver spoon dipping into a jar of honey. She could taste honey on her tongue, and the air in the apartment was suddenly thick and suffocating. She began to tremble. *Please, Vanessa, slow down. Be gentle with me.* She pulled her cardigan tighter across her chest. "Vanessa, I'm not sure—"

"It was that last morning we lived together as sisters, remember? We shared that room at the farm, that big attic room with the yellow flowered wallpaper. And very early that morning, you woke me up to tell me that Zed wanted me to come out to the barn. You were nervous. I was only eight, but I could tell. You couldn't look me in the eye."

The memory was wispy and vague, but it was there, and it was real. She remembered the anxiety—that same wired sort of urge to escape she felt now—but she could not recall its source. "The sheriff said he needed your help," she said uncertainly. It sounded more like a question than a statement. Was it the genuine truth, or a truth she had concocted?

"No," Vanessa said. "He said he needed your help. I went out there, and he said, 'Where's your sister? I like dark-haired little girls best. I told Claire I wanted her to come out here, but I guess she's a scaredy-cat. Sends her little sister instead. Guess you'll have to do.'"

Claire gripped the wrought-iron arms of the chair. "What are you saying? Are you saying he ... molested you? He wouldn't have. He was a nice man, from what I remember. He—"

"Don't act so damned innocent!" Vanessa rose to her feet. "Yes, he molested me. He raped me."

Claire drew back in her chair. "My God, Vanessa." She could not even entertain the idea. It was crazy. "Maybe you've remembered this wrong. It was so long ago, and you were just a child." Was it physically possible for a grown man to rape a child that young?

Vanessa stared at her sister. "I thought it must have happened to you, too. I figured that was why you knew not to go out there yourself."

"No." Claire shook her head. "Nothing like that ever happened to me. So if—when—I told you he needed your help, I couldn't possibly have known what he wanted." She looked down at her hands, afraid to continue. Yet she had to. She was desperate to cast doubt on Vanessa's story. When she spoke again, her voice was tentative. "Lately, I've discovered that I've twisted up some of my memories from back then," she said. "Could you possibly be doing the same thing?"

Vanessa paced across the floor. "Unfortunately, my memory of that morning is very clear, down to the last detail," she said. "It happened on that goddamned merry-go-round. On the chariot."

"The chariot?" Claire asked. Vanessa's memory *was* flawed. There had been no chariots on the carousel, only horses.

"I was eight years old," Vanessa continued. She was still pacing. "Do you know what that was like, what it *felt* like? Do you know the kind of toll that sort of experience exacts on an eight-year-old child?"

Claire would not think about it. She felt nauseated; swallowing was an effort. "Vanessa," she said, her voice strained, "we need to sort out our memories together. I think your memory is a little distorted. There were no chariots on the carousel, for example. Maybe what you think happened never did, and it's made you angry with me all these years, and I—"

"God, you remind me of Mellie." Vanessa folded her arms across her chest and stopped her pacing to stand close to her. Her smile was cynical. "You are fucking Mellie all over again, aren't you? I'd practically forgotten what she was like until you started talking."

"I'm not like Mellie." Claire felt an indignant innocence. Suddenly she saw her mother's face, as clearly as she'd ever seen it, smiling across the table from her in the farmhouse kitchen. Mellie was winking at her. And she could see a spoon being lifted from a jar of honey, a thick ribbon of amber spilling from the silver. The nausea teased her again, and she swallowed hard.

"It happened," Vanessa said. "You sent me out there, and the bastard raped me." She leaned against the wall, arms still folded. "As a teenager, I looked far and wide for the man who could purge that encounter from my mind. I had sex with everyone. Didn't matter who they were. I just wanted to find someone who could take away that pain."

Through the fog of nausea, Claire could see the slight shiver in her sister's lower lip, a barely perceptible betrayal of the fragility behind the tough exterior.

"I don't know what's fact and what's fiction anymore, Vanessa," she said. "If something really did happen to you, I'm terribly sorry." She reached up to touch her sister's arm, but her hand was shrugged away.

Vanessa drew in a breath, her lip quivering again. "Do you know how much I loved you when we were small?" she asked. "How much I looked up to you?"

Claire wanted to reach for her again, but stopped herself. "I don't remember much of anything from back then," she said. "I wish I did." She remembered being jealous of her golden sister. That was all.

"Well, you're lucky, I suppose." Vanessa picked up her purse from the sofa and slipped it over her shoulder.

Claire stood up slowly, afraid of getting sick. She stood between her sister and the door. "I'm going through a rough time, Vanessa." Her voice sounded weak. "The reason I'm separated from my husband and in this apartment is that I'm trying to figure out—"

"You wrote in a letter long ago that you had a child." Vanessa interrupted her. "A daughter?"

Claire's knees could no longer hold her up. She stepped away from the door to sit on the arm of the sofa. "Susan, yes. She's nineteen."

Vanessa looked at the floor with its thin, drab carpet. "I have a daughter too," she said. "Anna. Only I suppose that's not her real name. I've never seen her. They took her from me when she was born because I was just a kid myself, and I was drinking and using drugs and taking overdoses of sleeping pills and generally doing everything in my power to either erase my existence or make it somehow bearable." She looked out the window at the new buds on the maple tree, and Claire could see the shine of tears in her eyes. "I'm not saying that all of that is your fault," she said. "I blame you for one thing only. For betraying me."

"I didn't," Claire said, "or if I did, it wasn't inten—"

"You know they were lovers, don't you?" Vanessa asked.

"Who?"

"Mellie and Zed. That's why Daddy left."

Claire pressed her fingertips to her temples. Mellie and

the sheriff? "Oh, that's insane," she said. "You must be mistaken."

"I heard all about it from our father. Six days in the car with him on our drive to Seattle. I heard more than I ever wanted to hear."

"He never let us know where you were, Vanessa. Do you know that? We had no way of—"

"He's still doing it." Vanessa clutched her purse close to her side.

"Who? What?"

"Zed Patterson."

"Doing what?"

"Did you know he's now a senator from Pennsylvania?"

Claire shook her head blankly.

"Goes by Walter Patterson."

Yes, Claire thought. She'd heard that name before.

"A girl recently accused him of molesting her, but he got off because no one believed her story. I should have come forward to lend some support to her allegation, but I was a coward. Now though—" she let out a sigh. "I run programs for teenagers who were abused when they were younger, and now I'm going to testify on Capitol Hill to try to get funding for those programs. I'm going to come out in the open, for the first time, on all the crap I've carried around."

"What if you're wrong, though?" Claire asked, alarmed. "Or even if you're right and all of it did happen to you, do you actually want to dredge it up? Maybe you need to put it behind you." The old Claire was talking, she thought. How quickly she could regress to that comfortable state of denial.

She wasn't surprised when her sister shook her head

with disdain. "I'm through here," Vanessa said, walking toward the door.

Claire followed her. "Where are you staying?" she asked. "How can I get in touch with you?"

"I'm at the Omni Shoreham. But I don't see any point in us talking again. I've said all I want to say. I should have said it all years ago." She stepped outside, then turned to face Claire. "You know, maybe I'm the lucky one after all," she said. "At least I know who I am and what I did and didn't do. At least I know I have nothing to feel guilty about or ashamed of."

Vanessa didn't give her a chance to respond. Claire watched her sister walk out to the street and get into a waiting cab parked at the curb. Then she locked up her apartment and got into her own car, pulling out onto the road. The temptation to drive to the Fishmonger was strong, but she was already far too late. She would call Randy the instant she got in. She'd ask him to meet her for lunch in the theater. And she would not think about Vanessa's visit until she was safely with him.

She sped toward the foundation as though someone were chasing her, as though if she drove fast enough, she could leave the memories behind. But she couldn't. They were with her, edging in. And when she looked in the sideview mirror, it was filled with green.

Well, Claire was not off to a great start. Jon looked at his watch again and pursed his lips. She'd seemed so sincere about wanting to come back. Had she completely forgotten, or was she simply going to be abysmally late? And how much should he tolerate?

The door to his office suddenly burst open, and Claire

stood in front of his desk in her gray skirt and a red sweater. Her face was pale, and she was trembling.

"I'm sorry I'm late," she said, "but I need one more minute for a phone call."

He set down his pen. "Are you all right?"

"Yes. Fine. I'll be back in a sec." She turned to leave.

"Claire, wait." He wheeled out from behind his desk. "What's wrong?"

She ran a shaky hand through her hair, and he could see her debating between telling him and racing off to the phone. He felt as if they were both on the edge of a precipice. "What is it?" he asked.

She drew in a long breath. "I just spoke with Vanessa— my sister. She showed up at my apartment." She pressed her hand over her mouth as though she'd shocked herself with her words, and with a jolt, Jon noticed that she had taken off her ring.

He motioned toward the sofa. "Sit down," he said.

"No. I need to make a—"

"The phone can wait," he said, wheeling toward the sofa himself. "Come here."

She hesitated a moment before sitting down.

"Vanessa called the house for you a few days ago," he said. "I gave her your address. I thought she'd write to you, or call you here at the office. I didn't know she'd show up. I'm sorry. Maybe I should have checked with you first, but—"

"No, that was fine." She hugged her arms across her chest, shivering, hunching over as if her stomach hurt. "Oh, God," she said, "I feel so sick."

"Sweetheart." Jon wheeled close to her, resting his hand on her knee, and although her body remained stiff and tremulous, she offered no resistance to his touch. "What did she say that's got you this upset?" he asked.

She shook her head, eyes closed.

"Claire," he said. "Tell me."

"I'm afraid to talk about it," she whispered.

Jon gnawed on his lip, thinking that if Randy were sitting this close to her, touching her, she would be more than willing to talk. And if he were Randy, he would not be afraid to hear what she had to say.

"Tell me, Claire," he tried again.

With her eyes still squeezed shut, she began to talk, quickly, as though once she started she could not get it out fast enough. She told him about Vanessa's accusations, about how she had sent her sister out to the barn, where she was raped by the sheriff, Zed Patterson. Jon wasn't certain if he was listening to Vanessa's memories or Claire's, but he listened hard. He needed to know exactly where she was in the process of discovering her past.

"She despises me," Claire said when she'd finished giving him the account of Vanessa's visit. "I could see it in her eyes. She's hated me ever since that day."

"Is it true, though?" he asked carefully. "Do you think that what she said happened to her actually did happen? Do you think you meant to set her up?"

A tremor ran through her body, and she leaned closer to him, clutching his hand in both of hers. The gesture nearly brought tears to his eyes.

"I don't know," she said. "I was starting to remember some of it in the car on the way over here, but I feel like I'm trying to piece together a dream." She looked at him directly. "I've been remembering more and more lately," she said. It sounded like a confession.

"Yes." He nodded. "That's good."

She pressed his hand hard between hers and stared into space. "I know that the sheriff—Zed—was helping my grandfather that summer. Not with the carving, of course, but with the mechanical stuff. Grandpa was sick, I think, and Zed really worked hard. Oh!" She let go of his hand to hold her fists to the sides of her head. "I just parroted Mellie," she said. "Mellie used to say how hard Zed worked, wasn't he a great worker, etcetera. Maybe there was something between them."

He caught her hands again, holding them once more on her knee. Her fingers felt fragile beneath his. He hoped she would talk on and on and they could sit this way forever.

"What was he like, this Zed guy?" He wasn't certain how far to push her. How far would Randy push? "Was there any reason for you or anyone else to suspect he'd be abusive?"

"Oh, do you know who he is, Jon?" she asked suddenly. "I didn't realize this, but Vanessa said he's Walter Patterson, the senator from Pennsylvania."

Jon could not mask the shock in his face. "The victims' assistance guy?"

"I don't know about—"

"Yes, you do. Remember, he was a big supporter when we were trying to get the Americans Disabilities Act through?"

"Yes. God, I never realized . . . I don't believe . . . He was a nice man, I thought. My memory's vague, but I remember him giving me things. A doll, once—a Barbie—which, looking back, seems like kind of an odd gift from a man, but I thought it was great at the time. And he'd tell me I was pretty, but . . . I think I did feel a little uncomfortable around him. I can't put a finger on it. I can't remember.

Maybe I was picking up on whatever was going on between him and Mellie. But I *do* remember the day Vanessa's talking about. It started coming to me in the car driving over here." She suddenly froze. "But I don't want to think about it. I'm afraid to." She made a sound, a small whimper, like a hurt animal. "Oh, Jon," she said.

"What? Tell me."

She shook her head. "I'm afraid to remember, because I think I really did betray her."

"I'd like to hear about it," he said. "From your perspective, not Vanessa's."

"I can't."

Jon shut his own eyes, thinking of the phone call she was so anxious to make. "What does Randy do or say that makes it easy for you to tell him these things?" he asked. The words burned his throat.

Claire hesitated before she answered. "I don't know," she said. "He listens well, I guess. He asks questions." She glanced at him, a mild accusation in her eyes. "He doesn't try to change the subject."

"I'll listen very well," he said. "I promise." He lifted his hand to brush her hair back from her cheek. "Go ahead. What do you remember?"

She looked out the window as if she could see her story taking shape in the trees and the pond. "It was the night before my father took Vanessa away," she said. "Zed told me he could use my help in the barn very early the following morning. I can't remember why I was uncomfortable about it, but I know I was afraid to go. Somehow, on some level, I must have known what he was really after. Although I was only ten. I mean, how did I know that? But I did." She suddenly furrowed her brow. "Oh, Jon, maybe I'm making this up! Maybe Vanessa's planted the seed, and now I—"

He shook his head. "Trust yourself, Claire. Go on. What happened?"

She drew in a trembling breath, turning her hand so that her fingers were locked with his, and he ran his thumb over the pale band of skin where her ring had been.

"I was so afraid of having to go out to the barn in the morning that I couldn't get to sleep that night," Claire said. "And sometime during the night I must have gotten the idea to send Vanessa. In the morning, just like she said, I woke her up and told her Zed had asked for her to come out and help him." She leaned away to look at him. "Why did either of us have to go? Why didn't I simply roll over and go back to sleep?"

"I don't know."

"Maybe he told me I'd get in trouble if I didn't help him."

"What happened after you told Vanessa to go?"

"She left, and I remember going downstairs and sitting at the breakfast table with Mellie and my grandparents while she was out in the barn. My grandfather was eating eggs. I remember that because the smell made me sick." She looked at him. "I was very nervous, Jon. I remember being nervous."

He nodded.

"My grandfather called me 'Sunshine,' and I couldn't even smile at him. Then Mellie or someone asked me where Vanessa was and I told them she was out in the barn helping Sheriff Patterson. I think Mellie said something about what a good little girl Vanessa was, because I felt jealous. Oh!" She nearly smiled. "The honey!"

"The honey?"

"I've been having this flashback of a jar of honey and I think it's from that morning. We were eating English muffins, and I was putting honey on mine, letting it dribble from the spoon into all the little holes, and my grandmother told me not to play with it. And that's when Vanessa walked in the door."

Jon was astonished at the workings of her memory. If he hadn't known better, he would think this tapestry of scenes was nothing more than the creation of a fertile imagination.

"Mellie said, 'Good morning, Angel,' to Vanessa and offered her a muffin," Claire continued, "but Vanessa said she wasn't hungry. I couldn't look at her, Jon." She let go of his hand to press her fist to her mouth. "I just stared at my muffin, at the way the kitchen light was reflected in the little pools of honey."

For a moment, she seemed lost. He waited quietly, finally prompting her. "Claire?"

"I didn't like her," she said softly. "I still don't. She's gorgeous. That's a petty reason, I know, but she was so pushy and forceful and rude in my apartment."

He nodded, remembering Vanessa's cold voice on the phone. "Go back to that day at the farm," he said. "What happened next?"

"I think she asked if she could take a nap. Mellie was worried that she was sick and said she'd be up to check on her in a while. I remember wanting to get out of the house so I wouldn't have to see her or talk to her. I really remember this," she said, as if surprised by the clarity of her thoughts. "I remember thinking I would do everything I could to avoid being alone with her that day."

"Why?"

"Because I betrayed her. I sent her out to get hurt. I don't know how I knew that, but I did." She sat back fully on the couch, taking his hand with her, and he had to lean forward a little. "This is the first memory I've had where I can feel the emotion attached to it," she said. "Usually I just remember things in a dry sort of way. This is harder. I don't like it."

He didn't want her to leave the past. Not yet. Her story did not shock or even surprise him. He only wished it went farther than it did. "So did you manage to avoid her all day?" he asked.

She nearly laughed. "I managed to avoid her for the rest of my life," she said. "The day she went to the barn was the same day my father showed up and dragged her away." She shook her head, suddenly smiling. "The drawing of the robin," she said, cryptically. "I was coloring a picture of a robin when he showed up." She squeezed Jon's hand, leaning forward. "Things are starting to come together," she said. "The flashbacks are falling into place. I bet this was it—this thing with Vanessa. This must be what I've been hiding from myself all these years."

"Maybe," he said, although he knew better.

She slipped her feet from her shoes and drew them up on the couch, covering her legs with her long gray skirt. Resting her head on her knees, she shut her eyes. "This sounds terrible," she said, "but I remember being *relieved* when my father took her away. I was so afraid of talking to her or seeing her, that I was glad to see her go. With her gone, I could convince myself that nothing bad had happened. I could erase the whole memory. But I was thinking like a child—you know—I wanted that immediate satisfaction of having her gone. It never occurred to me that I might never see her again."

"You *were* a child, Claire," he said. He dared to lift his free hand to her head, to stroke her hair. Once, twice, three times. "You didn't intentionally set her up to be abused." He was playing her game, he thought. Denying any nasty intent, making the bad things go away with a few weak words of reassurance.

He could hear her breathing, but that was the only sound in the room. Her trembling had subsided, and he knew that soon she would pull her hand away. Damn Randy. Anytime he felt like it, Randy could touch her like this. He could run his fingers through her hair or feel the delicate weight of her hand in his. He could make love to her any time, any way she wanted it.

Claire lifted her head from her knees and looked at him. The color was back in her cheeks. "I feel better now," she said.

He could nearly make out his reflection in her eyes. He touched her cheek with the back of his fingers. "I'm sorry I haven't been there for you these last few months, Claire," he said.

"And I'm sorry I laid all this on you."

Jon shook his head. "What do you think will happen to me if you tell me terrible things? Do you think I'm going to crack up? Slit my wrists?"

She smiled weakly. "I don't know."

"Are you afraid I'll cry?" He tugged gently on a strand of her hair. "That might happen. I might cry if you tell me about something that hurt you. Would that be so terrible?"

She lowered her feet to the floor. "It's a habit, not telling you things that might upset you."

"Yeah, I know. But you don't need to protect me any-more, Claire. You don't need to keep your sad or angry or otherwise shitty feelings from me. I can handle them now, all right? Give me a chance to be there for you."

"That's what you said in your speech."

"My speech?"

"At G.W. I was there for your keynote speech—the one I was supposed to make with you. But you were really wonderful all by yourself."

He smiled, touched and surprised to learn that she'd been there. "But lonely, Claire," he said. "I was fine, but I was lonely up there on that stage. And that pretty much sums up my life lately. I'm fine—but lonely for you."

She smiled at him, then leaned over and hugged him hard. "I miss you too," she said, standing up, backing away from him, and she left his office quickly, anxious, no doubt, to make her phone call.

45

Vienna

Sitting behind her desk in her old office at the foundation, Claire found she had lost the sense of urgency to call Randy. The cloak of Jon's comfort was still warm around her shoulders. She'd been too shaken by Vanessa's visit to curb the flow of what she'd told him, but he had listened well, indeed. Had he always had that ability? Had she simply not given him the chance?

It was hard to focus on the monumental stack of files on her desk when thoughts of her sister still haunted her. She told herself she had to make a dent in the files before the eleven o'clock staff meeting, and so she was on her lunch break by the time she had a chance to call Randy. She had expected to eat lunch with Jon, as they used to, over the desk in his office. But he had scheduled a lunch meeting with one of their consultants—and without her. He did not even invite her to join them, which was probably wise. She did not have a good grounding in the project they were discussing, and she doubted she would be able to give the meeting all her concentration.

Randy was at the restaurant when she called. She could hear the clank of dishes in the background.

"How are things at the office?" he asked.

"Looks like everything ran smoothly in my absence." She drew sloping lines on the notepad in front of her, a string of slender snakes, reverse Ss, across the blue paper. "*I'm* not running too well, though. My sister stopped by my apartment this morning."

"Vanessa? You're kidding. Is that good or bad?"

"Well, it shook me up a bit. I'll tell you about it tonight."

"Do you need to talk now?" he asked. "Can you take a break? I could meet you someplace."

She felt a rush of tenderness at his concern. "Thanks for offering," she said. "It can wait."

After getting off the phone, she once again attacked the stack of work on her desk. Besides the files, there were memos to be read and forms to be filled out about issues and people she could barely remember.

So much had changed at the foundation in the last month. She felt like a visitor. The new receptionist at the front desk had not even known who she was when she arrived that morning. At the staff meeting, she'd initially listened to the esoteric chatter with a sense of alienation, and it was obvious that no one knew exactly how to treat her. Jon, though, set the tone with his laid-back, unflappable good humor, including her on decisions, asking the others to fill her in on their various projects. Pat spent a few minutes with her after the meeting, updating her on plans for the retreat, telling her how good it was to have her back. Still, Claire's sense of disorientation was almost dizzying. It was going to be okay, though. She simply needed to get her sea legs under her again.

As she pulled into Randy's town house parking lot that evening, she almost dreaded the recounting of Vanessa's visit. She no longer felt the need to talk about it. Randy began questioning her as soon as she was in the door. They sat in his dark and cozy living room, and he held her hand and furrowed his brow and listened closely as she repeated the incident to him. It felt like a mere updating, though. The telling had lost its emotion.

They went for a walk through his neighborhood before dinner, and she realized with some guilt that Randy had concerns of his own tonight. He'd gotten a call from LuAnne that afternoon. Cary was in trouble at school for beating up a girl. Never mind that the girl had been making fun of one of Cary's friends, a boy with burn scars on his face and hands. LuAnne wanted Randy to talk to Cary by phone that night. Claire held his hand as they walked, helping him plot his end of the conversation. She offered suggestions as best she could, trying to give him her full attention as he had so often done for her, but she could not stop thinking about Vanessa, in a hotel room not ten miles from her. She would have to call her, have to try. Surely their entire link as sisters could not be erased by an error in judgment made when she was ten. She could not discount the severity of that mistake, but wouldn't both their lives be richer by becoming part of each other's family?

After their walk, she helped Randy make dinner in his white and copper kitchen.

"I'm a bit bewildered," Randy said as he took a glass baking dish from one of the cabinets. "How come you're so calm about your sister's visit? It sounded extremely upsetting, yet you seem"—he shrugged—"almost complacent."

"I was beside myself this morning," she said, slicing mushrooms for their salad, "but then I told Jon about it. I was late to the office because of Vanessa, and I wanted to call you when I got in because I was such a wreck, but Jon stopped me to ask what was wrong, and I blurted the whole mess out to him. So I guess it doesn't seem so urgent now." The mushrooms were white and perfect, and she had sliced far more than they needed.

Randy's back was to her as he wrapped sole fillets in parchment. "So how did Jon react?" he asked.

She scooped the mushroom slices up with her hands and dropped them into the salad bowl. "Very well," she said. "He surprised me." She put a bowl of frozen spinach in the microwave and hit the defrost button. "I realized I've always kept things from him. Anything that might have upset him. Or upset us. I heard him speak the other day, and—"

Randy turned to frown at her. "You heard him speak? Where?"

She'd forgotten that Randy didn't know about the symposium at G.W. It had not felt like deceit on her part at the time, but now the small side trip seemed like a betrayal.

"I stopped by G.W. on Tuesday," she said. "Jon and I were supposed to be the keynote speakers at a symposium there. I wanted to see how he'd handle it alone."

"Oh." Randy rested his hand lightly against her back. "I didn't mean to jump on you."

"That's all right." Claire slipped the knife into a green pepper. "Anyhow, in his speech, he talked about being overprotective of your loved ones, not wanting them to suffer any more than they already have. He said that by protecting them, you don't give them room to grow or to learn how to take care of themselves. He was referring to me, I suppose. Or to both of us. We took care of each other extremely well."

Randy laughed.

"What's so funny?"

"You were very well trained. Mellie protected you the same way. It's all you knew how to do."

She set down her knife with a sense of defeat. "I don't want to be that way anymore."

Randy walked across the kitchen to the steps leading down to the basement and his wine cellar. "Don't worry, Claire, you're not," he said. "If you were still into protecting people, you wouldn't have told me how good you felt talking to Jon today." He disappeared into the basement, and she stared after him, trying to discern if his words had been meant as a compliment or if they were, instead, an expression of hurt. She had not known that Randy needed her protection.

She pulled the bowl of spinach from the microwave. The icy green block was still hard. Setting it on the counter, she began chopping at it, the knife in her fist.

Suddenly, her hand froze in midair, and the vertigo fell over her with such force that she had to lean against the counter. The bright green of the spinach made her stomach roil, and the knife shook in her hand. She wanted to drop it, but her fingers were locked in place around the handle. Frightened, she started to call for Randy, but stopped herself.

"Open your damn hand," she said out loud. She nearly had to pry her fingers from the knife. When it fell into the bowl, she backed away from the counter and lowered herself into one of the kitchen chairs.

Closing her eyes, she steadied her breathing. She tried asking herself the questions Randy might ask. Had she seen anything—any images from the past? No, she had seen nothing but the knife in her hand. That alone had been enough to sicken her.

And what did the knife remind her of?

Nothing. No, that wasn't true. She pictured the barn. The workshop. Carving. She could see herself in her grandfather's shop, carefully working the knife around a pattern in a block of balsa wood. That was a good memory, though. Nothing to bring on an attack of terror.

"Damn it!" She pounded her fist on her knee, tears filling her eyes. Wasn't she ever going to be free of this? She'd hoped her flashbacks had been linked to the incident with Vanessa. With that out in the open, they should leave her alone, shouldn't they?

She heard Randy on the basement stairs and quickly stood up again, wiping her eyes with the back of her hand. Gingerly, she removed the knife from the bowl before putting the spinach back in the microwave. She wouldn't tell Randy what had happened. She wasn't hiding it from him, not in any underhanded way. She simply needed to know she could do this on her own.

Randy called Cary later that night. He used the phone in the study, across from the master bedroom, where Claire waited for him under the paisley sheets and comforter. She could hear his side of the conversation, and she listened with admiration. Randy talked about loyalty to friends, options to violence, respect for the opposite sex. The conversation lasted a very long time.

When he came into the bedroom, he undressed quietly and climbed into bed without reaching for her. She looked over at him, at the faint shine of tears on his cheeks, and her heart broke.

She pulled close to him. "Cary will be all right," she said. "He sounds like a healthy kid who—"

Randy shook his head. "Do you hear yourself, Claire?"

She thought about her words. Empty, soothing words— the kind she was best at uttering. "Yes," she said sheepishly.

"And it's not Cary I'm upset about right now."

She ran her fingertips over his cheek. "What is it?"

He suddenly closed his arms around her, holding her so tightly she could barely breathe. She heard him swallow, and it was another minute before he spoke.

"I guess I've known all along that I was only borrowing you," he said.

"Borrowing me?" She lifted her head from his chest. "What are you talking about?"

"You've always loved Jon. I've been serving some need in you that you didn't think he could meet."

She wanted to protest, to offer him some sort of reassurance, but said instead, "I don't want to *need* either of you anymore."

"I don't regret a moment I've spent with you," Randy said, as if he had decided for both of them that their relationship was over.

She pulled back from him, sitting up.

"I was hoping your feelings about me would change," he continued, reaching toward her. His fingers came close to her satin-covered breast, but he lowered his hand to the bed without touching her. "Even after all this time, though, you still think of me as a brother."

"That's not true." She gently cradled his hand in hers, knowing that she and Randy were on new ground here, that in the next few seconds, the fabric of their relationship would stretch and give until it had taken on a different shape. She was ready for that; she felt profound relief that the time had come. "I think of you as a wonderful friend who's helping me through a terrible time." She touched the hem of the sheet where it lay above his waist. "I've felt dishonest, though."

"How so?"

"By becoming lovers."

"Oh." He shook his head. "Don't feel guilty. You've never led me to believe there was more between us than there was. You and I have had different hopes and expectations right from the start. We both knew that."

Her throat felt tight. "I don't want us to make love anymore," she said.

He nodded, squeezing her hand. Silence filled the room, and all Claire could hear was the sound of their breathing.

"Will you go back to Jon then, if he'll have you?" Randy asked finally, and the question surprised her because she had not even considered it an option at the moment.

"No," she said. "I just want to be with Claire for a while."

"Well, I admire you for that," he said. "And I'm selfishly very glad. I hope that means I can still see you. Can we still be friends?"

The thought of *not* seeing him hadn't even crossed her mind. "I'm counting on it," she said. She let go of his hand, folding her own hands together in her lap. "But right now, I think I'd better move to the bed in the guest room."

He nodded, a look of resignation on his face. "If you insist," he said.

She got out of the bed and let out a long breath, as if

she'd just endured some taxing physical challenge. "I love you, friend," she said, leaning over to kiss his cheek. "Thank you."

The bed in the guest room was cold, and she shivered as she slipped beneath the covers. She missed Randy's warmth and the comfort of his arms around her, but she knew she could not have continued the intimate side of their relationship much longer. It had not felt right to her. And after tonight, she would not sleep at his house again.

She could not fall asleep. Slowly, very slowly, the panicked confusion she'd felt while talking with Vanessa crept over her once more. She thought of how, when she'd had trouble sleeping, Jon would relax her with images of the carousel. Randy could never have done that. Even if she had told him what to say, it wouldn't have had the same effect.

Maybe she could learn to paint those serene and calming images for herself?

No. What was the point? After today, she doubted that thoughts of the carousel could ever bring her peace again.

46

Vanessa stood in front of the dresser mirror in her hotel room, stroking color onto her cheeks, smudging the liner beneath her lower lashes. She could see Brian's reflection in the mirror, and she watched as he shoved their room service trays to one side of the glass-topped table and spread out the Washington Post on the other. He made no comment about the fact that she had not touched the breakfast he'd ordered for her. He should have known there would be no way she could eat this morning.

In an hour, she would be meeting with Starla Garvey. How much detail would she be asked to provide? She was as ready for this as she would ever be, yet she wished she could simply talk about the AMC programs from the safety of her role as a physician.

She had decided to be somewhat cryptic in the facts she offered. She would say she could not remember her abuser's name—if indeed she'd ever known it—and she would not mention the carousel. The man was simply someone who had helped out on her grandparents' farm from time to time. She would stick to the facts that were important—those that would get her a slot in testifying in front of the committee the following day.

Her stomach was churning, and the makeup could not mask the pallor of her skin. The pale green suit looked crisp and cool in the mirror, though. A good choice. She turned to face Brian.

"How do I look?" she asked.

He lifted his eyes from the paper and smiled. "Incredible," he said, and she had to laugh.

"Great, but I'm trying to look *credible* this morning."

"You've failed miserably, then." He stood up and started walking in her direction when the phone rang. Her first thought was that the attorney was canceling their meeting. Tensely, she picked up the receiver from the dresser.

"Vanessa Gray," she said.

"Vanessa, this is Claire."

She gave Brian a look of distress. She should have expected this call. After riding away from her sister's apartment, she'd wondered why the hell she'd given her the name of the hotel.

"Hello, Claire," she said. "I only have a second. I'm on my way out."

Brian grimaced when he realized whom the call was from and took his seat at the table again.

"I need to see you," Claire said. "I could come into D.C. for lunch tomorrow, or we could arrange to meet at some other time if you'd prefer. But please, Vanessa, let's get together."

Vanessa sighed and leaned against the dresser. "There's

no point to us getting together," she said. "I've learned to exist without family and—"

"Maybe I could be a support for you while you're going through this thing with the hearing."

"Thanks, but my husband's with me." She looked at Brian, whose hazel eyes were wide and encouraging. "He's all the support I need."

There was hesitation on the line. "Lately . . . something happened to me a couple of months ago," Claire said. "I witnessed a tragedy, and since then I've been remembering things from our childhood. I always thought that everything was wonderful for us growing up. But I began to remember things that weren't so great, and I—"

"You'd better go, Van." Brian looked at his watch, and Vanessa missed some of what Claire was saying. She was interested, in spite of herself.

"It would help me so much to talk to you," Claire said. "To see what you remember. To compare and—"

"Claire, I really have to go. Maybe I'll get back to you."

She heard Claire's exasperated sigh. "I made a mistake, Vanessa, I know that," she said. "But I was *ten*. I didn't know what Zed Patterson wanted. I guess I figured it was something I should avoid, but when I sent you out to the barn, I didn't know for certain that something terrible was going to happen to you. And I'm not responsible for our father taking you away that day. I feel as though you're blaming everything that happened to you on me."

Anger flamed up inside her. "Look, Claire, you don't know what I went through. I can't expect you to know or to understand. But you're a reminder to me of the most horrific time in my life. I don't need that, all right?" She hung up and stared at the phone for a few seconds as if waiting for Claire to try again. But the phone did not ring.

Brian was at her side, squeezing her shoulders lightly. "Are you sure you want to burn that bridge?" he asked.

"I feel no love for her," she said. "I haven't had a sister in thirty years. I still don't have one, as far as I'm concerned."

He rubbed her arms through the suit. "I liked what you said about me being your support."

"And I meant it," she said softly. "You've been terrific." She tried to hold his gaze, but couldn't. She pulled away from him and walked over to the mirror to run the comb through her already well-combed hair. In the mirror, she caught the bewilderment in Brian's face as he sat down behind the table again. She simply could not talk to him about support right now. He would not support her if he knew the full extent of her plan.

As she climbed into the cab in front of the hotel, she recalled what Claire had said about her newly found memories. It wasn't so much the content of Claire's words that played through her mind as the confusion in her voice. The pain.

While riding to Claire's apartment the day before, she'd wondered how she would be able to confront her sister face-to-face. She was afraid that seeing the grown-up version of the little girl she had once adored would force her to soften her words to the point of losing her message. But it had not been a problem. There was so much of Mellie in Claire—so much denial and false cheer—that Vanessa had been able to quickly discard her, the way she'd discarded all memories of her mother. Mellie had been useless as a mother. Self-aggrandizing. Ineffectual. She had done nothing to protect her from Zed, and she'd done nothing to prevent Vanessa's father from dragging her away from her family and her home. Worse, she'd done nothing to track that little girl down, not until Vanessa was fully grown and well past the point of needing or wanting her mother. Equating Claire with Mellie, Vanessa had been able to let her sister have it with both barrels.

Yet, although she had said all she'd wanted to say to Claire, all she'd waited years to say, she had not felt quite as free and clean leaving her sister's apartment as she had expected. And now Claire was talking about unearthing old memories, and her voice was full of hurt.

So, as Vanessa rode in the cab through the streets of D.C., anticipating the interview that frightened her more than anything had frightened her in years, it was her sister she was thinking about and not herself.

Starla Garvey's office was sparely decorated, with no show of money or power, and that relieved Vanessa as she waited in the reception area. She might be able to like this woman, after all. Starla was an unpaid adviser to the committee; she must truly be dedicated to the importance of these hearings. It would be all right.

She'd been waiting ten minutes when a tall woman with teased, bleached-blond hair and heavily made-up eyes emerged from one of the inner offices and offered her hand to Vanessa.

"Dr. Gray?" The woman smiled.

"Yes." Vanessa shook her hand. "Are you? . . ."

"I'm Starla Garvey. Please come in."

Vanessa walked into the office in front of Starla Garvey, pleased to have a few seconds to wipe the surprise from her face over the attorney's appearance. She sat down on one side of a long conference table while Starla lowered her tight-skirted derriere into a seat opposite her. A tape recorder rested between them on the table.

"All right." Starla glanced at her watch. "As I think I mentioned to you on the phone, I already have my quota of witnesses. I understand, though, that you offer a different perspective—the needs of the adolescent, correct?"

Vanessa nodded. "The adolescent who was abused when she was younger."

"Right. So, I'm willing to hear what you have to say." Starla gave Vanessa a smile that was hard to read. "Are you ready?"

Vanessa nodded again, and Starla pressed a button on the recorder. "Go ahead, then. Tell me your story."

Vanessa wanted to slow things down. Talk about the weather. Anything. She locked her hands together in her lap. When she finally began to speak, her throat felt dry, as if her voice might fail her any minute, and she kept her eyes focused on the slow, steady circling of the tape.

She told Starla about the farm and how much she enjoyed her summers there with her grandparents. She felt happier during the summer, she said, because her father was with them only on weekends, thereby reducing the amount of time he and her mother were able to fight.

When she was eight years old, a young man from a neighboring town spent the summer helping her grandfather with work around the farm. One morning, he asked Vanessa's sister to help him in the barn, but her sister told Vanessa to go in her place, and the man raped her on the floor of the barn.

Starla surprised her by asking for a description of the inside of the barn.

"The floor was covered with hay," Vanessa blurted out, although she had never seen anything resembling hay in her grandfather's pristine barn. Yet it was the first thing that came into her mind, and now she could see the counterfeit image clearly—light pouring through the barn windows onto the golden hay, a pitchfork standing in the corner. The lie made it easier to describe the details of the rape. None of it seemed real now. She spoke clearly and factually, her eyes fixed on the hypnotic turning of the tape reels.

"Why didn't you tell anyone what happened?" Starla asked.

"He threatened me with further harm if I told," she answered honestly. She went on to describe how, later that day, her father split up the family and took her with him to Seattle. She did not see her family again.

She raised her eyes from the tape to Starla, who was taking notes, despite the running of the recorder. This had been quite simple, she thought. Not nearly as hard to talk about as she'd anticipated. Maybe because she was not telling the complete truth, and that made it seem almost like someone else's story.

She described her emotional and physical suffering from the trauma. She talked at length about how, as a teenager, she began hurting herself and sleeping around and using alcohol and drugs to try to erase the memories of the abuse.

Starla Garvey continued to listen attentively, nodding, her face solemn beneath the heavy makeup, and Vanessa knew, without Starla saying a word, that she had been there, too. There was a bond between the lawyer and herself. It made Vanessa wish she could be more honest with her.

Starla began questioning her about her work, and Vanessa slipped with relief into the role of the knowledgeable director of an AMC program.

When Vanessa had said all she could think of to say, Starla hit the button on the machine and smiled at her. "You're going to be excellent," she said.

"Then you'll use me?"

"Oh, absolutely." Starla leaned over her notes. "Now, here's the way this works. I'll prepare a transcript which you will then read at the hearing. I'll—"

"A transcript?" Vanessa had not counted on having to read her statement. But of course. That was the way these things were done. She should have anticipated it.

"Yes. It'll make it much easier on you, and copies of it will be distributed to the committee members, so they can follow along with you."

Vanessa forced herself to nod, to keep her face from giving away the fact that this was an unexpected development.

"Now"—Starla looked thoughtfully at her notes, rapping her knuckles lightly on the table—"ordinarily, your testimony would be vetted. You know, I would verify the facts of your story. I realize in your case we don't even know the identity of the perpetrator, but I'd usually check on the other facts to gain you credibility."

Vanessa's heart thudded miserably in her chest.

"Given your credentials, however, and the fact that we are in a major time crunch here"—Starla winked at her—"I think we can safely dispense with the vetting process, if you have no problem with that."

Vanessa shook her head. "No problem." She could barely get the words out.

"Fine." Starla stood up. "One more thing you should know is that the hearing will probably be televised, at least in part, on one of the cable channels. You'll barely know they're there, though."

Televised. Lord. "All right," she said.

She stood up and followed the attorney to the office door, where she turned to ask her, "What compels you to do this for no pay?"

Starla looked briefly surprised, then offered a small smile. "You know very well why I'm doing it," she said. "I've been watching you watching me, and I can tell that you know. It's just that you and your fellow witnesses have more courage than I do. I'm doing the little bit I can to contribute."

Oh, she liked this woman! Vanessa squeezed the attorney's hand instead of shaking it. She only hoped that Starla would be able to forgive her the following day, when she changed her story once again.

47

Washington, D.C.

Vanessa knew she was losing weight. She stood with Brian in one of the wide hallways of the Senate office building, waiting to enter the hearing room, and she felt as though the skirt of her green suit was merely hanging from her hips. She'd managed to get down half a baked potato at dinner the night before, but that was all she'd eaten since her meeting with Starla yesterday morning.

There were many other people in the hallway, so many that she had quickly given up trying to separate her fellow witnesses from the reporters and the members of a curious public.

Shortly before eight, a security guard opened the wide doors, and the crowd in the hallway funneled into the room.

Starla stood inside the door. She touched Vanessa's shoulder and told her where to sit.

Brian was allowed to sit with her in the second long row of chairs. Several other women shared the row with them.

The heavy-set, dark-haired woman sitting to her left smiled at her.

"Are you testifying?" the woman asked. Vanessa guessed she was in her early thirties.

"Yes," she answered.

"Me too." The woman held her hand toward Vanessa. "Maggie Rowan," she said.

"Vanessa Gray." Vanessa shook Maggie Rowan's hand. It was wet with perspiration. She imagined her own hand felt no different.

Starla and another woman sat in the first row, directly in front of Vanessa and Brian. Vanessa turned to look behind her. The room was quickly filling with people. She caught a glimpse of a television camera in the rear of the room, took in a deep breath, and reached for Brian's hand.

In the front of the room stood a long table, the half-dozen chairs behind it facing the crowd. A second, shorter table faced the first, and it was graced by a single chair. She would sit in that lone chair and face that long table of men—yes, Starla had told her the committee was entirely composed of men—and tell her story. She could still back out. Feign illness. No. She owed this to herself and to Brian, if not to the AMC programs. She rested her hand lightly on her flat belly. She owed this to the future. She closed her eyes and leaned her head on Brian's shoulder.

"You going to be all right?" he asked.

She nodded without lifting her head, and when she finally did open her eyes again, the committee members were entering the room. She watched as they took their seats. Some old, some young. Rickety or bulging or lithe. Most wore very serious, almost sour, expressions on their faces. They looked like unhappy men.

He sat near the center of the long table, fingering a wooden gavel. Senator Walter Patterson. He rummaged through the stack of papers on the table in front of him, rubbed his chin with his hand, turned to say something to the jowly gentleman on his left. He was quite thin. It was the thinness of a man who probably ran every morning, who ate right, who treasured his body and worked hard to preserve it. His hair was a graying blond, sparse, but well cut. Even from where she sat, Vanessa could catch the glint of blue in his eyes when he looked out toward the crowd. She forced herself to study him. She wanted to harden herself to the sight of him before it was her turn. She was scheduled to speak fourth, and she prayed that would be before lunch. She did not want to struggle through another meal.

Zed Patterson raised his gavel and brought it down hard on the table. He proceeded to tell the assembly the purpose of the day's hearings—to provide the committee with graphic evidence of the need for the Aid to Adult Survivors Bill. He spoke about the bill for a few minutes, his folksy style of speech making Vanessa's skin crawl, and then the witnesses began their testimonies.

Maggie Rowan was first. Her story was one of incest at the hands of an uncle, and it was ugly and sad, but nothing Vanessa had not heard dozens—hundreds—of times before. It looked like news to the committee members, though. They frowned and shook their heads and twisted their mouths in disgust as Maggie read word-for-word from her transcript, her eyes glued to the paper in front of her. Patterson followed along in the transcript as she read, occasionally raising his sharp blue eyes to the witness herself, listening attentively, nodding with sympathy.

Vanessa barely heard the next two witnesses. She

watched the clock on the far wall as the hands slipped past nine, then ten, and the reality of what she was about to do sank in. A small voice inside her head kept barking at her, "Are you crazy?" but the clock ticked on, and soon she had no choice but to take her turn in front of the committee.

Brian squeezed her hand as she rose from her seat, and Starla stood to touch her arm. "You're going to be fine," the attorney said.

Someone had placed her transcript on the table in front of her. Waiting to begin, she looked directly at Zed Patterson, searching for a sign that he recognized her, but his eyes only brushed over hers as he spoke to the senator on his left, who chuckled in response, jowls quivering.

She was told to begin. She licked her lips, took a breath, and started reading from the transcript.

"I was abused at the age of eight," she read. "Unlike your previous witnesses, my abuse consisted of only one incident. Yet it had tremendous repercussions for me, some of which I'm still dealing with."

She looked down at her hands where they were folded on the table, then up at the committee.

"During the summers of my childhood, I lived on my grandparents' farm in a small town in Pennsylvania called Jeremy."

The transcript read only "a small town in Pennsylvania." Zed Patterson, who had been jotting something on a sheet of paper in front of him, suddenly jerked his head up. His eyes seemed to focus on her for the first time, and she felt the quick beating of her heart in her throat.

"My grandfather carved carousel horses for a hobby," she continued, not reading from the transcript at all now. "He had actually built a carousel in the barn on his property."

Zed Patterson sat back in his seat, and the jowly senator lifted his copy of her transcript in the air.

"You're not following your printed statement, Miz, um—" He hunted through his papers for her name.

"Gray," she said.

"Yes. Ms. Gray."

"Is this information relevant?" one of the other senators asked. His thick eyebrows were knitted together in a frown.

Vanessa stole a look at Starla, whose mouth was open as if she wanted to speak but was not sure what to say.

"Yes," Vanessa said. "It's extremely relevant. Please bear with me."

"Go on." The senator unknitted his eyebrows and rested his arms on the table.

"The summer I was eight years old, my grandfather hired a young man to do some work on the carousel," she continued. "One day, the man asked my sister, who was ten, to help him in the barn. She didn't want to go and sent me in her place. I went out to the barn, and the man gave me a doughnut—chocolate-covered. He was disappointed I wasn't my sister, though. He said he preferred dark-haired girls—my sister was dark—but that I would have to do."

In the harsh overhead lights, Zed Patterson's face looked skeletal. The color had drained from his skin, which was pulled tightly over high, pallid cheekbones. His lips were a thin line of white.

"He then proceeded to tell me how pretty I was, and how smart," Vanessa said. "He asked me which was my favorite horse on the carousel, and then he lifted me onto it, his hands touching me between my legs, but I remember thinking, 'He's an adult. I can trust adults.' I'd been brought up thinking that all adults were honest and protective of children." She hesitated. "I was wrong, of course, but that's what I thought at the time. It would not have occurred to me that he might want to hurt me."

Vanessa stole another look at Starla, who was nearly as pale as Zed Patterson under her teased blond hair. Starla had to be wondering what had happened to the sunlit hay on the floor of the barn. What had happened to her excellent, unvetted witness?

"He started the carousel, and he stood next to me as the ride spun around. He was touching me, and I was beginning to feel afraid, but I didn't know what to do." Vanessa felt the first threat of tears. She would not let them out. She pressed her palms hard together in her lap. "As we were going around, he lifted me off the horse and took my hand and led me over to the chariot. He sat me down there and told me how beautiful I was and how excited I made him. I remember clearly that he used that word, 'excited,' because it seemed like a strange word to me at the time. I didn't know what he meant. He said he was going to do some things to me—to my body—and that I must never tell anyone. He was smiling and calm. He said some of the things might hurt a little, but he would try to be gentle. I started crying then, and he held me and told me I was brave, and he would try very hard not to hurt me any more than he had to." For a moment, Vanessa could not speak. She pressed her fingertips to her forehead, eyes down, and felt one tear, then another slip over her cheek.

Brushing the tears away with her fingers, she looked up again. "I was confused," she said. "He seemed so nice, and this seemed like something that had to be done. Like going to a doctor and getting a shot. An adult who had no choice but to hurt me."

The room was still, hushed. Although she could not see the crowd behind her, she imagined all eyes were riveted in her direction. She wished she could steal a look at Brian. She didn't dare.

"He laid me down on the seat of the chariot, took off my underpants, touched me, and then tried to insert his penis inside me. Which was, of course, difficult, and at that point he lost his tenderness and concern for me. He didn't seem to care if he was hurting me or not, and I started fighting and screaming. He held his hand over my mouth, though, and raped me. I had no idea what was happening to me. All I knew was that I felt as though I was being torn apart, from head to toe."

Vanessa looked at Starla again, trying to convey an apology with her eyes. "I told Starla Garvey, the attorney responsible for screening the witnesses presenting testimony here today, that I didn't know the identity of my abuser, other than the fact that he worked for my grandfather. Because I knew that if I told her, I wouldn't be allowed to testify. But I do know who he was. I have always known. He was the deputy sheriff of Jeremy, Pennsylvania, at that time, and today he is Senator Walter Patterson."

The room was deadly still for several seconds before Patterson let out a burst of laughter. "I beg your pardon?" He leaned toward her, smiling. "Want to run that by me again?"

"No." She drew in a deep breath, and along with it, a welcome sense of relief and power. "Running it by you once was difficult enough. I've been waiting a lifetime to do it. I never thought I'd get the chance. The statute of limitations has long ago run out for me." She leaned toward him over the table, locking her eyes with his. "This is the best I can do, and it feels great, you bastard."

Patterson's eyes widened. He raised the gavel from the table and banged it down hard. "Recess!" he proclaimed. But no one moved. The crowd behind her began to buzz.

"If only I'd had the guts to come forward when you were on trial for molesting that little girl last month." Vanessa had to shout above the din. "Maybe people would have realized she was telling the truth, and you'd be locked up by now." She was losing it. She could feel any semblance of poise or pride slipping away from her. Patterson crashed his gavel on the table again.

Vanessa stood up. "I fear for any child you have access to," she said. "I fear for your own chil—" Her microphone suddenly went dead, and her words were swallowed by the clamor. A security guard reached for her as Starla chased after the committee members who were filing quickly out of the room, several of them darting anxious looks in Vanessa's direction.

Brian was trying to get past the uniformed security guard, who was hanging on to Vanessa's arm but didn't seem to know what to do with her. Shaking the guard's hand from her arm, she reached for her husband, and she was relieved to see that Brian wore a grin. He pulled her into a hug.

"Holy shit, woman," he said into her ear, and she laughed.

The crowd was beginning to press around them, and the guard no longer seemed to know whether Vanessa was a danger to others or in need of protection herself.

"Can we get out of here?" she asked Brian.

He nodded. "Come on." With his arm around her, he led her quickly through the crowd. People followed them into the hallway, and she and Brian kicked into a run. They turned down another hall, where Brian yanked open a door and pulled her inside.

They were in some sort of broom closet. The light was off, but a small window illuminated shelves of cleaning supplies. The scent of bleach was strong. Brian was trying to still his own laughter as he pressed a finger to her lips to keep her quiet. In a few seconds, they heard the thunder of footsteps in the hall outside the closet.

Brian leaned against the wall and closed his arms around her. "That was the bravest thing I've ever seen anyone do," he said. "Was it impulse or did you plan it?"

"A little of both." She made a wry face. "I'm sorry I didn't tell you before I did it. I was afraid you'd—"

"You're right, I would have. Don't apologize."

He bent low to kiss her, and she thought of what else she hadn't told him. She could tell him now, but the time did not seem right. It could wait. She kissed him hard.

"I feel *good*," she said. "I feel happy."

He touched her cheek. "God, I'm glad to hear you say that. It's been a while."

"Did you see his face when I said the farm was in Jeremy?"

Brian laughed. "That was rich, but when you identified him as the guy, he looked like he was going to have a coronary. Like he *wished* he could have a coronary."

She started laughing herself, almost uncontrollably. "I got him," she said. "I nailed the bastard. And now I'm hungry."

The footsteps in the hallway had subsided, and Brian nodded toward the door. "Let's go," he said.

They walked calmly through the halls without encountering anyone who recognized her.

"You know what I feel bad about, though?" Vanessa said as they approached the exit.

"What's that?"

"I should have planned it better," she said. "Timed the revelation better. I never got to talk about how it affected me as an adolescent. Why we need AMC programs."

She pushed open the door, and they walked out into the sunlight—and the waiting jumble of television cameras and reporters. Brian wrapped his arm protectively around her shoulders, gesturing with his other hand toward the eager crowd. "I think you're going to have the opportunity to talk about whatever you like," he said.

48

Vienna

The sky was darkening outside the foundation windows when Jon appeared in the doorway to Claire's office.

"Patterson's called a press conference," he said. "Should be on in ten minutes. Want to watch with me?"

"*Yes.*" She was supposed to go to the Chain Bridge Theater tonight, early. It was opening night for the play Randy was directing, and she wanted to spend some time with him first, but she could not miss seeing the press conference. "I'll be right there."

It had been two days since the hearings on Capitol Hill, and Vanessa's outburst had been telecast over and over on the news. Claire had been shocked by the public reaction to her sister's allegations. The media was tearing her apart. The victim was being systematically beaten into submission, while no one cast a doubting eye in Patterson's direction. Even women's groups, which Claire had expected to rush to her sister's defense, were keeping silent, unwilling to derail the man they saw as their champion.

She'd left several messages for Vanessa at the Omni, but her calls had not been returned.

She had to admit that Vanessa did not make the most sympathetic victim. Her cursing at a much-loved senator did not play well with the public. Her past—the drug use, the teenage pregnancy, the alcoholism, all of which had been rapidly unearthed and paraded for the world to see—did not lend her credibility. It didn't matter that she was now a respected physician. That was not nearly as sensational as her sordid past. Besides, people *liked* Zed Patterson. After breathing a long, collective sigh of relief at his acquittal in the molestation case, Patterson's devotees did not want to hear any more allegations about his behavior.

In the *Post* that morning, a psychologist had written an article offering half a dozen motives for Vanessa's attack on the senator. The possibility that she might be telling the truth was not even considered. Vanessa had gotten a little too uncomfortably crazy during her testimony, Claire thought.

Somehow, a reporter had learned that Claire was Vanessa's sister. He'd contacted her, asking her to verify the information Vanessa had offered, and she had done so willingly. Yes, she'd said, Zed Patterson had worked for her grandparents, and yes, she had sent Vanessa out to the barn to help him that morning, not knowing there was any danger. And yes, she believed her sister's account of what happened. And although she carried with her the prestige of the Harte-Mathias Foundation, no one seemed to take her thoughts on the subject very seriously. Vanessa Gray was either a troubled woman who, in all innocence, had her facts twisted, or she was a clever zealot with some obscure political ax to grind against Patterson.

She had told Debra Parlow about Vanessa's visit, and she'd wept in the therapist's office for the sister she had lost and could not seem to regain. Ironically, that painful session had left her more comfortable with Debra, more trusting of her nonjudgmental support. Maybe someday she *would* be able to talk with Debra about her memories.

Claire walked into the lounge to find the TV on and Jon and Pat deep in conversation. They sat with their chairs facing each other, leaning toward one another, close enough to touch. Indeed, Pat had her hand on Jon's arm. Claire turned her eyes away, and Pat immediately let go of Jon and sat back in her chair.

"Hi, Claire." Pat picked up her briefcase from the floor, rested it in her lap, and wheeled past Jon toward the door. "I've got to get out of here," she said. "I'll have to watch the news tonight to see what Patterson has to say."

"'Night, Pat," Jon said.

"Good-night." Claire sat down in one of the upholstered straight-backed chairs by the table and looked up at the TV. A commercial was on, but the sound was off.

She felt Jon's eyes on her. "Do you believe Vanessa?" he asked.

The question surprised her. Of course she believed her. Yet wasn't there that little speck of doubt still lurking in the back of her mind? She didn't know Vanessa, and Vanessa was doing all she could to be certain they remained strangers. She was still bothered by Vanessa's continued allusions to a chariot on the carousel. And she didn't really know what had happened in the barn that day.

"I'm ninety-nine percent sure she's telling the truth," she said.

Jon looked at the screen, where a woman with deep

lines across her forehead was studying a bottle of cold medicine. "Well, I believe her one hundred percent," he said.

His words touched her. She studied his face. From
where she sat in the darkening room, the brown of his eyes
looked like amber, and she could see the full length of his
eyelashes in the light from the television. Silver-dusted hair,
high cheekbones, hollow cheeks. The tightness low in her
belly took her by surprise. Jon Mathias would still be sexy
when he was eighty.

A group of people suddenly appeared on the screen, a
few men and a woman standing behind a microphone-
littered dais in a room with baby blue walls. Jon hit the
sound button on the remote, and the muffled, cluttered
noise of a pre-press-conference crowd filled the lounge.

"I feel the need to share with all of you my response to
the allegations of Dr. Vanessa Gray." Zed Patterson let his
eyes roam over the unseen crowd. Next to him stood a
young, redheaded woman. Claire recognized her from pictures she'd seen in the newspaper. Patterson's wife, Penny,
age thirty-something, mother of his two young children.

"It took me a while to piece it all together," Patterson
said, "and I'll do my best to tell you all I know." He spoke
with an unhurried, easygoing style; there was a despicable
hint of a smile on his lips.

"I hate him," Claire said, the words surprising her. "I
hate this man."

Jon wheeled close to her chair and took her hand.

"I was indeed the sheriff of Jeremy, Pennsylvania, in
1962, the year in which Dr. Gray alleges the abuse took
place," Patterson said. "I was twenty-seven years old, a
young man with a penchant for law and order and a growing interest in our legal system. As many of my constituents

know, I did not come from a privileged background. My father was an automobile mechanic, and that was the first trade I learned. So when Vince Siparo, one of the farmers in Jeremy, was looking for a mechanic to help with the machinery that ran the rather amazing carousel he was building in his barn, I offered my services. Dr. Gray is accurate to that point. I did help her grandfather one summer—the exact year I couldn't say. Her grandparents were fine people. Fine, hardworking people."

He stopped to take a sip from a glass on the dais.

"I've racked my brain to try to remember more about the home situation there on the farm. I know Siparo's daughter and son-in-law were there from time to time, and I believe there were some children around. Boys, girls, I don't remember." He took another drink from the glass, and Claire pressed her hand to her mouth.

"He's lying," she said. "He knows perfectly well who was there. He gave me presents, Jon."

Patterson looked at his wife, who gave him an encouraging smile. "So that brings me to Dr. Gray's accusations," he continued, "and believe me, I've given this a lot of thought. Dr. Gray is in a position of responsibility and esteem in a children's hospital in Seattle. I can't—and none of us should—simply shrug off her serious accusations. I would guess that she sincerely believes what she is saying. Something probably *did* happen to her way back then. It just didn't happen at my hands. The mind works in funny ways. Maybe when she heard about the recent accusations against me, she made the leap in her reasoning that, since I was around then, I must have been the person who abused her. Otherwise, why on earth didn't she come forward with this some other time in the past thirty years?"

His wife nodded, shielding her eyes against the lights in the room.

"People know me and will continue to trust me as an advocate for the rights of abused women and children, and I think Dr. Gray is right—we *do* need to provide services for adolescents who suffered abuse in their younger years."

Penny Patterson nodded again, like a robot. Claire felt sorry for her.

"Therefore," Patterson continued, "I plan to have services for adolescents added to the Aid to Adult Survivors Bill. The fact is, despite all she's accomplished professionally, this one incident obviously did traumatize Dr. Gray to an enormous extent—as we all witnessed on the Hill on Wednesday." He offered a wry, condescending smile to the camera. "Although she was misguided, it must have taken great courage on her part to come forward in that way, and I must thank her for bringing the matter of how childhood abuse can wreak havoc on the adult to our attention so graphically."

"Oh, he's a flaming prick!" Claire said. She drew her hand away from Jon's to pound her fist on the table.

Patterson fielded a few questions after speaking, but only a few, and he said nothing new. His wife was asked to comment, and she said something about it being "fashionable" these days for "grown women" to accuse men of long-ago abuse, and how "such behavior" can steal the focus from "today's real victims."

"I simply don't understand Dr. Gray's motives," she added. "My husband is, I'm afraid, more tolerant than I am on this issue."

They watched in silence as the press conference came to a close, and Claire was aware of how dark the room had become with only the television for light. She could smell the soft scent of Jon's aftershave. On the wall, the clock ticked toward the hour of the play. Randy was probably wondering what had happened to her.

She touched Jon's arm lightly. "I have to go."

"To Randy," Jon said. He did not often mention Randy these days.

"It's the opening night of his new play."

"Ah."

Jon clicked off the television, and darkness swept across the room. Neither of them moved.

"Jon?"

"Mmm?"

"I want you to know that it's not physical with Randy." That was misleading, she thought. "What I mean is, that was never what motivated me, and—"

"Shut up, Claire."

She cringed. She was not saying this well. "You're the sexiest man I've ever known." She tried again. "I just want to be sure you know that my attraction to Randy had nothing to do with sex. It was a different sort of need altogether."

Jon wheeled over to the door and flicked the light switch on the wall. "See you Monday?" he asked. There were red blotches on his cheeks and neck, and she knew he wanted to be rid of her and her impulsive rambling.

She blinked against the sudden brightness in the room. She wished she could talk with him longer. She wanted to tell him she was trying to learn to take care of herself. It was hard, she would say. Scary.

But she stood up instead and, with a sigh, bent over to brush her lips across his temple.

"Monday, yes," she said. "Good-night."

49

Vanessa and Brian rented a paddleboat in the Tidal Basin Saturday morning, and as they pushed off from shore, Vanessa felt a welcome sense of isolation from the rest of the world. The cherry trees surrounding the basin had dropped their blossoms, which circled the water with a faded pink-and-white blanket. The sky was a rich, cloudless blue. Ahead of them, Thomas Jefferson stood silhouetted in his domed monument.

Late last night, they'd checked out of the Omni and into a smaller, more intimate hotel under Brian's name. They had lost the wolves, they hoped, and they'd called their respective employers to let them know they were taking a few more days off. The city was beautiful, signs of spring were everywhere, and they were determined to escape Vanessa's tormentors without having to leave Washington itself.

Out in the middle of the basin, Vanessa stopped pedaling. She slipped off her lightweight jacket and raised her face to the sun. Brian took her lead, taking off his own jacket, then putting his arm around her and letting the little boat drift idly in the water.

Reporters could be frighteningly quick and ruthless, Vanessa had learned. They had dug up enough information on her teenage years to fuel any argument against her credibility. And they were not her only tormentors.

Terri Roos had tracked her down the night before. Vanessa had already heard from a few other people in the network. Most expressed a stunned, but reserved, sympathy. Terri, though, was clearly angry.

"You put your personal agenda ahead of the greater good," she'd said. Vanessa had simply hung up on her.

Doug Jenks, the chief executive officer of Lassiter Children's Hospital, had called to tell her she should have thought through the potential repercussions of her testimony, both to herself and to Lassiter, before going public with her allegations. But it was the call from the reporter who said he had learned that she'd put a baby up for adoption twenty years ago—and was trying to track that young woman down—that propelled them into changing hotels.

"Please, don't," was all Vanessa had managed to say before her tears started. She was tired. Tired of the phone calls. Tired of the questions.

The one truly heartening call had come from Darcy, who'd cried on the phone and chastised Vanessa for not having told her. Brian suggested that if she returned the calls from Claire, she might find support there as well. He was probably right, but she did not have the strength to talk to her sister right now.

"I'll call her when we get back to Seattle," she promised. And she would. Her anger toward Claire was gone, and she realized it had been misdirected all along. In its place was a mounting sympathy. Claire was battling old memories. Vanessa had seen too many women in the midst of that fight to be able to shrug off her sister's suffering. But she could not deal with it now.

The boat rocked lightly in the basin, and the sun warmed her face, and despite the trauma of the past few days, Vanessa felt more at peace with herself than she had in a long time. She'd done what she had to do. If they believed her, fine. If not, what did it matter? It was obvious to her, if to no one else, that she had scared Zed Patterson. He was going to include aid for adolescents in his bill just to keep her off his back.

"Let's not go back to shore," Brian said.

She rolled her head to his shoulder. "Never?"

"Maybe to eat every once in a while. That's all."

"Maybe to see a doctor," Vanessa suggested.

"A doctor?"

"I'm a week and a half late."

Brian's arm tightened around her shoulders. "Stress?"

"Could be. I've been under a little."

They were quiet for a moment. She could feel Brian absorbing the news, and she smiled to herself.

"Have you ever been a week and a half late before?" he asked.

"Never."

"Van." His voice was thick, and she put her arms around him and held him close to her as their boat drifted gently under a cloudless sky.

50

Winchester Village Amusement Park, Pennsylvania

Winchester Village was deserted. Claire and Randy walked between the skeleton of a sprawling roller coaster and an enormous sky-scraping claw that probably held cars full of screaming teenagers in the summer. The amusement park was not due to open until late May, and it had the feel of a ghost town, lifeless and forgotten. It was hard to picture it alive.

She'd had no trouble at all getting permission to enter the village out of season. She'd called the public relations department for the park and spoken to a man named Scott Merrick. She'd told him she was the granddaughter of Vincent Siparo and that she had not seen his carousel since her childhood. She asked if there was a chance she could see it now, and Merrick told her she would be welcome anytime. He was clearly a carousel enthusiast, and they chatted on the phone for several minutes about the Siparo horses of her great-grandfather's era. Merrick had ridden them as a child, he said. He could barely tell the difference between the horses carved by her grandfather and those carved by her great-grandfather, except for the signature floral decorations that adorned the Joseph Siparo bridles. This man did indeed know his painted ponies.

He wanted to be with her when she saw the carousel. She could tell by the way he was talking. "I'll show you how we've restored the horses," he said. "True to your grandfather's colors and designs. We even used the gold leaf like he did."

"Mr. Merrick," she began, "would it be too much to ask if I could see the carousel alone? You see, I think it's going to be a little emotional for me. Would you mind very much?"

Merrick had hesitated, and she could almost hear the disappointment in the silence. "Of course. You stop by the office here, and I'll give you the key to the carousel house."

She had intended to make the trip by herself, but Randy asked to join her, and she was glad for his company. Over the past week, she had watched him wrestle with the new boundaries of their relationship as he tried to determine how close to her he could sit, how intimately he could touch her. She appreciated the effort he made to keep their friendship alive despite the limits she had set on it.

They had left Virginia shortly after breakfast that morning and arrived at Scott Merrick's office close to noon. Merrick had warmly shaken her hand before pressing the key into her palm. She'd brought him a gift from the old photograph album, a picture of her grandfather carving a horse head in the workroom of the barn. Merrick had been ecstatic. He would blow it up, he said, and hang it on the wall of the carousel house.

"If you'd let me come with you, I could turn the carousel on for you," he negotiated. "Otherwise, you'll only get to see it standing still."

"That's fine." Claire had smiled at him, the key burning in her palm. "That's all I need."

The carousel house was at the opposite end of the park from the office. Claire held tight to the key as she and Randy walked among the hibernating rides and boarded-up concessions. She had to stop herself from running now that she was this close.

"I wonder if I'll be disappointed," she said to Randy. Maybe Titan would not be as beautiful and noble as in her memory. "You know how the things you thought were so wonderful when you were a child turn out to be smaller and less spectacular than you remembered?"

"Right," Randy said. "I know what you mean."

They rounded a huge covered platform of some sort, and the white carousel house suddenly sprang up in front of them. The building looked as though it had barely survived the winter. The white paint had a definite grayish hue. Scott Merrick had said the house was due to be painted in a few weeks.

The building was fronted by three wide garage-type doors. Apparently the rear of the building remained permanently closed, although the hundreds of small windows would let in light. With the key, Claire unlocked the center door, and Randy helped her roll it up. Directly in front of her, as he had always been in the barn, stood Titan, nostrils flaring, gold mane glinting in the spring sunlight.

"Oh." She took a step backward to study the horse, and her concern about being disappointed vanished. Titan was magnificent, his windblown mane wilder than in her memory. His huge brown eyes were stormy. His well-shaped head was lined with veins, and his gold-trimmed English saddle had the mellowed gloss of well-worn leather.

"Give me the key," Randy said. He took the key from her hand and opened the other two doors while Claire simply stared. Before her was an entire collection of crazy-maned, prancing, snorting, pawing, untamed horses. She wondered why as a child she had felt no fear of these frenzied animals. There was no denying that she felt a thread of fear now.

As dingy as the outside of the building was, the inside was spotless and glowing. Once the doors were fully open, shards of sunlight cut across the colors. The glossy paint and gold leaf and the oval mirrors on the inside rounding board made her squint.

The mirrors.

She looked away from them quickly, and she kept her face lowered as Randy took her hand and they began circling the carousel.

"The side of the horse that faces out is called the romance side." Claire could barely get the words past the knot of fear in her throat. The damn mirrors. She tried to keep her voice even. "That's where all the decoration is, on the romance side. All the identity that's shown to the world." She stepped onto the platform, pulling Randy with her, and walked among the horses to show him their plain sides. "The real horse is back here," she said.

Randy was clearly enchanted. "It's incredible to me that one man carved all these horses by hand." Randy stroked his fingers over the intricate plated armor covering the side of a black stallion. "What skill."

Ahead of her, Claire caught sight of something nestled among the horses. She let go of Randy's hand, still keeping her eyes lowered, and walked toward the glossy green shape.

A chariot. Indeed, there was one. The carved wood of its sides was gently sloping, the shape disturbingly familiar; she had been doodling the curved line of that wood for months. The chariot was short, but wide, with one broad seat upholstered in brown leather. The wood was painted a deep green, and a gold dragon and a woman dressed in white gossamer were carved into its elegant romance side.

Randy had caught up with her, and she gripped his arm.

"What is it?" He followed her eyes to the chariot.

She could almost smell the strong, spicy cologne. She could almost feel the scratch of an unshaven cheek against her face. She could hear the kind words.

You're a beautiful little girl. I love dark-haired little girls. And you're smart, aren't you? Smart and pretty. Easy to love.

One meaty hand held her down—gently, yes, but holding her all the same—while the other touched her where she didn't want to be touched. She could feel the buttons of his green shirt pressing against her skin.

I won't hurt you. That doesn't hurt, does it? It feels sort of good, doesn't it?

Claire forced herself to look up. Above her, the gridwork of the carousel formed a pattern like the cobweb of a spider. The wavy oval mirrors were filled at first with green, then with her face, a child's face. He was nuzzling her, his hand tugging down her pants. Her eyes in the mirror were filled with a confused sort of terror.

Claire backed away from the carousel, nausea quickly building inside her.

"Claire." Randy touched her shoulder. "What's the matter?"

"Close it up, Randy," she said, turning away. "Please just close it up." She crossed the platform and stepped out into the sunlight. A bench was nearby, and she somehow managed to reach it before her vision blurred and blackened. She sat down, lowering her head to her knees. She could hear the doors rolling shut over the carousel, over Titan, over the chariot, and she covered her ears with her hands.

She straightened dizzily as Randy walked toward her. He stood behind the bench, resting his hands on her shoulders.

"You saw a ghost," he said.

She nodded. "He did it to me, too," she said softly. "Zed Patterson. I must have known what he wanted with me that morning in the barn, because it wouldn't have been the first time. I sent Vanessa instead. I was scared. I couldn't go through it again." She turned to look up at him. "How could I possibly have forgotten?"

Randy walked around the bench and sat next to her. "You grew up in a family that taught you how to forget anything unpleasant and put a candy-coated lie in its place. They just forgot to tell you what to do when the coating wore off."

They sat quietly, Claire with her back to the carousel house. They had planned to get a hotel room somewhere nearby and stay the night—in separate beds—before driving back to Virginia, but now she wanted to escape this place. She wanted to leave the carousel and her memories here in this winter-dead park she would never visit again.

And there was something else she wanted. Something Randy knew before she did.

He took her hand and rubbed the back of it. "Do you want to see Jon?" he asked.

She nodded. Yes. She wanted more than anything to see her husband.

51

Vienna

From the window in the kitchen, Jon saw Claire's car pull into the driveway. He was surprised. She'd told him she would be gone this weekend—away with Randy, no doubt. The man with whom she supposedly had no physical relationship.

He was making chili for a potluck at Pat's that night, and he was stirring the pot when Claire walked through the back door. She gave him a weak smile and burst into tears.

His heart contracted sharply. Had something happened to Susan? He could not bring himself to ask that question.

"What's wrong?"

She pulled one of the chairs from the kitchen table and sat down, digging a tissue from her purse.

"I went up to Winchester Village to see the carousel," she said, "and I remembered something."

Jon lowered the heat under the chili and pushed his chair closer to her. "Go on."

She twisted the tissue between her fingers. "Zed Patterson did it to me, too," she said. "I remembered it vividly."

He listened as she described what she'd remembered. If she wondered why his face registered no shock, she didn't say. She was too lost in the past to notice. He reached up once to brush away the tears that she'd needed to cry for a very long time. Tears for a little girl who, in many ways, had never been allowed to grow up.

When she was through talking, she blew her nose, swept back her hair, and sat up straight. "I made a decision driving back to Virginia," she said. "I'm going to go public with this. Vanessa's getting my support whether she wants it or not."

She was very close to the truth, he thought. Close enough for him to fill in the gaps without harming her. He touched her knee. "I think that's fine," he said slowly. "I think it's important for you to do that, but . . . Claire? What more do you remember?"

Her eyes widened in exasperation. "What do you mean?" she asked. "Isn't that enough?"

"How did your grandfather die?"

She frowned. "You've asked me that before, Jon, and I told you, I don't know. How is that relevant? All I remember is that he sort of . . . disappeared. No one ever really talked about it. Eventually I realized he was dead."

"Don't you think that's a little strange?"

"My family was a little strange."

Jon sighed. He reached his hand toward her. "Come here, Claire."

She hesitated.

"Please." He leaned forward to take her hand, and she let

herself be pulled onto his lap. She sat woodenly, though. He rested his hand lightly on her back.

"I'm not certain if I'm doing the right thing in telling you this," he began. "I'm not certain if I've done the right thing all along, but I'm not going to play your mother's game any longer."

She looked at him. "What are you talking about?"

"You remember when Mellie was living here? How I spent a lot of time with her because I was sick and home from work for a while?"

"Yes. I was glad to see you two getting close."

"We did get close. And Mellie told me a lot, Claire. I guess something happens to people when they know they're going to die."

A look of alarm passed over Claire's face. "What did she tell you?"

"She said how glad she was that you'd found me. That she thought I was a good person and a good husband."

Claire's eyes filled again, and she raised her arm to circle his shoulders. "You were," she said. "You are."

"She said that she'd been afraid you would never be able to find happiness as an adult because of all the trauma you'd endured as a child. She told me it had taken every ounce of her creativity to prevent you from being permanently scarred."

"Her creativity?" Claire wrinkled her nose. "What was she talking about?"

"Think about it, Claire. Think of all that happened in your family that you remember so little about. You forgot those things because Mellie made sure you would. She told me she worked hard to twist things around, so you'd forget the bad and remember it as good, or at worst, benign."

Seems like I was always having to cover things up, Mellie had said to him. *Claire made it easy, though. She always wanted to believe me.*

Claire shook her head. "No wonder I've been feeling so insane lately."

"Do you want to hear what I know?" he asked.

She nodded uncertainly.

He wrapped his arms around her and held her close as he told her what Mellie had revealed to him.

He had pressed Mellie to elaborate on the truths she'd claimed to have twisted, and she'd finally relented, swearing him to secrecy. "It could only damage Claire if she knew," she'd said.

The tale Mellie told began several weeks after Vanessa's abduction by her father. Mellie's father—Claire's grandfather—was suffering from phlebitis and emphysema that summer and was not able to work much. On one particular day, however, he asked Mellie to go out to the barn with him to help him carry some tools back to the house.

Mellie had trembled as she related the story to Jon. "I knew Claire was in the barn, helping the deputy sheriff, Zed Patterson, with something on the carousel," she'd said. "At least that's what I thought she was doing. But when my father and I walked into the barn, we could see that Zed and Claire were on the seat of the chariot. I didn't get a good look. I just remember that Claire was lying down, and Zed was sort of kneeling over her. But Daddy got a look, all right. He was a gentle man, a teddy bear, but he flew into a rage the likes of which I'd never seen before. He started beating on Zed, bloodying his nose, but he was no match for a man in his twenties. Zed got the upper hand right away. He wasn't really punching my father, but he was shoving him around. Poor Daddy with his bad legs. He kept falling down and struggling to get up again. I tried to get between them. I wanted to kill the bastard myself."

Mellie had hung her head then, shamefaced. "You see," she'd said, "I'd been having an affair with Zed. I thought he was so charming. I was touched that he gave my girls—especially Claire—so much attention, when her father gave her so little."

After a minute, she continued her story. "Claire was kneeling on the chariot. There was terror in her little face. She loved her grandpa more than anyone. More than me, I think. It must have upset her terribly to see him getting shoved around that way. I told her to run and hide, and she scooted past all of us and ran into the workshop. I thought she was safe in there. Then, all of a sudden ... " Mellie's voice trailed off, and Jon had to prompt her to get her talking again.

"All of a sudden, Claire ran out of the workshop and over to where the men were fighting. She was so fast, I couldn't stop her. She reached them just as Zed pushed my father for the last time. Daddy fell to the ground, cracking his head on the platform, and Claire charged at Zed, screaming like a soldier in battle. It was only at the last second that I realized she had one of Daddy's carving knives in her hand. She ran at Zed and got him in the groin. His pants were up and zipped, but she got him good, and there was blood everywhere. On the floor of the carousel. On the horses. On Claire. I thought I'd never get the mess cleaned up." Mellie broke down then, and it was a few minutes before Jon could force himself to coax her to continue.

"I told Claire to run to the house and call an ambulance, and she took off," Mellie said. "I tried to help my father, and Zed took the opportunity to make a run for it. When Claire got back to the barn, I could already hear the sirens in the distance. I closed the barn doors and wouldn't let her in. I told her Grandpa was going to be okay, but that the ambulance would take him to the hospital for a few days just to keep an eye on him. Actually, they told me later he'd died of a heart attack before he even hit the floor."

"Why did you lie to her?" Jon had asked Mellie, incredulous.

"How could I tell her the truth? Look at what had happened to this child in the space of a few weeks. She'd lost her sister and her father, then her grandfather. She'd stabbed a man. She'd been . . . molested"—Mellie winced at the word—"who knows how many times. Looking back, I realized that morning was probably not the first time it happened. Zed was always after her to help him in the barn. I had to protect Claire from as much as I could."

Silence filled the room when Jon had finished telling Claire all he remembered of Mellie's story. Claire was leaning against him. She was shaking, and he felt the rapid beat of her heart against his ribcage. He rubbed his hand up and down her arm as the silence stretched on.

Finally, Claire spoke. "My mother was so crazy," she said softly, her voice thick with tears. "And she left a few things out, I believe, when she told you that story. Unless I'm making it up." She pressed her hand to her head, and Jon caught her fingers and drew them down to her lap again.

"Trust your memory, Claire," he said. "I think it's growing more accurate by the minute."

"Well, I *do* remember the fight she was talking about. I remember the blood." She sniffled. "Remember the blood on porcelain? The flashback?" She did not wait for his answer. "It wasn't porcelain after all; it was Titan." She took in a breath. "I also remember my mother screaming at Zed, something like, 'What were you doing to her?' and he answered, 'It's her fault,' pointing at me. 'She's always after me.' I guess I thought it *was* my fault. When Grandpa fell, I thought somehow I was to blame."

"Oh, Claire." He hugged her hard. Her body quaked with her weeping.

"And you know what?" she asked after a moment. "Grandpa never came back from the hospital, and no one said a word about it. Mellie and Grandma, as far as I can remember, never shed a tear in front of me, and somehow I knew better than to ask where he was or why he didn't come home. If I asked and the answer was bad, they might remember it was my fault."

They sat quietly for a few minutes. Jon was not anxious to move. Claire was leaning heavily against him now, and he would hold her as long as she would allow it. After a while, she spoke again.

"Why didn't you ever tell me any of this?" she asked.

Jon sighed. "I was afraid it would do more harm than good. You always seemed so content with your life, and I loved your cheerfulness and your spirit. I didn't want you to change. When you started having flashbacks, I thought of telling you, but Pat said people need to work through repressed memories at their own pace, and I was frankly glad to be taken off the hook. I knew Randy was helping you sort through the past in a way I didn't have the guts to do." His eyes suddenly burned, and he pressed his lips to her shoulder. "I've been afraid, though, Claire. I've been so afraid of losing you to Randy for good." He felt the warmth of tears on his cheeks. "Have I lost you?"

She sat up straight to look down at him. Her nose was red, her own eyes brimming. "You asked me once what Randy did that made it so easy for me to talk to him," she said. "I think I said that he listened well or something like that, but I know that isn't it. It's not anything Randy does that makes it easier. It's that I can tell him about terrible things that happened to me, and it doesn't hurt him the way it hurts you." She brushed her fingertips across his wet cheek. "He doesn't cry when I tell him sad things. He doesn't love me the way you do, Jon. And I don't love him the way I love you." She kissed him softly. "You haven't lost me. That is, if you still want me after all I've put you through."

He pulled her close enough to bury his face in the valley between her shoulder and throat. "I still want you, Harte," he said. "I never stopped wanting you."

They held each other awhile longer. He heard Claire's breathing grow even; felt her relax in his arms. And when she spoke again, her voice had lost the sound of tears.

"Where did that courageous little girl ever go?" she asked.

Jon smiled to himself, turning his head to kiss her throat. "She's right here," he said. "She's right where I want her."

52

Washington, D.C.

Brian had stopped packing. Vanessa stepped out of the bathroom of their cozy hotel suite to find him staring out the window, the suitcase only half filled on the bed.

"We've got to get going." She tightened the bath towel across her chest. "The guy at the front desk said the airport traffic's unpredictable."

Brian turned to face her. "I changed our flight," he said. "We're not leaving until tonight." The light from the window behind him made his features dark and unreadable.

She frowned. "Why would you do that?"

Brian stuffed his hands into his pants pockets. "Because your brother-in-law called and asked us to come to a press conference this morning. Claire is planning to make some sort of announcement."

"About?"

"He didn't go into it. He just said he really wishes we'd be there."

Vanessa lowered herself into one of the armchairs by the window. In the distance, the Washington Monument nearly glowed in the sunlight. Brian had changed their plans, radically, and she wondered why she felt so little annoyance at him for not consulting her. She tried to muster up a solid sense of indignation, but it remained small and petty and not worth expressing. Still, a press conference?

"I've spent the last few days going out of my way to avoid the media," she said, her voice flat. "And now I'm supposed to voluntarily sit in a room full of reporters?"

Brian sat down on the edge of the bed next to her and squeezed her arm. "They won't be there to see you," he said. "They'll be there for Claire."

She shook her head, her damp hair chilly on her shoulders. What was Claire up to? She remembered her sister's allusion to old memories and the pain in her voice, and she felt an unexpected desire to protect her from harm. Claire did not know how ruthless the press could be.

"You've accomplished what you wanted to on this trip," Brian said. "You did most of what you needed to do. But there's one final obstacle you need to take care of, and that's you and Claire." He squeezed her arm again. "We're going to this press conference."

She reached out to lock her hand with his. She and Claire were no longer children, no longer filled with childhood fears and fantasies and rivalries. And there was one thing Vanessa now knew with absolute certainty: Her sister was not her enemy.

"Yes," she said. "We're going."

53

Vienna

Jon sat at the long table at the front of the foundation's main conference room, watching as reporters filed in and took their seats. Next to him sat Vanessa Gray, pale and fragile and silent. She and her husband had arrived only minutes earlier, and they had merely nodded to him and Claire as they sat down. Jon saw Vanessa's eyes dart around the room. He could not blame her for her apprehension. He reached for her hand and squeezed it.

"I'm glad you came," he said. "Thank you."

Claire sat to his right, engrossed in conversation with Steve Ackerson, the foundation's attorney, whom Jon had insisted she consult. Steve was not at all happy about this press conference and had demanded to be with Claire as she spoke. Only if he'd let her speak without interruption, Claire had said. She'd requested the same of Jon. She wanted to do this alone. Jon understood. He admired her for doing it at all.

It was hardly Claire's first press conference. At least ten

times in the past, reporters had converged on this room at the foundation to hear about the development of a new program or some other topic of interest to the foundation. Still, Jon could tell she was nervous. She had stayed at the house with him the night before, and she had been unable to sleep. They had made love, which made her alternately giddy and weepy and very, very tender toward him. It had not eased her nerves, though, and now she kept unconsciously groping for his hand, holding it for only a second or two before pulling her own hand away. Her voice was breathless as she talked with Steve, and she kept checking her watch. On Jon's other side, Vanessa rocked her foot frenetically beneath the table. He was sandwiched between two human bundles of anxiety.

Perhaps twenty-five reporters were seated in the room, and there was a steady buzz of chatter, which quickly abated when Claire stood up behind the microphone-studded podium.

"Thank you all for coming," she began. Jon shifted his chair away from the table a bit so he could more easily see her face. Next to him, Vanessa did the same.

"I am, as you all know, the sister of Dr. Vanessa Gray, who recently accused Senator Zed Patterson of having abused her when she was eight years old." Whatever nervousness Claire had exhibited before starting to speak had disappeared. A sheet of paper rested on the podium in front of her, but she did not glance at it. "My sister and I have been estranged since the time of her abuse," she continued. "We were separated by our parents, Vanessa living in Seattle with our father while I lived here in Virginia with our mother." Claire spread her hands out on the sides of the podium. Her wedding ring glittered in the overhead light.

"For the past several months, I've been trying to make sense of some long-forgotten memories from my childhood," she said. "I recently visited Winchester Village in Pennsylvania, where the carousel built by my grandfather is housed, and I remembered very vividly that I, too, was molested by then deputy sheriff Walter Patterson on the carousel."

A surge of whispering swelled in the room but faded quickly as Claire spoke over it.

"This occurred at least two times that I remember," she said, "but I believe it probably happened more often than that. I realize that my sister's allegations have not been taken seriously, and it's with some apprehension that I go public with this information myself. But I feel that I must, not only to lend credibility to Vanessa's statements, but also to alert others to the fact that Senator Patterson does indeed have a history of pedophilia. I doubt very much that Vanessa and I were his only victims, and I hope that by our coming forward, other victims will be given the courage to do so as well. Pedophilia is not an illness that goes away on its own, and I'm concerned about the possibility of other children being at risk in the presence of the senator."

She glanced down at Jon. He smiled at her, and she looked out at the reporters again.

"I'll take your questions now," she said.

A woman wearing thick glasses stood up in the third row. "Forgive me, Ms. Harte," she said, "but your coming forward at this time seems a bit suspicious. Your sister makes some allegations against Senator Patterson and, suddenly, you claim to remember something similar happening to you. Can you offer us any proof at all that what you're telling us actually took place?"

"I have no proof other than my words and Vanessa's," Claire said. "There *were* two witnesses to one of the incidents of abuse. Unfortunately, both of those people, my mother and my grandfather, are dead." Claire drew in a breath. "After visiting the carousel and recalling the abuse, I told my husband what I'd remembered. He then told me that shortly before my mother's death, she revealed to him that she and my grandfather had walked into the barn one day to discover Mr. Patterson molesting me on the carousel. My mother described an incident to my husband, which I remembered only as my husband repeated it to me. She said that after she and my grandfather found us on the carousel, a fight broke out between the sheriff and my grandfather. During that fight, Mr. Patterson knocked my grandfather to the floor and I . . . " Claire's voice failed her for the first time. She looked down at the podium, and Jon felt a film of sweat break out on his back as she raised her eyes to her audience once again. "I got one of my grandfather's carving knives," Claire said, "and I stabbed the sheriff with it." Jon could see tears in Claire's eyes. "I loved my grandfather very much," she said. "I think I was trying to protect him, but he died of a heart attack during the fight. My mother never pressed charges against Sheriff Patterson, for reasons of her own. She was the type of person who distorted the truth in an attempt to protect her children from pain. She made sure I forgot what had happened, but the incident came back to me as my husband told me about it."

There were a few seconds of silence in the room. Looking at the faces of the reporters, Jon knew that for perhaps the first time they were beginning to doubt Patterson's slick and convincing rebuttal of Vanessa's allegations.

A second reporter stood up, this one an obese middle-aged man.

"How can you explain the fact that Senator Patterson has made victims' rights his pet project?" The man wheezed as he spoke. "Not to mention all the work he's done for women and children?"

Claire leaned into the bank of microphones. "Only the senator can answer that question," she said. "I can speculate, but I'd like to stick to what I know as fact during this conference, rather than conjecture."

A black woman sitting in the middle of the room stood up. "You said you"—the woman looked down at her notes—"stabbed Senator Patterson with a carving knife. How serious was the wound and where was he cut?"

"He was cut in the lower abdomen or groin area, and I remember a lot of blood," Claire said. "I don't know if the wound was very serious, however."

Jon stole a look to his left, at Vanessa. Her round blue eyes were on Claire. The fingers of her right hand were pressed to her mouth, while her left was tucked snugly into her husband's hand on the table.

The questions continued for a few more minutes, skeptical questions, stunned questions. It was obvious that Claire had shaken up this room of reporters. Whether they believed her or not was unclear. Jon was not certain it was important.

Steve Ackerson suddenly stood up, leaning across Claire to speak into the microphone. "That's all the questions Ms. Harte-Mathias will take today," he said. "Thank you very much for coming."

Claire raised her hand to keep the reporters in their seats. It was obvious she had something more to say.

"I don't know if I've been fortunate or unfortunate to have blocked these memories from my mind all these years," she said. "All I know is that my sister has done the suffering for both of us." She glanced in Vanessa's direction. "I feel as though it's long past time for me to take on my share."

Steve set his hand on Claire's shoulder, turning her, and quickly ushered her from the room, out into the hallway. Vanessa and Brian followed, with Jon behind them in his wheelchair. By the time Jon reached the hallway, Vanessa and Claire were embracing. He was anxious to touch Claire, to tell her how much he admired her for what she had done, but he could see that he would have to wait his turn. It was going to be a long time before anyone could pry these two sisters apart.

54

McLean

She had left only a few things at Randy's town house. Some articles of clothing, a few books, and some CDs— Chopin, mostly, which Randy certainly did not want and in which she found she had little remaining interest. Randy was waiting downstairs while she packed in the guest room. He had the television on, and she could make out the sounds of the midday news. She knew what the top story was—she'd been listening to it all morning: Penny Patterson had taken a nearly fatal overdose of sleeping pills. She'd been found in her Pennsylvania home by a friend very late the night before. She had called the friend earlier in the evening, sounding despondent. She was crying, the friend reported, and was saying, over and over again, "Zed has a scar. Zed has a scar." No one had any doubt that the scar to which she referred had been given to him long ago by a frightened and furious knife-wielding ten-year-old girl. Claire's sense of vindication could not erase the sympathy she felt for Penny Patterson.

Back in February, Claire had borrowed one of Randy's sweatshirts. As she walked into his bedroom to put it away, she could hear him in the kitchen downstairs, making a racket with the pots and pans. Cary was due to arrive later that afternoon. He and Randy were going to make cookies, Randy had told her, to celebrate spring. She was glad Cary was coming. It would make things much easier on Randy to have his son with him today.

She opened the middle drawer of his dresser where he kept his sweatshirts and spotted a folded sheet of paper tucked between the shirts and the side of the drawer. She pulled the paper from its niche. It was covered with tiny handwriting, in green ink, and the signature at the bottom of the page made her gasp. *Your sister, Margot.*

She sat down slowly on the edge of the bed, and flattening the page on her lap, began to read.

Dear Randy,

You always hated this picture frame. When you gave me the photograph, you said it should have a nicer frame, and you'd comment on it every time you visited me. But you never brought a new frame. So I figure they will give you this picture, and the frame will bother you enough to change it, and when you open up the old frame, this letter will fall out. I hope you find it sooner instead of later.

Well, I bet you are surprised to know that I actually heard the things you said when you visited me. You probably thought I wasn't listening, but that is one thing I am good at, Randy. Listening. And I heard every word you ever said to me. And so did Charles. Charles is always with me, and he speaks to me often. I know you probably think that's crazy, but I don't care. Charles is here. I don't see him, but I hear him. He still talks in his child's voice. He's always saying how good it is where he is now, how peaceful. There is music all the time. I know he wants me to come there, but he is not very pushy. I think the time is right, though, so here is this letter. I can't leave it out for someone else to give you, because it's important that only you get to see it. Only you and I know what really happened that night. Charles and I have forgiven you. Maybe I should have said that to you out loud sometime. Maybe that would have helped you. I almost did that one time you cried when you visited me. Remember? But somehow I could never get the words out. I only wish I'd lived long enough to see you forgive yourself, Randy. I don't think you'll ever be happy until you do.

Charles's death did the same thing to you that it did to me. It made us both scared of loving somebody, right? I'm in here, where I don't have to worry about it much. But you've had chances and you've blown them. Those girlfriends you used to tell me about. The ones you broke up with when you thought you were getting too close to them. That was a long time ago—bet you're surprised I remember!! And LuAnne. You think she left you cause of your heart, but I know what you're like. You probably never let yourself really love her, did you? Never got really close enough to make her feel loved. You're so afraid of taking a chance with somebody, Randy. I hope you don't hold back that way with your little boy. Cary, right? You showed me a picture of him once, but I didn't look at it, remember? I was afraid he might look like Charles.

I have some advice for you, Randy. First of all, get out of your house. I know you're hiding in there like you've always done when you get depressed. So LuAnne is gone. Look at it as a lesson. Get out and meet some people. Get out of your shell. You're probably saying, "Look who's talking." Well, I'm in a pretty thick shell, that's true, but it's what I want. It's not what you want, though. I know that about you. You're a caring person or you wouldn't still be hurting so much about Charles after all these years. You like people and you have lots to give them, but you're just scared to do it because they might fall off a bridge or leave you. Right? And they might!! No guarantees. But it'll be worth it. I'm not talking about finding a lover, necessarily. Just one person or even a bunch of people you can love and get close to. Get involved with them. Listen to them. Make a difference in someone's life and it'll make a difference in yours. Please, Randy. I can't bear to think about you being miserable for the rest of your life.

As for me, don't you dare get depressed over what I'm going to do. I'll be happier by the time you read this letter. Happier than I've ever been.

I love you, you know. I'm sorry I never said it to you. I guess you are not the only one afraid to take that risk. See what we've missed out on?

Well, tomorrow night I will fly from the bridge in Harpers Ferry. I've dreamt of doing that for years. It is supposed to snow like it did that night. Won't that be beautiful? And Charles will be waiting for me. The music will be waiting.

Your sister,
Margot.

Claire sat numbly on the edge of the bed, the letter flat on her knees. Even when she heard Randy begin to climb the stairs, she made no move to return the sheet of paper to its hiding place.

Randy stood in the doorway. His eyes lit on her face first, then dropped to the letter before returning to her face again.

"I'm sorry," she said. "I was putting away your sweatshirt and the letter was there, and when I saw it was from Margot, I had to—"

He held up a hand to stop her. "I thought of telling you about it many times. I'm not sure why I didn't." He moved toward the bed and sat down next to her, draping an arm over her shoulders. "Well, Claire," he asked with a sigh, "did I make a difference in your life?"

"You did what she told you to do." Claire bit her lip. "You took a risk and now I—"

"And there were no guarantees," he interrupted her. "I knew that going in. I told you, I have no regrets."

She pressed her hands together above the letter. "I hope your experience with me doesn't send you back to your shell again."

He shook his head with a grin. "You were my dress rehearsal, Claire," he said. "Now I'm ready for opening night."

Claire smiled, then looked down at the wrinkled paper. "When did you find this?" she asked.

"Between the time you gave me the picture and the time I called to ask you to meet me for lunch. I felt ready then to hear what Margot had said to you on the bridge, but I also remembered you mentioning your sister. I knew you were upset about her and needed to talk, but it never would have occurred to me to encourage you until I read Margot's letter."

Claire shook her head. How different the last few months would have been if Randy had not discovered this letter. How different for both of them.

She ran her fingertips over the fine green handwriting. "Is there any more news on Penny Patterson?" she asked.

"It sounds like she's going to be all right."

Claire felt the dark cloud lift from her shoulders. "That's a relief."

"I doubt very much she'll be standing by her man after this, though," Randy said.

"I certainly hope not."

"I'm glad you're standing by yours though." Randy gave her shoulders a squeeze.

"You are?" she asked, although she was not surprised to hear him say that.

Randy nodded. "You know, don't you, that Jon is probably the least handicapped of the lot of us?"

She nodded, smiling.

A buzzer suddenly went off in the kitchen.

"First batch of cookies." Randy stood up. "I couldn't wait for Cary."

She watched him leave the room and listened as he walked down the stairs. She opened the drawer again and rested the sweatshirt on top of the others. Then she folded Margot's letter in fourths and tucked it back where she'd found it. She would leave it there, in case Randy ever needed to remind himself of his sister's advice. She doubted he would have to, though. He had embraced her counsel well enough the first time.

55

Harpers Ferry, West Virginia
January 1994

Outside the High Water Hotel in Harpers Ferry, the snow fell softly, steadily, while inside, the annual conference of the Washington Area Rehabilitation Association was winding down. Everyone was joking about the fact that for the second year in a row, the hotel had conjured up a snowstorm to prevent the attendees from leaving, forcing them to keep their rooms an extra night. No one minded, though. The hotel was warm and cozy, and the setting was beautiful, high above the dueling rivers. No one minded at all.

The fire raged in the stone fireplace of the lobby, where Claire and Jon sat with a group of their colleagues. They'd called Susan over an hour ago to let her know they would not be coming home tonight. Susan, home for the holidays, would be returning to William and Mary the following day and, like last year, Claire and Jon would be unable to see their daughter before she left. Yet they had not even considered driving in the storm. Claire had simply extended their reservation at the hotel, and Jon had simply expected that of her. The roads were treacherous tonight.

Claire looked across the circle of her friends to try to catch Jon's eye. He was already looking at her, though, looking and smiling, and he nodded in the direction of the elevators.

She returned the nod and stood up, and they made their way through the crowded room, saying good-night to the people they passed, wishing them pleasant dreams.

Mary Drake stopped them at the elevator, grabbing Claire's hand. "I admire you two so much," she said. "Your workshop yesterday was the best you've ever done."

"We enjoyed yours, too," Jon said.

"Come on," Mary chided him. "You know what I mean. Before, when you two talked, you were great and an inspiration to us all, but everyone always thought, well Jon and Claire can make it work because they don't have any problems."

Claire laughed and rested her hand on Jon's shoulder.

Mary shook her head. "I have to admit you shook me up a little when you started speaking so candidly about what this year's been like for you. But it was terrific. You gave everyone a different perspective and a different kind of hope."

"Thanks, Mary," Claire said sincerely. They'd been hearing much the same message from other attendees since their workshop the day before. The truth was, she and Jon knew no other way to handle their presentation than with absolute honesty.

They took the elevator to the top floor. They were in the same spacious turret room they'd had the year before. The queen-sized bed was cradled in the circle of windows.

All the shades were raised, and the sky outside was black, the falling snow barely visible.

Jon wheeled into the bathroom while Claire tried to reach Vanessa one more time on the phone. Vanessa was to have arrived in D.C. earlier that day, with Brian and two-month-old Catherine in tow. Claire had called her sister's hotel a half-dozen times, but apparently the weather had caused some delays at the airport. This time, though, the hotel staff put her call through to Vanessa's room, and her sister answered almost immediately.

"We're still in Harpers Ferry, Van," Claire said. "I'm sorry. I'm not sure I'll be able to make it back in time for the meeting tomorrow."

"Don't worry," Vanessa said. "There was a message for me here at the hotel saying the meeting's been postponed till Wednesday. The weather's horrendous. Nobody's going to make it in tomorrow."

They'd set up this meeting over a month ago with Senator Christine Warrick, the feisty new sponsor of a revamped Aid to Adult Survivors Bill. With a little luck, the bill would make it through this year. It had lost its chance the year before. Zed Patterson's grim-faced admission of "a problem" and his subsequent entry into a treatment program for pedophiles had ironically stolen the focus of attention from the bill he'd sponsored. But the three wary women and two frightened children who came forward with their own stories of abuse at Patterson's hands left Claire and Vanessa no doubt at all that they had done the right thing. Jon had promised Vanessa that the foundation would keep her AMC program afloat until a more appropriate source of funding came through.

She and Vanessa spoke on the phone awhile longer,

mainly about Catherine, who was proving to be a good-natured traveler in the face of adversity.

"I can't wait to see her," Claire said.

"She looks like you, Claire."

"Like *me*?"

"Yes. Honestly, she does. I thought maybe I was imagining it, but Brian noticed it too. It's great. I feel like I've got you with me all the time."

Claire smiled to herself. "You do, you know."

"Yeah," Vanessa said, "I know."

Jon was already in bed by the time she got off the phone. She told him about Vanessa's side of the conversation while she put away her clothes. Jon listened, his back propped up against the pillows, and Claire saw the smiling impatience in his eyes as she folded her sweater, hung up her skirt.

"Come to bed, Claire," he said.

She closed the closet door, then walked over to her side of the bed and turned off the lamp on the night table. The room was plunged into darkness, and as she stood between the bed and the curved wall of windows, she felt her eyes drawn outside. With the light off in the room, she could see the steady fall of snow, thick and gray above the icy rivers. And she could see, far in the distance, the haze-covered lights of the bridge over the Shenandoah. For a moment, she was caught in a trance. She was not in the room at all, but out there on that bridge, shivering against the cold and snow, suspended high above the river.

"I'm waiting for you, Harte." Jon's voice came softly through the darkness, and she drew in a breath and slowly turned away from the windows, away from the distant string of lights. And as she slipped into bed next to her husband, she offered a silent prayer of thanks to Margot St. Pierre.

Acknowledgements

One of the greatest pleasures in writing a novel is the opportunity to talk with people who know things I do not, and who are more than willing to supply me with the knowledge I need for the creation of a fictional world. For their information and advice, I am indebted to Darlene Atkins, Rita Hagler, Sharon Lieblich, Maureen Lynch, Ken McLaughlin, Dottie and Bill Perry, and Katherine Young.

I am also grateful to Joann Churchill, Elizabeth Hain, David Heagy, Mary Kirk, Peter Porosky, Suzanne Schmidt, and Laura Schmitz for reading various drafts of *Brass Ring* along the road to completion.

And for their enthusiasm, trust, and candor, I owe special thanks to B.J. Campbell and Bruce Scott.

To discover more about your favourite author

DIANE CHAMBERLAIN

visit

www.dianechamberlain.com

You can also find her on

Facebook at www.facebook.com/
Diane.Chamberlain.Readers.Page

Instagram @diane.chamberlain.author

Twitter @D_Chamberlain